At Some Disputed Barricade

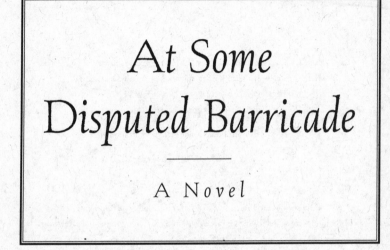

At Some
Disputed Barricade

A Novel

ANNE PERRY

BALLANTINE BOOKS · NEW YORK

2008 Ballantine Books Trade Paperback Edition

Published in the United States by Ballantine Books, an imprint of
The Random House Publishing Group, a division of Random House, Inc., New York.

BALLANTINE and colophon are registered trademarks of Random House, Inc.

Originally published in hardcover in the United States by Ballantine Books, an imprint of
The Random House Publishing Group, a division of Random House, Inc., in 2007.

Library of Congress Cataloging-in-Publication Data
Perry, Anne.
At some disputed barricade : a novel / Anne Perry.
p. cm.
ISBN-13 978-0-345-45659-5
ISBN-10 0-345-45659-9
I. Great Britain—History—George V, 1910–1936—Fiction. 2. World War, 1914–1918—
England—Fiction. 3. Chaplains, Military—Fiction. I. Title.

PR6066.E693A94 2007
823'.914—dc22
2006049880

Printed in the United States of America

www.ballantinebooks.com

2   4   6   8   9   7   5   3

Text design by Julie Schroeder

To my brother, Jonathan,
army surgeon

At Some Disputed Barricade

ONE

*T*he sun was sinking low over the waste of no-man's-land when Barshey Gee staggered up the trench, his arms flying, his boots clattering on the duckboards. His face was ashen and streaked with mud and sweat.

"Chaplain! Snowy's gone!" he cried, bumping into the earthen wall and stopping in front of Joseph. "Oi think he's gone over the top!" His voice was hoarse with helplessness and despair.

That morning Snowy Nunn had seen his elder brother sawn in half by machine-gun fire in yet another pointless attack. It was now late July 1917, and this mid-Cambridgeshire regiment had been bogged down on this same stretch of ruined land between Ypres and Passchendaele since the beginning, those far-off days of courage and hope when they had imagined it would all be over by Christmas.

Now mutilation and death were everyday occurrences. The earth stank of three years' worth of latrines, poison gas, and corpses. But it was still different to see the brother you had grown up with reduced to bleeding jelly in front of your eyes. At first Snowy had been too stunned to do anything, as if the sheer horror of it had paralyzed him.

"I think he's gone over," Barshey repeated. "He's lost it. He's gone to kill the whole German army himself. They'll just wipe him out." He gulped.

"We'll get him back," Joseph said with far more certainty than he felt. "He might have been taken back to the first aid post. Have you—"

"Oi looked," Barshey interrupted him. "And in the cookhouse, and Oi looked in all the dugouts and the holes big enough for anyone to crawl in. He's gone over the top, Captain Reavley."

Joseph's stomach clenched. It was pointless to cling to hope they both knew was futile. "You go north, I'll go south," he said briefly. "But be careful! Don't get yourself killed for nothing!"

Barshey gave a bark of laughter so harsh it was almost a sob, and turned away. Joseph started in the opposite direction, south and west toward the place where a man could most easily go over the parapet and find the shelter of what was left of the trees—shell-torn, blackened, and mostly leafless, even now in full summer.

" 'Evenin', Chaplain," the sentry said quietly from his position on the fire step, peering forward into the gathering gloom. The German guns were rumbling sullenly, starting the night's barrage, flashes from their muzzles red. The British answered. There were Canadian and Australian regiments up in this section, too.

"Evening," Joseph answered. "Seen Snowy Nunn?" He had too little time left to afford discretion. Grief had shattered all sense of self-preservation. Of course Snowy had seen men killed before: burned, drowned, gassed, frozen, or blown to pieces, some caught on the wire and riddled with bullets. But when it was your own brother, there was something that tore you in an inner way that nothing else could reach. Tucky had been his childhood friend and protector, the companion in his first adventures, the one who first told him daring jokes, the one who had stood up for him in the school playground. It was as if half his own life had been destroyed obscenely right in front of him.

Joseph had seen Snowy's face, and known that when the first numbing shock wore off his emotion would turn to rage. He had just expected it to take longer.

"Have you seen him?" he asked the sentry again, this time more sharply.

"Don't know, Captain Reavley," the sentry answered. "Oi bin watching forward."

"He hasn't done anything," Joseph said, clenching his teeth to keep control of the helplessness rising inside him. "I want to get to him before he does!" He knew what the man was protecting. Joseph was an officer and a priest, tied to the command by both rank and conviction. There were whispers that men in the French army had already mutinied, said they would hold their positions but would not launch any attack. They had demanded improved rations and whatever humanity of treatment was possible in this universal misery. Thousands had been charged, and over four hundred had been sentenced to death, but so far apparently very few had actually faced the firing squad.

In the British Army the losses had been equally appalling. Men were exhausted and morale was low, but as yet no mutiny. Now there was talk of another push forward against the German lines and there was no heart left for it. Everyone had seen too many friends dead or crippled to gain a few yards of clay, and nothing had changed, except the numbers of the dead. The sentry's sympathies were with the men, and he was afraid.

"Please!" Joseph said urgently. "His brother was killed and he's in a bad way. I need to find him."

"And tell him what?" the sentry said raspingly, turning at last to face Joseph. "That there's a God up there who loves us and it'll turn out all right in the end?" His voice was raw with misery.

Joseph had not expressed that sentiment in a long time. Certainly such words were no help. Young men of nineteen or twenty who had been sent out to die, in a hell those at home could not even imagine, did not want to be told by a priest almost twice their age, who had at least had a chance at life, that God loved them in spite of every evidence to the contrary.

"I just want to prevent him from doing something stupid before he's had time to think," he said aloud. "I know his mother. I'd like to get one son back to her."

The sentry did not answer. He turned back to face over the parapet again. The sky was fading into a soft, bright peach trailed across by a wisp of scarlet cloud, still burning in the sun. There were a few naked trees in Railway Wood to the west, silhouetted black against the hot color, more ahead over the German lines beyond Glencorse and Polygon Woods. That was the direction toward which they'd mount the attack.

"Oi don't know," the sentry said at last. "But you could troy Zoave Wood." He jerked his hand to the right. "There's one or two decent places over there you could sit boi yourself. If that was what you wanted."

"Thank you." Joseph moved on quickly. Ahead of him he heard rats' feet scraping along the boards. The trenches were full of them, millions scavenging among the unburied dead. Men went out at night, Joseph often among them, and brought back the bodies, the living first, then what dead they could.

He passed the dugouts off to the side where stretchers and extra first aid supplies were kept, although each man was supposed to carry with him at least the basics to stanch a wound. It was getting dark and occasionally star shells burst above, briefly lighting the mud with a yellow-white glare, leaving men in momentary blindness afterward.

He still did not know what he was going to say to Snowy when he found him. Perhaps there was nothing more he could do than be there, sit with him in the long agonized silence. Snowy probably would not ask him the impossible questions. He had ceased to imagine there were any answers, and certainly none that Joseph knew. Snowy was over twenty, a veteran. Most of these boys coming out now had been taken from the schoolroom. When they were broken and dying, it was their mothers they called for, not God. Out here what was there to say to God? Joseph was not sure how many people believed in such a being anymore, or thought that if He was there, then He was just as helpless as everyone else.

The trench walls were deep here, the sides firmly riveted with wood.

He passed a couple of men squatting on their heels over a Dixie can of tea.

"Seen Snowy Nunn?" he asked, stopping beside them.

One lifted a pale face, smeared with mud, a long scar across his cheek. Joseph recognized him as Nobby. "Sorry, Cap'n, not lately, poor sod. Tucky were a good chap." There was no horror in his voice and his eyes stared beyond Joseph into a distance no one else could see.

"Thanks, Nobby," Joseph acknowledged, and moved on quickly. There were more sentries, a group of men telling tall stories to each other and laughing. Somebody was singing a music hall song with risqué alterations to the words.

Joseph passed an officers' dugout, its entrance down steep steps. It was narrow as a tomb, but at least it was safe from sniper fire, and in the winter as warm as anyone could be in the frozen earth. He emerged from the confining walls of the trench into Zoave Wood. Most of the trees here were blasted or burned, but a few still had leaves. Beneath them the earth that normally was covered with undergrowth was trampled flat. The front line passed right through what was left of the wood.

He stood close to the trunk of the nearest tree and felt its rough bark against his back. If Snowy was here in these few acres behind the line it was just a matter of walking quietly, crisscrossing it like a gamekeeper looking for a poacher. Except that Snowy would probably be motionless in his grief, alone, growing cold even in this summer night because he was exhausted not in body but in heart. Perhaps he was consumed by that terrible, inexplicable guilt that survivors feel when for no reason at all they live on after those they loved have died.

Joseph started to walk, placing his feet softly on the bare ground. The wind stirred in the few remaining leaves, and shadows flickered, but he could hear nothing else above the noise of the guns. It was a warm night and the stench of the dead mixed with that of the latrines was thick in his throat, although these days he hardly noticed it. It was there all the time. You had to get right away from the lines, into one of the towns, perhaps in an estaminet, and smell cheese and wine and sweat before you lost it. Fortunately there was opportunity for this in places like Poperinghe or Armentières and the small villages within a few miles.

Something moved to his right. It must be a soldier. There were no animals left, and even birds would not come this close to the lines. He turned toward the figure and walked zigzag from tree to tree. It was a while before he saw the movement again. It was not Snowy. The man was too tall.

The sky was completely dark now, the only light emanating from gun flashes and star flares. They made the trees black and filled the spaces between with jagged shadows as the rising wind swayed them to and fro. The summer heat could not last. Soon there would be rain, maybe a thunderstorm. It would clear the air.

He almost stumbled on them: five men sitting in a slight hollow, facing each other and talking, all of them dragging on cigarettes, the brief glow marking their positions and momentarily showing a cheek or the outline of a nose and brow. At first he could not hear the words, but at least one of the low, emotion-charged voices was familiar: It was Edgar Morel, one of his own students from Cambridge days.

Joseph dropped down to his hands and knees to be less obvious, and crept forward soundlessly, keeping his movement steady so he didn't catch anyone's eye.

Morel drew on his cigarette again. The burning tobacco glowed red, showing his gaunt features and wide, dark eyes. He was speaking urgently and the anger in him was clear in the rigid lines of his shoulders and chest as he leaned forward. His captain's insignia gleamed for a moment, then the darkness returned and the smoke he blew out was almost invisible. Joseph could smell it more than see it.

"They're going to send us over the top again, toward Passchendaele," Morel said harshly. "Thousands of us—not just us but Canadians, French, and Aussies, too. It's all just as bloody hopeless as it's always been. Jerry'll pick us off by the hundreds. It'll wipe us out. There's almost nothing left of us already."

"They're all barking mad!" Geddes said bitterly. He was a lance corporal with a long, thin face. The hand holding his cigarette was shaking. It could have been nerves, or shell shock.

Somebody else lit another and passed it across. The man who took it thanked him and took a long drag, then coughed. Joseph stiffened, his stomach knotting. It was Snowy Nunn. He could not see the white blond hair under his helmet, but he recognized his voice.

"They've bin saying all summer that we're going," the fourth man said wearily. "Can't make up their bloody minds. But when did they ever know their arse from their elbow anyhow?"

"The twenty-first of March, loike clockwork," Snowy said quietly. "First day of spring, an' over we go. They must think Jerry doesn't have a calendar or something." He took in a deep, rasping breath, his eyes filled with tears. "What for? What's the point?" He stopped, his voice choking off.

The man next to him reached out and put a hand on his shoulder.

"The question is, what are we going to do about it?" Morel looked from one to the other of them, his expression unreadable in the darkness, except for his mouth, an angry line in the glow of his cigarette. "Are you willing to be driven over the top to get slaughtered for no bloody reason? The French aren't, God help them."

There was a bark of laughter. "You reckon it's better to be tried and shot by your own? You're just as dead, and your family's got to live with the shame."

"It's show," Morel argued. "The French aren't going to shoot more than a dozen or two. But that isn't the point." He leaned forward, his body no more than a deeper shadow in the gloom. He spoke with intense earnestness. "Jerry's a hell of a lot better prepared for us than we thought."

"How d'you know that?" Geddes demanded. "What makes you God Almighty? Not that I've got any time for generals, or anybody else who thinks he's better than his neighbor 'cos he was born with a silver spoon in his mouth."

"Because I was questioning a prisoner a couple of days ago," Morel answered sharply. "The Germans know we're coming."

"I forgot you speak bloody kraut," Geddes said angrily. "Is that what you went to Cambridge for?"

A voice in the darkness told him to shut up.

"The point is, I do," Morel answered.

"The point is, did you tell anyone?" one of the others asked. "Like Penhaligon, for example."

"Of course I did!" Morel spat. "And he passed it on up. But they don't want to know. Most of us are going to die anyway," he went on urgently. "I'd rather go for a cause I believe in than be sent over the top because some damn fool general can't think of anything except the same futile slaughter, year after year, no matter what the intelligence tells him. We're no closer to winning than we were in 1914. I'm not sure that the Germans are our real enemies. Are you? You've fought opposite them for the last three years, captured some of them. I'm not the only one who's talked to them. Our sappers have been in tunnels so close under their lines they can hear them talking at night. What about? Killing us? No, they aren't! Ask any of the sappers, they'll tell you they talk about their homes, their families, what they want to do after the war, if they live through it. They talk about friends, who's been killed or wounded, how hungry they are, how cold, how damn wet! They make rotten jokes just like ours. And they sing, mostly sad songs."

No one argued.

"I don't hate them," Morel went on. "If I had the choice, I'd let them all go back to the towns and villages where they belong. I hate the bastards that sent them. What if we copied the French, and told the generals to fight their own bloody war!"

There was a stunned silence.

"You can't do that," Snowy said at last. "It's mutiny."

"Afraid of being shot?" Geddes asked sarcastically. "Then you're in the wrong place, son. An' you know that as well as I do."

Snowy did not answer. He sat without moving, his head bent.

"I'll fight for what I believe in," Morel went on. "It isn't this senseless death. The land stinks of it! The best men of our generation are sacrificed for nothing! The generals commanding this farce haven't any more idea of what they're doing than their poor bloody horses have! Somebody's got to stop it while there's still anyone alive to care."

Joseph was sick at heart, and his legs were cramped where he was crouching to the earth. He had felt the anger in the men for months, the growing helplessness since last summer, but still he had not expected anything so overt, not from a man like Morel. He had known him since 1913 when Joseph had first come back home to Cambridge after his wife's death. The loss of Eleanor had left him too crippled in faith to lead a parish anymore. He had retreated into teaching. The theory in academic study of biblical languages was so much easier than trying to face the crises of love and faith, doubt, loss and disillusion that were part of the practice of religion.

He moved his leg, kneading the muscle to get rid of the pain. He should have realized that if anyone finally rebelled against the slaughter it would be Morel. Joseph's job had been to try to teach eager, intelligent young men such as he to think for themselves! University was only partly about acquiring knowledge. Mostly it was about learning how to use the mind, refine the processes of thought.

He felt the steel against his cheek, cold as ice. He froze. Somehow the Germans had gotten a raiding party through the lines. Then he realized that if that were true, the men smoking a few yards from him would have been the first to be seen. He relaxed and tried to turn and see who it was, but the pressure increased.

Morel stood up and came toward him. He stopped about five feet away and struck a match. It flared for only a moment before the breeze blew it out, but long enough for him to recognize Joseph.

"What are you doing here, Captain Reavley?" he said coldly.

The rifle barrel moved away from his cheek, now that the man holding it knew who he was, and Joseph rose to his feet also, easing his aching muscles. It was strange how in the broken woods, earth bare even in high summer, they faced each other like strangers. All memory of being master and pupil had vanished.

There was no corresponding ease in Morel's stance. His face was almost invisible. It raced through Joseph's mind to behave as if he had heard nothing of their talk of mutiny, but he knew Morel would not believe him. Even were it true, he could not afford to take the risk.

"Captain Reavley?" Morel repeated, his voice harder.

"I was looking for Snowy Nunn," Joseph replied. He outranked Morel and he was several years older, but he was a noncombatant, a chaplain rather than a fighting soldier. And perhaps out here in the woods, without a gun, that was irrelevant anyway. If Morel was really thinking about mutiny then all discipline and respect for rank were already gone. Would he shoot a chaplain, a man he had known for years?

Death was all around them, hundreds of men, sometimes even thousands every day. What did one more matter? Unless it was your brother—like Tucky Nunn? Then it ate inside you with a grief almost like madness, as if your own life were being torn apart. Friendship was the only sanity left.

"I know he came out this way," Joseph went on.

"Come to say a prayer?" Morel asked sarcastically, his voice shaking a little now. "Don't waste your time, Captain. God's gone home; the Devil is master here. Don't bother telling Snowy that. He knows."

"Don't decide for me what I am going to say, Morel," Joseph responded curtly. "That is arrogant and offensive."

A star shell went up and burst with a brief flare, showing the slight surprise on Morel's face, and then the anger. "And you were just—" The rest of whatever Morel said was lost in the roar of gunfire less than fifty yards away. The light died and they were in darkness again.

Joseph made up his mind quickly. "Are you planning mutiny, Morel?"

"So you heard!" Morel said bitterly. "I think you'd have left me some doubt. That wasn't very clever, Chaplain. I should have realized that when it came to it, you were just as stupid as the rest. I used to admire you so much." There was a regret in him now, a loss so deep it was as if all the world he had loved had finally slipped from his grasp, the very last vestige gone in this ultimate disillusion.

"You called me *chaplain*," Joseph reminded him. "Had you forgotten I am a priest? What you tell me in confidence I cannot repeat to anyone at all." He breathed in and out quickly. "Let's see how stupid you are, Morel."

Snowy had stood up as well, but he did not move. He was facing toward them although it was impossible to tell how clearly he could see them.

"Not stupid enough to trust one chaplain with a loyal conscience and not enough brains to see that this is just a futile slaughter now." Morel's voice was sharp with emotion. "We won't win, we'll die for nothing. Well, I won't! I care, Chaplain, whether you do or not! I won't see these men sacrificed on the altar of some idiot general's vanity. I don't believe in God. If He existed, He would put a stop to this. It's obscene!" He spat the word as if it were filth on his lips. "But I care about my men, not just the Cambridgeshires, but all of them. We've already lost Lanty and Bibby Nunn, Plugger Arnold, Doughy Ward, Chicken Hagger, Charlie Gee, Reg, and Arthur." His voice dropped. "And Nigel. The only good I know of is to be sane, not to kill and not to be killed."

"That would be best," Joseph agreed, struggling to keep himself steady. Morel had named all the men from his own village deliberately. "But that's not on offer right now," he said. "Your choice is whether to trust me and let me walk away, or shoot me, and then shoot all the others who saw you do it. Is that what you want for them?"

"I won't shoot them!" Morel said derisively. "They're in it just as much as I am."

"Oi in't," Snowy said from close to Morel's back. "Not if you shoot Captain Reavley, Oi'm not. That's murder."

Joseph waited. There was a lull in the gunfire and he could hear the wind sighing in the branches. Then the crackle of machine guns burst out again and the deeper roar of the heavier shells from far behind the lines. One exploded five hundred yards away, sending the earth flying forty feet into the air.

"Some poor bastard's got it," Morel said quietly. "Aussies along that way. I like the Aussies. They don't take damn stupid orders from anybody. Did you hear about them striking up their band every time the sergeant told our boys to drill in the sun, just to keep them busy? The Aussies couldn't play 'God Save the King' to save themselves, but they made such a row banging and squealing on every instrument there is that the sergeant had to give up. I hope that's true."

"Yes, I heard," Joseph answered. He smiled with a bitter grief in the darkness, but no one saw him.

"Is it true?" Morel asked.

"Yes." He had no idea, but he wanted it to be, not only for himself but for all of them. He looked at Snowy, who had moved a step closer.

Morel was still hesitating. Should Joseph take the risk of moving to ease his limbs? One of the other men, indistinguishable in the dark, had his rifle in his hands, pointed loosely toward Joseph.

Snowy turned to him. "Goin' to shoot me, too, are you? What for? Going over, or not going over? Or you just want to shoot someone, an' Oi'm an easy target what won't shoot back? 'Cos I won't. Not at me own mates."

"Get out!" Morel said sharply. "Get out, Reavley, and take Nunn with you."

Joseph grabbed Snowy by the arm and, almost pulling him off his feet, set out as fast as he could over the rough ground, snarled with tree roots, back toward the trench again and the cover of its walls.

"Thank you," he said when they were finally safe below the parapet.

There was no life in Snowy's voice. "Couldn't let 'em shoot you," he said flatly. "Moi fault you were out there."

"Just came to see if you wanted company."

"Oi know," Snowy replied. "Oi seen you do it for hundreds of other men. There in't nothing you can say. Tucky's gone. Reckon we'll all be gone in another month or two anyway. Good night, Chaplain." And without waiting to see what Joseph might say, he turned and walked down the connecting trench toward the supply lines, keeping his balance on the duckboards with the ease of long practice.

It was a fairly quiet night, just the usual sporadic shelling and occasional machine-gun fire. Joseph never forgot the snipers and as the summer dawn came early, he kept his head well below the parapet in the forward trenches.

Fresh water and rations came up and the men stood to. There were all the usual drills, inspections, cleaning of kit, patching up of walls breached during the night. It was still hot and the lice were making men scratch their skins raw.

The mail came, and those with letters sat in the sun with their backs to the clay walls and read. For a few moments they were in another world. Fred Arnold, the blacksmith's son from St. Giles, roared with laughter at a joke and turned to Barshey Gee next to him to pass it on. They were friends. Both had lost their brothers here, in this regiment.

There were other brothers as well, Cully and Whoopy Teversham. At home their family had a long and bitter feud with the Nunns over a piece of land. Out here it was all absurdly irrelevant.

Tiddly Wop Andrews, good looking but painfully shy, was reading a letter for the third time, blue eyes misty. It must be a love letter at last. Perhaps he could write what he could not say aloud. Joseph had tried many times to help him put his feelings into words, but of course he would not say so now. The men teased each other mercilessly, perhaps to break the tension of waiting for the next burst of violence.

Punch Fuller was sitting with his back to the clay wall and his face up to the sun. He would get his large nose burned if he was not careful. Joseph told him so.

"Yes, sir, Captain," Punch said, and took no notice at all. He had long learned to ignore remarks about his most prominent feature. He closed his eyes and continued to make up even bawdier verses for "Mademoiselle from Armentières" than the classic ones, trying them out to himself in a surprisingly musical voice.

Joseph came to the end of the connecting trench and walked toward his dugout. Officers had a little privacy, cramped but comparatively safe under the ground. Gas was the worst threat because it was heavy and sank into any crater or hole. But it was unlikely to land this far back.

Just before he reached his dugout he met Major Penhaligon, his immediate commander. Penhaligon was about thirty, eight years younger than Joseph, but today he looked harassed and hollow-eyed. He had cut his cheek shaving and not had time to deal with it. A smear of dried blood marked his skin.

"Ah, Reavley," he said, stepping in front of Joseph. "How's Snowy Nunn? Did you see him? That was too bad. Tucky was one of the best."

Tucky's cheerful face was as clear in Joseph's mind as it must have been in Snowy's. They were alike, with blunt features and fair hair, but Tucky had had the confidence, the brash good humor, always ready to seize a chance for anything. He had been wiser than some men thought him, steadier in a crisis. He had helped Joseph more than once with a word of advice, a well-timed joke, an earthy sanity that reminded men of home, laughter, the things that were worth loving.

"Yes, sir," Joseph replied. Death was death. It should not be harder for one than another, but it was. "Snowy's taking it badly."

Penhaligon had no idea what to say, and it showed in his eyes. He felt it his duty to try; both brothers were his men. He struggled through the weariness and the knowledge of the campaign ahead of them for something to say that would help.

It was Joseph's job to break the news of loss to people, and think of a way to make it endurable when they would never really get over it, without unintentionally sounding as if he neither understood nor cared. It was his job to steady the panic, create courage out of terror, help men believe there was a purpose to all of this when none of them had any idea if there really was. He had no right to leave it to Penhaligon.

"I talked to him," he said. "He'll be all right. Give him a little while, but . . . keep him busy." Should he say more, ask Penhaligon to give Snowy some duty that would guard him from Morel's path?

"We'll all be busy soon enough," Penhaligon said with a twist of his mouth. "There's going to be a pretty big push forward, starting in a day or so."

"They've been saying that ever since the spring," Joseph replied truthfully.

"Mean it this time," Penhaligon told him, his eyes steady, trying to see if Joseph understood him beyond the mere words. "Afraid you'll have a lot to do."

The morning sun was hot already, but Joseph was chilled inside. He wanted to tell Penhaligon that the men were not ready, some of them not even willing anymore. He had no idea how many others there were like Morel.

Joseph became aware that Penhaligon was watching him, expecting him to speak. He wanted to warn him about Morel, but he had given his word that it ranked as a confession and was sacred. But Penhaligon was commanding a unit with an officer in it who was trying to subvert the entire campaign. Did what Joseph had overheard amount to mutiny? Or was it still only an exaggerated example of the kind of grumbling that was everywhere? The men were exhausted, emotionally and physically—and casualties were almost uncountable. What man of any spirit at all would not question the sanity of this, and think of rebelling against a useless death?

"Chaplain?" Penhaligon prompted him. "Is there something else?"

"No, sir," Joseph said decisively. Morel had not spoken of any specific intent, simply complained of the violent senselessness of it all. Men had to be free to do that. Even if he thought of anything like refusing to obey an order, he was a Lancashire man born and bred, the Cambridge-shires would never follow him against other Englishmen. "Just thinking about what lies ahead, that's all."

Penhaligon smiled bleakly. "It'll cost us a bit, but apparently it'll be a real strategic advantage if we take Passchendaele. Damned if I know why. Just one more wretched hell, as far as I can see."

Joseph did not answer.

The advance began the next morning, July 31. Judith Reavley stood with the men eating their last hot breakfast before the ration parties returned. Her stomach, like theirs, burned with hot tea and the fire of a tot of rum. At ten minutes to four, half an hour before the summer sunrise, the whistles blew and she watched in awe and misery as almost a million men moved forward over the plowed and torn-up fields, slick with mud after the occasional drizzle of the last few days. They threw up pontoons over the canals and poured across the water and up the other side. They moved on through the few still-standing copses of trees and small woods. The noise of guns was deafening and murderous fire mowed down whole platoons, tearing them apart, gouging up the earth.

By midmorning it began to rain in earnest, and a mist descended so that even four or five hundred yards away she could see that the outline of Kitchener's Wood was no more than a smudge in the gloom.

Two hours later she was struggling to drive her ambulance over the sodden, rutted land to get it as close as she could to the makeshift first aid post to which the wounded were being carried. The road was bombed out and there was nothing but a track left. The shelling was very heavy and in the rain the mud was getting worse. The heavy clouds made it gray in spite of it being close to midday. She was afraid of being bogged down, or even tipping sideways into a crater and breaking an axle. It took all the strength she had to wrestle with the wheel and to peer through the murk to see where she was going.

Beside her was Wil Sloan, the young American who had volunteered at the beginning of the war, long before his country had joined only a matter of months ago. He had left his hometown in the Midwest and hitched a ride on the railroad to the East Coast. From there he had worked to earn his passage across the Atlantic. Once in England he had offered his time—his life, if need be—to help the troops in any way he could. He was not the only one. Judith had met several American drivers and medical orderlies like Wil, and nurses like Marie O'Day, doctors, even soldiers who had enlisted in the British Army, simply because they believed it was right.

Since January America itself had joined the Allies, but there were no American forces in this stretch of the line.

She knew there were shadows in Wil's life. His blazing temper had run out of control more than once before, and had finally forced him to leave his home. He had never told her how serious the breach had been, but he had hinted at it. Perhaps because they were close enough friends that honesty compelled him, he could not pose to her as an unblemished hero.

Now he was sitting beside her, calling out warning and encouragement alternately as they bucked and slewed over the rough ground, trying to discern through the mist and rain where to stop for the wounded.

"There!" he shouted, pointing to what looked like a level spot slightly below a rise in the slope. There was a mound of some sort, and a man standing near it, waving his arms.

"Right!" she answered, but her voice was drowned by a shell exploding fifty yards away, sending mud and earth up like a gout of water. The debris fell on them, battering the roof and sides of the ambulance and flying in, striking both of them through the open part of the front above the windshield and the door.

She kept on with her hand on the accelerator. There was nothing to gain, or lose, by stopping before they reached the post. Finally she slithered to a halt, a few yards short of the level she had been aiming for. Almost immediately a soldier was beside her, shouting something she could barely hear, and gesticulating behind him.

Wil leaped out and splashed through the mud and rain to start helping the first wounded into the back. He would take only those too badly injured to walk. They could carry five, maybe six at the most. God only knew how many there were. He could do something to stanch bleeding—pack a wound, put on a tourniquet—but that was about all. If an artery was lacerated very often a man bled to death and there was little anyone could do about it. But if a limb was torn off completely, the artery constricted and the blood loss was far less. If they could prevent him dying of shock, there was a good chance of saving him.

Now Judith kept the engine running while Wil and several other men loaded in the wounded. As soon as they gave the signal, she could turn and begin the difficult journey back to the nearest clearing station. She had already made two trips, and she would go on as long as she could, all day and all night if necessary. She did not think that far ahead. One ambulance had been blown to pieces already today, killing everyone in it, and a crater had broken both axles of another.

Wil shouted and she felt the jolt as the door was slammed shut. She moved her hand and accelerated. The wheels spun, sending mud flying. She tried again, and again, then reversed before she could get them to grip.

The journey back was a nightmare. Twice, shells exploded close enough to them to batter them with debris. Once they got stuck, and Wil and the two injured who could stand had to get out to lighten the weight. By the time they reached the clearing station, one of the wounded men was dead. Wil had done everything he could, but it was not enough.

"Shock," Wil said briefly, his face drawn under the smears of earth and blood. He shrugged. "Should be used to it," he added, as if it were self-criticism, but his voice wavered.

She smiled at him, and said nothing. They knew each other well enough that he would understand, remember the words from the countless times they had done it all before.

They went back again and again all day, breaking only long enough to eat a little bread and a tin of Maconachie's stew and hot tea out of a Dixie tin. It all tasted of oil and stale water, but they barely noticed.

By dusk, they were unloading wounded and helping to carry them into a makeshift operating theater in a tent somewhere in an open field. Everything was shrouded in rain. She could see a copse of trees about fifty yards away, but she had no idea which of the many woods it was. All that mattered was to get the men to some kind of help.

Inside the tent, medical orderlies were looking at the newcomers, trying to assess who to treat first, whose wounds could wait, and who was beyond saving anyway. The injured half-sat, half-lay, ashen faced, waiting with the terrible, hopeless patience of those who have looked at horror so often they can no longer struggle against it. They were trying to absorb the reality that their arms or legs were gone or their intestines spilling out into their blood-soaked hands.

Judith was half-carrying a man whose left leg was ripped open by shrapnel which they had bandaged as well as they could. His more important wound was his left arm, which was gone from the elbow down.

The surgeon came over to her. His coat was soaked with blood, his fair hair plastered back. His eyes were sunken and dark-ringed with exhaustion. She had worked with him countless times before.

"We've done what we can, Captain Cavan, but he was injured several hours ago," she said. "He's pretty cold and shaken up." It was a magnificent understatement, but everyone dealt in understatement; it was a matter of honor. Ask any man how he was, and he would say, "Not too bad. Be all right in a while," even if an hour later he was dead.

"Right." Cavan acknowledged her with a brief smile, a momentary warmth to the eyes, then he moved to the other side of the man and supported him over to the corner inside the tent where he could lie until they could take him onto the table. "Come on, old son," he said gently. The man was perhaps seventeen, his beard hardly grown. "We'll have you sorted in a minute or two."

"Don't worry, sir," the man responded hoarsely. "It's not too bad. Actually I can't feel it much. Leg hurts a bit." He tried to smile. "Suppose I won't be playing the violin now."

Cavan's face registered a sudden pity.

"Sorry, sir," the man apologized. "I never played it anyway. Don't like the piano much, either, but my mam made me practice."

Cavan relaxed. "I expect she'll let you off now," he said drily. "Wait there and I'll be with you in a minute." He eased the man down gently, then turned back to Judith.

She read in his eyes the struggle to conquer the emotions that wrenched at him. There was no time, and they served no purpose. The only help was practical, always practical: clean, scrub, stitch, pack a wound, find something to take the edge off the pain, ease the fear, move to the next man. There was always a next man, and the one after, and a hundred after him.

Judith turned and went back to help Wil with the next casualty.

Ten minutes later a VAD nurse with a plain, sallow face handed her a mug of tea. It was sour and oily, but it was hot and someone had been thoughtful enough to lace it with about half a shot of rum. It loosened some of the knots inside her.

Another ambulance arrived and she helped them unload it. The men were badly wounded and the driver had caught a piece of shrapnel in the shoulder.

"You can't go out there again," he said, wincing as he tried to lift his arm. "Jerry's putting up a hell of a barrage and we're too close to the front here. They'll probably have to evacuate this as it is. They'll need us for that, after they've patched up the worst. It's a bloody shambles. Thousands are dead, and God knows how many wounded."

Judith walked back into the tent and over to the table where Cavan was stitching up a lacerated arm on a soldier with dark hair.

"Another lot, sir," she said quietly. "Looks to be three bad ones, and the driver's got a shrapnel tear in his right shoulder. He says it's pretty grim out there, and Jerry's coming this way, so we'll probably get told to retreat. Do you want us to stay here and help if we have to go suddenly?"

"I've got men I can't move," he replied without looking up at her. His voice was very quiet. "We'd better see what we can do to defend ourselves. If it's only the odd raiding party we'll be all right." He tied off the last knot. "Right, soldier. That'll do. You'd better start making it back. That bandage'll hold till you get to the hospital."

The man eased himself off the table and Cavan put out his arm to steady him. "Go with MacFie over there. You can hold each other up. You'll just about make a good man between the two of you."

"Yes, sir. Thank you, sir." The man swayed, gritted his teeth and went gray-white. Then he steadied himself and, swaying a little again, made his way over to MacFie.

Cavan started with the next man. The one after that was beyond his help. Judith brought him a mug of tea. "If you survive it, it'll make a new man of you," she said wryly.

"Then you'd better get a river of it." He took the mug out of her hands gently, his fingers over hers for an instant. "We're going to need a whole new bloody army after this. God Almighty! Whose idea was this attack?"

"Haig's, I imagine," she replied.

"I'd like to get a scalpel to him sometime," he responded, pulling his mouth into an expression of disgust as he swallowed the tea. "This really is vile! What the hell do they put in it? No, don't tell me."

"I could do it with a bayonet," she replied bitterly.

"Make the tea?" he asked in surprise.

"No, sir, perform a little surgery on General Haig."

He smiled and it softened his eyes. She could glimpse the man he would have been in peacetime, at home in the green fields and quiet hills of Hertfordshire. "Good with bayonets, are you, Miss Reavley?" he asked.

"I thought all you had to do was charge, shoulders down and your weight behind it," she replied. "Isn't it enthusiasm that counts rather than accuracy?"

This time he laughed and his fingers rested gently on her arm. It was just a brief contact, almost as if he had changed his mind before he completed the movement. Only his eyes betrayed the warmth within him. "Those guns sound closer. Perhaps you'd better start getting the wounded out of here and back to the first aid posts."

"They're no closer than before, sir," she told him. She was as used to the sound of them as he was.

"That's an order, Miss Reavley."

She hesitated, wondering whether she dared defy him, or if she even wanted to. It had been the worst day's casualties she had experienced so far, even worse than the first gassings two years ago, but leaving now would look so much like running away.

"Take those men back." He still spoke sufficiently quietly that only she could hear. "Get them to the hospital now, while you can."

"Yes, sir." Reluctantly she turned, still feeling as if she were somehow deserting her duty, being less brave, less honorable than he was. She had gone only as far as the entrance flap of the tent when she heard the shots. This time there was no question that they were rifle fire and much closer than the German line. The next moment she saw them: a dozen German soldiers running toward her out of the gloom, rifles in front of them, bayonets fixed.

Wil Sloan dropped to the ground and she felt almost as if she had been hit herself. She stood frozen. A bullet tore into the canvas and she dived forward and ran to Wil, falling almost on top of him. It was idiotic to try to save him—they would all be dead in minutes—but still she grasped his shoulders to turn him over, needing to see where he was hit.

"Get off me, you fool!" he growled. "I need to get the gun up!"

She wanted to slap him out of sheer relief. "What gun?" she demanded furiously. "If you've got a gun, don't bloody lie there, shoot someone!"

"I'm trying to! Let go of me!"

She obeyed immediately and he hunched up onto his elbows and knees. There was far more gunfire now. The other ambulance driver was firing back and there were more shots from the far side beyond the tent.

"Get the ambulance started," Wil told her. "We'll get everyone out that we can. It'll be a hell of a crush, but we'll get most of them, with two vehicles. Hurry. Don't know how long we can hold them. This could be just the first of bloody thousands!"

She obeyed and, bending low, ran back to the tent. Half the wounded were gone already. All those who could stand had rifles. Cavan was at the operating table, still working. A man lay on it bleeding heavily, his belly ripped open. The anesthetist held the ether, but he was shaking so badly the mask seemed to jiggle in his hand.

"You've got to get out!" Judith shouted at them. "We've got two ambulances. We'll get everyone in. Just hurry! There are at least a dozen Germans broken through and only five or six of us with guns. We can't hold them off much longer."

Cavan did not look up from his work of stitching. "We can't go yet, Miss Reavley," he said steadily. "If I leave this man, he'll die. So will the others who have just been operated on. The journey under fire will tear their sutures open. Tell the men to stand fast. Then come back and help me. I'm afraid my orderly is dead."

It was only then that Judith noticed the body on the floor. When she had turned to go outside five minutes ago he had been assisting Cavan. The bullets that had torn through the canvas had struck him in the chest.

"Be quick," Cavan added. "I need you back here. I can't keep on much longer without help."

"Yes, sir." She swiveled and went out, almost bumping into a lance corporal with a heavily bandaged leg. He was kneeling against a packing case firing round after round at the raiding party. One moment they were visible through the drifting rain only by the flicker of their rifle fire, then suddenly the wind gusted and they could see them clearly, more than a dozen of them pressing forward.

"Captain Cavan says to stand fast," she said loudly. "Tell the ambulance drivers we've got to fight."

He looked at her incredulously, his face slack with disbelief.

"You heard me, Corporal," she replied. "We've got wounded men to defend."

He swore under his breath, but he did not argue. "You'll 'ave ter tell 'em yerself, miss. Oi can't move. Oi don't mean Oi won't. Oi can't!"

"Sorry," she apologized, and bending low again she scrambled over to Wil and repeated Cavan's order to him.

"*Stand fast?*" he repeated incredulously. "You English!" He aimed the rifle again. "Remember the Alamo!" he shouted, and fired. In the distance someone fell.

She gave him a pat on the shoulder and went back to the tent to help Cavan. She knew enough about field surgery to pass him the implements he asked for, even though she could not keep her hands steady. When she tried to thread the needle for him it was hopeless.

"Hold this," he ordered, indicating the surgical clamp in his hand buried deep in the abdominal wound.

She took it and it slipped off the flesh, blood spurting up hot, catching her across the face. She had never been more ashamed of her inadequacy.

Cavan took the clamp from her and grasped the flesh again.

"Swab it," he commanded.

She prayed under her breath and cursed herself. She tried to still her breathing, control her muscles. She must not be so stupid, so ineffectual. This was a man's life she was holding. Her fingers steadied at last. She mopped up the blood, then threaded the needle and passed it to him.

He glanced upward and met her eyes. His look was warm for an instant, then he took the needle. She reached for the clamp.

The gunfire started again, louder and more rapid than before, volley after volley. It sounded as if it was just outside the tent flap. Cavan did not hesitate in his slow, steady work. "Keep swabbing," he told her. "I need to see what I'm doing."

A spray of bullets shredded the tent wall and the anesthetist collapsed silently, buckling to his knees, then sliding forward, his back scarlet. Through the ragged tear stepped a German soldier, rifle pointing at Cavan. Behind him were two more, their weapons pointing at Judith also.

"Stop!" the leader said clearly in almost unaccented English.

"If I do, he'll bleed to death," Cavan replied without looking up, his hands still working. "Swab, please, Miss Reavley."

Imagining the bullets crashing into her, bringing instant white-hot death, Judith obeyed, soaking up the blood within the wound.

"Stop!" the German repeated, speaking to Cavan, not Judith.

"I have two more men to operate on," Cavan replied. "Then we will withdraw."

There was more rifle fire outside. Someone cried out. The German turned away.

Cavan went on stitching. He was almost finished. The bleeding was contained.

The German looked back. "Now you stop."

The tent flap opened and one of the wounded men stood there. He was swaying slightly, blood streaming down his tunic where his left arm should be, a revolver in his right hand. He raised it and shot the first German soldier through the head. The other two fired at him at the same moment, hurling him back against the canvas. He was dead before he touched the tent wall, and slithered to the floor.

Cavan swung round and dived toward him, hands outstretched.

"It's useless!" Judith shouted at him. One of the other soldiers raised his gun to aim at Cavan. She reached for the instrument tray, picked up a scalpel and drove it into the man's neck. His bullet went through the ceiling.

Cavan was half on top of the dead soldier on the floor. He knew he could do nothing for him. It was his gun he was after. He rolled over, covered in blood, and shot the third soldier through the head.

The second one, gasping and spewing blood from his neck wound, staggered back through the tent the way he had come.

The gunfire outside never ceased.

"We have two more wounded we might save." Cavan clambered to his feet, shaking, his face white.

"Only one now," Judith corrected him. "Can . . . can we hold them off?"

"Of course we can," he replied, his breath ragged, swaying a little. "But we've lost a scalpel."

Joseph heard about it in the morning, standing in the wreckage of the forward trench, the parapet collapsed, mud up to their knees.

"It's about the only good thing, Captain Reavley," Barshey Gee said to him grimly as they stopped working on rebuilding the trench walls for a moment. "He's some doc, eh, Cavan? There he was, cool as a cucumber, stitching away like there were nothing going on! An' your sister with him.

An' that Yank ambulance driver, too." Barshey was a tall man with thick hair. Before the war he had been slender; now he was gaunt and looked years older than twenty-four. "Got 'em out, they did. Didn't leave a single live one behind."

Joseph felt a wave of gratitude that Judith was still alive. It was so powerful he smiled fatuously in spite of his effort not to. He forced himself not to think about her most of the time. Everyone had friends, brothers, someone to lose. It would cripple one to think of it too much.

"I'm afraid Major Penhaligon's dead, sir," Barshey went on. "Pretty well half the brigade dead or wounded. The Canadians and the Aussies got it hard, too. Word is we could have lost around fifty thousand men. . . ." His voice choked, words useless.

"This summer?" Joseph said. It was worse than he had thought.

"No, sir," Barshey said hoarsely, the tears running down his cheeks. "Yesterday, sir."

Joseph was numb. It could not be. He drew in his breath to say "Oh God," but it died on his lips.

The battle of Passchendaele raged on and the rain continued, soaking the ground until it oozed mud and slime and the men staggered and sank in it.

On August 2, Major Howard Northrup arrived to replace Penhaligon. He was a slight man, stiffly upright with wide blue eyes and a precise manner.

"We've a hard job ahead of us, Captain Reavley," he said when Joseph reported to him in his dugout. He did not invite Joseph to sit, even though he was obliged to bend because of the low ceiling.

"It's your job to keep up morale," Northrup went on. He appeared to be about twenty-five and wore his authority heavily. "Keep the men busy. Obedience must be absolute. Loyalty and obedience are the measure of a good soldier."

"Our losses have been very heavy, sir," Joseph pointed out. "Every man out there has lost friends. . . ."

"That is what war is about, Captain," Northrup cut across him. "This is a good brigade. Don't let the standard down, Chaplain."

Joseph's temper flared. He had difficulty not shouting at the man. "I know it is a good brigade, sir," he said between his teeth. "I've been with them since 1914."

Northup flushed. "You are a chaplain, Captain Reavley, a noncombatant officer. Morale is your job, not tactics. I don't wish to have to remind you of that again, or in front of the men, but I will do so if you make it necessary by questioning my orders. Thank you for your report. You are dismissed."

Joseph saluted, then turned and went out, blind with fury.

TWO

"Mr. Corracher, sir," Woodrow said, opening the door to Matthew Reavley's office and showing in a man in his early forties who was dressed formally in a dark suit. His hair was smooth and sleek, off his brow. Normally he would have been distinguished looking, but today his features were marred by anxiety.

Matthew stood up and offered his hand.

Corracher took it so briefly it was barely a touch.

"Thank you, Woodrow." Matthew excused the clerk. "Sit down, Mr. Corracher. How can I help you?" That was a euphemism. Matthew was a major in the Secret Intelligence Service and Tom Corracher a junior cabinet minister of great promise. However, now he was sweating, in spite of the fact that the room was not overly warm. He had asked for an urgent appointment with someone in charge of counterespionage in London, and since America's entry into the war in January Matthew's duties were more general than previously, when America had been neutral, and German diplomacy across the Atlantic and sabotage of American munitions supplies a more immediate concern.

Did Corracher really have anything to say, or was he one of those who jumped at shadows? Many people were. The news was bad almost everywhere. Naval losses were mounting all the time and there was no end in sight. It seemed as if every day ships were going down somewhere. Britain was blockaded and in some places rations were so short the old, the weak, and the poorest actually died of hunger.

The news from the Western Front was devastating, and only moderately better in Italy, the Balkans, the Middle East, and Egypt. In Russia the tsar's government had fallen and been taken over by the revolutionaries under Kerensky. Perhaps Corracher was merely reflecting the nation's grief? He had a reputation for courage and a degree of candor. To Matthew it looked as if he might have been overrated in both.

"What can I do for you, Mr. Corracher?" he repeated.

Corracher drew in a long breath and let it out slowly. He had the air of a man about to be sent over the top to face enemy fire. Considering the real loss of life in Passchendaele, Matthew's patience was fast dwindling.

Perhaps Corracher saw it. "I have been in Hungary recently," he began. "I am not sure if you are aware of it, but the political situation there is very volatile. Losses in the Italian Front have been critical and it looks as if there may even be revolution there also—as well as in Russia, I mean." He took a deep breath and steadied himself with an obvious effort. "I'm sorry. I am not making a great deal of sense."

Matthew did not argue.

Corracher began again. "There is more unrest in Hungary than many people are aware of. A very strong element wishes to break away from the German- and Hungarian-dominated rule by Austria and become independent. If they did so, that would radically alter the balance of power in Southeastern Europe. The whole Balkan peninsula might be persuaded to ally with Italy and strengthen it against Austrian oppression." Corracher smiled bleakly. "I see from your face that you appreciate at least some of what I am saying."

"I do," Matthew conceded. "Unfortunately that is not my area of expertise. I have been—"

"I know," Corracher cut in. "America. But if my information is correct, you have also done some subtler and more dangerous, shall I say politically complicated, work here in England." The nervousness had returned even more markedly. His body was rigid, his hands locked around each other, stiff fingered, and the sweat glistened on his face.

Matthew was aware of the silence in the room and the faint sound of footsteps beyond. Corracher was a cabinet minister, but he could still tell him nothing.

Corracher licked his lips. "There are men in this country, highly placed, who did not wish us to go to war against Germany, and do not now wish us to win. They do not wish us to lose, of course, but would rather we made an even-handed peace." He was watching Matthew intently.

Matthew knew that far better than Corracher possibly could have. His own parents had been murdered in 1914 in order to regain a copy of the proposed treaty between King George and the Kaiser that his father had found and taken. It would have allied Britain with Germany in an empire that would have dominated the western world. But he had hidden it too well, and Matthew and Joseph had found it on the eve of the outbreak of war. But John Reavley had warned them that the conspiracy ran so high that they had not dared to trust anyone. Since then the man behind it—they referred to him among themselves as the Peacemaker—had maneuvered ruthlessly to end the war, even at the cost of Britain's surrender. He had been willing to kill to achieve it, a lesser sacrifice for a greater cause. But Corracher could not know any of this.

"Indeed," Matthew said as noncommittally as he could. It was hard to keep the emotion out of his voice. The memory could be pushed to the back of his mind, but the pain was always there: his parents crushed to death in a car wreck, then Cullingford murdered in the street; last year Blaine—and all the other men sacrificed to that terrible cause.

But Matthew had identified the Peacemaker, and the Peacemaker was dead now. It was a nightmare that came back to him waking or sleeping, heavy with the knowledge of betrayal and counterbetrayal. None of it had anything to do with Corracher.

"If you have come to tell me that, Mr. Corracher, it is unnecessary," he said aloud. "We are aware of it. The most powerful man behind such a sentiment is dead. He was killed at sea, in the Battle of Jutland, last year."

None of the fear left Corracher's face; if anything, it increased. "Possibly." His voice was flat.

"I was there. There can be no doubt." Matthew remembered the German destroyer looming out of the darkness, the earsplitting sound as the huge twelve-inch naval guns on the deck of the *Cormorant* exploded, the searing fire belowdecks, magazines on fire, the stench of burning corticine, shattered glass, and smoke. Most of all he remembered Patrick Hannassey's face as he stood with the prototype of the missile guidance system in his arms and hurled it down. He had turned to leap to the German ship that had rammed them and been carried away and back again by the sea, crashing into them over and over. Matthew had lunged after Hannassey. He could not afford to let him go with the knowledge he had of their scientific failure. He had locked with him, struggled, and won. He could still see Hannassey going over the side, whirling for an instant in the air, lit by the flames of the burning ship, arms and legs flailing. Then the German destroyer had heaved up on the wave and smashed into the *Cormorant* again, crushing Hannassey like a fly.

Corracher was staring at him, eyes wide. "Oh . . ." he gulped. "Then he . . . he can't have been alone in the cause."

Matthew's emotions were too raw with the memory for him to argue. Hannassey was the only man he had ever killed with his own hands, but it was the knowledge of what happened to Detta that wounded him. She was the Peacemaker's daughter. Of course long before he knew that, he had known she was an Irish Nationalist, just as she had known he was in British Intelligence. They had used each other. That did not stop him from loving her, or feeling the pain twist in his gut because he had beaten her at the game of betrayal. Her own people had crippled her in punishment for losing. Beautiful Detta—who had walked with such dark and subtle grace.

"Exactly what is it you want to tell me, Mr. Corracher?" Pain was jagged in his voice. "There have always been traitors and profiteers. Unless you come about someone of whose acts you have proof, there is nothing I can do. Perhaps it is a police matter rather than intelligence?"

Corracher appeared to come to some decision. The embarrassment in his face was acute, but this time he did not hesitate.

"I have worked hard and had some success in persuading the independent elements in Hungary to swing to the allied side. But they are my contacts, my mother's family, and others they knew among the Hungarian aristocracy, who trust me. But I have been a voice within the cabinet against any kind of softening or appeasement," he went on. "One of the few left." He swallowed with difficulty, as if his throat was tight. "I am about to be charged with a crime I did not commit, but the evidence against me is overwhelming. Mr. Lloyd George will have no choice but to dismiss me from office, and leave the criminal prosecution to take what course it will." His voice cracked. "It is unlikely that I will escape prison. But even with the best legal defense I can find, if I am cleared it will not remove the slur from my name, or the suspicion that I was guilty."

Matthew felt the anger grow within him. If the man really was innocent, it was appalling. "I'm sorry," he said sincerely. "How can Intelligence help you? Do you know who is behind it?"

Corracher's eyes reflected an emotional exhaustion that was crippling. "If you mean names, I have no idea," he replied. "I don't believe there is anything you can do. I'm not seeking your help, Major Reavley, I am giving you information. I am not the only person to whom this has happened. Other men with views inconvenient to some have left office for one reason or another. Kemp was killed in a zeppelin raid last autumn. Newell resigned, no real reason given. And Wheatcroft is threatened with a scandal which will destroy his life."

Suddenly Matthew's attention was total. A coldness settled inside him. In the instance of Wheatcroft, he knew exactly what Corracher was referring to; word of it had crossed Matthew's desk. Alan Wheatcroft had been accused of acts of gross indecency with another man much younger than himself. It had not been proved, and he had protested his innocence, but whether anyone believed him was almost irrelevant. When the accusation became widely disseminated, as inevitably it would, his career would be finished.

"What views did the other three have?" he asked. The belief that he knew was not sufficient.

Corracher smiled bitterly. "Kemp's sister married a Belgian. All her family was killed in the first German advance. He wants crippling reparations. Newell was something of an expert in Russian affairs. Wheatcroft is different." A flicker of puzzlement lit his eyes for a moment. "I'm not sure what interest he would be to anyone else. Maybe there's something about him I don't know."

Matthew's mind was racing. Had the Peacemaker been alive he would have seen a pattern in it, but Hannassey was dead. Matthew had seen his body crushed beyond recognition. Nothing could have survived that impact.

"Do you understand me, Major Reavley?" Corracher said quietly, leaning forward across the desk a little, his hands clenched white.

"Yes," Matthew answered, drawing his attention back. "Yes, I do, Mr. Corracher. I can look into the other cases, but tell me about yours." He was aware that it would be difficult for Corracher, and embarrassing, but he could not investigate without the facts.

Corracher was very pale and his hands were locked till the knuckles were white.

"It is extremely sordid," he said huskily. "I am actually being charged with blackmail."

Matthew was startled. "You mean someone is saying that *you* are a blackmailer? Not that you are being blackmailed . . ."

"That's right." Two spots of color stained Corracher's cheeks.

"Who is saying this?"

Corracher bit his lip. "Mrs. Wheatcroft."

"Mrs. Wheatcroft?" Matthew was incredulous. "Alan Wheatcroft's wife? For God's sake, why? Hasn't she got more than enough trouble already?"

"That's it." Corracher all but swallowed his words. "She is saying that I blackmailed Alan after creating the situation with which he was charged. He claims it never existed in reality. I set it up in order to take money from him." He stared at Matthew with desperation. "I can see how his wife would wish that that were true, but it is not. I knew nothing at all about it until the police accused me! I was as shocked as anyone."

"Do you imagine that Wheatcroft told her that?" Matthew asked. His pity for Corracher was intense, but far greater than for any one man was the threat he implied to the integrity of government and the country in general. The only way to fight it was to find the truth.

Corracher frowned, struggling with his own emotions. "I could understand his wanting to find any way of escaping the charge. He must have been desperate. Anyone would be. But why say it was me? Why not one of his closer friends, somebody more likely?"

"For example?" Matthew pressed. He loathed doing this—it was personal in the most distasteful way—but to evade it now out of squeamishness would make it worse.

Corracher looked embarrassed. "Well there are people with . . . connections to that sort of thing. I mean . . . men . . ." He tailed off miserably, as if the air in the room oppressed him.

Matthew was less delicate. "Who prefer other men rather than women," he finished for him. "But presumably are discreet about it. Yes, of course there are. You think one of them may have set up the scene, or possibly was himself blackmailed into it?"

"It seems probable," Corracher conceded.

"Any idea who?"

"No. I . . . I could give you a list of names of those whose nature I am aware of, but it seems a despicable thing to do." His face registered his disgust at the manipulation of a shared vulnerability in such a way.

"I'm only interested in finding who set up the Wheatcroft scandal and blamed you," Matthew said vehemently. "If you are right, then someone is effectively ruining both of you. They are robbing the government of the men most likely to fight for a lasting peace. One that will prevent enemy alliance with future elements in Germany which would allow the same thing to happen again. God knows, we need a just peace, but not a weak one."

"That is why I came to you, Captain Reavley," Corracher said, his eyes meeting Matthew's again. "I don't believe it is coincidental. Whoever has created the evidence that makes me look guilty has been very clever. There's no way I can fight against it without betraying other good men and raising doubts about other men's personal lives."

Matthew saw it very clearly. It was simple and supremely effective. Like a slip noose, every movement against it pulled it even tighter. "Tell me about Wheatcroft," he asked. "Exactly what is he accused of doing? Where? Who else was involved, and what part are you supposed to have played? What evidence is there, written or witnessed? Is any of it true, even the bits that merely support or contribute?"

Corracher was deeply unhappy. He began slowly, hesitating as he searched for words, too embarrassed to look up. "Wheatcroft is accused of having solicited a sexual act with a young man in a public lavatory near Hampstead Heath. He lives not far from the heath and was walking his dog, which he does regularly. He had been seen talking to the same young man at least twice within two or three hundred yards of the place a week or two earlier. He says that this man simply asked him directions and he gave them."

"Both times?" Matthew interrupted.

"Yes. It was quite late, at dusk, and he was apparently lost."

"What does the young man say?"

Corracher's face tightened. He looked up quickly, then away again. "That's the thing. He's a friend of mine, at least his father is. I've known him in a casual way most of his life. He's a bit wild. He's run up a degree of debt that he can't pay, and it would be difficult for his father to come up with that much."

"I take it he says Wheatcroft approached him?" Matthew concluded.

"Yes."

"And it couldn't be true?"

"He says I told him to say it!" Corracher's face was scarlet now, but the anger in him was painfully real.

"Give me times, dates, and names," Matthew said gently.

"There's more." Corracher's voice was husky. "Wheatcroft says I asked him for money to keep it quiet, and he paid me a hundred pounds, but when I came back for more he told me to go to hell. And that was when I told Davy Pollock—the young man in question—to report it to the police. There is a hundred pounds in my bank that I can't account for. Wheatcroft said he put it there the day after I demanded it, and he has the paying-in receipt."

"How are you supposed to have asked for it?" Matthew asked.

"In a typewritten note."

"Which I imagine he gave to the police?"

"Yes."

"Write down everything you can think of, Mr. Corracher, including where I can reach you at any time, and I'll do everything I can to expose the truth," Matthew promised.

"Thank you." Corracher seemed relieved that at last someone appeared to believe him. He rose to his feet a little unsteadily and offered his hand, then withdrew it and turned to the door. Was he afraid Matthew would decline to shake it? It was a mark of how deeply he already felt tainted by the charge.

After he had gone, Matthew read all the information, made the briefest of notes himself, then left his office to begin his inquiries.

Outside the air was close and heavy, as if waiting for thunder. The streets were quiet compared with peacetime. Petrol was scarce and expensive, and the army had first call on good horses. There was something heartbreakingly drab about the quiet women waiting in queues or patiently walking along the pavements. The omnibuses had women conductors. One passed Matthew as he waited on the curb to cross. The driver was a woman also, her hair drawn back off her face and tied behind her neck. The girls who worked in munitions factories had actually cut theirs short. It was too easy to get it caught in the machinery and literally have one's scalp torn off.

No one seemed to wear red or pink anymore, as if it were somehow indecent in the face of so much loss.

Matthew crossed the street and reached the other side, stepping up onto the pavement past a group of white-faced women, silent, each lost in her own world. There were such groups in every town and village all over Europe, waiting for the casualty lists. In some places where a whole brigade had been wiped out, every house in street after street would have the blinds half drawn and stunned, white-faced women would sit in the August heat and wonder how they were going to face tomorrow, and all the tomorrows after that.

Too much had been paid to allow this ever to happen again, anywhere, for any reason. To appease now would be to make this terrible sacrifice meaningless. That thought was not bearable.

He walked past them to the top end, caught an omnibus to Hampstead Heath, and climbed the steps to the upper deck. He sat alone, his mind turned inward.

He barely glanced at the streets he passed through. They were gray and dusty, the city trees in full leaf between the occasional stretch of fire-scarred rubble where a zeppelin had bombed.

Was it possible that Hannassey had left some legacy behind him? Matthew had never imagined that the Peacemaker worked alone, but he had believed that the Peacemaker was not only the brain of the conspiracy, but the heart and the will of it also. Was he wrong? Was there still someone with the skill to concoct a plan like this and carry it through?

Had the Peacemaker designed it and left the instructions before his death?

He dismounted at Hampstead Heath and walked to the police station. With his credentials, it was not difficult to find a senior officer willing to tell him about the alleged incident, the young man involved, and his debts.

"Miserable business," Inspector Stevens said unhappily, sitting behind a desk piled with paperwork. He stirred a tin mug of tea to dissolve the sugar in it.

Matthew had declined the offer of tea.

"Could it have been a misunderstanding on Wheatcroft's part?" he asked. "Unwise, perhaps, and young Pollock jumped the gun a bit?"

"Of course it could," Stevens answered. "Pollock withdrew the complaint anyway. Said he was put up to it when he was drunk and only half knew what he was saying." His bland face registered a weariness and unutterable contempt. "Young waster should be in the army, like everyone else!" He could not disguise the bitterness and the grief in his face. For a moment it was embarrassingly naked. Matthew did not need to ask where his own son was, or if he was still all right. The answer was stifling, like the hot air in the closed room.

"Why isn't he in the army?" he asked, because he needed to know more about the boy.

Stevens shot him a look of disdain. "If someone propositioned him, it'd be the first time he bloody complained about it!" he said hoarsely.

"Obvious he was willing?" Matthew asked.

Stevens raised his eyebrows. "You mean should Wheatcroft have known what he was and kept clear? Not necessarily. He wasn't refused by the army for that. Flat feet! That's what it says on the forms. But that isn't the point. Wheatcroft said the whole incident never happened, and Pollock changed his story. Said Corracher put him up to it."

"Could that be true?"

"God knows!" Stevens replied. "I doubt it. Wheatcroft denied that Corracher tried to blackmail him at first, and then he refused to say anything at all. Seemed in a blue funk to me. Sweating like a pig and white as paper." He ran his hand over his face, rubbing it hard. "He wanted to withdraw the whole thing, let it go, but his wife was furious, determined to charge Corracher, in case it ever came up again. Prove once and for all that he was a vicious liar."

"Professional rivalry between the two men?" Matthew asked.

Stevens looked genuinely surprised. "Political? You mean for office? Never thought of that, but I don't think so."

"What do you think?"

Stevens rubbed his face again and moved his eyes to meet Matthew's. "Honestly? Ever met Mrs. Wheatcroft? Formidable woman. Beautiful as cut glass, and about as comfortable. My guess would be that Wheatcroft behaved like a fool, refused to do the honorable thing and own up to it. Took the way out by blaming Corracher, until the alternative became facing his wife over it, and her public embarrassment if it became known. If he denied it to her—and maybe quite honestly—it might have been no more than an indiscretion. Then she insisted on taking the way out offered by blaming Corracher. Or at least he didn't have the courage to deny that it was him. Poor devil!"

"Corracher?"

Stevens looked at him bleakly.

"Both of them. But it's only my guess. Could be wrong. I don't know Corracher, except by repute. And I've long ago learned that damn near anyone can surprise you—for better *or* worse."

Matthew did not press him any further. He thanked him, asked him for David Pollock's address, and went to see him. He was a handsome, rather effeminate young man. However on looking at him more closely, Matthew realized that that effect had been achieved more by allowing his hair to grow longer and wearing a loose shirt like an artist's smock than by the basic cast of his features. At first he affected a slight lisp, but as soon as he became angry he forgot it.

"Of course I didn't!" he said furiously. "It's all lies! That damn politician put me up to it. Scared me silly. Thought I was going to be accused of . . . of being a . . ." He did not finish the sentence, as though the thought were too repellent for him to speak it. "The army refused me because I have flat feet! I couldn't march if my life depended on it."

Matthew did not bother to respond. He did not know the truth of his fitness, or his honesty. Nor did he care. It was not his job to chase cowards. It was Corracher who mattered, and the possibility of the Peacemaker's plans still alive, still working their slow poison.

He did not believe Pollock, but neither could he prove him a liar. All he had achieved was to substantiate what Corracher had told him.

He left and walked back across Hampstead Heath in the late, thundery dusk. The leaves seemed to shiver in the heavy air and the breeze smelled of rain.

He turned it over in his mind. Was this plot a legacy of the Peacemaker? Or was it possible that Hannassey had been the tool, not the principal of the conspiracy? It was now a year since the Battle of Jutland, and Matthew had basked in a certain kind of peace. He had heard about the punishment of Detta and it had hollowed out a new place of pain inside him, but he had known it would come, even if not in so savage a form. He had found a degree of calm inside himself knowing that the man who had caused the death of John and Alys Reavley had finally met his own death. He was both horrified and satisfied that Hannassey's end, too, had been violent, even that Matthew himself had caused it. He had had no moral alternative but to kill him, and when he had woken in the night, sick and sweating at the memory, that knowledge had enabled him to sleep again.

And there was the infinitely larger issue of the Anglo-German alliance, which the Peacemaker had so nearly brought about, with its monstrous dishonor. Now that, too, was laid to rest.

Except that perhaps it was not. The removal from office of four junior but highly effective members of the government was exactly the sort of thing the Peacemaker would do, and the skill and subtlety of the method suited his style. It was only by chance that the plot had come to Matthew's notice. Now he realized with a chill that there may have been other plots during the year since Jutland, successful ones that he had not recognized because his assumption that the Peacemaker was dead had blinded him to even considering such a thing. He would have to rectify that fault urgently.

The next day he began inquiries about the death of Kemp in the zeppelin raid. No one had considered it suspicious at the time. There had been many deaths in such raids; his was simply more notable because of his position. Where he had lived was a matter of public record.

"Could it have been murder?" Matthew asked the fire warden who had been first on the scene.

"Murder?" the man looked startled, as if Matthew had said something in bad taste. "Call it that if you like, sir, but it's better just to say it's the war. Murder's sort o' personal. It's this way for everybody at the moment."

"What I mean, Mr. Barker, is could he have been killed by some other means and left with the casualties, to hide the fact that in his case it was murder?" Matthew explained.

Barker was taken aback. "Oo'd want ter do a thing like that?"

"Most people who have power also have enemies," Matthew said evasively. "Is it possible?"

Barker still looked confused. " 'Ow would I know, sir?"

"Where was he found? Inside the house? Under rubble? With other people or alone?" Matthew elaborated.

"Alone. In the street just outside the 'ouse," Barker replied thoughtfully. "You sayin' as 'e were put there, an' we reckoned as it were the bombs wot killed 'im, but it weren't? Yer never goin' ter prove nothin' now!"

"I daresay not. I'd just like to know."

"Then 'e could a' bin. Or not."

"Thank you."

About Newell he could learn nothing. Reasons of health were given for his resignation, but no one had any knowledge of what illness it might be. Newell himself refused to see or speak to Matthew, claiming that he was not well enough, and had nothing relevant to say.

Blackmail again? Possibly. Its particular nature did not matter. Matthew was now certain in his own mind that there was a concerted plan to get rid of ministers who were individually able to affect the course of war, through diplomatic skill or connections, whether it was the Peacemaker who was behind it or not. The nation was exhausted with the loss of men, with shortages of food, fuel, and luxuries of all sorts, with the drabness and ever-present fear of bombing. They dreaded even greater hunger, and ultimately invasion and conquest. Perhaps after that might come civil war, Briton against Briton as some surrendered, believing it the lesser evil, and others fought on until the slaughter and defeat were total.

But Matthew still found he was striding out even more rapidly, with his anger against the Peacemaker, alive or dead, so hard inside him it hurt his chest to breathe.

Now he had enough information to report his findings to Calder Shearing, the head of his branch of Intelligence.

"Morning, Reavley," Shearing said as Matthew came into his office. "Anything on the sabotage in the factory in Bury St. Edmunds yet?" He looked up from his desk. He was a man of barely average height. His black hair was receding severely, but his face was so dominated by his dark eyes and powerful, expressive brows that one did not notice the expanse of his forehead. His nose was aquiline, his lips delicate and unusually sensitive.

"Yes, sir," Matthew replied, still standing at attention. One did not relax until Shearing gave his permission to. "I have sufficient evidence for the police to deal with it now."

"Then give it to them," Shearing ordered. "There's plenty more to be getting on with. There's an unusually high number of accidents at the munitions factory in Derby—Johnson Heathman and Company. I—"

"I'll give it to Bell," Matthew interrupted him almost without realizing that he did so. "Tom Corracher came to see me two days ago with something far more urgent."

Shearing's brows rose and his eyes were bright and cold. "More urgent than sabotage of our munitions factories, and yet you left it for two days to come and tell me?"

Matthew remained at attention. He had worked with Shearing since before the war, and at times their tacit understanding of each other was like the best sort of friendship. They did not speak of emotions. Even last week when they had sat up all night together over merchant shipping losses, bruised at heart over the deaths of hundreds of men, no words had been necessary. To Matthew these losses were infinitely more vivid since his experiences during the Battle of Jutland. Now he knew the slow, crawling fear of night patrol when the enemy could be anywhere under the dark water and fire, explosion, and drowning came without any warning at all. He knew the head-splitting noise of the great guns, the smell of blood and fire.

And he knew what it was like to sink an enemy ship and watch it go down, with a thousand men just like yourself, to be buried in the darkness of the ocean forever.

What he did not know was anything of the nature or the passions, the background, the home or family of the man sitting behind the desk now, waiting for his explanation. He did not even know if Shearing had ever personally seen anyone die. Perhaps for him it was numbers, something all in the mind, like a chess game.

There was one picture in Shearing's office, a painting of the London docks at twilight, and nothing else that betrayed his taste, his feelings, his own inner life. There were no books except those of a professional nature; no novels, no poetry. There were no photographs on the desk or the walls. He never mentioned his family, if he had any, or where he lived or had grown up, his school or university—nothing.

There had been many times when Matthew had wondered if Shearing himself could be the Peacemaker, before he knew it was Hannassey. It was a fear that had gripped him with an acute sadness. He had wanted to like Shearing. He found it easy to admire him. The suppleness of his mind, his occasional dry wit, the self-mastery and the dedication which kept him at his desk all day and half the night. It was the ability to trust him that had eluded Matthew, until Jutland had proved that the Peacemaker was Hannassey. Then suddenly relief, sweeter than he had expected, swept away suspicion. Now the trust was eroded again. Still he had no choice but to tell Shearing what he was doing; to attempt it secretly would betray his doubt, and he could not afford that.

"Reavley!" Shearing's voice cut across Matthew's thoughts impatiently.

"Yes, sir!" Matthew snapped his attention back. "It was a story I needed to investigate before I brought it to you. I couldn't judge the importance of it without making some careful inquiries."

"And you found it true." That was a statement.

"It seems to be."

"Then sit down, man, and tell me!" Shearing snapped. "Don't stand there like a damn lamppost!"

"Yes, sir." Matthew pulled up the chair and sat down. He recounted everything that Corracher had said, and how much of it he had been able to verify.

"And you believe that the removals of these four men are connected?" Shearing asked when Matthew finished. "Who do you consider responsible? Hannassey is dead."

"Yes, sir," Matthew responded, knowing the words were meaningless.

There was a wry amusement in Shearing's eyes. "One of his disciples taken his mantle of power?"

"I don't know, sir. That is first among the many things I would like to find out. But whoever it is, his purpose seems to be broadly the same, and his skill is obviously formidable. And I'd like to save Corracher, if possible."

Shearing's mouth pulled tight. "Not likely," he said bitterly. "If the man behind this is as clever as you think, he'll have made provision for Corracher fighting the charge. Wheatcroft's wife has powerful family connections. They'll all want to believe her, and take the blame off Wheatcroft, true or false. Think carefully before you act, Reavley—and keep me informed. You might end by making it even worse."

It was a dismissal, but Matthew refused to stand up. "Are you telling me not to do anything, sir?" he said between his teeth.

"No, I'm telling you to use your brain, not your emotions!" Shearing said tartly. "Be as angry as you like. Go home and smash the china, swear at the neighbors, punch the furniture. Then grow up and do your job."

Matthew sat motionless.

"Now!" Shearing shouted suddenly. "It's a filthy thing to do! It's deceit and betrayal and it soils everything it touches. Don't sit there like a grave ornament! Do something!"

"Yes, sir." Matthew stood up. Quite unreasonably, it made him feel better to see Shearing's temper snap, too, and to know that under his tightly controlled surface he was just as furious and offended as Matthew himself.

That evening the man whom Matthew had referred to as the Peacemaker stood at the window of an upstairs room in his house on Marchmont

Street, only a few miles away from Matthew's flat. He was waiting for a visitor and uncertain when he would arrive. It was no longer possible to rely on steamers or trains. The German Grand Fleet had not left harbor since the Battle of Jutland, but U-boats still patrolled the seas, necessitating that British warships guard troop carriers bringing back the wounded from France and Flanders.

It grew darker. The soft colors of the sky were fading, light reflected on windows opposite. The fire watch would be out soon, looking for zeppelins, waiting for the explosion of bombs. The streetlamps would make the city an easy target from the air.

His hands clenched and unclenched, his nails digging into his palms when he saw a taxi slow as it passed his house, then speed up again. He had known it would not be Richard Mason; he would not be foolish enough to get out right at the door. However, he would be tired after the long, dangerous, and heartbreaking journey. He might be careless. He had been once before.

The Peacemaker drew the curtains closed and turned away from the window, impatient with himself and the emotion raging inside him, which locked the muscles of his arms and chest, making them ache. Mason, the man he was waiting for, was possibly the best of all the war correspondents. He had sent dispatches from all the places where the fighting was fiercest: France, Flanders, Northern Italy, Bulgaria, Palestine, and Mesopotamia. He did not quote figures of men dead or wounded, or yards of mud-soaked land gained. He wrote with passion of individual experience, one act of heroism, one victory, one death. He described the weariness, the disgust, the hunger he himself felt, or the laughter, the letters from home, the silly jokes and terrible food. He hid nothing. Through the human suffering and tragedy of a few he painted the whole. In his words the destruction of Europe, now spreading across the Near East, North Africa, India, and America as well, was brought to life.

The Peacemaker had always known that the human cost of war was beyond measuring. As young men during the Boer War, he and Mason had both seen the concentration camps, the brutality, the degradation of the spirit. They had not known each other then, but the experience had given them a common goal. Both were consumed by an ideal that war should never be allowed to happen again, but the Peacemaker was willing to go to any lengths. One man, ten men, a hundred were a price not worth the counting if it could prevent the slaughter of ten million and the ruin of nations.

The Peacemaker had conceived a plan, and but for a collision of events no one could have prepared for, he would have succeeded. The treaty that would have bound Britain and Germany in an alliance unbeatable by any other axis of nations had been found by John Reavley, and seeing its potential with short-sighted patriotism rather than a world vision, he had stolen one of the copies to expose it. There was no time to write it out again, and have the kaiser sign it. The assassination in Sarajevo had altered everything. Even killing Reavley had not retrieved the document, and the buildup to war had become unstoppable.

Of course he had tried to find ways to bring about peace since then—he had never stopped trying. It had become a passion that devoured everything else in him, overtook his life and cost him every other wish or dream, every principle or ideal he had treasured, certainly all personal happiness. But what was that when balanced against the ruin of Europe and its centuries of beauty, its magnificence of thought, its philosophy and dreams, not to mention the loss of human life?

Every attempt had been foiled either by tides of circumstance or the intervention of an individual. In at least three instances that he knew of he had been frustrated by the sons of John Reavley, who were still bent on avenging his death, and still held his foolish idealism.

After the first poison gas attack in the trenches at Ypres in 1915, and the slaughter on the beaches of Gallipoli, Mason had written a brilliant article exposing the arrogance and extreme incompetence of the command in the second instance. Joseph Reavley had been briefly at Gallipoli also. He had pursued Mason back toward England and finally caught up with him in an open boat in the English Channel when they had survived the sinking of the ship they had been in.

What conceivable part of Reavley's shortsighted philosophy could have changed Mason's mind and persuaded him to abandon not only his article but also the entire cause? It had taken the Peacemaker more than a year to win him back and make him see the greater cause again.

It was Matthew Reavley who had caused the death of Patrick Hannassey, but this had not been unwelcome. Hannassey had been extremely useful, but by the summer of 1917 he was becoming a liability—greedy and unreliable. Corcoran had been one of the Peacemaker's successes. Other plans were almost ripe as well.

So he paced the floor of his room trying to compose his mind as he waited for Richard Mason and the report he would bring from Russia, and even more important, from Germany itself. The Peacemaker had seen a year ago that the key might lie in the deluge that was about to break over the tsar's government and bring it to an end. Now it had happened. Kerensky was in control now. He was a man of vision and humanity, a man of compromise. Lenin was there now, too, and Trotsky—but they were extremists. In time they would take Russia out of the war. There would be no more Eastern Front to bleed away German strength and crush its men with the deadly cold and hunger, and the useless marches and sieges that had ruined every army that had tried to conquer that vast country. Dear God, even Napoleon had learned that at crippling cost. Did the kaiser really delude himself he could do better?

God knew Germany tried hard enough to keep the United States out of the war, knowing how their strength would renew the almost beaten forces of Britain and France. Until January of this year, 1917, they had succeeded. But Zimmerman, the German foreign secretary, had sent that idiotic directive to Mexico to attack the United States. The telegram had somehow found its way to President Woodrow Wilson. America had had no choice but to declare war on Germany and join the Allies.

Tens of thousands more lives would be lost as the war dragged on for another year, and another. The blind, insensate stupidity of the leaders who sacrificed men for nothing but their own arrogance, their petty "little England" mentality, brought the hot rage to his mind. The sweat stood out on his body and he could feel his heart pounding. Britain and Germany were natural allies. Together they could have brought peace and safety to half the world, prosperity and civilized government, and the highest culture mankind had ever seen.

Instead Britain in its imperial conceit had loosed a storm of destruction that threatened to bring back the Dark Ages, and leave Europe all but uninhabited, except by the old, the crippled, and the lonely women whose men were buried in the blood-soaked earth.

He steadied himself with difficulty, breathing in slowly and out again, counting the seconds. There was still hope. He must be in total control when Mason arrived.

He heard another car go past and whirled around to stare at the door, then was furious with himself for giving in to such impulse.

And it was meaningless. Mason would not drive past this house. He would stop at least a hundred yards away.

Then there was the knock on the door.

"Come," he said quietly.

The manservant came in. "Mr. Mason is here, sir," he said respectfully. "Would you like tea, or perhaps a glass of whisky? There is Glenmorangie in the decanter, sir."

"Bring tea and then leave us," the Peacemaker replied. Mason would be tired and cold. There might be something to celebrate later, but not yet. It depended very much on what news he also brought from Germany.

"Yes, sir."

Mason's footsteps sounded on the stairs, and a moment later he came into the room. He was thinner than when the Peacemaker had last seen him, but he still moved with a certain grace in spite of the fact that he must have been exhausted. It was an energy of mind rather than of body that kept him going. It burned in his dark eyes now, and the power of his emotion was suggested in the lines of his face, the broad cheekbones and wide mouth.

"Have a seat, Mason," the Peacemaker said calmly, as if it were only days since they had last seen each other, and not months. "I've sent for tea, but if you'd rather have whisky, it's here."

"Tea, thank you." Mason sat down in the armchair opposite him, and only as he eased himself into it did his tiredness show. There was clearly a stiffness in his back, and the light of the lamp above the mantel accentuated for an instant the hollows around his eyes.

"Bad journey?" the Peacemaker asked, also sitting.

Mason did not hide his feelings; perhaps he couldn't. "Trains are full of wounded," he replied, his voice quiet and precise as always, but the pain in it undisguised. "Mostly from Passchendaele. Hundreds of them, gray-faced, staring into space. Some are straight from the schoolroom—fifteen, sixteen, slaughtered before they've tasted life." He stopped abruptly, his breathing ragged as he tried to block the memory from his mind and think of the present: the Peacemaker and the quiet rooms where at least for a few hours he was comfortable and safe.

There seemed nothing to add, and trivialities would have been offensive to both of them. They waited a few moments with no sound but an occasional car in the street and the steady ticking of the clock on the mantel. It was now completely dark outside. The manservant brought tea and sandwiches, apologizing for the liberty.

"Fish paste, sir, and cucumber. I hope it is acceptable?"

Mason gave him a bleak smile. "After the rations I've had, it's food for the gods. Thank you."

"You're most welcome, sir." He inclined his head, then withdrew, closing the door.

The Peacemaker passed the tea and pushed the plate of sandwiches toward Mason. His stomach was tense and his mouth dry, but he sat calmly, as if there were all the time in the world. He would not ask for the article yet, with its encoded message from Berlin. He forced himself to wait until Mason had eaten, before he spoke again.

"What is the news from Russia?" he said when finally Mason put down his cup. "Has the revolution progressed since you were there before?" He made it sound as if he were no more than interested, not that the fate of the war might depend upon it.

Mason's face was motionless, looking within himself, as he answered. "Yes, it has progressed, not as I had hoped. Kerensky is an intelligent man, a visionary, a moderate who wants to build the new without destroying the old."

"The tsar will not give in," the Peacemaker said with some distaste. He had little respect for Nicholas II, or for his tsarina Alexandra and her absurd dependence upon the filthy monk Rasputin. "What is Kerensky doing to hasten his complete control? He cannot wait forever!" His voice was sharper than he had meant it to be. With an effort he steadied it. "Russia is bleeding away in this senseless war, just as we are. And God knows their people deserve freedom from the centuries of oppression they have suffered. Don't tell me about the hunger and the deaths on the Eastern Front, or the poverty across the land. Any dispatch can tell me that. What is the mood in St. Petersburg? Moscow? Or Kiev? What of Lenin, or Trotsky, or any of the men of real vision? When will they move to take over the leadership?

Mason was somber. He met the Peacemaker's eyes at last. "I wish I didn't have to say this," he answered quietly, "but Kerensky is out of his depth. He is in many ways a man of both vision and morality, but history has overtaken him. He has neither the fire nor the obsession to match the mood of the people now, or their needs. It has passed beyond his kind of moderation."

The Peacemaker sat still. Suddenly the restlessness was gone inside him, replaced by something like a solitary fire. If Mason was right about the mood in Russia, then his hope would be realized, perhaps soon. With the Eastern Front no longer a threat, Germany could turn all its men and forces toward the west. The German plan to ship Lenin into Russia in a sealed train had worked. They were on the brink of harvesting its fruits.

"I see," he said aloud. He had never intended to tell Mason anything of the secret diplomacy that had brought some of this about. Mason hated war with a passion and a horror equal to anyone's, but he was an Englishman, and the thought of England beaten would reach his emotions with unpredictable effect. It was prudent that he know only what was necessary. "You look tired," the Peacemaker went on. "Have you an article for me?"

Since the American entry into the war in January he could no longer route his communications with Berlin through Washington. Now he relied on Mason to meet secretly with Manfred von Schenckendorff in any of the neutral territories Mason visited. He encoded his information within his articles, so nothing could ever be betrayed, and gave them to the Peacemaker on his return. The Peacemaker altered them slightly to remove the information and gave them back. It worked in reverse with copies of notes as if for an article yet to be written.

Mason pulled half a dozen slips of paper out of his pocket and passed them across.

"Thank you." The Peacemaker accepted them. He had difficulty keeping his fingers from shaking, but he forced himself to leave the papers closed. He would read them later, alone.

"I wish I could say there is nothing urgent to discuss, and allow you to rest," he said quietly. "But Passchendaele is a disaster." He had no need to act to thicken his voice deliberately with pain; it was real enough, gouging into him, bringing back memory of Africa and a wave of nausea at sight of the dead, obscene and helpless. "It looks as if it is going to be worse even than the Somme," he went on hoarsely.

Mason must have caught the sudden, ungoverned pain in him. "I know," he answered softly.

The Peacemaker straightened a little in his chair, needing to mask the nakedness of his momentary lapse.

"Of course you do—at least from the figures, and the trainloads of wounded you'll have seen. But that is not all. It is not widely known, at least to the public, but part of the French army mutinied. . . ."

Mason jerked his head up, his eyes hot and angry. "The poor devils had just cause," he said, as if the Peacemaker had leveled an accusation.

The Peacemaker nodded slowly. "I know that. They are brave and patriotic men, like ours, but their conditions are intolerable, and now they are being driven onto the enemy guns in pointless suicide. And it's happening again all along the Flanders Front. We need an honest voice to tell us what is happening to our own men. This is no longer a war of the people, Mason, it's become a senseless destruction the leaders are too blind or too incompetent to put a stop to. Get a good night's sleep. See me in the morning and I will give you back your article. Then go to Ypres again. Forget the propaganda and the figures, and what the commanders say. Find the truth of what the men who are fighting and dying really think. We have to know!" Without realizing it he leaned forward. "We have the moral need to know, and they have the moral right that we should. If you won't speak for them, who will?"

Mason did not argue. "I'll go tomorrow night, after I've reported to my paper," he said simply. His face hardened as he smothered the weakness within himself, the momentary faltering, the longing to turn away. "There's no reason to delay."

"Good," the Peacemaker said simply. He looked at the empty tea tray, sandwiches all eaten. "Would you like a Glenmorangie?"

"Yes," Mason accepted. "Yes, I would."

Richard Mason was not the last visitor to the house in Marchmont Street that evening. At close to midnight, after he had read the article and deleted Schenckendorff's message the Peacemaker stood in the dark before the uncurtained window, his mind racing with new ideas. Hope had rekindled in him for an end to the madness of the battlefield. It might even be that the ordinary soldier himself at last could take control of his destiny. Most men who were actually commanded to kill the enemy, to fire the bullets, to let off the gas, who charged with the bayonets fixed, had no personal enmity toward the German soldiers in the lines opposite them. They knew they were just ordinary men like themselves. If the French could mutiny, then surely so could the British. Mason would bring him back the truth of morale in Flanders. Then perhaps there would be an end to it.

There was a knock on the door again, tentative at this late hour.

The Peacemaker swung around angrily. "What is it?" he demanded. He was inwardly exhausted by the unceasing emotional soar and plunge between despair and the blindness and the folly of those with whom he had to work. Time and time again he had been on the brink of success, the beginning of the end, only to have it dashed from his hand. "What is it?" he said again.

The manservant opened the door, looking apologetic. "It is a gentleman to see you, sir. He won't give his name, but he says it is to do with a certain event on Hampstead Heath. Shall I ask him to leave, sir?"

"No. Tell him to come in," the Peacemaker said quickly. "Do not disturb us. We shall require no refreshment. You may retire. I shall show him out."

"Yes, sir. I'll send the gentleman up."

The man who arrived a moment later was thin, with a dark mustache and large, red-knuckled hands. He closed the door behind him. He met the Peacemaker's eyes without flinching, as if they were equals. The Peacemaker did not like him. They were on the same side by force, not idealism. There was no passion for humanity in this man, only for him-self and his own profit, but he was useful. "Yes?" he said curtly.

"Corracher's been talking to someone in the Secret Intelligence Ser-vice," the man told him. "He's seen the pattern, and it looks as if he could make a fight of it."

"Rubbish!" the Peacemaker snapped. "He'll only dig himself in deeper. No one's going to believe him."

"This man did," his visitor replied. "Started asking a lot of ques-tions, getting police records—times and places. He was very thorough."

The Peacemaker felt a tiny flash of anxiety, nothing more than a cold touch inside, there and then gone again. "Any idea who it is?"

"The man from Intelligence? His name is Matthew Reavley." The man said it without expression, as if it meant nothing to him.

"Thank you." The Peacemaker's voice was little more than a whisper, and he stood perfectly still in the room. Reavley again. The name was like a curse. He cleared his throat. "I doubt he will do anything, but I will at-tend to it. I am obliged to you that you had the foresight to tell me. Good night." He led the way down toward the front door, holding it open for the man to leave, then he locked and barred it behind him.

He returned to the upstairs room with an inexplicable sense of loss. It disturbed him. Of course Matthew Reavley would have to be killed. There was now no choice. Getting rid of ministers like Corracher was vital to the peace negotiations when they came. His Hungarian connec-tion had proved far better than the Peacemaker had foreseen. He was striving for unity! A single state, led by Britain and Germany. A renegade Hungarian leadership waiting to break up the old Austro-Hungarian Empire was the last thing needed.

It was also vital that the right men guided the peace. After the defeat of the generals on both sides, the ordinary men might still ally and lay the foundations of an empire that would begin to rebuild with justice, bring order and finally prosperity again and beauty out of the present chaos.

Why should he grieve that it cost the life of Matthew Reavley? That was a sentimental weakness he must not allow himself. He was bone weary, but far deeper than that he was heartsick. What on earth was one life more? Passchendaele was costing thousands a day! Every day!

But London was still outwardly civilized, so it must be done with care. He would set the act in motion tomorrow, speak to the right man for the task. If he allowed personal regret of any kind to hold him back he was despicable, not fit to lead. The best men in the country had lost sons and brothers.

He sat down at his desk and encoded a short letter to Manfred for Mason to take tomorrow. Manfred von Schenckendorff had been the Peacemaker's ally from the beginning, when it had still seemed possible that they might have won peace with honor, and avoided this whole misguided tragedy of war between two nations who should have been brothers—together. Manfred would understand the pervading sense of loss he felt that he had to destroy a good but stubborn man, as he had had to destroy Reavley's father before him. He would so much rather have won him to the cause.

This new turn of events with Corracher had left him no choice. Manfred would appreciate that; they had always understood each other in the subtler ways of honor and logic and the wounds of unnecessary tragedy.

He walked over to the gramophone, wound it up, and placed a record on it: Beethoven, the last quartets, composed after he was deaf—complex, subtle, marvelously beautiful, and full of pain.

THREE

*R*ichard Mason walked along the rutted and cratered road in the steady rain. The sky was leaden and the rumble and crack of gunfire was mixed with occasional thunder. The few trees still left standing had branches torn from them, lying rotting on the ground. His clothes were sodden and sticking to him and his feet were covered in the thick Flanders mud. It seemed to be everywhere. The unhedged fields swam with it, the ditches were awash, and it lay thick and churned up across the way ahead.

He had passed more troops going forward, more wagonloads of ammunitions and supplies. And of course there were columns of the walking wounded, moving slowly, awkward with pain, their eyes unfocused in that strange, blank stare of those who have seen hell and carry it within them. Some had their eyes bandaged, and stumbled forward, arms outstretched and hands on the shoulder of the man in front of them. Mason turned away, choked with grief.

He was less than two miles from the trenches now. He could smell the familiar stench of death.

What could he write that would be new about any of this? Were there really rumors of mutiny, or just the usual complaining that was part of any life? Possibly it was little more than a good-natured sympathy for the French.

An ambulance passed him, loaded with wounded, and he glanced at the driver. Every time he saw the high, square outline of an ambulance he thought of Judith Reavley and finding her before on a stretch of road just like this. It was knotting his muscles and making his chest ache, as memory of her always did, quickening the blood and stirring him with a deep, unsettling hunger. Then, she had been slumped over the wheel of her ambulance, motionless at the side of the road.

At first he had been terrified she was actually dead. His relief when she opened her eyes and looked at him had been like warmth on freezing limbs. Then she had spoken and he realized the vibrancy was gone from her voice, the passion. Even the anger was snuffed out. Something beautiful was broken. He had never hated the war as savagely as he had at that moment. All the injured men and riddled corpses he had seen had not moved him any more deeply. She had symbolized all that was precious in living: the laughter, the courage, and the strength.

He had managed to see her twice since then, once in Paris, very briefly and almost by accident. The second time, in London, was a great deal more by design.

It seemed a long time ago now, and unconsciously he quickened his step, almost unaware of the soaking rain.

Half an hour later, he reached the dressing station behind the supply trenches. It was on the third line back from the forward trenches on the edge of no-man's-land. The large tent was half supported by wooden walls at one side, and like everything else, was awash with mud. Through the gray air of late afternoon it was easy to imagine the dusk settling, although at this time of the year it would be hours yet before sunset.

Mason walked across the duckboards at the entrance and into the yellowish light of the lamps over the operating tables. He could smell blood and disinfectant. There were half a dozen men sitting on the floor, backs against packing cases. Two or three were drinking hot tea from tin mugs, their faces white. The others simply stared ahead of them into the distance as if they could see farther than the canvas wall or the darkening, rain-soaked air outside.

Another man lay on the table, the scarlet stump of his right leg making his injury hideously apparent. The surgeon working on him did not even look up as Mason came in. The anesthetist glanced at him, saw he was standing upright, and returned his attention to the patient.

A middle-aged medical orderly came over to him, his face lined with exhaustion. "Where are you hurt?" he said with little sympathy. His time was too precious to waste on the able-bodied.

"I'm not," Mason replied, understanding his feelings. "Richard Mason, war correspondent."

The orderly's face softened. "Oh. Come to see Captain Cavan? Up for the V.C., he is." There was pride in his voice and his head lifted, the weariness gone for a moment.

Mason changed his mind instantly about what he had been going to say, so that when he answered it had become the truth. "When he's got time. Are those men waiting for the ambulance?" He realized with a sudden grip like iron in his stomach that he did not know for certain if Judith was still alive. Ambulances were shelled like everything else. Drivers could be killed or injured. Just because someone was unhurt a week ago did not mean they were safe now.

"Yes," the orderly replied. "Shouldn't be long."

"Still got the American driver, Wil Sloan?" Mason pursued. It sounded as if he was looking for a story, even though his voice cracked a little. "Or did he go over to the American forces now they're in it, too?"

"They're not along this stretch," the orderly told him, his lips thinning for a moment. "We're all men who've been here from the beginning: English, Welsh, Canadians, French. Quite a few Aussies and New Zealanders, too. But Sloan's still here. At least he was this morning."

Mason did not ask what he meant. He had seen the casualty figures. His mouth was dry. "And Judith Reavley?" His heart pounded so he could hardly draw his breath as he waited the long seconds till the orderly answered. He realized how stupid the question was. Would the man even know one V.A.D. driver from another, or care, in this hell?

The orderly smiled, perhaps seeing Mason's emotion raw in his face, unguarded until too late. "Must have been a demon on the roads in Cambridgeshire, that one! She certainly is here."

Mason smiled back. He thought of saying something about his intention of writing an article on women in the battlefield, and then stopped himself in time. It would be absurd, and certainly wouldn't fool the orderly. "Thanks," he said simply. He accepted a hot cup of tea, which tasted of oil and dirt, and sat down to wait for a chance to speak to Cavan, and with the knowledge that in the next few hours Judith would come to this station.

The shelling grew heavier, but was still falling some distance from them. More wounded came in, but most of the injuries were superficial. Cavan acknowledged Mason briefly. He finished his operation on the man who had lost his leg, but could not leave him until the ambulance came. The rain never ceased its steady downpour, drumming on the canvas roof and adding to the already swimming craters outside. The wounded men's hair was plastered to their heads, their faces shone wet, their uniforms stained dark. Some were covered in mud up to their armpits and must have been manually hauled out of the shell craters before they could drown.

It was nearly an hour before the ambulance arrived. They did not hear it in the noise of guns and the beat of rain. Mason noticed the movement at the entrance and looked up to see Wil Sloan. He looked tired, pale-skinned, and filthy, but had the same cheerful smile on his face that Mason remembered from a year ago. "Hi, Doc," he said casually, looking across at Cavan. "Anyone for us?" His eyes went to the man on the table, who was still mercifully unconscious.

"Have you got a driver?" Cavan asked. "Someone'll have to sit with him. He's in a bad way."

Sloan's face tightened and he nodded. "Sure. If anyone can get us through this bloody bog, it's Judith . . . Miss Reavley."

Mason's heart lurched.

The ghost of a smile touched Cavan's face. "You're picking up our bad language, Wil? You'll shock them at home. I'll help you carry him out." He turned back to the table, his shoulders bent a little, a long smear of blood down his arm.

Mason stood up quickly. "I'll give you a hand," he offered. "I'm doing nothing. I'll get the stretcher."

Wil followed Cavan inside to help the other men who would take up the rest of the space in the ambulance. It would be only those who could not walk.

The minute Mason was outside the shelter of the tent the rain drenched him again. He could hardly discern the square outline of the ambulance through the gloom. His feet slipped in the mud and he found himself floundering. God knew what it must be like trying to struggle through it with ninety pounds of equipment and ammunition on your back and a rifle, knowing the bullets and shrapnel could tear into you any moment.

He saw Judith step out of the driver's seat of the ambulance and come forward to help him, mistaking him for a wounded soldier. He straightened up, feeling foolish. He wanted to think of something engaging to say, but his mind was racing futilely.

"There's an amputee coming out on a stretcher," he said instead. "Still unconscious. We're bringing him now. Wil Sloan's going to have to ride in the back—" The rest was cut off by the roar and crash of a shell landing five hundred yards away. It sent a tower of earth and mud high into the air, which rained down on the roof of the tent behind them, and onto the ambulance with the dull thud of metal.

Judith took no notice at all. Her face showed surprise and an instant of pleasure as she recognized him, then she went straight around to the back of the ambulance and opened the doors. She pulled out the stretcher without waiting for his help. She was swift, efficient, even oddly graceful.

Next moment Wil Sloan was there as well and all their thoughts were overtaken by the need to load the unconscious man. They carried him as carefully as possible in the wind and rain, and then had to decide which of the others were most in need of riding along with him, bearing in mind that there had to be room for Wil also.

"How's the road, Miss Reavley?" Cavan asked Judith when they were ready to go. The rain had eased a little but the heavy, overcast sky had brought darkness early and they were no more than outlines in the gloom.

"Bad," she answered, her voice strained with anxiety. "But there's no choice." She knew the amputee had to reach a hospital soon if he was to live.

"Wil can't leave him," Cavan warned her. "I'm sorry." They stood a yard away from each other and neither made a move or a gesture, but there was an intense gentleness in Cavan's face in the headlights, and Judith's eyes did not once waver from his. Mason saw it and was stung by a surge of jealousy so powerful it clenched his whole body. He was astonished at himself.

"Can I help?" he said immediately. "I can speak to you another time . . . sir."

"Yes," Cavan said. "Ride in the front with Miss Reavley. If there's a wheel to be changed, or debris to move from the road, she'll need another pair of hands." He did not ask Judith; it was an order.

"Yes, sir." Mason was pleased to obey. He splashed around to the other side and climbed in.

Cavan bent and cranked the engine, and it fired easily. Judith slipped in the clutch. There was a violent spurt of mud and they were jerked backward. Mason was startled, thinking she had forgotten which gear she was in.

She laughed. "On a slope," she explained. "Going uphill the tank drains backward and we get no power. Drive in reverse and we're fine. I'll turn here." She stopped and slewed around as she spoke, her hands strong on the wheel, muscles taut, then she drove forward along the dim, cratered road.

Every now and then star shells went up, lighting the landscape with its jagged tree stumps and erratic gouges out of the clay now filled with mud and water. There were wrecked vehicles by the side of the road and here and there carcasses of horses, even sometimes helmets to mark where men had died. Broken gun carriages and burned-out tanks showed up in the glare, and once the barrel of a great cannon projecting from a crater angled at the sky. Then the shell would fall and the darkness seemed more intense, in spite of the headlights, which showed little more than the slanting rain and the wilderness.

"How on earth do you know where you're going?" he asked her incredulously.

"Habit," she said frankly. "Believe me, I know this stretch of road better than I know my own village. Only trouble is we can't get Jerry to put the craters in the same place each time. He's a damn awful shot. All over the place like a drunken sailor."

He forced himself to smile, although he knew she could not see him, and the lunacy of the whole thing almost choked him. Didn't she see it, too? Was she deliberately blinding herself to it in order to survive? How could anyone tolerate being imprisoned in this, knowing the rest of the world was clean and sane? Somewhere beyond the endless violence, dirt, and incessant noise there were cities and villages where the sun shone, women wore pretty dresses, and people picked flowers, talked about crops and church fêtes, and gossiped. They ate around tables, washed in clean water, and slept in beds.

Another ambulance passed, lurching over the ruts, going toward the front line. For a moment its headlights lit Judith's face as she raised her hand in salute. He saw her high cheekbones and beautiful, vulnerable mouth. She looked older, more finely honed by horror and exhaustion, but the spirit was back as he had first known her.

He was amazed. How did she do that? Did she simply refuse to think? Had she no idea what was going on everywhere else, the suffering and monumental loss, the crushing futility of it all?

They barged over a rut and came down hard. Mason felt the bones of his spine jar. What must it be like for the injured men in the back, especially the one he had seen operated on?

He could not see Judith's face anymore as they lurched forward. He could just make out her shoulders as she clung on to the wheel, struggling to keep the vehicle on the road. The rain was harder again.

It was she who broke the silence.

"Did you come here to interview Captain Cavan?"

"Not particularly," he replied. "It seemed like a good opportunity. Does he deserve the V.C.?"

"Oh, yes." She could not keep the lift of excitement out of her voice as if there were new hope, and new life because of it. "His courage was extraordinary."

He had known she would say that and it frightened him. It was so easy! One man's heroism changed nothing, it was just a candle lit against the night. It would be quenched by the next gust of wind, and then the darkness would seem even worse. She was still just as naïve as ever. How many other men and women were there here just like her, believing the impossible, giving their lives pointlessly to defend a mirage?

"Did he really hold off a German attack practically single-handedly, and save his patients?"

"Not single-handedly," she corrected him. "We all fought. But he commanded. He was the one who defied them and refused to leave."

"We?" His voice was hoarse. "Are you speaking figuratively? You weren't there?" he insisted. He did not want it to be true because of the danger to her, but as much as the knowledge of how close she had come to death, he did not want her to have been part of Cavan's heroism.

"Yes, I was there," she replied as if it still surprised her. "We were caught off guard. We didn't expect the attack. It was well behind the lines."

He was stunned. A shell exploded to their left, flinging mud up against the side of the ambulance and across the windshield. They lurched badly. Judith swore and wrenched the wheel over, trying to right them again. He leaned across and put his weight against it, his hands touching hers.

"Thank you," she said matter-of-factly.

He did not reply, moving his hands away again and straightening himself in his seat. Suddenly he was acutely conscious of her, the mud and bloodstains on her gray dress, the curve of her cheek, the startling strength in her arms.

Ten minutes later they reached better roads which were still water-logged, but without the shell holes, and they picked up speed. The rain eased until it was no more than a fine mist like a veil across the head-lights, forever shifting and parting to show trees black against the sky. When they moved through villages, they found that a few buildings were burned out but most still stood, windows curtained against showing light. No one was in the streets.

"Have you been in France?" she asked him.

"Not lately," he replied. "I was on the Eastern Front, up in Russia."

"Is it as bad as they say?"

"Probably. Kerensky's trying hard, but he's changing too little. The time for moderation is gone. They want extreme now, someone more like Lenin or Trotsky. The hunger's appalling." He told her of individuals he had seen—the poverty, the hollow faces, the emaciated bodies. He said far more than he meant to, needing her to feel what he had, both the anger and the pity. He glanced sideways at her face, trying to read the emotions in it as she listened to him, seeing her expression fleetingly as they passed the lights of other vehicles. "Everybody's sick of the war," he finished.

"Only a madman wouldn't be," she replied, leaning forward to peer through the gloom. "But some things are necessary. Fighting is terrible. The only thing worse is not fighting." There was no doubt in her voice, no wavering.

"Is it really better to fight?" he challenged her. "Always? Even at this cost?" His voice was harsher than he had meant it to be because his own certainties had been torn away, leaving him naked, and he hated it. "And do you really know enough about the French to judge?" The instant the words were out he regretted them. He wanted her as she had been the first time he had met her, ignorant and brave, luminous with her own belief, even if it was absurd, and wrong. It was what made her beautiful. "I'm sorry. . . ." he started.

"Don't apologize. Not to me. At least you have the courage to say what you believe."

Should he answer her with the truth? He had seen the conditions in France, the unimaginable losses, the destruction, and it lacerated him with pity.

He did not want a division between them. He wanted her to care for him, to love him, but what use was that if he hated himself? What could he win with lies?

"It isn't always the enemy you have to fight," he said, weighing his words. "The French had reason for what they did. Enemies can be behind you as well as in front. The soldiers were mostly peasants, not revolutionaries at all. They objected to unfair rations and curtailed leave. New recruits were treated with favor while long-serving men were sent back to almost certain death, knowing their families at home were left to go hungry. Those who were excused from military service profiteered at their expense. Leave for agricultural purposes was based on political favoritism. They were willing to fight, and to die, but they wanted justice. I don't see that as cowardice, or disloyalty."

She remained silent, accelerating the ambulance over the smoother road. The rain had stopped and there were rents in the clouds. The moonlight showed the summer trees, heavy boughed and glistening as the headlights caught the wet leaves.

"I didn't know that," she said at last. "Poor devils. Do you think they'll be executed?"

He heard the pity in her voice, but no anger that he had shattered her illusion. He reached out his hand to touch her, lay his fingers on her arm, then changed his mind and withdrew it. He did not want to risk being rebuffed. He knew how it would hurt.

"Only a few," he answered her question. "Enough to make an example."

She said nothing. A few minutes later they pulled in at the hospital. From then on everyone was busy helping to unload the wounded. The amputee was still alive, but very much weaker, and in great pain. The only thing that Judith or Mason could think about was getting him out of the ambulance and into a bed as easily as possible.

After the men were all unloaded, Judith was standing with Mason when Wil Sloan emerged from the side door of the hospital ward into the cobbled yard. He looked almost ghostly in the lamplight.

Judith went over to him and locked her arm in his, leading him across the yard to the ambulance. "Let's see if there's somewhere open for a glass of wine and a sandwich," she said.

"It's half past one in the morning," he pointed out with a tiny smile.

She gave a shrug. "So we'll find someone who'll let us use their kitchen to make our own. We've got to sleep somewhere. Can't go back to the trenches until I've cleaned the ambulance and got some more petrol anyway." Mason had followed her. "Do you want to go back?" she asked him.

"Better than walking," he replied. "Unless, of course, you'll be shot for giving a civilian a ride?"

She gave him a quick smile. "We can always poke you with a bayonet, and put you in the back," she offered. "Then you'll be genuinely wounded!"

He was too tired to think of an answer.

Mason woke at five to find Wil Sloan's hand on his shoulder, shaking him gently. It was already daylight and the ambulance was clean and refueled. There was time for bread and tea, and then they were in the yard beside the ambulance and ready to go again.

Judith looked tired. In the morning light, which was harder and colder than the dusk of yesterday, he saw the fine lines in her face and the shadows around her eyes. She was twenty-six, but she could have been ten years older. Her dress was plain gray and completely without adornment.

The hem was still crusted with mud, but now he could see that the bloodstains were old and had already been washed many times. They were too soaked into the fiber ever to be removed.

She saw him watching her and gave him a tiny, self-conscious smile.

He remembered their first meeting with a catch in his throat that was as sharp as pain. It had been in 1915, in the Savoy Hotel. She had been dressed in a blue satin gown that had hugged her body and she had walked with a grace that had forced him to look at her. She had been angry, mistaken about almost everything, and utterly beautiful, enough to charm any man and stir forgotten hungers inside him.

Now the feeling was quite different. It was nothing to do with laughter or conquest, but a need within himself for something tender and clean, and immensely vulnerable, still capable of pain, and hope.

"Not quite the Savoy, is it?" she said drily, as if she had read his thoughts.

He felt the heat in his face. He wanted to look away from her, and could not. She would be gone too soon!

She was embarrassed also. "Come on!" she said quickly. "Get in!"

They spoke of general things. She asked him more about other battlefronts he had seen and he found it easy to tell her. He felt no more need to hide his feelings or his knowledge of casualties. He tried to describe the ravaged beauty of northern Italy with its exquisite skies over Venice and Trieste; the courage of partisan fighters in the mountains of Albania, particularly some of the women he had seen, struggling to get medical supplies to the wounded.

He even found himself explaining some of the moral dilemmas he faced as to how much or little he should tell the truth of certain events in his articles.

She listened with interest—and understood enough to offer no solutions.

It was a windy day with only a light rain. When they were two or three miles from the front, they saw a gun carriage on its side and a soldier standing beside it waving his arms in desperation. There were three others behind him near the gun and two horses harnessed to the gun carriage.

Judith pulled the ambulance to a halt as close as she could and the soldier was at her side immediately.

"Can you 'elp me, miss? Private 'Oskins is 'urt pretty bad. That bloody gun just pitched back into the mud and none of us could shift it, even with the 'orses. 'E's gonna die if we don't 'elp 'im. Both 'is legs is bust an' 'is back's gorn. I dunno 'ow ter move the thing wi'out makin' it even worse. Please . . ."

Judith turned off the engine. "Yes, of course we will," she said, climbing out without hesitation. "Come on." She gestured to Mason, then hurried around to the back just as Wil Sloan opened the door and looked out. "We need help, Wil," she told him. "Man trapped under a field gun. You'd better get tourniquets, and splints, and a stretcher." She turned to Mason. "You come with me." It was an order. Without seeing if he would obey, she picked up her skirts and waded through the ditch, in water up to her thighs. With a hand from the soldier she climbed out, then floundered across the thick, plowed clay to the crater. There, the other soldiers were trying to hold the gun from sliding even deeper, keeping the weary, patient horses leaning against the harness.

The injured man was almost submerged in the filthy water. Another man, who looked to be no more than sixteen or seventeen, held his head up, his eyes wide with terror. He was losing. He could feel the weight of the man slipping out of his grasp, slimy with mud and blood, and he was helpless to prevent it.

Mason dropped in beside him without even thinking about it, and grasped them both. They were freezing. The shock of it took his own breath away. A moment later Wil Sloan appeared with the stretcher. Judith was giving orders. "Hitch it tighter, move forward, slowly! Steady!"

There was a great squelch of mud and running water. Someone shouted, and the gun reared up. Mason put all his strength to pulling the wounded man, lost his footing, and fell back deeper into the crater himself. He thrashed around, suddenly terrified of drowning also. The clay held him. Water was in his eyes, in his mouth, over his head. It was vile, stinking of death. Someone caught hold of him and he was in the air again, gasping, filling his lungs. His hands still held the blouse of the wounded soldier. Wil Sloan was heaving on them both and one of the other soldiers as well.

They scrambled up onto the bank. Without even examining the wounds, Wil was binding tourniquets. Judith still held the horses.

"Hurry!" she shouted. "This gun's going to slide backward any minute. I'll have to cut the horses loose or they'll go, too!"

"Stretcher!" Wil bellowed. Mason staggered to his feet and grasped it. Together they rolled the wounded man onto it, and then raised it up. They were a couple of yards clear when Judith cut the harness. The gun and carriage both fell back into the crater, sending up a wave of mud and water that drenched them, even at that distance.

"What the bloody hell are you doing?" a voice shouted furiously.

Mason looked at the captain who stood on the side of the road glaring at them. He was a slender man, his wide, dark eyes seeming overlarge in his haggard face.

"Whose damn fool idea was it to take a gun across a field full of mud?" he demanded.

The corporal snapped to attention as well as he could, standing in the gouged-up clay and over his knees in mud. "Orders of Major Northrup, Captain Morel. I told 'im we'd get stuck, but 'e wouldn't listen."

Morel turned to Judith. "Get that man to the nearest field station. Cavan's only about a mile forward. Be quick."

"Yes, sir." Judith waved at Wil to go on, then climbed into the ambulance, her sodden skirts slapping mud everywhere, and took her place behind the wheel. "Will you have one of the men turn the crank for me?" she requested.

Wil slammed the door shut from inside with the wounded man. Morel himself turned the crank and the engine fired.

Judith looked quickly at Mason and he shook his head. There was a story here he had to find, and perhaps to tell. He hoped she understood. There was no chance to tell her.

She nodded briefly, then gave all her attention to driving.

Mason stood in the road and watched them go. He would speak to Cavan another time.

Captain Morel was tight with fury. His features were pinched and white except for two spots of color on his cheeks. His movements were jerky, his muscles locked hard.

"Leave it, Corporal!" he shouted at the man with the gun. "Save the horses and get them out of there."

"But, sir, Major Northrup told us—"

"To hell with Major Northrup!" Morel snapped back, his voice shaking. "The man's a bloody idiot! I'm telling you to get the horses out and rejoin your platoon."

The corporal stood where he was, torn with indecision. Mason could see that he was terrified of what Northrup, who outranked Morel, would do to him for disobeying his order.

Morel saw it, too. He made an intense effort to control his fury. His face softened into pity so naked Mason felt almost indecent to have seen it. He wanted to look away, yet his own emotion held him. He was involved whether he wanted to be or not. Equally, he was helpless. This was one tiny instance of idiocy in a hundred thousand times as much.

"Corporal," Morel said quietly, ignoring the rain running down his face. "I outrank you and I am giving you a direct order. You have no choice but to obey me, unless you want to be court-martialed. If Northrup questions you, tell him that. I'll answer for it; you have my word."

The corporal's face flooded with relief. He was no more than eighteen or nineteen. "Thank you, sir." He gulped.

Morel nodded. "Do it." He turned away, then, realizing Mason was still there, he faced him. His eyes were hard and belligerent, ready to attack if Mason criticized him.

Mason looked at him more closely. Everything about him spoke of a terrible weariness. He was probably in his mid-twenties, a public school boy, and later, judging by his accent, a student at Cambridge. A wounded idealist, betrayed by circumstances and blind stupidity that no sane man could have conceived of.

Mason thought of all the Frenchmen, also betrayed and slaughtered. Would the man in front of him mutiny, too? There was a rage in him too fragile, too close to snapping.

"Who are you and what do you want?" Morel demanded.

"Richard Mason, war correspondent," Mason replied. "Who is Northrup?"

Morel let out his breath slowly. "Major Penhaligon was killed on the first day of Passchendaele. Northrup's his replacement."

"I see."

"I doubt it." Morel glanced up the road the way the ambulance had gone. "You'll have to walk. Follow the stench. You can't get lost. Although it doesn't matter a damn if you do. It's all the same."

"I know."

Morel hesitated, then shrugged and turned away back to his own men and the staff car still parked on the edge of the road. After the driver cranked it up, Morel climbed in and they drove off.

Mason started to walk.

How should he write up this incident? Should he record it at all? It was a classic example of the idiocy of some of the officers now in command and, as always, it was the ordinary men who paid the price. Thanks to Judith's intervention, this one would only have two smashed legs. He might even walk again, if it hadn't caught his back as well. Others would be less fortunate.

He could see Judith in his mind's eye, ordering the soldiers to lift, stand, hold. Her voice had been perfectly calm, but he had seen the tension in her. She knew what she was doing, and the risks. If one of the horses had slipped or she had lost control of it, the gun carriage would have rolled back into the crater and crushed the soldier to death.

She had not seemed to give reason even a passing thought. Morel's fury had had no visible effect on her. She could have been a good nanny watching a small child throw a tantrum, simply waiting for it to pass before she told him to pull himself together and behave properly. It had not entered her head to rebel against the madness.

Why not? Did she lack the imagination? Was she conditioned to obedience, unquestioning loyalty no matter how idiotic the cause? Perhaps. John Reavley had stolen the treaty, and she was his daughter. Joseph Reavley was her brother. Maybe sticking to ideals regardless of pain or futility, in defiance of the evidence, was considered an evidence of faith, or some other virtue, in the family? She had been taught it when she was too young to question, and now to do so would feel like a betrayal of those she loved.

Mason's feet hurt in the wet boots, and he was growing cold in spite of the exertion of walking. Two years ago Joseph Reavley had followed him from the shores of Turkey right to Gibraltar, then out into the English Channel. After the U-boat had sunk the steamer, they had ended in the same open boat in the rising storm, trying to make for England.

Would Joseph really have let them both drown rather than surrender his ideals to fight to the end? That one article, had Mason written it, might have ended the recruitment of hundreds of thousands of men, God knows how many of them dead in the two years since.

Yes, Judith was probably just like Joseph.

Mason remembered with surprise how he had believed Joseph then. For a brief time he too had understood the reasons for fighting. They seemed to embody the values that made all life sweet and infinitely precious. Indeed, was life worth anything at all, worth clinging to without them?

How many more had given their lives, blindly, heroically, since then? For what?

What would happen if he wrote that honestly, put quixotic sacrifice in its place? It was meaningless in the long run, no comfort to the hundreds of thousands left all over Europe, whose sons and husbands would never return, lonely women whose hearts were wounded beyond healing. Judith would think him a traitor—not to the cause, but to the dead, and to the bereaved who had paid so much.

He realized only now, in the wind and rain of this Flanders road where the stench of death was already knotting his stomach, that her disillusion in time would be a pain he would never afterward be free from. It would be one more light gone out forever and the darkness would be closer around him than he could bear.

Joseph came out of his dugout at the sound of Barshey Gee shouting almost incoherently. Gee swung around as he saw Joseph. His face was red, his thick hair sodden in the rain.

"Chaplain, you've got to do something! The major's told us to go back out there and get the bodies, roight now!" He waved his arm toward the front parapet and no-man's-land beyond. "We can't, not in that mud! In the loight. Doesn't he know we'd do it if we could?" His voice was hoarse and half choked with tears. "Jesus! Fred Arnold's out there! Oi've known him all moi loife! Oi got stuck up a tree—scrumping apples in old Gabby Moyle's orchard. It was Fred who got me down before Oi were caught." He drew his breath in in a gasp. "Oi'd go if there were any chance at all, but that mud's deep as the hoight of a man, an if yer get stuck in it you've no chance. Jerry'll pick us off like bottles on a wall. Just lose more men for nothin'."

"I know that, Barshey," Joseph said grimly.

Barshey was shaking his head.

"Oi refused an order, Chaplain. We all did. He can have us court-martialed, but Oi won't send men out there." His voice was thick with tears.

"I'll talk to him." Joseph felt the same anger and grief hot inside him. He had known Fred Arnold, too, and his brother Plugger Arnold who had died of his wounds last year. "Wait here." He turned and strode back toward the officers' dugouts where he knew Northrup would be at this time of day.

All dugouts were pretty similar: narrow and earth-floored. There was room enough for a cot bed, a chair, and a makeshift desk. Most officers made them individual with odd bits of carpet, pictures of home or family, a few favorite books, perhaps a wind-up gramophone and several recordings.

Entrance was gained down steep steps and doorways were hung with sacking to keep out the rain.

"Yes, Chaplain?" Northrup said as Joseph answered the summons to come in. Northrup looked harassed and impatient. He was sitting in the hard-backed chair in front of the desk. There were half a dozen books on it, which were too worn for Joseph to read the titles. There was also a picture of a woman with a bland, pleasant face. Judging by the age of her and the resemblance about the set of eyes and the high brow, it was his mother.

Joseph disliked intensely having to speak, but he had no choice.

"Sir, I understand you ordered Corporal Gee to lead a rescue party to find the dead or wounded in no-man's-land."

"Of course I did, Captain Reavley." His voice was faintly patronizing, even if he did not intend it. "We can't leave them to die out there. Or fail to bring back the bodies of those who have. I regret that the corporal refused a direct order. I've given him half an hour to get his courage back, but if he doesn't, I'll have to put him on a charge. This is the British Army, and we obey orders. Do you understand me?"

Joseph wanted to tell him that the French command had driven its own men to mutiny, but he knew it would be disastrous to do that now. Northrup was thin-skinned enough to regard it as a personal insult and react accordingly.

He kept his temper under control with difficulty. "Sir, I've known Barshey Gee most of my life, and served beside him since 1914. He's one of the bravest men in this regiment, and if he could have gone out there without sacrificing his men pointlessly, then he would have. One of his closest friends was lost last night. . . ."

Northrup's face was hard, his pale blue eyes hot with anger. "Then why doesn't he get out there and look for him, Chaplain?"

Joseph had to struggle to keep his voice level. It was hard to breathe without gasping. "Because it's been raining for a week, Major Northrup," he said with elaborate patience that grated in spite of his effort to be civil. "The men are being sucked down into the mud and drowned! The craters are ten or twelve feet deep and no one can keep their footing for more than a few minutes. A soldier with full equipment hasn't got a chance. He'd be stuck fast, a sitting target. He's not willing to sacrifice more men pointlessly."

"Recovering the wounded is not *pointless,* as you put it, Captain Reavley." Northrup's face was white, his hand on the desk pale-knuckled and trembling. "I would have thought that, as a chaplain, you of all people would have known that! Think of morale, man. That's your job. I shouldn't have to do it for you!"

"I am thinking of morale, sir." Joseph's words came between clenched teeth. "Court-martialing one of our best soldiers because he won't lead his men on a suicidal mission is going to do infinitely more harm than the losses overnight."

Northrup glared at him. His certainty had evaporated, and he was doubly angry because he knew Joseph could see it.

"Sir!" Joseph started again, unable to hide his emotion. "These men have been here for three years. They've endured hell. Every one of them has lost friends, many of them have lost brothers, cousins. Their villages have been decimated. You know nothing of what they've seen, and if you want their respect, then you must also show them the respect they deserve."

Northrup remained silent for several minutes. Joseph could see the struggle in his face, the anger at being challenged and the fear of weakness. "Other men have gone out," he said finally. "That puts paid to your argument, Reavley."

"And have they come back?" Joseph asked. He sounded challenging and he had not intended to be. He sensed Northrup's need to prove himself right and that he might dig himself in if he felt threatened, and yet he had gone too far to stop.

"Not yet," Northrup said defiantly. "But Eardslie's a good man, an officer. He didn't refuse to go."

Nigel Eardslie was another of Joseph's students from St. John's, before the war: a sensitive, intelligent young man, a good scholar, and a close friend of Morel's. Suddenly the argument with Northrup was pointless. What did it matter who won it or who lost it? All he could think of was Eardslie and his men out in no-man's-land in the mud.

"It's not raining now," Northrup added, as if that vindicated him.

"It's not the rain that matters, it's the mud!" Joseph snapped. "If you'll excuse me, sir, I'll see if I can help." He did not bother to explain any further. Northrup was out of his depth and afraid to show it. Joseph saluted and left, pushing the sacking aside and climbing the steep steps up to the air again.

It took him nearly half an hour to make his way to the forward trench. The duckboards were awash, some floating knee-high in the filthy water. Others were almost waist-high, clogged with the bodies of dead rats, garbage, and old tins. The leg of a dead soldier stuck out from the gray clay of the wall. There were patches of blue sky overhead, but Joseph was cold because he was wet to the skin.

Going uphill slightly, he came to a relatively dry stretch and several groups of men cleaning equipment, telling bad jokes and laughing. One had his shirt off and had scratched his flesh raw where the lice had bitten him. Another had coaxed a flame inside a tin and was boiling water. Some were reading letters from home. Five of them could not have been over seventeen. Their bodies were slight, smooth-skinned, although their faces were hollow and there was a tight, brittle tension in their voices.

A hundred yards farther on he came to a connecting trench. Huddled along it, their backs to the walls, were a dozen men. He recognized Morel. He was standing a little apart from the others, bracing himself against the earth, his head back in a blind stare upward. The angles of his body were stiff, almost as if he were waiting to move, yet afraid to.

Joseph felt his chest tighten and his breath grew heavy in his lungs. He tried to go faster but the duckboards had rolled and were broken, and his feet could get little purchase in the mud.

No one took any notice of him when he stopped. He knew most of them. Bert Collins was there, caked in mud, his right arm blood-soaked. Cully Teversham and Snowy Nunn stood together with Alf Culshaw, who was smaller, narrow-chested, dapper when he had the chance. He always managed to scrounge whatever you wanted from rations—for a consideration, of course. He looked grim and tired, and there was a bandage wrapped tightly around his left arm. Stan Tidyman for once was not talking about his favorite food. He was shoulder to shoulder with George Atherton, who could mend anything if you gave him pliers, a bit of wire, and the time. The last one was Jim Bullen.

It was Cully who saw Joseph first, but there was no smile on his face. He did not even speak. No one saluted or came to attention.

Morel turned slowly but it was several seconds before his eyes focused and he recognized Joseph. His expression did not change. Snowy Nunn also stared unblinkingly.

They were covered in mud, wet to the waist, or—in the cases of Cully Teversham and Stan Tidyman—up to the armpits; all except Morel. In a blinding moment, Joseph understood: Barshey Gee had refused to take a party into no-man's-land to look for survivors and bring back what dead they could find, but these were the men Nigel Eardslie had led.

"Eardslie?" Joseph's voice was hoarse, almost unintelligible, except that they all knew what he was asking. He gulped air. "Wounded?"

"Dead," Morel said huskily. "There wasn't enough of him left to bring back. You want to bury one arm, a foot, Chaplain? Couldn't even tell if it was left or right." He could not control the tears running down his face.

Joseph was furious, raging against believing it, as if to refuse to acknowledge the fact could stop it being true.

"You went?" he said incredulously. "For God's sake, what's the matter with you?" He flung his arms out toward the sea of stinking, gassoaked mud beyond the hastily thrown-up line. Then words choked him and failed.

"No, of course I bloody didn't!" Morel shouted back at him, his voice so high-pitched it was almost a scream. His chest was heaving and he seemed hardly able to breathe. "That idiot Northrup ordered them and told them it was mutiny if they refused, and he'd charge them. And the stupid bastard would have, too!"

Joseph was overwhelmed. Grief and a terrible sense of helplessness stunned him. He had nothing left to say, no answers anymore. He stared at Morel and saw at the same time the young man he had first met at St. John's: careless, hot-tempered, quick to laugh, and possessed of a hard, supple intelligence. The idealist in him was bruised to the bone, scorched with pain at the loss, and at the monstrous stupidity of it. Everything in Morel's nature and his education told him it was his responsibility to stop it. He was bred to lead, to answer for actions and pay the price of them. It was naked in his face now, and he was teetering on the edge of mutiny. He would take Snowy with him—that was clear, too—and possibly several of the others.

How could Joseph tell them there was a God who cared? He felt his own belief slipping out of his grasp. He closed his eyes, his mind crying out, "Father, if You are there, if You still remember us, do something! We're dying! Not just smashed and bleeding bodies, we're dying inside. There's no light left."

"What do you say now, Reverend Reavley?" Morel's voice cut across his mind like a knife edge.

Joseph opened his eyes and wiped a muddy hand across his face. "Barshey Gee refused to go," he answered. "Northrup'll have to back down. Did you find any wounded still alive?"

"Of course we bloody didn't!" The tears streamed down Morel's face. "Those that weren't blown apart are drowned! And Northrup won't back down. He'll crucify the lot of us, if we don't get to him first. There's no point in waiting for God—Chaplain! How long does it take you to realize that there's no God there? No God that gives a damn, anyway." He turned and walked down the trench, blundering into the walls, bruising himself without knowing or caring.

Joseph had nothing to say. It even stole into his mind that perhaps Morel was right.

FOUR

*F*our nights after Eardslie's death, Northrup led a major assault. The rain had eased a little, but the water did not soak away through the thick clay of Passchendaele. It lay coating the paths and filling the craters and trenches.

Gradually they inched forward. The guns roared all night, and star shells lit up the sky. The landscape looked like the surface of the moon. It was hard to believe anything had ever lived on it, or would again.

They were long past midsummer and the days were shortening. The dawn was heavy and dull, a drifting mist and occasional rain obscuring most of the newly gained land. The woods ahead, beyond no-man's-land, were not even a darkening of the gray. It was ideal for going out to search for wounded.

"Bloody Jerry won't see anyone in this," Barshey Gee said cheerfully, swinging his rifle over his shoulder. "Ready, lads?"

"Roight," Cully Teversham agreed. Behind him Stan Tidyman, John Geddes, George Atherton, and Treffy Johnson nodded.

"Captain?" Barshey looked at Joseph.

"Of course." Joseph led the way up the fire step, across the parapet and down onto the slimy mud on the other side. They had to be careful because the winding path through the craters and bogs changed with every bombardment. Bodies floated beside it, grotesquely swollen, and the stench of rotting flesh and effluent flooding over from the latrines was hanging in the almost motionless air.

They went in twos, one man to help the other if either lost his footing. They spread out to cover as much ground as possible. No one spoke. The misty rain would probably deaden sound, but it was not worth the risk.

Cully Teversham went with Joseph. He was a big man with ginger hair that even the army barber couldn't tame and hands that dwarfed everything he held. He moved calmly, picking his way, testing the ground under his feet, always looking ahead and then to the sides.

A long spike of barbed wire caught around Cully's leg and he stopped, bending slowly to cut himself free. Joseph helped, and they moved forward again.

Ahead and to the left they saw Geddes and George Atherton. They were no more than shapes in the gloom, identifiable only by Geddes's stiff shoulders and the swing of his arms.

It was half an hour before they found the first wounded man. His side was torn open by shrapnel and one leg was broken, but he was definitely still alive. Awkwardly, slipping and floundering in the mud, they got him back across the parapet and to the dressing station behind. Then they went back to look for more. The mist was clearing, and in another hour their camouflage could be gone.

This time they were more certain of the path, and the urgency was greater. Joseph moved ahead, his feet sucking and squelching, tripping over occasional broken equipment, spent shells, and now and then part of a corpse. He was sweating. It was warmer and there were patches of blue sky above.

He saw the body before Cully did. It was lying on its side, looking as if it were asleep rather than dead. There was no apparent injury. Joseph quickened his step, slithered the last few feet, and bent over him. It was then he saw the crown on one shoulder. It was a major! He turned the man gently, trying to see who it was, and where he was wounded. It was Major Northrup.

Cully was at his shoulder. "In't no good, Captain. Look." There was no emotion in his voice. He was pointing at the man's head.

Joseph saw. There was a small blue bullet hole in his skull, just above the bridge of his nose, exactly in the middle.

"Sniper," Cully remarked. "Damn good shots, some o' those Jerrys.

Mind, I suppose he were pretty far forward. Clean way to go, if you've got to, eh?"

"Yes," Joseph agreed. It was. Far better than being gassed, coughing your lungs up, drowning in your own body's fluids, or being caught on the wire, riddled with bullets, and hanging there perhaps for days till you bled or froze to death. But that was not what was in his mind. Why had none of his own men brought Northrup back? Surely they had seen him fall? But no one had even reported him missing.

"Let's get him back," he said grimly.

"Yes, sir," Cully said obediently.

It was an awkward journey and as the sky cleared and the heat burned through, the ground steamed gently. But the cover it offered was too little. Shots began to ring out, shells and sniper fire starting to miss them too narrowly.

They reached the forward lines, then the parapet, and rolled over into the shelter and filth of the front trench. Hands reached out to help them.

"He's dead," Cully said matter-of-factly. "Can't do nothing for him, not now."

"The major!" Stan Tidyman said in surprise. "Well Oi never!"

"Now we'll have to get another one," Tiddly Wop Andrews remarked. "Can't be worse than this, though, can he?"

Barshey Gee fished a sixpence out of his pocket and slapped it on the fire step. "Sixpence says it can," he said with a smile. "Oi'll be happy to lose."

The others laughed.

It was Joseph's duty to report the death to Colonel Hook at the regimental command. Northrup would have to be replaced. Headquarters might send someone, or it might be a field promotion of someone already with them, but he had no time to think about it. Please heaven it would not be Morel. Joseph still did not know what to do about him, how to help or where his first obligation lay. Morel was angry at Northrup's incompetence and his arrogance at refusing to be helped by a man from the ranks, even when he was right. But he was far from the only experienced man to feel that. And he was grieved at Eardslie's death. They had been friends for years.

Geddes and Bill Harrison helped Joseph carry Northrup to the table in the first aid post. He would be buried close by, probably tonight. Precious transport had to be kept for the wounded.

He thanked them and Harrison remained behind. "Can I help you, sir? Tidy him up a bit?"

"Thank you," Joseph said. It was a grim task, but he had done it so often it was almost mechanical now. Such decencies really were for those left alive who would know, a rather pointless exercise in humanity, as if it could make any difference. Northrup was beyond help, and no one else cared. It was a pretense that in the seas of blood each death was somehow important. The whole of the Western Front was strewn with broken bodies; many of them would never be found. He had presided at burials where there was little more to identify than a handful of dog tags.

Still he accepted the offer, and together they straightened his uniform, took off the worst of the mud and washed his face. Northrup looked frightened. There was no resolution or peace in his pinched features.

"Reckon as he saw it coming, don't you, sir?" Harrison asked with a touch of pity. Perhaps now that Northrup could do no more harm he felt free to treat his weaknesses with humanity.

Joseph looked down at the corpse. He closed the staring eyes. "Yes," he agreed. "It looks like it."

"Poor devil," Harrison said bleakly. "Is there anything else I can do, sir?"

Joseph found his throat dry, his hand trembling a little. "No, thank you. This is just routine. I'll have to go and tell Colonel Hook, but I'll make Northrup look a bit better first."

"Yes, sir." Harrison saluted and left.

When Joseph was certain he had gone he looked again at Northrup's face. Even with his eyes closed, the fear was still there, ugly and painfully naked. How long would it be before Harrison realized that Northrup could not possibly have seen the sniper? Any German must have been at least five hundred yards away from where they had found Northrup's body. Had Northrup simply panicked under fire? Please God that was it!

Please God? Did he think God was listening after all? Joseph had wanted Northrup removed before he killed any more men with his arrogant stupidity, but not this way!

He slid his hand under Northrup's head and felt the exit wound. The bone was splintered, hair matted with blood and brain. There was no point in trying to wash it off. Simpler to bandage it briefly, decently. Make him look whole.

He took off the tin helmet and washed that clean. He stared at it. There was no scar, no mark on the metal where the bullet had exited. Where was the bullet? Fallen out onto the ground, or inside his clothes?

The answer was obvious but he still resisted it. There must be another explanation.

Deliberately, methodically, he examined the rest of the body. There were no other injuries on him, except for a chafing at the wrists. It was not much more than red marks and a little broken skin, as if he had been firmly tied, but not harshly.

Joseph knew it before he forced himself to accept it. Old memories flooded into his mind of finding another body and bringing it back, and then realizing it was not a casualty of war but murder. That time he had at first assumed a German soldier had held the dead man's head below the water. This time he knew straightaway it was his own men who had killed Howard Northrup. But now, two years and thousands of deaths later, Joseph would be a great deal more careful what he did about it. The grief of that time, and the guilt of his own part in it, still haunted him. Before he reported this to anyone, he would learn more about Northrup's incompetence, how serious it was, how many lives it had cost, or had appeared to cost, and whose. He would look further than an instant judgment of what seemed to be justice. He was wiser now, more aware of the complexity behind an apparently simple act. These men lived in circumstances unimaginable to those who had originally written the rules. How could any sane man have conceived of this horror, let alone framed laws to meet its needs?

He reached for a wet rag and was making sure the crowns on Northrup's epaulettes were clean, when he saw Richard Mason standing in the doorway. His dark face which concealed so much emotion was set in lines of tense expectancy.

"Hello, Mason," Joseph said with slight surprise. The last article of Mason's he had read had been sent from Russia. "There's nothing new here. You could copy what you put last time, just change the casualty figures."

Mason's mouth tightened in the barest of smiles. He came farther into the room. "Was he alive when you found him?" he asked.

"No." Joseph knew in that moment that he would give Mason no information he did not have to. He needed time. He liked Mason personally; they had struggled through the nightmare of Gallipoli together, and then the storm in the English Channel, but Mason was a war correspondent. He would publish the truth of a situation, no matter how hideous, if he believed it served a greater good. Perhaps that was right, but Joseph had already learned how hard it was to judge where a path might lead, and that it was too late to be sorry afterward. Very little was simple.

Mason was looking at him, eyes unwavering. "Sniper?"

"Looks like it," Joseph said. He knew it was a lie, but he needed to learn more before he committed himself. "Why? Are you going to write an obituary for him?"

Mason smiled this time, but there was no light in it, no humor. "Do you think I should, Reverend? What should I say? Killed in the line of duty, Passchendaele, the eighth of August, 1917. Not exactly individual, is it! I could write that for tens of thousands of men. They're all unique to those who loved them, someone's only son, only brother, husband, fiancé, friend." His eyes widened and his voice became harsher. "What should I say about Northrup? That he was an arrogant fool and his men hated him? His death may save the lives of a few poor devils he'd have sent over the top uselessly?"

"If you set yourself up to judge one man, then you need to judge them all," Joseph replied, this time facing him without flinching. "Do you feel you have the right or the ability to do that, Mason?"

Mason's mouth turned down in a wry wince. He leaned against the upright of the tent flap and put his hands in his pockets.

"Of course I don't. That wasn't really my point. I notice that you question my right to say so, but not that it is true."

"I question your right to come to that conclusion," Joseph corrected him. "But I don't really care what you think, only what you say."

"And you don't want me to say that Northrup was an incompetent officer and it's a blessing for his men that he's dead?" Mason raised his eyebrows. "His men are saying it themselves."

"Possibly," Joseph agreed. "To each other, but they wouldn't write it down, or repeat it where his family will hear."

"Perhaps that's the problem?" Mason suggested. "We cover the errors, however disastrous, if it's going to hurt someone's feelings, especially if that someone is an officer."

"We do it for the dead, whoever they are," Joseph corrected him again.

"Ah." Mason smiled. "That's the point, isn't it? Now he's dead, his mistakes die with him. He's no more danger, so why cause unnecessary pain?"

Joseph was beginning to feel cold in spite of the August sun burning outside and the close, overwarm air. "What is it you want, Mason? As you said, the man was arrogant and a fool, but he's dead. Do you feel some moral obligation to soil his name and make his family's grief the greater, just because it's true? What about the families of the men who died because of his ignorance or bad judgment? Do you think knowing that will help their pain?"

"That's what it's about, isn't it, Chaplain? Pain to other people?"

Joseph stared at him. The fierce intelligence in Mason's eyes did not allow him to delude himself any longer. "Part of it, yes."

"And is covering their sins the part you've taken on yourself?"

"Northrup's sins are not my business, Mason," Joseph told him. "Neither are they yours. He can't do any more harm now."

Mason straightened up. "It won't work, Reavley. I'm not referring to Northrup's sins, and you know that. I'm talking about how he died. I saw you look at the helmet. The bullet wasn't there, was it?"

"Probably fell out." Joseph still tried to evade the issue.

Mason walked over to the table and looked down at Northrup's face. "He was shot by his own men, or at least by one of them. And the others are covering for him. You know that. Are you going to lie, by implication, so they escape with murder?" Now he was looking at Joseph, his eyes searching Joseph's, probing for honesty. "Does war really change things so much, Chaplain?"

"I don't know what happened yet," Joseph answered him. "I want to find out before I jump to conclusions."

"Liar," Mason said quietly. "You want to find out if it was one of the men from your own village who killed him, so if it was, you can protect him."

Perhaps a year ago Joseph would have lost his temper. Now he kept it tightly governed. "I want to find out what happened before I set in motion a chain of events I can't stop or control," he said gravely. "Perhaps moral issues are all black and white to you, although I doubt it. I know you've been prepared to sacrifice one goal to attain another." He was referring to their argument in the Channel two years ago, and the implicit fact that Mason would allow some of his own countrymen to be killed in order to save the vast majority. Or was he naïve enough not to know decisions like that faced military commanders every week?

Mason smiled. The expression softened his face, changing him. "But we are not the same, Reavley. I'm a war correspondent. I can observe, tell stories, ask questions. You're a chaplain, supposedly a man of God. People think you know the difference between right and wrong. They look to you to tell them, especially now when the world is falling apart. If you won't stand, Reverend, who will?" There was mockery in his face, but a wry, self-conscious sort of hope as well. He wanted Joseph to have the certainty and the faith he did not. He might have denied it—Joseph believed he would have, because it was too precious to put to any test. Fragile as it was, ephemeral, he would be lost without it.

"I did more than that before," Joseph answered him. "And I'm not sure whether I was right or not."

"Northrup was murdered." Mason bit his lip. "If he hadn't been, you wouldn't argue the issue now, you'd just deny it."

"I've only just seen the helmet." Joseph told the truth, but it was still a prevarication, and the moment he had said it he was sorry. He should have known what to do, if right and wrong were as clear to him as Mason seemed to imagine. And not only Mason. Many of the men thought he should not be confused, as they were. They wanted answers, and felt let down if he could not give them. Priests were God's authority on earth. For a priest to say he did not know was about the same as admitting that God Himself did not know; that He had somehow become confused and lost control. Life and death themselves became meaningless.

Mason was waiting.

"You are not naïve," Joseph told him. "Your faith doesn't rest on me. Don't blackmail me with it. I don't know what happened to Northrup. Of course his own men might have killed him. It happens. I'd like to know more of the circumstances before I report it to Colonel Hook."

Mason's eyes were steady, unblinking.

"Why? In case the man who did it is someone you like, whose father and brothers you know? Or are you afraid the morale of the whole brigade will crumble if you tell the truth?"

"Aren't you?" Joseph continued. "Or is that what you want? Truth at all cost? Whoever pays?"

"Who pays if the chaplain condones men murdering one of their officers because they don't agree with his orders?" Mason asked.

"Is that how you see it?" Joseph said tensely. "If it's as simple as that to you, maybe you should be the chaplain. You seem to have right and wrong very clearly labeled. You know far more about it than I do?"

Mason shrugged. "No. But I know what the men will say, and so do you. If you let Northrup's death go, who's next? I haven't any faith that what we're fighting for is worth the price. I think the whole bloody nightmare is madness. If I believed in the devil, I'd say he's taken over." He spread his strong, supple hands. "This has to be as close to hell as it gets. But you believe in something. You don't have to be here. You could have stayed at home and looked after a nice quiet parish in the countryside, comforted the bereaved, and kept spirits up on the home front. But you're here. Why? Just going down with the ship because you don't know what else to do? Can't find a way to admit you were wrong, or can't face telling the men that?"

He had touched a nerve. How many nights had Joseph wrestled in prayer to find some sense, some light of hope in the endless loss? If God really had any power or cared for mankind at all, why did He do nothing?

Was Northrup's murder just one more ugly and senseless tragedy for him, for his family, and most of all for the man who had pulled the trigger? Or would it be the catalyst for a general mutiny against the senseless daily slaughter?

Joseph could divert the attack against himself by attacking Mason in return, but it answered nothing, and Mason would know it, just as he knew it himself.

"You seem to think I should be the judge of what to do," he said slowly. "And yet you have decided for me, before either of us knew what happened, or what result will come from pursuing it."

"I know what result will come from not pursuing it," Mason told him. "And so do you. Either you tell Hook, or I do."

Joseph did not put him to the choice. If Hook had to be told, it would be his way.

"You're quite sure, Captain Reavley?" Hook said unhappily. He was a lean man who had been spare to begin with and was now almost gaunt. He had been twice wounded, and the way he stood betrayed every so often that his shoulder still ached.

Joseph had said only what he had found, without drawing conclusions. "Yes, sir."

"Any idea who is responsible?"

"No, sir. I'm afraid Major Northrup angered quite a few of the men."

Hook gave him a dour glance. "He angered the whole bloody lot, Reavley. That isn't what I asked."

"I have no idea which of the men is responsible."

Hook stared at him. His eyes were shadowed. He had seen too many of his men die, and he was helpless to do anything but go on ordering them forward in endless attack after attack. He wanted to avoid this one further pointless grief. He sighed. "See what you can find out when you have the chance." He waited, trying to gauge if Joseph understood him.

"Yes, sir." Joseph came to attention. "As soon as I have the opportunity."

Hook relaxed a little. "I'll write to his father. I should do it myself. Thank you, Reavley. You can go."

Two days later, on the tenth of August, the rain burst like a monsoon over Ypres and Passchendaele, running in rivers down the slopes of the slight hills, filling the trenches till men were waist-deep in it. The fields became quagmires, latrines flooded, stores were ruined and swept away. In every direction one looked was water and more water.

Men made jokes about collecting animals.

"Anybody give me two cows for two rats?" Cully Teversham asked hopefully.

"Two cows for twenty rats?" George Atherton improved the offer, then laughed with the odd, jerky sound he always made.

"Oi'd give you all the sodding rats in Belgium for two cows," Tiddly Wop Andrews retorted.

"I've already got all the sodding rats in Belgium!" Geddes said bitterly.

Into this morass came General Colin Northrup to mourn the loss of his son. He arrived in the middle of the afternoon, climbed out of his car, and stood in the torrential rain as if completely unaware of it, his back ramrod stiff, his face ashen.

It was Joseph's task to meet him. Apart from his obvious grief, and his rank, the general was instantly recognizable because of his physical resemblance to his son. His coloring, the angle of nose and jaw, the steady blue eyes were all the same. Only his mouth was different. There was none of his son's indecision in it, none of the hesitation or lack of fire.

Joseph saluted him and received a smart salute in return.

"If I can be of any service to you, General Northrup, I am at your command. May I extend the condolences of the whole brigade, sir. We all feel his loss."

"I'm sure you do," Northrup said quietly, his voice raw with hurt. "I understand he is the second commanding officer you have lost in a short space of time."

"Yes, sir." It seemed ridiculous to equate Northrup with Penhaligon, but only to Joseph who knew them both and had liked and admired Penhaligon. He struggled to find anything to say that would be even decent, let alone helpful. He understood grief. He had lost his wife, Eleanor, in childbirth in 1913, and his son as well, then both his parents had been murdered by the Peacemaker's agent the year after. God knew how many of his friends had also died since then. There was not a man here who could not name a dozen they had lost. He knew no one could ease this man's grief, but he could at least not insult him with dishonesty. "It always hits the men very hard. I'm sure you know that they often cover their feelings with jokes. It's the only way to hold on to sanity."

"Yes." Northrup swallowed. "Yes, I know that, Chaplain. I don't expect to see the loss I feel in anyone else, nor will I mistake levity for lack of respect. They did not have time to know him as I did, or what a fine man he was."

"No, sir. We have a dugout for you, if you'd like to stay, but I daresay you would prefer to see his grave, and then decide for yourself what to do next. When you are ready, I'll show you. It's . . . it's quite a decent place. We have very good men there."

Northrup's face was set so hard the muscles in his jaw quivered and a nerve ticked in his temple. "Show me my son's grave, Captain Reavley."

Joseph obeyed. It was over a mile's walk through the drenching rain, but Northrup was too lost in his grief to be aware of physical discomfort. When they reached the place, which was filled with makeshift crosses, its earth newly turned, they stood in silence. Joseph already knew where Major Northrup's grave was among the thousands. He took the general to it, then left him alone with his thoughts. Joseph, too, had agonizing memories that made him appreciate solitude. Half the men who had left England with him lay covered in this earth.

He waited until the general moved at last, stiffly, as if all his body ached and his joints pained him. Northrup could not have been more than in his early fifties, but he seemed an old man.

"Thank you, Captain," he said courteously. "He was my only child."

There was no answer to give that had any meaning. Joseph treated it with the dignity of silence.

The battle continued unabated. Joseph sat in his dugout, the endless rain beating unheard on the roof above him. It was difficult to keep the water from running down the steps and inside.

He had already written the day's letters of condolence, five of them to the same small village half a dozen miles from St. Giles where he lived. He did it now almost as if in his sleep. He could no longer think of anything individual to say, even though he had known each of the men.

Now it was time to answer his own mail, the first chance he had had in several days. He picked Matthew's letter off the top of the pile. It was general news, gossip about people they both knew, what was on in the theater or the cinema, a book he had wanted to read but could not find, an art exhibition everyone was talking about. It was not the facts that mattered but the pleasure of hearing from him, the familiarity of the phrases he used; as for everyone, it was the contact with home and people he loved.

He wrote back with all the harmless news he could think of, the bad jokes and the opinions, the rivalries and the generosity.

He replied similarly to his sister Hannah at home in St. Giles. She, of course, had written to him about the village and the people they both knew, but mostly of her children and the odd scraps of news about her husband, Archie, at sea in command of a destroyer.

She described the late summer trees, the gold of the fields, how untidy the garden was, and regretted that she could think of no way to send him raspberries, which were now ripe.

He smiled as he thanked her. Then he told her about Tucky Nunn, and asked her particularly to do what she could for his mother. Not that there was anything, but one had to try.

He wrote also to Hallam Kerr, the vicar in St. Giles who had been so utterly useless last year when Joseph had been home recuperating from injury. Then Kerr had sputtered platitudes, out of touch with any kind of real emotion. By the time Joseph left, Kerr had begun to grasp reality and find the courage to face it. Since then he had matured into a man who was usually adequate, and sometimes superb, but good or bad, he no longer ran away or hid in meaningless ritual answers.

He could not offer Kerr advice, nor did he need it; he simply reaffirmed friendship.

The most difficult letter to answer was the last he had received from Isobel Hughes. In 1915 her husband had been killed and Joseph had sent his condolences along with the official notice of bereavement. She had written back to thank him, and a warm and honest friendship had developed between them. Often he had found he could tell her of his feelings more openly than he could anyone else. Her answers, her faith in him and her easy, natural stories of her own life, hill-farming in Wales, had been a balm to him on many long and bitter nights.

Her last letter had woken in him almost a sense of betrayal. He was aware how ridiculous that was, and yet it was taking time for the smart to go away. He had never met her, and yet he had been taking some part of her affection for granted.

Now she had told him, perhaps a little awkwardly, maybe not soon enough, that she had met a young man, invalided out of the army, and was falling in love with him, and he with her.

Joseph sat in his rickety chair, holding the notepaper in his hands and reading her words again. What was he losing, exactly? More than a correspondent? He knew Isobel Hughes's ideas, nothing more. That was not how love worked, not really. Did he want comfort, or did he also want the urgency, magic, the beating heart?

Could he fall in love again, after Eleanor?

Yes, if he was honest, he could. Was that a betrayal, too? Was that what he was afraid of? He wanted someone safe, so he would never risk that sort of pain again.

There it was, in the open. Fear. He was looking for safety.

He took out the pen again and wrote: *Dear Isobel,* and then quite easily the words came to wish her happiness, and rejoice with her.

Then he wrote to Lizzie Blaine, the widow of the young scientist who had been murdered in St. Giles last summer. It was she who had told him how Hallam Kerr had grown more than Hannah had, or anything Kerr himself had written. But then Lizzie was blazingly honest, even when she was the one most hurt by it. And she was brave. Her husband's death had been appalling, but she had never flinched from seeking the facts, facing them wherever they led. It was not that she was not afraid, he had seen it in her eyes, her hands gripped on the steering wheel of her car as she had driven him on his quest both of pastoral care and of investigation, his injuries having prevented him from driving himself. She was deeply afraid. But she had a wry, self-mocking humor and a courage that forced her forward, whatever the price.

He could not remember that time with its horror and its burning disillusion without thinking of her also, and the companionship they had shared in such quiet adversity was a balm to the pain of it, a bright thread woven through the darkness, a loyalty amid the betrayal.

He wished he could tell her of Northrup's death and the things he was afraid of now, but military censorship would only cut it out. He knew better than to try. Instead he told her how much he missed the richness of summer at home, the quiet lanes, the smell of growing things, the sight of horses leaning into the plow, men laughing over pints of ale after the work was done, faces burned by the sun.

He missed the silence. His ears ached for it. He missed dew on the grass, and the smell of clean earth. He told her all of that, more clearly than he ever had before, and setting the words down almost brought it within his grasp again.

There was a sharp rap on the wood by the sacking curtain, jerking him back to the present. The moment he answered, General Northrup came in. Joseph was startled, having assumed that he had left. Now his face was as pale as before, and his body as stiff, but his eyes were hot with anger. He did not attempt to conceal it, but stood swaying very slightly on the damp earth floor, his hands locked behind his back. He spoke before Joseph could rise to his feet.

"Captain Reavley, I have to tell you that I find morale among your men so low that they have descended to the grossest disloyalty toward their officers. There is a laxity that I cannot and will not tolerate." He spoke very clearly, enunciating each word. "I have even heard oblique suggestions that my son was less than competent in his command. It is a slur on the name of a fine man who gave his life in the service of his country, and it is ... obscene." He took a deep breath. "In the name of decency it must cease. The men responsible for such traitorous talk must be identified and punished." He drew his shoulders back even further. "I am disappointed in you, sir, that you did not take action sooner than this to stop such infamy."

Joseph was standing now. He felt the heat burn up his cheeks, not for shame that he had not defended Major Northrup, but because he had allowed himself to hope that the general would leave without hearing it.

"Perhaps you believed that you were being loyal to Colonel Hook," Northrup went on. "You are mistaken. The ultimate loyalty is to the truth. You do the army no service by keeping silent while slander and betrayal go on. As a man of God your duty is to the highest principles of honor. Your own convenience is nothing." He sliced his hand in the air, then put it back stiffly to his side again. "You have let down your cloth, sir. I will not permit you, or any man, to dishonor my son. Do you hear me?"

"Yes, sir." Joseph's mind raced. How could he respond to this man who was so deeply outraged by what was essentially the truth? If only right were as clear as General Northrup imagined. Did one place ideals of truth before compassion for men? This was a hell where just to survive took all a man could dredge up out of his soul. Hope and sanity were lights on a hill the other side of the abyss.

Northrup was waiting for an answer. His son was dead and his grief was insupportable. What good was forcing him to see the truth?

"Well?" Northrup's temper broke. "Don't just stand there, man! Account for yourself!"

How many explanations were there that would not wound irrevocably? They would sound to Northrup like lies and excuses anyway.

"I'm sorry, sir," Joseph began. "Major Northrup replaced a man deeply respected. It was after that that we suffered a great many losses, both wounded and dead. Some of the men blamed Major Northrup for giving orders that cost many of those lives."

"Rubbish!" Northrup snapped. "To blame an officer for necessary orders is close to mutiny, sir. Which you must know as well as I do! You may be a man of the cloth, but you are in the army. How long have you been out here?" His eyes narrowed and he looked Joseph up and down critically.

"Since September 1914, sir," Joseph answered him equally curtly.

Northrup swallowed. It was far longer than he had been there himself. In that instant Joseph knew it, and Northrup saw that he did.

"With these same men?" Northrup asked more quietly.

"Yes, sir, those that are still alive. A lot of them are replacements, recently recruited. Half the old regiment's gone."

Northrup sighed, his face ashen. He swallowed convulsively. "They are still at fault, Captain. They have no right to question an officer's order in the field. That is not the worst of it. I have . . . I have even heard suggestions that his own men are glad he is dead." He did not add the last fearful thought to that, but it was in the air unsaid.

Joseph had to face it. "If you are asking what I think you are, sir, then that is nonsense. There is always some degree of loose talk. The men are facing death. Most of them will not come back, and they know it. They have two or three weeks to live, at most. Some will die easily, by one bullet through the head, like Major Northrup. For others it will be far harder. I think we should ignore the more foolish things that are said."

General Northrup's voice was hoarse. "Do you? Do you indeed? Well, I do not. Stupidity I can allow. They are, as you say, ordinary men facing a grim death. But I will not have my son's name slandered. And if you will not stop it, then I will speak to Colonel Hook."

"General Northrup!" Joseph knew the man was going to provoke the very disaster he most feared. Of course he could not bear to think his son was a fool, or that his men had hated him, but by forbidding them to say so, he would force the truth into the open. Someone's temper would snap, and he would say it simply to defend himself or, more probably, to defend someone else.

"What is it, Captain?" Northrup said tersely.

"Sir, you can command men to obey you, and shoot them if they don't. You cannot command them to respect you. That you have to earn, especially after you have given orders that have cost lives and achieved nothing."

Northrup's face mottled dull red. "Are you saying that my son gave such orders, Captain Reavley?"

"I'm saying that no one can govern what the men think, sir. When people speak foolishly, because they are exhausted, beaten, and afraid, it is better to overlook—and forget."

"That is the coward's way, sir," Northrup replied. "If you will do nothing, then I shall speak to Colonel Hook. Good day, Captain Reavley." He turned and went out without a salute, leaving Joseph standing alone.

That night the bombardment was heavy. The rain never ceased. It looked like it would be the wettest August anyone had ever known. By morning the casualties were heavy, some of them from drowning.

By midday Joseph was so bone weary his body ached, his head throbbed, and his eyes felt as if they had burning grit in them. His clothes were stiff with blood and his skin was rubbed raw.

He had worked with Cavan in the field hospital most of the night, helping in every way that he could. The man seemed never to cease working. His eyes were bloodshot, his face ashen, but he moved from one broken body to the next like a man in some terrible dream.

That afternoon Joseph was standing in the supply trench, eating a heel of bread and trying to keep it out of the rain, when Barshey Gee came up to him.

"Sorry, sir," Barshey said, screwing his face up. "Colonel Hook would like to see you, sir. Right away." He looked unhappy. There was a scar down his cheek oozing blood which was washed away instantly. His right arm moved awkwardly because of the thickness of the bandage beneath his tunic.

Joseph put the rest of the bread in his mouth. "Right," he acknowledged.

"Sir . . ." Barshey began, then stopped.

"Yes?"

"General Northrup's with him, Chaplain." He said no more, but Joseph understood. There was no avoiding it now.

"I'll do what I can," Joseph promised. He knew Barshey would understand what he meant.

Hook was waiting for him in the command dugout. General Northrup was sitting on the other decent chair, which left an old ammunition box for Joseph to sit on, after he had saluted and been told to be at ease. It was hot and airless inside the confined space, but it was relatively dry.

Northrup looked like a man who had won a bitter victory, exhausted but justified.

"Captain Reavley," Hook began miserably, "General Northrup informs me that there is considerable talk among the men that his son, Major Howard Northrup, did not die as a result of enemy fire."

Northrup shifted his weight in the chair impatiently, but he did not yet interrupt.

Hook was aware of it. "If that is so, of course," he went on, "then it is an extremely grave matter. . . ."

Northrup could not contain himself any longer. "It is more than grave, Colonel Hook," he cut across him. "It is murder, plain and simple. It means you have men who under ordinary law are guilty of the most terrible of all crimes, and under military law are also guilty of mutiny, and must face a firing squad."

Hook kept his courtesy with a very obvious effort. He remained looking at Joseph, as if desperate for his help. "If that is so," he continued, "then it is, as General Northrup says, a capital crime. I can't imagine why any of our men would do such a thing." He spoke carefully, enunciating every word. "Major Northrup had been here only a matter of a week or two. I can't think how he could have made an enemy of that depth in so short a time."

"Of course he didn't!" Northrup snapped. "Your men are out of control! On the verge of mutiny. Major Northrup exerted some discipline, perhaps for the first time, and they resented it. Or possibly there was mutiny planned, and he discovered it, and would naturally have had them arrested and shot. Have you considered that? It is a perfectly obvious motive. A child could understand it." His eyes were watery and he blinked several times.

"Even a child would require that you prove such a thing before exacting punishment," Hook told him, then turned back to Joseph. "Captain, I regret the necessity for this, most particularly now in the middle of one of the hardest offensives we've ever experienced, but I have no alternative other than to investigate the possibility of a crime, even though I do not believe it to be so."

Joseph understood exactly what Hook was saying. Everything about it was bad. Even the suggestion of such a crime would damage morale irreparably. It was already fragile with the appalling losses, the failure to make any significant gain of land, the disastrous weather, the whispers of mutiny among the French troops—even if there was very little real evidence. Even though at least outwardly the men condemned the idea of mutiny, inwardly they had a profound natural sympathy.

And the additional tragedy was that in Northrup's efforts to avenge his son's death and protect his reputation, he was actually going to expose him far more. Now only his own immediate men knew he was incompetent. Soon his name would go down in history as having provoked a murder among the very men he led, murder in order to save their own lives from his stupidity. Joseph knew there was a pity in Hook that wanted to rescue Northrup from himself.

"Yes, sir," he said aloud. "I can see that such rumors, however untrue, must be investigated and silenced, one way or the other."

"One way or the other?" Northrup challenged him sharply, swiveling in his chair to face him. "There is only one way, Captain Reavley, and that is with the truth, and the justice that comes from it."

"I meant, sir, whether there is any charge resulting from what we find, or if it is no more than careless talk," Joseph corrected him. "I've heard nothing more than the usual grumbling and bad jokes. The men always complain, usually about petty things. It's a way of making it bearable."

"I am perfectly acquainted with front line humor, Captain," Northrup said bitterly. "It does not extend to blackening the name of a dead officer."

Hook drew in his breath, but Joseph preempted him. He looked at the general. "What are they saying of Major Northrup that is more than the usual complaints that fly around of any officer, sir?"

Northrup's face was bright pink, his cheeks burning. "That he was an incompetent officer and gave orders that cost lives unnecessarily," he said between his teeth, his voice trembling. "It is to cover their own cowardice."

"My men are not cowards!" Hook said furiously, his thin body stiff, the color rising in his haggard face. "And deeply as I regret the death of your son, sir, I will not tolerate any man, of any rank, saying that they are. That is inexcusable, even in grief."

Northrup glared back at him. "If they murdered my son in cold blood, then they are worse than cowards, sir. They are traitors!" His voice trembled. "And I will see every last one of them shot. Do you defy me, Colonel Hook?"

Hook was shaking. "No, sir, I charge you to make your accusations after they are proved, and to treat my men with the honor they deserve unless and until that time."

"Then prove it!" Northrup's voice was close to a shout. "Don't hide behind your chaplain's protection. Institute a proper inquiry."

"By whom?" Hook could not keep the sarcasm from his tone. "I have no fighting men to spare . . . sir! Captain Reavley is the best man to do it. He is both liked and trusted, and he has known most of these men since they joined up. If anyone can find the truth and prove it, he can!"

"I want military police," Northrup replied, gulping. "The chaplain is not qualified to investigate murder, and his profession makes it impossible either to be practical and insist that men speak to him and answer his questions, or that he should repeat what they say if they do. He might very well learn the exact truth, with a confession, and be unable to act on it."

"That's my answer, General Northrup," Hook told him. "If you want to take it to the general in command of the Ypres Salient, then you must do so. I think it extremely unlikely he will spare men at the moment to investigate any front line soldiers on the possibility that there may, or may not, have been a crime, when there is no evidence beyond some ugly talk."

"We'll see," Northrup retorted, rising to his feet. His face was ashen but for the flaming spots of color in his cheeks.

"Sir!" Joseph stood up, turning toward Northrup and barring his way out. "Major Northrup was very new to this section of the front. He made some bad decisions, specifically sending men out across no-man's-land to look for wounded or dead when the weather and visibility made it recklessly dangerous. No one was rescued, and Lieutenant Eardslie, a well-liked and decorated officer, was killed. I would rather not have told you that. All men make mistakes, but this was a particularly foolish one, and he was told by the experienced men here that it was wrong, but he wouldn't listen."

Northrup was shaking; his whole body trembled. He stared word-lessly at Joseph, grief and incredulity naked in his face.

Joseph was furious with him and pitied him at the same time. It was a uniquely painful conflict within him.

"If I investigate his death, sir," he continued, "I shall bring my find-ings to Colonel Hook, and any stories that are unnecessary to repeat, I shall make no written record of, and repeat them to no one. I think it would be wiser, and fairer, if we were to learn all we can before we make any decisions at all."

Northrup stood silently for so long that Joseph thought he was not going to answer, then finally he spoke. His voice was hoarse, little above a whisper.

"Do so. But I will see my son's name cleared, and if any man in the British Army, whatever his rank or his record, had a part in his death, I will see that man shot, and alongside him anyone who defends him or lies for him." He snapped to attention, then before anyone else could speak, he strode the three steps to the entrance and went out.

"Thank you, Reavley," Hook said with intense feeling. "For God's sake, be careful what you find. We're losing thousands of men a day to the Germans, or to the bloody rain. The men are on their last legs. Most of them will be killed anyway. The French weren't cowards; they were just driven beyond human endurance. But Northrup looks readier to face a firing squad himself than see the truth, God forgive him."

"Yes, sir. I'll be very careful," Joseph promised. He gave a very faint smile. "I've done this before."

Hook looked up at him. "Oh, yes, the murder of that bloody awful correspondent, Prentice, or whatever his name was, in 'fifteen. I heard about it. You didn't ever find out who killed him though, did you?"

Joseph did not answer him.

Hook put both his hands over his face and let his breath out slowly. "I see."

Joseph knew it would be difficult even to find a place where he could make himself heard, never mind to frame the questions. He was acutely conscious of disturbing men in their few moments' peace to ask pointless questions. And if he was honest, he was not sure he wanted the answers. He had been just as appalled by Northrup's stupidity as they were. He had prayed for some kind of release from it—but not this.

He began with Tiddly Wop Andrews. He found him standing on the fire step up to his knees in water, drinking tea out of a Dixie can. It was early evening.

"Hello, Chaplain," Tiddly Wop said between the bursts of artillery fire. He always spoke quietly. He was a handsome man but profoundly shy. "Looking for someone?"

Joseph was on the trench floor. The duckboards had been swept away and he found it difficult keeping his balance in the mud. Because he was lower than the fire step, he was up to his thighs in it.

"Anyone who might know exactly what happened to Major Northrup," he replied.

Tiddly Wop grinned. "He got shot," he replied cheerfully. "That's one Jerry whose hand Oi'd loike to shake. Moight even give 'im a cup o' moi tea!" He pulled a face. " 'Cepting Oi' wouldn't want ter poison the poor bleeder."

"Don't pretend you don't know." Joseph kept his own face straight with an effort. "The general thinks he was shot by one of our men. Colonel Hook has asked me to make inquiries."

Tiddly Wop's blue eyes opened wide. "You going to, then?"

"If he was murdered, don't you think I should?" Joseph countered.

Tiddly Wop thought about it. "You know, Chaplain, Oi used to think Oi knew pretty good what was roight and what wasn't. But nothing much looks the same as it used to. Oi'm not so certain anymore." He frowned. "Oi hated Major Northrup 'cos of the men who died 'cos he wouldn't listen. Oi didn't shoot him, but if Oi knew who did, Oi'm not saying Oi'd tell you. Oi 'spect Oi'll be facing whatever judgment there is in a few days, an' most of moi mates with me. Oi'd rather answer to them than to General Northrup."

So would Joseph, but he could not admit it. He did not know what to say.

"If Oi knew, and Oi told you, what'd you think of me?" Tiddly Wop asked gravely.

"Maybe it's just as well you don't know," Joseph answered him. He would never be sure if that was the truth or not, nor did he wish to be.

"Chaplain," Tiddly Wop started as Joseph turned to leave.

"Yes?"

"It's koind of hard at the moment. Oi'd be careful if Oi was you . . . about asking, Oi mean."

"Yes, I know what you mean. Thank you." Joseph waded away, sliding and squelching through the mud.

He sat in his dugout the second evening, tired and cold to the bone because he was wet. He had spent two days asking questions and heard more stories of Northrup's ignorance. There was little sympathy for him, sometimes even open hostility without any disguise that Joseph was wasting his concern on the dead instead of doing what he could for those still alive. He had no argument to rebut it: simply that Colonel Hook had ordered it, and better he than the military police.

Night had come, violent and full of pain. The next day had been the same. A few yards were gained, and they were closer to Passchendaele than before. But another thousand men were dead, with twice as many injured.

He had been told stories of Northrup's last leadership of the men into no-man's-land. No one had seen him fall. No one had been there at the time. Everyone accounted for everyone else. Friendship and its loyalties were the beacons that towered above the darkness. Joseph knew they were lying because in several instances they actually contradicted each other in their eagerness to protect everyone. He realized with surprise that he would have accepted it all and relayed it to Colonel Hook exactly if he had thought there was the slightest chance of his believing it.

He shivered and stared around him. He had lived in this hole in the ground for more than a year, like some hibernating animal. Half a dozen of his favorite books were here, his picture of Dante, the writer of *The Divine Comedy.* Could his vision of hell have been as bad as this reality?

What of Dante's beliefs, his searing portraits of good and evil? Would he be so certain of it if he had seen this welter of terror, heroism, loyalty, and death? Joseph wasn't. He ought to be unequivocally for the law, sure of the few absolutes of justice and the perceived order that had sustained them for more than a thousand years.

Surely there was a constant morality, values beyond any questions, no matter what? Were the truths that spanned the abyss not the surest evidence of God's existence, and His continuing governance of the world? Sometimes in darkness such as this they were the only evidence.

He was lying to himself. The sure theories of the past broke before the need to save lives now, to understand whatever it was that had happened to Howard Northrup, and to the men who had brought it about. The answers did not obey rules. Compassion, loyalty to the living who trusted him to understand, swept away the old faith in rules.

Or was it just a simple and very human matter of who you liked, and who you didn't, who belonged to your pack, the old bonds of loyalty again? He had prayed for understanding, some answers to make the slaughter comprehensible, so men at least knew what they were dying for, and he had received this, which only made it worse.

There was a parcel from Hannah with cake, raspberry jam, a bundle of books, and new socks. There was a note with it where briefly, almost self-consciously, she described the familiar, heart-stopping beauty of the countryside, the harvest-gold fields, the soaring poplars, leaves fluttering in the sunset breeze, the heavy elms, skirts down to the ripe corn heads, the starling whirling across the evening sky.

He pulled out paper to answer her, and wrote possibly too much. Sharing his confusion with her only made him see more clearly how uncertain he was, and his reasons sounded like excuses. In the end he tore it up. It sounded too much as if he were expecting her to find a solution for him. He would thank her properly later.

Instead he wrote to Lizzie Blaine again. He smiled as he remembered how quick she had been to understand last year, how she had had the wisdom not to offer false comfort when he had at last found the awful answer, and had to accept it, and his deep and bitter disillusionment.

The physical pain of his shattered arm and ripped-open leg had almost gone; only now and then did it ache and remind him. But the wound to his faith in people and in his own judgment, the destruction of old loves and old certainties would not ever be forgotten. The truth about Shanley Corcoran had broken something in him.

Lizzie knew that things were never solved, only a little better understood, the doubts faced, courage gripped a little more tightly. It was easier to admit to her than to Hannah that he was troubled by his own sympathy with the men more than the law, that he could conceal the truth, turn away from it, in the needs of mercy.

Perhaps he cared less what she thought of him than he did about Hannah. Or it could be that Hannah was his sister, and might need to believe that he knew more of the answers than he did. He had been there all Hannah's life, when so much else had been ripped away. She had found the loss of her mother particularly hard. And the war had taken all the old certainties she had loved, the way of life she had grown up believing would last forever. She was not like Judith, hungering for adventure. She loved the sweetness of what she had, village life, her home and family, giving the quiet service of a good neighbor—food for the hungry, time with the lonely, a quiet hand for the sick or afraid. She did not want glory; she wanted peace and the assurance of a tomorrow.

There was none, especially for a woman whose husband was at sea, whose eldest son was fast approaching the age when he could join the navy also—not to speak of both a brother and a sister on the Western Front.

To Lizzie he would not matter so much, and he could write honestly, without fear of hurting her. Her friendship seemed a clean and precious thing. He wrote with ease.

*M*atthew spent a wretched afternoon at the police station with the officers in charge of prosecuting Alan Wheatcroft, and now of prosecuting Tom Corracher as well. He had hoped they would have some information to indicate who had set the scandal in motion, and that it would eventually lead back toward the Peacemaker. Matthew was more and more convinced it was he behind the dismissal of all four ministers.

"Sorry, sir," the young policeman said with extreme discomfort. "We'd 'ave 'eld off if we could. Fine man, Mr. Wheatcroft. Rather not know these things, as long as no one's 'urt. But we 'ad no choice."

"Really? Someone important, Constable?" Matthew had asked hopefully. "I thought it was the boy himself who complained. And you believed him?"

"It was, sir. That's the thing of it." He looked apologetic. "You see, it wasn't the first time we had a complaint about Mr. Wheatcroft. First time the boy was younger, and we thought as possibly 'e'd got 'old o' the wrong idea, so to speak. It was all dealt with very quietly. We couldn't do it a second time."

"Oh!" Matthew was startled. It was not something he had foreseen at all. "Who knew of this original claim?"

"No one, sir. For the boy's sake, we said nothing."

"But possibly his parents knew."

"His father, sir. We didn't want to distress his mother with it."

"What was his name?"

"I can't tell you that, sir. Discretion, confidence, you understand?"

Matthew had not argued. It would be easy enough to get to know from Wheatcroft himself tomorrow. There was now no way of avoiding seeing him.

However, before he did that, there was one last man he would see who had known Wheatcroft as a student in Cambridge, fifteen years ago: Aidan Thyer, Master of St. John's. It was a calculated risk. Matthew had once believed Thyer himself might be the Peacemaker. He certainly had both the intelligence and the influence. He had been a brilliant scholar in his youth, and now as master he had the position and the charisma to mold generations of students who would be the future teachers, philosophers, scientists, and governors of the nation. He might even have access to members of the Royal Family and friends in power throughout Europe and the Empire. And of course he was a Cambridge man whom John Reavley would have known. He was fluent in several languages, an idealist with a vision quite broad enough to have conceived the Anglo-German Empire the Peacemaker envisioned.

Was he also ruthless enough to commit murder to bring it about? In the name of peace, in the cause of saving the millions of lives already lost, and the bleeding away of thousands more every day across the Channel, would he have destroyed a few, a handful?

Somebody had!

Matthew left the police station and walked quietly up the street. The August afternoon was still and damp, the road surface glistened in the late sun, and after the downpour the gutters were running deep. There was little traffic. People either took the underground trains or walked where possible.

He wished he could go to the cinema and escape for a couple of hours. He would sit in the dark with strangers and laugh animatedly at Charlie Chaplin, with his absurd walk, his cane, his courage, his defiance, and the individuality that would not be crushed. Or at Fatty Arbuckle and his fights with custard pies that were so brilliantly choreographed they were almost like ballet.

Or perhaps it would be fun to see a real melodrama. Someone had told him that Theda Bara would soon be appearing in *Camille*. That would be something to see.

He crossed the road, oblivious to a speeding motorcar. The vehicle passed him by mere inches, and he staggered, lost his balance, and tripped. There was a screech of tires and brakes as he sprawled into the street, wrenching himself so hard his shoulder was twisted in its socket.

An engine accelerated and tires squealed again.

Struggling to catch his breath, he started to clamber to his feet, feeling more than a little ridiculous. Anger boiled up inside him.

Someone offered him a hand and pulled him up. It was an elderly gentleman with a white mustache and military bearing.

"That was a close shave, sir," he said with a shake of his head. "Damn fool driver! Must have been drunk as a newt. Are you all right? You look a trifle shaken."

Matthew was damp from the pavement and there were smears of mud on his elbows and knees. His left foot was wet where he had stepped in the gutter, but other than the wrench to his shoulder and a few bruises, he was unhurt.

"Yes, sir, thank you. I didn't see him coming at all." He felt extremely foolish.

"You wouldn't, sir," the other man said crisply. "Come round the corner driving like a Jehu! Straight for the pavement. If it weren't ridiculous, I'd say he was aiming straight for you. I'd thank your stars, sir, and go home and have a hot bath, if there is such a thing available to you, and a large whisky."

"Thank you," Matthew said sincerely. "I think that's exactly what I will do."

But when he was back in his flat, sitting in the armchair with a single lamp shedding a soft light over the familiar room, and a glass of whisky in his hand, he was still cold, and his mind was racing. Was it possible that the incident in the street was not an accident?

Surely not? It was just somebody drunk, or even distracted perhaps with bad news. There was certainly enough of it about. Matthew was angry because he had been frightened, for a moment, and made to look vulnerable and ridiculous.

He telephoned Aidan Thyer and made an appointment to see him the next day. There was no point in wasting time going all the way to Cambridge, and then finding that Thyer was too busy to see anyone, or even not there at all. But telephoning did mean he was warned. If he was the Peacemaker, then he might already know what Matthew was doing, and the reason he was coming.

If it proved to be Thyer it would hurt Joseph. He had liked the man and trusted him. It would be a double betrayal because of Sebastian Allard's death as well, and the manner of it, as well as the murder of John and Alys Reavley.

Matthew went over in his mind yet again the course he had followed in seeking the Peacemaker. It had to be someone with connections to the Royal Families of both Britain and Germany. Although since the king and the kaiser were first cousins, with Queen Victoria as a common grandmother, a connection with one might well open doors to connections with the other. He had also to be a man of extraordinary intelligence, boundless ambition, an understanding of world politics, and an idealism he could follow with ruthless dedication regardless of all cost.

Because John Reavley had found a copy of the treaty that proposed this monstrous alliance, and been murdered in the attempt to expose it, the Peacemaker had to be someone who knew him sufficiently well to predict his actions, even his daily routine.

But Matthew and Joseph had considered Aidan Thyer, Master of St. Giles; Dermot Sandwell, senior government minister and confidant of royalty; and Ivor Chetwin, Secret Intelligence agent and longtime friend of John Reavley, until an ethical difference over the morality involved in spying had divided them. Matthew had once dreaded that it might be Shanley Corcoran, brilliant scientist and lifetime friend of John Reavley. He had not even dared suggest that to Joseph. It would have wounded him desperately. But then Corcoran's betrayal last summer had wounded him even more deeply. And he was dead now, hanged for treason.

Matthew sipped the whisky again, and did not taste it. He barely felt its fire slip down his throat. He himself had been sure it was Patrick Hannassey who had been the Peacemaker, and he had seen him die. Even up to a couple of weeks ago he had believed it was he. But this new conspiracy was too like the Peacemaker's work to cling on to that false comfort anymore.

And of course there was always his own superior, Calder Shearing. Matthew liked Shearing. He understood his sudden explosions of temper when stupidity caused unnecessary loss. He admired both his intelligence and his emotional energy, the strength of will that drove him to work until he was exhausted, the patience to pursue every chain of reasoning, to wait, to watch and go over and over details meticulously. He was honest enough to admit his errors, and he never took credit for another man's work. But more than any of these things, Matthew liked his dry wit, the laughter he saw in Shearing's eyes even when the appreciation was wordless.

None of these things altered the fact that even after five years working with him, he did not know anything about Shearing beyond those boundaries. He seemed to have no personal life. He never spoke of family either past or present. He was widely knowledgeable but he never spoke of a school or university. Nothing seemed to be known of him but the present.

Could he be the Peacemaker? Yes, of course it was possible. The thought was both frightening and painful, like so much else.

"Matthew! How good to see you." Aidan Thyer came into the Master's Lodge sitting room, his hand outstretched. He was a slender man with flaxen-pale hair, which flopped forward onto his brow, and a sensitive, highly intelligent face. Matthew remembered now with sudden regret that Thyer's beautiful wife, Connie, had loved another man. It was honor and probably affection that kept her loyal. But it was not love, and Thyer knew it.

"How are you, sir?" he asked aloud, taking Thyer's offered hand. The courtesy title came to him naturally. Matthew had not studied at St. John's, but the respect for a master of college was innate.

"Well, thank you," Thyer replied. "Although the casualty lists are worse than any nightmare. I heard just the other day that Nigel Eardslie was lost in Passchendaele. He was one of Joseph's students, you know."

"I'm sorry." There was nothing more to say.

"Sit down." Thyer waved to a chair, and took the one opposite. "I'm sure you must have lost friends as well. There's no one in England who hasn't. Europe has become an abattoir. But no doubt you didn't come here to discuss that. What can I do for you?"

"Alan Wheatcroft was a student of yours some time ago," Matthew began. Thyer knew he was in intelligence; there was no purpose whatever in being overdiscreet.

Thyer sighed. "Unfortunate," he said quietly. "Yes, I heard about it, of course. Very foolish. End of a fine career."

"You think he was guilty?" Matthew asked.

"Probably of nothing more than indiscretion," Thyer replied. "And a startling naïveté. What did he imagine a good-looking boy was doing hanging around in a public toilet? He should have given the boy a wide berth and not even spoken to him, let alone indulged in a conversation."

"And Corracher?"

"Corracher? Tom Corracher?" Thyer's fair eyebrows rose. "How is he involved?"

"Wheatcroft's defense is that the whole episode was set up to blackmail him, by Tom Corracher," Matthew replied.

Thyer was incredulous. "For God's sake, what for? Money?"

"Yes, to begin with. Once you've paid money to keep quiet over something, then you establish a precedent. It's as good as an admission. After that, other things can be asked for: favors in office, information, the right vote. The list is endless."

"What a damnable mess." Thyer's face was filled with distaste but his eyes never left Matthew's. "What is it you imagine I can do that would be of service to intelligence?"

"Wheatcroft is going to take Corracher down with him," Matthew began.

"You don't think Wheatcroft will survive this?" Thyer asked. "No, probably not. That sort of mud sticks once it's public." He pulled his mouth down at the corners. "Still, if he was ill-advised enough to get caught out in such behavior and leave himself open to blackmail, then guilty or innocent of the charge of approaching the boy, he's guilty of unforgivable stupidity."

"Apparently his wife is very handsome, and an heiress, and he has two sons," Matthew pointed out.

"Yes, of course," Thyer said guardedly, a shadow of pain crossing his face. "If he loves her, or his sons, he may be far more concerned with their feelings, and belief in him, than any continuance in high office. Blaming Corracher might seem the obvious escape."

Matthew looked at him. If he were in truth the Peacemaker, and had engineered this whole tragedy, knowing each man's weaknesses, then he was a superb actor. But the Peacemaker was superb. Time and again that had been only too evident.

"Do you think he's deliberately lying in order to save himself?" Matthew asked. "It's a pretty filthy thing to do."

Thyer stood up, walked over to the French windows and looked out. The lavender was buzzing with bees; the scent of flowers and crushed herbs filled the air. Beyond the hedges, the mellow walls of St. John's rose into a blue sky. It had looked like this in 1914, and probably in 1614.

"If you don't know that men lie and betray when they are frightened of losing what they most want, Matthew, then you are unfit for intelligence work—or much else," Thyer said softly. "The average priest or schoolteacher would tell you as much."

"It doesn't occur to you that Corracher could be guilty of blackmail?" Matthew asked.

"Frankly, it doesn't. I know Wheatcroft. He is . . . susceptible," Thyer said regretfully. "Can you help Corracher? Is that why you are interested?"

"Partly." Should he tell Thyer the truth, and see what his reaction was? Saving Corracher was important. Finding the Peacemaker might be vital. Or was he allowing his own vendetta to blind his judgment? Had he lost perspective?

Thyer did not prompt him, but waited quietly, his fingers propped in a steeple, the sunlight shining on his pale hair.

Matthew plunged in. Caution had gained him nothing. "The rest is to see if you consider it likely that there could be someone else behind it, pulling the strings, as it were."

Thyer looked startled. "I have no idea. To what end? Do you imagine Wheatcroft is sufficiently important that someone would do all this in order to get rid of him? Why, for heaven's sake?"

"Both Wheatcroft and Corracher," Matthew pointed out. "I think possibly Corracher is the more important."

Thyer was suddenly motionless. Matthew could hear the birds singing outside.

"Do you mean a German, or at least a German sympathizer?" Thyer said slowly.

"They were two of the strongest standing in the way of a settlement of peace before total obliteration of one side or the other," Matthew pointed out.

Thyer sighed. "Do you really think that is realistic, Matthew, after all we have lost? Is there not too large a section of the country who have paid in blood for victory, and will feel betrayed by any government that settles for less?"

"Does that make them right?" Matthew parried.

Thyer was watching him almost unblinkingly, his pale eyes brilliant. "It makes them the voice of the majority," he said. "And whether that is correct or not, it is moral, since we are a democracy."

"Is government to follow rather than to lead?" Matthew asked.

Thyer thought for several moments. "In matters where it is the people who have fought and died, yes, I think perhaps it is. Government may argue a case for something different, or lay before them arguments, facts, and reasons, but in the end we must abide by their decision. And before you argue that point, consider the nature of leading without reference to public wish. Would that not be dictatorship? I imagine most dictators believe themselves to have superior wishes to those of the people, and certainly superior information. That may even be true in the beginning, but eventually it leads to government by oppression rather than consent, and finally to tyranny."

He flexed his fingers as if they were stiff. "And it is also supremely impractical," he added with an oddly gentle smile, "unless you have a very great force at your command. And believe me, we have all had enough of bloodshed. We do not need civil war after this ... if there is an afterward? From what I read, a German victory is far from impossible. We seem no closer to defeating the kaiser than we were in 1914, and half of an entire generation is mutilated or dead. What man who has seen this war in its hideousness will ever return from it whole in mind, even if his body seems preserved?"

Matthew did not answer. Either Thyer was far from the Peacemaker in his philosophy, or his mask was impenetrable. Matthew was driven back again to consider Dermot Sandwell, or Shearing. He had excluded Sandwell once, because evidence had made it seem impossible, but everything within him recoiled from believing it was Shearing.

And yet in his own way the Peacemaker had begun as an idealist. It was not his ultimate aim—peace—that was intolerable, it was the means he was prepared to use, even from the beginning, to obtain it: a betrayal of France and eventually of America, and dominion, in the cause of an enforced peace, that would extend across half the world. Was that better or worse than war?

"Could there be someone behind Wheatcroft's accusation against Corracher?" he asked aloud.

"Of course there could," Thyer replied. "But I have no idea who. I can make some highly discreet inquiries, if you wish?"

How much was there to gain, or to lose? Matthew had committed himself already. "Thank you," he said. "Yes. But be careful, they will think nothing of killing you, should they feel you threaten them."

Thyer gave the ghost of a smile. "War is full of death," he said very softly. "It is an occupational hazard."

Since he was already close, Matthew took the local train to Selbourne St. Giles and spent the night in the old family home with Hannah. It was her husband Archie MacAllister, who had commanded the *Cormorant* at the Battle of Jutland, where Matthew had killed Patrick Hannassey, just before the burning ship had gone down. Several times he had drifted in and out of consciousness before being picked up. He still woke in the night fighting for breath, beating his way out of a darkness that threatened to crush his lungs, his face, everything in him that longed for life.

It had given him a new closeness to Archie and an understanding of both the horror and the comradeship of the men who faced the real violence of the war, not just the crushing fear of defeat that came from knowing the casualty figures better than most people. He saw reports that the public did not, and knew the shortages, the ever-shifting political alliances and the new threats internationally. He read the reports from agents in Europe and the rest of the Empire.

Before the Battle of Jutland he had only imagined the numbing horror that Joseph saw every day in the trenches. He had had no experience of the exhilaration and the horror of battle, no idea what it did to the mind and body to watch another human being—a man with whom you had shared jokes, food, the long tension of waiting—broken to a bleeding, unrecognizable pulp at your feet. He had never even imagined physical pain of that degree, the indescribable noise, the smell of blood and burning flesh.

After supper he sat quietly with Hannah in the soft summer dusk and watched the last light fade beyond the elms. The fields lay wide and quiet. The garden was overgrown. She had not had time to pull weeds, or to prune, and there were no young men to hire. They were either dead or in France, or like Archie, at sea. There were no delivery boys anymore, hardly any men in shops or banks or even on the land, only those too old to fight, or too ill. Women did the work now, in hospitals, factories, and farms, and they had no time for private gardens. They drove buses, cycled all over the place delivering things. He saw dozens of them on the country roads or out in the fields.

Hannah knew that Matthew's visit was not simply for pleasure. "The Peacemaker again?" she asked with a twisted little smile. She knitted automatically as she sat, the needles almost soundless in her hands.

He had not told her about Hannassey, at least not all. He still found it hard to talk about. Part of the pain he felt was because of the price Detta had paid. She had been spying for her cause, just as he was for his. One of them had had to lose. If it had been he, and he had done so deliberately, then he would have betrayed both himself and his country.

"I thought he was dead," he replied to Hannah's question.

"I know you did," she said with a tight little smile. She was looking more like her mother as she reached her mid-thirties. Something of Alys Reavley's inner calm was there in her features in repose. Matthew liked it, but it tugged at memories, reminding him of an old safety that could never return.

"Then why do you ask?" he said aloud.

"There's an excitement inside you, an edginess," she told him. "And what else would bring you back here now?"

"Any number of things," he said.

She looked up from her work. "You mentioned St. John's. Is that to do with Aidan Thyer? Do you still think it could be him?"

He was startled. Had he been so transparent?

She continued knitting, the faint click of her needles an intensely comfortable sound in the quiet room. All three children were upstairs, either in bed or doing homework.

He thought of denying it.

"It doesn't matter." She dismissed it. "I expect you can't tell me. Just don't lie."

"I don't know whether he is or not," he admitted. "I thought I knew who it was last year, and that he was dead—after Jutland. Now things have happened that make it look as if I was wrong, and he's still alive."

She looked up quickly. "Be careful, Matthew!" There was fear in her voice, and in her dark eyes so like Alys's.

He did not think of her words again until two days later. He had returned to London the morning after and pursued all the further information he could. It was distasteful, the sort of investigation into who had been seen offering or accepting illicit sexual activity that was one of the sadder and grubbier sides of police work. But he needed to know if Wheatcroft was guilty of seeking an escape from scandal by trying to blame Corracher, saying that he had deliberately set a trap for him in order to blackmail him, and he was entirely a victim. There seemed no doubt he had behaved extremely foolishly, at the kindest judgment. But was his blaming of Corracher a ploy he had thought up for himself? Or had the idea been planted in his mind, directly or indirectly, by someone else?

The only way to answer that was to see Wheatcroft himself, in spite of all his excuses that he was ill and had nothing to say. Matthew used the power of his Intelligence authority to force the issue. Even when he arrived at Wheatcroft's house, the servant at the door, an elderly, obviously infirm man, refused to admit him.

"No, sir," he said resolutely. "Mr. Wheatcroft is unwell, sir. He is not receiving visitors. Doctor's orders."

"I am from the Intelligence Service, and my orders supersede the doctor's," Matthew answered. "I can return with the police, if you oblige me to resort to such extremes. But I am sure that since you are as patriotic as the next man, you would wish Mr. Wheatcroft to assist the country's forces as much as he would wish to himself."

"Well . . ." the man said, confusion filling his face. "I . . . I'm sure I would, but I have my orders, sir. I can't just let anybody in here because they say so!" But he backed away several steps to allow Matthew to enter the hallway, and closed the front door behind him. It was a larger house than average, graciously furnished. Even in these restricted times, the marks of elegance were easy to see: the paintings, the gilt-framed mirrors, the crystal vase of roses on the table near the bottom of the stairs below the carved newel post.

"Sir!" The manservant's voice rose a little in protest as Matthew came farther in.

A door opened and a slender woman in a fashionable blue dress stood in the entrance. She was handsome in a fair, brittle way, but Matthew did not mistake the delicacy of her coloring for any fragility of mind or will.

"Mrs. Wheatcroft?" he asked, stepping around the manservant.

"Of course," she said coldly. "Oh, do be quiet, Dobson," she said to the manservant. "I can see what has happened." She waved her hand in dismissal without looking at him. "Who are you?" She regarded Matthew's uniform with distaste. "What are you doing forcing your way into my home?"

"Captain Matthew Reavley of the Secret Intelligence Service, Mrs. Wheatcroft," he replied. "I am sorry for disturbing you, but matters have arisen about which I need to speak to Mr. Wheatcroft."

"I'm afraid whatever you have to ask him will have to wait!" she replied. "My husband is unwell, as I believe Dobson has already told you."

"It is a matter of information necessary to the Intelligence Service, Mrs. Wheatcroft," he insisted. "It cannot wait."

She looked at him icily. "My husband has served his country all his adult life, and been repaid for it by vile accusations which are distressing to him and to all his family. Now you come here and push your way into his home demanding he answer your questions? You are brutal, Captain . . . I forget your name. The answer is no. You will have to wait for a more fortunate time."

"Reavley," he said again. "Undoubtedly your husband has served his country. So have we all. Some of us are fortunate that it has cost us no more than a little discomfort. I have a brother in the trenches at Passchendaele, and a sister out there driving ambulances for the few wounded they have some chance of saving. Now go and find Mr. Wheatcroft in his bedroom, and tell him I need to see him immediately. He may come down, or I shall go up."

She glared at him, her body trembling, searching wildly for an answer to hold him at bay, and finding none. She wheeled around, her skirt swinging, and marched away.

Five minutes later she returned. Without speaking she led Matthew up the stairs and across a spacious landing whose long windows gave a view of a sunlit lawn. Then, after a brief knock, she opened the master bedroom door. She stared at Matthew, leaving him to go in unannounced.

"Thank you," he said pointedly. He closed the door behind him, but he did not know if she waited outside it.

Alan Wheatcroft was sitting in a chair by the window, not in a dressing gown as Matthew expected, but fully dressed. He was ash pale and his skin shone with sweat. For a minute Matthew wondered if perhaps he really was ill, then he saw the hands clenched, white-knuckled, and decided it was more probably fear that made the man look so wretched.

"I'm sorry to disturb you, Mr. Wheatcroft, but the matter cannot wait." He spoke very quietly, only sufficiently to be heard, aware that Mrs. Wheatcroft might be only just beyond the door.

"My wife said so." Wheatcroft also kept his voice low. "Although I can't imagine what I might know that would be of interest to the Intelligence Service. I haven't been in my office for . . . for several weeks." His hands clenched even more tightly on the rug over his knees.

Matthew sat on the edge of the bed, more to avoid towering over him than for comfort. "It is nothing to do with your office," he replied. "It is a matter of possible treason."

"Treason!" Wheatcroft was stunned. There was no comprehension in his eyes, not even fear, simply total bewilderment. "I know nothing about anything remotely treasonous. I haven't been out of my house since . . ." He drew in his breath sharply and then let it out without finishing his sentence.

"Since you were accused of approaching a young man for homosexual favors at the men's convenience on Hampstead Heath," Matthew completed it for him.

A tide of color washed up Wheatcroft's neck and face. He started to speak, and stopped again.

"I'm sure the charge is profoundly embarrassing," Matthew said with some sympathy. "Any man would find it so. Whose idea was it to save your reputation by saying that Tom Corracher set up the whole scene in order to blackmail you?"

Wheatcroft stared at him in horror, as if Matthew had physically struck him.

"Presumably not only to salvage something of your career, but to save your wife's feelings," Matthew added. "Whether you actually approached the boy or were merely naïve is not my concern. I don't wish to know."

"You . . . you are assuming . . ." Wheatcroft began.

"That it was not your idea? Yes, I am," Matthew agreed. "Your record up to this suggests you are a man of honor."

"I did not approach that boy," Wheatcroft said in a whisper. "I . . . I may have been foolish, but that's all! It is . . . inadvisable. Perhaps I deserve to lose my government position for such stupidity. That I can accept. But I have committed no crime!"

"No," Matthew agreed. "But blackmail is very definitely a crime, and you are accusing Corracher of that. If he is found guilty then he will not only lose his position, he will go to prison."

Wheatcroft looked so wretched, it was hard to believe he was not physically ill. "What has that to do with Intelligence? What is it you think I know? For God's sake, don't you think I've done enough to him? I don't believe he's a traitor. I've nothing more to say about it."

"I don't believe so, either," Matthew responded. "I don't know who it is behind the charge, but I believe you can help me find out."

Wheatcroft did not look up. "If I knew of any treason, I'd have reported it! I haven't sunk so low as that."

Matthew felt brutal, but there was no alternative. Neither affection nor pity were excuses to add to injustice. "What made you think of accusing him of blackmail?"

"I . . ." He stopped.

"Didn't," Matthew finished for him. "Someone else suggested it to you?"

"It wasn't that . . . simple!" Wheatcroft's face was ashen and glistening with sweat. "Corracher came to see me a couple of days after . . . after the . . . event. We quarreled over something else, stupid. They were putting a man called Jamieson to take over my work temporarily. Eunice, my wife, seemed to . . . she . . . assumed the quarrel was about the incident. She leaped to conclusions. I . . . I allowed her to. It . . ." He gave up helplessly. His eyes beseeched Matthew to understand without forcing him to put it into words.

Matthew felt both disgust and pity. Wheatcroft was trapped. It was his cowardice in allowing himself to be used in turn to trap Corracher that Matthew despised.

"Withdraw the charge," Matthew told him. "I doubt you can restore his career. People don't forget. But you can save yourself some honor out of it."

"I can't!" Wheatcroft protested. "It would be as good as saying that I was guilty! And before God, I wasn't!"

"And it is unjust to be punished for something you didn't do?" Matthew had asked.

"Yes! And my family ruined!"

"I imagine Tom Corracher feels the same way."

Wheatcroft stared at him as if he stood on the edge of an abyss.

Matthew opened his mouth to apologize, then said nothing. He could not withdraw his words. They were true. There was some agony within Wheatcroft that he could not share—a guilt, a fear for himself or for others—but Matthew could not let him escape it at the price it would cost.

Did Wheatcroft know who had manipulated his wife? Probably not. Certainly he would not tell Matthew. He remembered her icy face, the fear in her and the immediacy to attack. She would tell him nothing, maybe even warn the Peacemaker, knowingly or not.

He left the Wheatcroft house with a feeling of oppression and went back to his office.

* * *

He worked late to learn all he could about Eunice Wheatcroft, searching for a connection to anyone who might be the Peacemaker, dreading the link that would tie them, however tenuously, to Shearing. But if it was there, whatever it cost him, he could not look away.

By the time he left he was tired. His neck and shoulders ached with tension and his mouth was dry. He walked outside in the dark to get a bus home. He alighted two or three streets away and took a shortcut through an alley to save himself a hundred yards.

He heard the noise behind him. It was no more than a loose pebble kicked, but he swung around, losing his balance a little. A figure fell hard against him and metal clanged on the brick.

Some deep memory of those last minutes on the *Cormorant* awoke in him the feel of Hannassey's relentless strength as they struggled at the railing with the German destroyer looming out of the darkness. He lashed out hard and straight with his left fist, all his weight behind it. It connected with the man's face and he felt bone break. Still he followed it with a lunging kick to the groin and the man went down, letting out a scream that was almost instantly choked with blood.

Matthew hesitated. He must have broken the man's nose. Should he stay and see if the injury was worse than that? What if he couldn't breathe—if he died?

He looked down. He could see little more than movement, a writhing on the pavement. Perhaps the man was reaching for whatever had fallen and clanged against the brick. A knife? Matthew turned and ran, feet echoing on the alley cobbles until he emerged into his own street.

Even upstairs in his flat, with the door locked, he found he was shaking uncontrollably. The memory of the violence washed over him until he was gulping for breath. It was as if he could feel the strength of Hannassey again, the struggle, then the sudden victory. In his mind he saw Hannassey falling, spinning, arms and legs wide, until he hit the dark water, and a moment later the German destroyer squashed him like a fly.

Matthew poured himself a whisky, spilling a little, and tossed it down his throat so its fire could calm his stomach. He had not killed the man in the alley; he had seen him still moving frantically, arms groping.

If Matthew had not hit back, then it would be he who was lying on the cobbles, possibly bleeding to death.

Was that what it was? An attempt to murder him? Was that really why he was shaking like this, because he knew it was not a robbery? Thieves might knock you over the head; more likely they would simply lift your wallet without you knowing it. The car driver the other day was not an accident, either.

Did this mean that at last he was enough of a nuisance to be worth killing? Even too close to the truth to be left alive? That made his heart race with excitement.

Was the Peacemaker Aidan Thyer after all? Or Calder Shearing? That was an ugly and viciously painful thought—one that made nausea grip his stomach and the sweat break out on his body. It was a strange friendship, almost tacit, and yet its depth was uniquely precious. There was a wealth of understanding between them that needed no words, and the comfort of that was immeasurable, the betrayal would be infinite. He remembered Joseph and Corcoran, and then pushed the thought from his mind.

Or could it be Dermot Sandwell, in spite of Matthew having ruled him out before? That would be far more bearable. Or someone he had not even thought of yet, but somehow had come close to without realizing it?

In Marchmont Street, the Peacemaker was woken in the small hours of the morning by his manservant. He dressed because he would not receive any visitor at the disadvantage of not being properly clothed.

He knew as soon as his guest entered the upstairs sitting room with its graceful proportions and lean, elegant furniture that the news was bad. The man who stood in the center of the floor reeked of failure.

The Peacemaker waited for him to speak.

"He got away," the man said simply. "I thought my fellow was good, but he said Reavley fought like a tiger. Broke his nose and ruptured his spleen. He's lucky to be alive."

The Peacemaker was astonished. "Are you sure he had the right man? Reavley's a thinker, not a doer."

"I'm perfectly certain," the man replied. "He's been followed on and off for weeks. Discreetly—he was never aware."

The Peacemaker raised his eyebrows skeptically.

"He wouldn't have gone alone down an alley at night if he'd been aware he was followed, . . . sir," the man replied.

The Peacemaker was annoyed with himself. He had allowed the failure to kill Reavley to rattle him, and now he had displayed a weakness in reasoning in front of this man, a rat of a creature who must be kept under tight control. He loathed having to use such people, and the necessity that drove him to it.

"You have failed twice," he pointed out. "I cannot afford a third error. Leave him alone. I shall think of a way of dealing with him that does not depend upon your very dubious skills. I'll send for you if I need you again."

The man opened his mouth to argue, then met the Peacemaker's eyes, and changed his mind. He left without speaking further.

The Peacemaker returned to his bed, but sleep eluded him. It required all his concentration and discipline of mind not to allow the Reavleys to dominate his thoughts and become an obsession. They were a nuisance, but peripheral to his main activities. The great cause was peace: first with Germany, then with the world. Never again would there be pointless slaughter like that going on at this moment at Passchendaele. The thought of it was enough to make humanity tremble and weep.

It was the night after that, with the air close and damp, and promising thunder, when Richard Mason returned from the Western Front and reported in the upstairs room. His face was gray with exhaustion. He had obviously shaved hastily and cut his chin. But it was the emotional tension in him, the grief in his eyes, the nervous tic at his temple that moved the Peacemaker to pity and a sense of the enormity of the horror. Mason had seen almost every battlefield of the war, not only in Europe but in Russia and the Middle East. He had never looked as haunted as he did now.

"Sit down," the Peacemaker said quietly. "Whisky? Tea? Have you eaten? What can I get you?"

Mason smiled bleakly. It was no more than a bare curving of the lips, hardly noticeable. "Tea would be nice. I can't afford to be light-headed. And a sandwich. Bread that isn't moldy. And a clean cup to drink out of."

The Peacemaker rang for the manservant. They spoke of trivialities until the food and drink came and they could close the door and be assured of privacy. He allowed Mason time to eat and drink before he approached the subject of his report.

"Thank you," Mason said. He met the Peacemaker's eyes. "It's beyond description. It's beyond human suffering. It is hell itself."

"But you have come with something to tell me." The Peacemaker had seen it in Mason's patience, his assurance. He had watched the man report on one atrocity after another over years, and he knew every mood of his mind and read its reflection in his face. Mason had brooding, sensitive features, powerful and yet more expressive than perhaps he himself realized. The depth of his emotion was mirrored too easily.

Now he answered slowly, measuring his words. He described Howard Northrup and his appointment to replace the much-respected Penhaligon. With no more than a trace of anger, he told of his stubborn incompetence. Watching him intently, the Peacemaker saw in Mason not only fury but pity as well for a man placed beyond his depth both of experience and of character.

Then, still slumped in the armchair, Mason told of Northrup's body being found with a single bullet through the brain, fired from right in front of him, and Joseph Reavley's unsuccessful attempt to learn from the men exactly what had happened.

"Reavley, the chaplain?" The Peacemaker kept his voice devoid of emotion with the greatest effort. He had not forgotten how Mason had thrown away his article on the nightmare of Gallipoli, with all its propaganda value, because of Reavley's sense of futile, narrow patriotism. "And what did Reavley find?"

Mason laughed. It was a jerky, painful sound that said more vividly than words how lacerated he was inside. "Nothing! Which I imagine was what he wanted, and intended. He's learned since Prentice's death. He's investigating because he has to. Neither he nor the Colonel wants anyone charged. The whole army in that section is facing slaughter. It will take both genius and lunacy to keep them facing forward and over the top,

God help them! And God forgive us!" He left the words brittle and sharp in the air, unsaid between them, that they could have prevented it all, if any of their plans had succeeded.

"There's open talk of mutiny, and it won't take much to bring it about," he went on. "Then they'll have to fire on their own men. They'll have no choice." There was absolute certainty in his eyes. "Reavley will have more sense of right and wrong, and of survival, than to find anything."

"Write your article," the Peacemaker said earnestly. "Write up the action in which the surgeon saved his men. In the men's own words: all their comradeship, loyalty to each other, their courage, and how they were betrayed by arrogant and incompetent leadership. For readers far away from the battle you must write the tragedy of it, and the sacrifice. Paint the loss as you saw it."

Mason stared at him, eyes shadowed and uncertain. "The noise, the mud, and the slaughter are unimaginable."

"But of course," the Peacemaker said grimly. "If we here at home knew what it was like, without the poetic words of sacrifice and honor to gild it for us, we would never allow it to go on. We would be sick with shame that we had ever tolerated it in the beginning. We sit in clean withdrawing rooms of quiet houses and weep into our handkerchiefs, and we talk to each other about glory. Write it as it is, Mason! For the love of God, write the truth!"

Mason sat still, the trouble still heavy in his face.

The Peacemaker leaned forward. "I know the figures, Mason. I know we have barely gained a few yards of mud at the price of a hundred thousand lives. It has to stop. The government won't do it; they've staked too much on victory to settle for less than that now. They're old men, dedicated to war. We need new men, with a vision of peace and the courage to pay what it costs in pride." For an instant he thought of Wheatcroft and Corracher standing in the way, young men with old men's vision. But they had been dealt with! Eunice Wheatcroft's pride would see to that. "But they can't do it without the truth," he went on, intent upon Mason again. "Doesn't the vast mass of our suffering people deserve to decide on truth, not lies? If not for them, then for the men you've seen paying the price of their folly. Is their enemy really the German soldier opposite, suffering the same hunger, the same horror and pain? Or is it the blind cowards behind them driving them forward?"

The argument died in Mason's eyes. The Peacemaker saw it and knew he had won.

Matthew reached a decision. Detection of facts had achieved very little. All his inquiries into Eunice Wheatcroft's connections had gained him nothing. He still had no proof who the Peacemaker was. He would carry the battle to Sandwell, and perhaps spur him to action, which would show him innocent or guilty.

He contrived to have himself invited to a dinner party Sandwell was giving at his home in order to discuss intelligence matters. As a senior minister, it was part of his responsibility. This was an elegant occasion with all the glamour and discreet good taste of the years before the war. The meal was abstemious, as became men who led a country where some of the poor actually starved. The talk was somber. There was no pretense made that victory was certain, only that surrender was unthinkable. The dead had paid too much for the living to betray them.

After the coffee and brandy had been served, Sandwell rose to his feet. He was slender, almost gaunt now, his fair hair gleaming in the subdued light from the lamps. He asked the others to excuse him, and gestured to Matthew to follow him into one of the smaller side offices.

It was tidy, gracious, and sparsely furnished. Sandwell sat down in one of the armchairs and invited Matthew to the other. He crossed his legs, his polished shoes shining for an instant as he moved. His eyes were almost electric blue, curious, amused. He waited for Matthew to speak.

Matthew began his well-rehearsed discourse. "Thank you, sir. I'll not waste time with prevarication. I imagine you are aware of the original prosecution against Alan Wheatcroft, and now that against Tom Corracher as well?"

"Naturally," Sandwell agreed. "Is that of interest to the intelligence service?"

"I believe so. Corracher is not guilty of any attempt to blackmail Wheatcroft. The accusation is Wheatcroft's way of escaping the consequences of either a very naïve action, or possibly a minor offense, but one with major effects upon his career, and probably more important to him, his marriage."

Sandwell was watching Matthew intently. Matthew tried to read the emotion in the brilliant eyes, and could discern nothing. It was like looking into a mirror.

"You mean Wheatcroft laid the charge of blackmail falsely, as a way of becoming victim rather than offender?" Sandwell grasped it immediately. "I'm surprised. It shows rather more nimbleness of mind than I thought he possessed."

Matthew smiled in spite of himself, and saw the answer in Sandwell's face.

"Yes, sir, I think it does, which is why I believe the idea may not have originated with him."

"I assume you asked him?"

"Yes. He told me it was his wife's suggestion."

"Ah. The redoubtable Eunice."

"You know her?" Suddenly the air was electric. Had Sandwell stiffened? Was Matthew at last facing the Peacemaker in a ridiculously civilized, lethal fencing match with words? Or wasting time talking in riddles to an innocent man?

The Peacemaker was an idealist: passionate, ruthless, believing utterly in his cause. He would crush Matthew as he had his father, with regret, but without hesitation.

"Do you know Mrs. Wheatcroft, sir?" Matthew reiterated.

"I have met her," Sandwell replied. "But I was speaking of her reputation. Elegant but chillingly cold."

"My impression exactly," Matthew agreed. "I think if I were Wheatcroft I would not wish to incur her displeasure, let alone her contempt."

"Sufficiently to accuse a friend of blackmail, falsely?" Sandwell asked with a lift of surprise. "That is a particularly squalid thing to do."

"It is a particularly squalid charge," Matthew pointed out.

"I don't see how it concerns Intelligence, even so. Or what I could do to be of assistance."

Matthew had hoped the question would arise and he had prepared for it. "Tom Corracher is an able man, with unique connections in Hungary. We can't afford to lose him so easily. Apart from the damage to morale of such a sordid scandal just now when the army is taking the most hideous losses. We need strength and honor at home."

"I see." Sandwell sat silently for some time. Footsteps sounded in the corridor outside, and a burst of laughter came from the dining room where the men were still passing the port and brandy.

Somewhere a clock chimed and then struck eleven.

"You wish me to intervene on Corracher's behalf. I assume you believe him innocent? Although perhaps that is not the major issue. You are right, a scandal would damage morale when we are too vulnerable to bear it easily. Thank you for bringing it to my attention, Reavley. I shall do what I can. Your argument is persuasive." He smiled and rose to his feet, holding out his strong, narrow hand with its long fingers.

Matthew took it, still not certain what he had learned. "Thank you, sir."

They stood for a moment, neither moving. Then Sandwell let go and turned to the door. Was his smile a shade less certain? Or was it only a change in the light and Matthew's imagination?

Matthew was a little late the next morning and was still eating a slice of toast when the telephone rang. He picked it up to hear Shearing's voice. It sounded tense and very formal, as if he might have been aware of being overheard.

"Morning, Reavley. Will you go to Wheatcroft's house, please. Immediately. Take full identification with you."

Matthew drew in his breath to ask why, and then let it out again. "Yes, sir."

He took his car this time. A taxi would have had to fight traffic just the same, and he knew London almost as well as any cab driver. It took him half an hour, even though he had to break the speed limit in several places and cut a dozen red lights too fine.

He was met at Wheatcroft's door by an elderly policeman who was well past the age at which he would usually retire. He looked distressed, which was sufficient to warn Matthew that whatever had happened was very grave.

"Yes, sir?" the sergeant said stiffly.

"Captain Reavley, Intelligence Service," Matthew identified himself.

"Yes, sir. Sergeant Roberts. I was expecting you. Mr. Wheatcroft's in the bedroom, sir. But there's no question how it happened."

"How . . . ?" Matthew began.

"Suicide, Captain." Roberts swallowed. "There's a letter. Wife said it's his handwriting, and we compared it with other papers we know were his. There's no doubt."

Matthew felt a wave of guilt rise up and choke him, tightening his chest till he could hardly breathe. He was gasping, his lungs struggling for air.

"You all right, sir?" Roberts's voice came from a distance.

"Yes, thank you. What did the note say?"

"That he was innocent, but he couldn't face the shame of the prosecution. That he'd been haunted over a piece of foolishness, his career was finished and there was no use or happiness left for him. For his family's sake he wasn't going to begin on a downward path which had no end."

Matthew cleared his throat awkwardly. "Those words?"

"Yes, sir. The note's up there beside him. Room's locked. Doctor's with the wife. Very strong woman, taking it with great courage, no hysterics, but looks like she should be buried alongside him, right enough, poor thing."

"Thank you." Matthew held out his hand for the key, then turned and walked up the stairs, leaving the sergeant at the bottom. He knew where the bedroom was. It seemed only hours since he had been there.

He opened the door, fumbling for a moment before he could turn the lock, then went in and closed it behind him. The curtains were drawn to a twilight gloom, but rather than pull them back he switched on the electric light.

Wheatcroft was lying on top of the bed. He had either not undressed last night or he had risen and dressed this morning. He had apparently shaved also. Matthew touched the bloodless face. It was cool. Had he died hours ago? He looked ravaged now, wasted as if by disease, his flesh sunken.

Was it despair that had driven him to this? And how would it reflect on Corracher? Was that another blow waiting to fall? This certainly would not stop the prosecution.

He picked up the note. It was quite long, and not addressed to anyone in particular—not even to his wife, as might have been expected. It mentioned his work and how he had believed in it, and that his successor, Marlowe, lacked the connections in Hungary to carry it through.

After that, it was pretty much as Roberts had said. He proclaimed his innocence and said he could not face the humiliation and would not publicly fight a battle he could not win, but significantly, he did not blame Corracher.

Matthew folded the note and put it in his pocket. He searched the papers, letters, notes of meetings, diaries, but there was nothing else there to help or hurt Corracher's cause.

Finally he left to go back and report to Shearing. He felt miserable, guilt-dogged, and yet confused as to what he could or should have done differently. Perhaps Wheatcroft was guilty after all, and the whole thing was a catalogue of small errors and profound tragedies, and the Peacemaker had simply seized the opportunity to use his weakness and destroy Corracher with it.

Was this suicide now a result of Wheatcroft's guilt over accusing Corracher? He had not openly admitted the lie; perhaps that was too much to ask, for his family's sake. But the prosecution against Corracher would have to be dropped.

Another victim of the Peacemaker, intentionally or not.

Had Matthew's conversation with him provoked the guilt? Or had it been brought about subtly, ruthlessly, by Sandwell, after Matthew's discussion with him last night? Probably he would never know.

SIX

By now Joseph had concluded his fruitless questioning about Northrup's death. He had gone through the motions so that Hook could tell General Northrup honestly that they had done everything they could to ascertain the truth of his son's death. But if anyone had known it and was willing to speak, they must have been among the casualties, which increased by the thousands every day.

After seventy-two hours Joseph went to see Hook in his dugout. It was yet another gray morning, with a weeping pall of cloud across the sky. The rain seemed to have soaked into everything. There was no dry ground, no food or equipment untouched. Everything dripped and was clammy to the touch. Bread was moldy before it arrived at the forward trenches, battle tunics never dried out, socks and boots were permanently sodden. Men's hair was plastered to their heads, and their pale skins shiny wet, streaked with mud and blood.

Joseph slipped on the step and jarred himself against the wooden lintel on the way down to the dugout. Hook looked up as he heard him and called out to come in.

"Morning, Reavley," he said a little huskily. His face was colorless and lined with exhaustion.

Joseph let the sacking fall back over the entrance and stood to attention.

"Morning, sir." He gave the casualty figures as he knew them, and mentioned the names of those men he was aware Hook had known personally. Then he moved on to close the issue of Northrup's death. "I've made all the inquiries I can, sir. If it was the sort of thing we feared, no one is saying anything. Of course it shouldn't have happened, but in the face of the circumstances, I strongly recommend that we close the issue. There seems to me to be two possible answers: either the whole thing is no more than loose talk by men angry and demoralized, speaking out of turn. This could be the best answer for all of us, especially Major Northrup himself. Or there was a piece of very regrettable indiscipline, but those concerned are themselves dead now. We can't now determine what it was, and in respect to Major Northrup, who can't defend himself, we should mention it no further."

Hook regarded him with a bitter humor in his eyes. "You did actually ask?"

"Yes, sir." That was the truth, although he had neither expected nor wanted an answer.

"Thank you, Reavley. I'll inform General Northrup. I don't imagine he'll be pleased, but he'll have to accept it."

But Northrup did not accept it. He sent for Joseph personally and demanded a more detailed explanation, and there was nothing Hook could do to protect him from it. It was in Hook's dugout again, in the early afternoon. Joseph had spent almost twenty hours helping wounded and dying, endlessly carrying stretchers. He had struggled through the mud and round the awkward corners of the few trenches that were still negotiable in the ever-deepening water. He had watched young men he knew and cared for die in indescribable pain.

He had managed to snatch a couple of hours' sleep, his body bruised, wet to the skin and shivering. Now he fumbled to straighten his clothes, splash his face with moderately clean water, and report back to Hook again. There was no time to shave, none even to try to light a flame and heat water for a cup of tea.

Outside, the earth smelled of death. The light was gray and the air close and warm.

Inside the dugout one oil lamp was burning, the light red and green on the backs of a pile of books. He saw General Northrup immediately. He looked thin, a little stooped; his face was tight with anger.

Joseph drew himself to attention, pulling his shoulders back with an effort. The muscles in his body shot through with pain and he could not fill his lungs with air.

Hook's voice was rough-edged. "I gave your report to General Northrup, Captain. However, he has made certain inquiries himself and he is not satisfied that we have exhausted all possibilities."

"I know of no others, sir," Joseph said doggedly. He knew that Hook was prepared to back him, and the men.

Northrup did not wait for Hook to reply but cut across him looking straight at Joseph. There was both pain and contempt in his voice. "I can understand your desire to shield your men, Chaplain. I even have some sympathy with your reluctance to believe any of them capable of such a crime. But if we have any right to claim that we fight for civilized values, a way of life acceptable to man and God, then we do not look away from the truth because it is not what we wish it to be or find comfortable to deal with."

Joseph was speechless with fury. The word *comfortable* was a blasphemy in this blood-soaked gateway of hell. He croaked the word, almost unintelligibly, like an animal sound in the back of his throat.

Hook heard the warning in it, the self-control fraying and coming apart. He intervened. "Chaplain, General Northrup has been speaking to the men also, and he believes that Corporal Fuller may have been involved and knows what happened. He insists that we ask him, under pressure if necessary."

"Punch Fuller?" Joseph was startled. "I haven't seen him for days. He must be . . ." he blinked, trying to hold back his emotion. "Among the dead." He had liked Punch with his pleasantly ugly face and his inexhaustible memory for the words of every song, orthodox and otherwise.

A nerve twitched in Northrup's cheek. "He is not dead, Chaplain! Not even wounded. Corporal Fuller is on leave in Paris, and no doubt enjoying himself. If we fight for anything, it must be for honor. If we have lost that, then there is nothing else left worth winning—or losing." His voice thickened. "I will not bury my son the victim of a cowardly murder and keep silent about it. I do not know if you would—that is not my concern—but if you would, then I pity you, and those who love or trust you I pity even more. What use are you to your men, sir, if you have neither the courage nor the strength to uphold the truth or the honor of the God you chose to serve?"

"General . . ." Hook began to protest, leaning forward a little, his skin yellow now in the lamplight.

Joseph could not allow Hook to fight in a defense he was not prepared to make for himself. "General Northrup." He turned to face him. "If Corporal Fuller knows something of Major Northrup's death, then with Colonel Hook's permission, I will go to Paris, find him, and learn what it is. Supposing you believe *that* is of more service to my men than remaining here to help them." He stared at Northrup's tired, wounded eyes without wavering.

Northrup blinked.

It was Hook who answered. "I think you had better try, Reavley. You could get a little sleep on the train, some dry clothes, maybe hot food. Give it a couple of days anyway."

"Yes, sir. Immediately?"

"Might as well," Hook replied. "If Fuller comes back and you miss him, you might not get another chance." He gave Northrup a sidelong glance, but Northrup was impervious. He could see only justice; the near certainty of death in battle seemed not to touch him.

"Yes, sir." Joseph saluted and left.

He was tired enough to sleep most of the journey from Ypres to Paris, jammed into a seat between other soldiers going on leave, a few staff officers, and several silent and uncomfortable civilians in cars rattling and jolting over the tracks. He was barely aware of them. Exhaustion lent him a few hours of oblivion, and when he finally disembarked at the station and pulled his thoughts together it was to consider at which of the many places the men on leave stayed in Paris he should begin to look for Punch Fuller.

He had heard many of the men joke about the music halls that were still open, the nightclubs, the cafés, and the brothels.

He stood on the platform outside the railway station looking at the street, hearing the clip of horses' hooves and the hiss of tires on the wet cobbles, the blare of motor horns and someone singing loudly and off-key, miserably drunk. A boy with a cap too large for him was selling news-papers, black headlines counting more losses at Passchendaele, Verdun, the Somme, and right along the front. A group of sailors swung by, with trouser legs flapping around their ankles. An ambulance passed, driven by a woman.

Joseph felt an overwhelming sense of being lost, even though he had been to Paris many times, both before the war and then on leave. He had spoken French passably since school. It was not that he did not care about France, or appreciate the country's wit, history, and culture; he just ached for the familiar, the idioms of his own people. He longed for things he did not need to think about, places his feet would find un-guided. He was too tired to begin a search for one man in all this weary, grieving city that had lived the last three years with the enemy on its doorstep, trying to keep a brave face while smiling at disaster, pretending it wouldn't really happen. God knew how many of its sons would never return. Did they hear the guns in their sleep?

It would be dusk soon. He must find a billet of some kind for the night, maybe three nights. He did not really want to find Punch Fuller, but he had to try. Damn Major Northrup for his stupidity, a father too blind to let his son lie buried in peace.

He found a room; it was small and expensive, but quite clean. The landlady made him an omelette with herbs and charged for it extortion-ately. But it was the best meal he had eaten since the early spring and he told her so with gratitude. There was no tea, and the coffee was bitter, but at least it was served in a cup, not a Dixie can, and there was no taste of oil to it.

He slept late, vaguely discomforted by the physical ease of a bed, and the silence compared with the guns he was used to. It should have wrapped him round in peace, but it didn't.

He went out again, asking first at the half dozen or so small hotels he knew the men used when in Paris. He kept his chaplain's collar showing to allay suspicion that his search had any ill intent, but it didn't help. He spoke of Punch Fuller by name, and described him fairly closely: his long nose and sharp chin, his slightly rolling walk, his ready wit. They all stared at him with blank faces, many openly hostile.

Then he tried the cafés, bars, and other drinking places—all without success. By near midnight again he was nursing a glass of rough red wine in a nightclub in the cellar of one of the older hotels. There were several other British soldiers there. They seemed determined to stay awake for every precious hour of leave, savor it to the last breath of smoky, wine-filled atmosphere, hear every aching note of the music from the three-piece band. A middle-aged woman with a thin body sang in a languorous voice filled with heartbreak.

Suddenly Joseph could no longer keep from his mind the awareness of how everything had changed since he was last here on leave himself, too short a time to go home. It was only three months ago, but now it was all just a little shabbier; a few more chairs were broken and not mended, and the tables more deeply scarred. Windows were cracked, lamps missing pieces of colored glass. It was this room he could see as he sat, but in his mind it was everywhere. Coffee was thin and bitter. Women's faces were bleak, numbed with loss. Clothes were patched and repaired, the few shreds of style left a little more desperate. Outside there was uncollected rubbish blowing in the gutters, and windows were boarded up where there was no glass to mend them.

The comradeship was still there, the anger and the pain, and a shred of the old ironic wit. But the shell was thin, and too near to breaking.

Joseph sipped his wine again and watched the group of Tommies at the bar. None of them looked more than twenty, several far younger, maybe sixteen or seventeen. They were laughing too loudly. They thought they were pretending to be brave, knowing that tomorrow or the next day they were going back to be killed. Joseph knew the courage was real—but behind the stupid jokes, white faces were slicked with the sweat of uncertainty and fear. Finally, Joseph realized, each man was desperately alone.

The three-piece band started a Cole Porter song. Porter himself was somewhere here in Paris, so Joseph had heard, but he would be in a better place than this, more sophisticated.

He should start looking for Punch Fuller again. He had to tell General Northrup that he had tried. Stupid man. The truth would hurt everyone, himself most of all.

And yet Joseph knew that some Englishman had shot Major Northrup on purpose, to save him from bringing on them even more destruction, and more of his friends sacrificed for nothing. Did duty require you to die pointlessly? If Punch were to ask him that, what would he say?

He had no idea. Too many of the old certainties were gone. Once he would have known exactly what to say to Morel about honor and leadership. Now he understood Morel's belief that his duty was toward the men whose lives were in his charge, to save them from incompetents who would take their loyalty and sacrifice it hideously and for nothing, unaware even of what they were asking.

He had tried again to argue with Morel. He could hear the words in his mind—"You can't lead them to mutiny! Think what it means. They'll be shot."

"How terrible," Morel had said sarcastically. "Good men shot."

Joseph had floundered, seeking something to say, a core of belief within himself to cling to and give him fire and conviction. He had found nothing sure enough, and Morel knew it as much as he did. He had failed.

He felt a hand on his shoulder and looked up to see a man smiling at him. He was tall and dark with a long nose and a mercurial, ironic laughter in his eyes. Just now there was a strange gentleness in him, an instant of naked emotion.

"Sam?" Joseph's voice was hoarse. Amazement and joy welled up inside him. It was Sam, wasn't it? Sam Wetherall, whose grave he had wept over, even though he knew it was not his friend's body in it, but someone else's wearing his tags. They had arranged it. It had been the only answer to Prentice's death and the knowledge afterward.

Sam grinned. "You look like hell, Joe. But it's still good to see you. Don't make a fuss."

Joseph's heart raced with fear, hope, intense, pounding relief. There was no question anymore. Sam was alive. "What are you doing here?" He managed the words although his lips were dry and his throat tight. Sam was not in uniform. "Are you on leave?" Surely he could not have left the army, even in his new identity, not deserted? It wasn't possible, not the Sam he knew. He realized he was shaking with fear. His belief in Sam was one of the few certainties he relied on. He did not want it tested.

Sam eased himself into the stool beside him. "Took a leaf out of your brother's book," he said very quietly.

Joseph stared at him, struggling to understand. Intelligence? But Sam was a sapper, one of those who dug under the enemy lines, listened, set mines, blew up defenses. Perhaps the tight spaces and the claustrophobia had gotten to him at last. It got to most men, sooner or later. Too many were buried alive in collapses, drowned in the mud and debris, crushed by falls.

He found himself smiling simply because Sam was alive. Memories poured back of conversations they had had on the line in 1915, when it had all been so new. They had thought then that the war wouldn't last a year. It had been talk of glory, of heroism and sacrifice. Now it was just death, endlessly and pointlessly ever more death. The soldiers were even younger.

"Here in Paris?" he asked aloud, his voice almost level.

"Mostly." Sam's eyes were far away for a moment. "How's the regiment?" He did not ask for anyone by name, but Joseph thought of the men Sam had known who were dead now. There was no need to tell him.

Sam interrupted his efforts to concoct a good answer. "You were never a good liar, Joe. Who's gone? Everyone?"

"No!" Joseph denied too quickly, thinking of those whose comradeship had been so precious. "Only a few: Tucky Nunn, Eardslie, Chicken Hagger, Lanty and Bibby Nunn both, Doughy Ward, both the Arnold brothers."

Sam's hand tightened on his arm. He said nothing. He had never wasted words.

The barman poured him some absinthe and he ignored it.

"I'm looking for Punch Fuller," Joseph said quietly.

"Deserted?" Sam said with slight surprise. "Poor sod. Is that really the best use they can find for you, to send you to Paris after the poor devils that reached the end of the line?" He frowned. "If he's really cut and run, Joe, there's no point in finding him. He's a casualty of war. You can't save him."

"No, he's not a deserter," Joseph said slowly. Perhaps he should not tell Sam about it, but he knew he was going to. He had no idea what Sam had done in the dreadful years since they had parted, just before Sam went over the top that day in spring of 1915. But he was the same man with whom he had shared the chocolate biscuits, sitting in the dugout, and told stories of the laughter and the memories that mattered, of the England they loved and the past that was slipping a little further away each day.

Sam was waiting, watching him. His face was leaner than before, more deeply lined. Joseph could barely even guess at the pain losing his identity must have caused him, hollowing out places of loneliness, character, and grief he could not imagine. He could never return to England, the familiar hills and fields, the villages, the rhythm and music of speech, the common history that framed even the simplest things.

Had Joseph been wrong to offer that way out? He had so desperately wanted Sam to live, and the decision had seemed right at the time, the only thing possible.

"We had an incompetent officer shot," he said aloud, looking at Sam again. "It might have passed off without any fuss, considering the overall losses, but another damn war correspondent saw it and left me no way out. The man's father is a general, and he's determined to see justice done and his son's good name reinstated, and of course whoever murdered him tried for it, and face the firing squad."

"What has Punch Fuller got to do with it? Don't say you're playing detective again, Joe!"

"Not willingly," Joseph answered, more memories almost drowning him. If he had been wiser last time, Sam would still be in the British Army, under his own name, and if he survived the war, free to go home to his brother.

Sam saw it in his eyes. He smiled. "Don't blame yourself for being who you are, Joe. I don't. I never wanted you to betray yourself, and that's what it would have been."

"I don't want to know who killed Northrup," Joseph retorted. "And I already know why. The man was a fool, and dangerous."

"All this old question of loyalty," Sam said softly. "Do you violate the old standards to save your friends? Or do you keep your conscience, and let them die?"

"I used to think I was sure of lots of things," Joseph answered ruefully. "Now I'm only sure of the values of humanity, of courage and honor and pity. Keep your word whatever it costs. Face forward, even if you're so terrified your guts turn to water. Help someone if you can, anyone, doesn't matter who they are or what you think they've done. Don't think, just help the pain. Stay with them, don't let go. Don't judge."

Sam's eyes were very gentle.

"And what happens if you go back without finding Punch Fuller?" he asked.

"General Northrup will go on looking for whoever killed his son, and trying to prove it was murder, until one day he finds out his son was an ass and the men hated him. Then he'll pin the blame on someone and his vengeance will be satisfied."

"You mean he'll settle for lies as long as he extracts the solution he wants?"

"Something like that."

"I assume you've already considered blaming someone who's dead?" Sam asked. "God knows, there must be enough of them."

Joseph smiled, aware of the irony. "Yes, I thought of it. But I wouldn't have much chance of getting away with it if I don't have any idea what actually happened. Punch Fuller might be able to tell me that."

Sam rolled his eyes very slightly. "Come on, Joe! If he does, it'll be in the nature of a confession! You won't be able to use it. For God's sake, have a little sense!"

"I won't be able to use it to prove anything," Joseph agreed with a pained smile. "But then I really don't want to!"

Sam's eyebrows rose.

"Don't you? You'll let them get away with murdering an officer because they think he's incompetent! God, you have changed!"

Joseph realized with a sense of amazement that in spite of the mockery, the chaffing, and the laughter, Sam wanted Joseph to cling to his belief. That he didn't share it, or professed not to, was irrelevant. Perhaps as long as Joseph did, Sam felt there was something certain. As a last resort, something to trust. When everything else was destroyed, then perhaps it would stand.

Maybe that was what a chaplain's job really was—not to teach others to believe, but to be seen to believe oneself. To stand not so much for a specific faith, but for the endurance of faith, for its power to outlast everything else. He must do it now, a gift for Sam, after all he had taken away from him.

"It's a matter of weighing one loyalty against another," he began delicately. "It's a matter of the men's loyalty to each other, after three years in the trenches living together, and before this is over, dying together. Weigh that against Northrup's answering for the truth of his incompetence, and I'm not so certain whoever did it was wrong that I'd be willing to force the issue and see them hang for it. Especially now. You may not know it here in Paris, but the whole of the British line is too close to mutiny to stomach a glaring injustice like that. I don't know if I'm right, Sam. There are a lot of things I don't feel so sure of that I'd ask another man to pay the price of it. I'll pay it myself. I want to know what happened. When I do, I'll go back and tell Colonel Hook—and General Northrup, if he wants to know."

"Are you sure the dead officer was an idiot, more than most?" Sam asked thoughtfully.

"I am. I saw some of his handiwork myself. Nigel Eardslie died as a result of it. Edgar Morel is ready to lead a mutiny, I think."

Sam smiled and his eyes were surprisingly bright. "I apologize. You haven't changed. Just a little more complex, that's all. You'll make a regular Jesuit, if you survive the war."

"Jesuits are Catholic," Joseph pointed out, but a tiny flicker of warmth was back inside him. "Can you help me find Punch Fuller? You must know Paris a hell of a lot better than I do. Have you got people I can ask? I haven't much longer to look."

Sam sat still for several moments before he answered. "Yes, there's someone I can ask," he said at last. "If I tell her you need to know for a good reason, she'll help. But you'll have to trust me, Joe. No questions, nothing reported to anyone, not to prove a point, not even to save a man's life. There are far more lives hanging on it. Your word?"

"My word," Joseph agreed, holding Sam's gaze.

Sam considered the absinthe for a moment, and decided against it. He put a few coins on the counter, then stood up, and Joseph followed him out of the club and up the narrow steps into the street. It was dark and still raining very slightly, a sort of drifting mist that covered every-thing with a sheen that gleamed bright and wet in the few lights that were still on.

"You all right to walk?" Sam asked quietly. "It's mostly alleys. We need to cross the river."

"Of course I'm all right to walk!" Joseph said tartly, but without ill temper. "Carry you, if you need it!"

"We have some problems," Sam said cheerfully, his voice on the edge of laughter in the dark. "Don't always know who our friends are. Keep up, and say nothing."

They went together through the old part of the city, along alleys and byways that predated Napoleon's grand redesign—places that echoed to the footsteps of revolutionaries, and had run with blood then. Now they held the furtive whispers of different secrets, fears, and griefs.

They crossed the river to the Île de la Cité. The rain had eased, and the water glistened in the faint moonlight. A string of barges was black on its shining surface. Everything was wet. A thin strain of a saxophone drifted and was lost. Someone laughed.

Sam spoke to someone, their voice murmuring, and a few minutes later they crossed the river at the far side onto the left bank. There were more whispered exchanges with people, sometimes no more than a few words.

It must have been after two in the morning when at last Sam led the way down steep flagged steps into a cellar. One flame burned in a glass lamp, leaving most of the room in shadows.

"Monique?" he said in little more than a whisper.

She answered him in French, only one word to acknowledge that she was there. Joseph, straining his eyes to discern through the shadows, was certain there was at least one more person there.

"We need to find a British soldier," Sam told the woman and who-ever it was beside her. "This is Chaplain Joseph Reavley. I've known him since 'fifteen. You can trust him."

"Deserter?" Monique asked. "If so, I'm surprised you came. I can't do that, and you know it. Not when he has information about German plans. Sapper, is he?"

Joseph drew in his breath to speak, then remembered he had promised Sam to remain silent.

"Knows the truth of an execution," Sam replied. "Wants to avoid the wrong man going to the firing squad. Better right now if no one does. Man from a Cambridgeshire regiment—name of Punch Fuller. On leave in Paris right now."

The woman turned to look very carefully at Joseph, moving the light closer, studying his face. He did not avert his gaze but looked back at her. She was beautiful, in a soft, intense way, with a strong nose, wide, gentle mouth. Her cloud of dark hair accentuated the pallor of her skin and the shadows around her eyes.

She turned back to Sam. "You swear for him?"

Sam did not hesitate. "Yes."

Monique turned to the man beside her and for a moment the light swayed a little toward him. Joseph had a glimpse of wide, light gray eyes and a thin face of extraordinary intelligence; then Monique moved the light away and everything became indistinct again.

"If he is still in Paris, we'll find him," Monique answered. "Have lunch in the Café Parnasse at one o'clock."

Sam thanked her and took Joseph by the elbow, leading him back up the steps into the street again. "Where are you staying?" he asked.

Joseph told him.

"I'll take you back close enough for you to find your way. The Café Parnasse is in the Rue Mazarin, near the river. Be there. That's the best I can do for you."

"Thank you."

Sam did not ask him what he would do if he discovered Punch Fuller was involved with the murder of Northrup. It was a delicate balance between them, understood that even if he were, Joseph would not instigate any court-martial that involved him. The success of the intelligence network for which Sam worked depended upon freedom of information, and trust that it was never used for police work, for private gain, or for vengeance.

From the very little Sam had said, Joseph assumed that what they dealt in was information about German troop movements. Sam had made a laughing reference to carrier pigeons, and Joseph knew their use in war. He could only imagine the courage and patience of scores of men and women posted all over Europe watching, listening, making notes, and risking their lives to report everything to one source, here in Paris, where it could be collated to form a picture.

They walked together speaking little. There was too much to say, and too little time even to begin. Perhaps most of it they already understood, and the rest did not matter tonight. Facts, details were irrelevant. They had the same understanding of the enormity of the change since the comparative innocence of the time when they had fought in the same trench, side by side.

Joseph asked a few questions about Paris, although nothing that could be secret; he simply wanted to picture Sam's life.

"Do you get reasonable food?"

Sam shrugged. "Most of the time. Better than you do! I'd back any Frenchman alive against an army cook, any day of my life!"

Joseph smiled, but he heard the moment of hollowness in Sam's voice. He remembered the chocolate biscuits Sam's brother had sent, and the rotten, scalding hot tea.

"It's important work," he said, then wondered if it sounded condescending. "And dangerous. It must be hard to know who you can trust. At least I know which way the enemy is." Then he wished he had not said that, either. The old comradeship was so precious that the memory of it now seemed almost like golden days, and yet those days had frequently been nightmare awful.

"It's which way he's going next we're working on," Sam said drily. "It's a sort of mental puzzle putting the pieces together. There are some decent chaps, and women, too. Different kind of courage. Paris isn't home, but it has charm, like a beautiful woman who falls ill. It's worth fighting to see her recover, get back the color and the wit again, to see her dress with style."

"See you in the Café Parnasse, after the war!" Joseph said impulsively.

Sam slapped Joseph on the shoulder, gently. "Done!" he agreed. "First anniversary."

They came within sight of Joseph's lodging. Sam gave a small salute,

a smile, and without any more words he was gone into the shadows. The
night was empty again, the warmth and the safety of it gone.

Joseph went to his room. The chill in his flesh—into the bones—
had nothing to do with the weather, or even his tiredness: It was a knowledge of loss.

Punch Fuller was in the Café Parnasse at one o'clock. He was flirting
shamelessly with a French girl who was perhaps no more than fourteen, a
beautiful, self-possessed child-woman with a magnificent head of curly
hair. She was very patient with him, brushing him off with easy skill.

"Hello, Punch," Joseph said when he was almost beside him. "May I
have soup and bread, please, mademoiselle?" He sat down on the seat
next to Punch.

Punch was startled. "Hello, Chaplain! You come to keep me out of
the paths of sin? That's downright unsporting of you." He looked at
Joseph narrowly to see if he understood that it was a politely worded request to go away.

Joseph smiled. "I didn't find you by accident, Punch. Colonel Hook
sent me."

Punch froze, not even turning his head toward Joseph. He was
twenty-three, plain with his hooked nose and sharp chin, but quick-
witted and an easy, loyal friend. "Who's that then?" he said guardedly.

Joseph had intended to be direct; he needed Punch to believe him.
"Because Major Northrup's father, General Northrup, is tearing the regiment apart determined to find out who shot his son," he replied.

"Oi got no oidea who that'd be, sir," Punch said immediately.

"No, of course not," Joseph agreed. "Nor have I. Not sure that I really
want to. The man was an ass. But the thing is, the general isn't going to go
away until he has an answer, even if it's a wrong one, and some innocent
man ends up before a firing squad."

Punch turned to look at him, his blue eyes troubled. "So what is it
you reckon Oi can do about that then, sir?" The suspicion was sharp in
his face that Joseph was trying to manipulate him into giving someone
away.

Joseph had his answer planned. "He won't leave until he gets an answer. I want to find one he'll accept, and stop looking."

"Loike wot, Chaplain? If it weren't a Jerry, it had to be one of us."

"True," Joseph conceded. "With our casualty rate, probably someone who's dead, too, by now."

"Roight." Punch nodded. "But still won't be very good for his family, though, will it? An' d'yer think the general'll believe it? Sort of convenient, don't you think? An' apart from that, Chaplain, who's going to tell him a loi? You aren't!"

Joseph was both pleased and frustrated by Punch's faith in him. The next part of his plan was very carefully judged. "I realize you don't know exactly what really happened, Punch," he began. "But let's create a sort of working model, for something that's close enough people would believe it. The major was a liability. He didn't know what he was doing, and he wouldn't be told. It cost several good men's lives, plus a smashed leg here and there, the odd amputation."

"That's roight," Punch agreed guardedly. "We all know that."

"So far General Northrup doesn't," Joseph corrected him. "He's still denying all such accusations."

"So whoi does he think we shot him, then?" Punch said reasonably.

"That's a good point," Joseph said vehemently. "I can find chapter and verse of that easily enough. And when I do, the people who suffered most, or those whose friends did, are going to be suspect. That's the reason I haven't made a point of looking very hard so far. I hoped he'd realize it's going to be ugly. Do as much damage to his son's reputation as anyone's. But he isn't listening."

"Don't necessarily follow!" Punch protested. "You can't say as it was this man or that just because of who got killed!"

"I know that."

"Could've been lots of people!" Punch emphasized.

An idea was crystallizing in Joseph's mind. "Do you mean lots of people together, Punch, or just any one of lots of people?"

Punch was thinking hard.

Joseph waited.

"How would it be . . ." Punch said very slowly, "if you was to tell him that it was lots of men, dozen or more. Not one man gone mad who wanted to murder him, but a dozen who'd all had enough, and could see that more an' more men were going to get killed if the major didn't stop and listen to someone with experience? And it was only meant to scare some sense into him."

"How was shooting him going to scare sense into him?" Joseph said dubiously.

"Not shoot him, Chaplain. Set up a trial, loike. Make him sit an' listen to what a fool he was, evidence. Foind him guilty of incompetence, causing other men's deaths, an' pretend to shoot him. Scare the hell out of him." He studied Joseph's face earnestly, searching for understanding.

It was beginning to be very clear. "You mean a kangaroo court-martial?" Joseph said very softly.

"I'm only suggesting it!" Punch protested. "D'you think the general moight believe that?"

"Private soldiers court-martialing an officer?"

"Not just privates, nor corporals neither."

"Officers?" Joseph was not really surprised. "Captain Morel?"

"An' Captain Cavan. He were the one who had to amputate poor Matheson's leg, just 'cos that idiot sent him to cart a bloody great field gun through the mud. Everyone told him it was dangerous!" He stared at Joseph, challenging him to argue.

Joseph sat numbly, no longer even aware of his surroundings. It was worse than he had thought. They were speaking theoretically, but both knew that what Punch was really saying was the truth. If Cavan had been involved and Northrup ever found out, it would be a court-martial that would tear apart more than just the regiment. Cavan was one of the best surgeons on the Ypres Salient, and one of the bravest men. His recommendation for the V.C. had heartened every man who knew him. If he were now court-martialed for Northrup's murder, it might be the final grief and absurdity that would break the spirit of some, and ignite others to the mutiny that had lain just beneath the surface in men like Morel. There wouldn't be a serving soldier on the front who wouldn't think Cavan was worth ten of Northrup, whatever the law said.

"Captain Reavley?" Punch said anxiously.

"Yes. Yes, I see. It was designed to frighten Major Northrup. What went wrong?"

"Oi don't know, sir. Oi swear."

"Thank you."

"You aren't going to go an' tell Colonel Hook what Oi said, are you? Oi'll deny it, sir." His eyes were angry and frightened.

"No, I'm not," Joseph said sharply. "I told you I wasn't. But I can't find a story the general will believe if I don't know what the truth is. This way none of the facts anyone can discover will prove it false."

"Roight. Yes, I see. Thank you, Chaplain."

It was dusk as Joseph left in a staff car returning to the front. The air was motionless, wet and close to the skin. The sky leached the last tones of warmth out of the waterlogged land. Thin vapors of mist provided a curious softness but hid none of the desolation: the broken trees; the bare, scorched wreckage of houses and farms; the litter of broken guns and vehicles on the roads.

The car was on a cratered road now, and he smelled the familiar stench long before they reached even the outpost farthest back. The first star shells were bursting, and gradually the sound of the heavy guns blurred one raid into another. A stray eighteen-pound shell exploded fifty yards away, jarring the earth and sending eruptions of heavy Flanders clay high and dark into the air. Most of it was far in front of the car, over the woods toward Passchendaele itself.

As he alighted, he thanked the driver who had given him a lift, glad of a few hundred yards to walk. He felt battered by the noise, as if it were a physical assault, but he needed the time for a last arrangement of thoughts in his mind.

He found Hook in his dugout. He was looking at maps, although he must have known the whole of the Ypres Salient better than he knew his own garden. The photograph of his wife had been moved to the top of the gramophone, as if both had to be forgotten for the moment.

"Ah, come in, Reavley," he said, looking up as if relieved to forget the advances and retreats for a while. "Did you learn anything?"

"Yes, sir," Joseph replied, letting the sacking fall closed over the doorway and standing to attention as well as he could. It was raining again outside and his boots were heavy with mud, his legs soaked almost up to the knee. "I found Punch Fuller, and he told me a good deal of what happened."

There was no light in Hook's face. "As a confession?" Clearly he hoped it was; then Joseph could not tell him.

"No, sir—more or less theoretically, the sort of thing that could have happened," Joseph answered unhappily. He stood to attention, refusing to sit. "I really think, sir, that General Northrup would prefer not to know this," he said very clearly. "And it would serve no purpose at all to tell him. The major was an arrogant and inexperienced officer who inadvertently caused the deaths of several good men, and the serious injuries of others. It provoked intense ill feeling among almost all the men, not just an odd one here or there. Any action you take is going to have to involve at least a dozen men, sir. And I have reason to think that his actual death was not intended but was an accident."

Hook looked weary. He gestured to Joseph to be seated on an upturned ammunition box.

"You can't have it all ways, Reavley," he said. "Either a dozen men were involved because he had angered them beyond their control, or his death was an accident. Which was it? And if you're going to say it was an accident, then you are going to have to produce the man who fired the shot, and prove its accidental nature. What the hell was he doing pointing a loaded weapon at an officer anyway?"

"I don't know who did it, sir," Joseph said honestly. It was the one part of the story he had no need to blur.

"Don't play games with me, Reavley!" Hook snapped. His uniform was crumpled and bloodstained. His face was haggard with exhaustion. "I've got men dying out there by the hundreds every day!" His hands were trembling. "I need to get Northrup off my back and out of the way! Either you know what happened or you don't! What did Fuller tell you? You said a dozen men. Do you mean a kangaroo court-martial?"

There was no point in denying it. Hook obviously knew. Joseph felt the net of circumstance tightening around him, but he was determined to give Hook a way out. "Yes, sir, but only with the intention of frightening him into taking advice in the future. Not to kill him."

Hook's face was pale, his mouth pulled down with grief. "Who was involved, Reavley?" His voice dropped. "I have to know."

Joseph looked straight back at him. He would not make the same mistake this time. He was prepared to lie, evade, whatever was necessary, and live with his conscience. "I don't know, sir. Fuller told me what happened, not who was concerned. And I promised him I'd not betray him. I think the men may know, sir, but no one will say. You can't blame them if their loyalty to each other is greater than to some military principle of obedience to an incompetent officer who, out of sheer stupidity, is going to cost the lives of their friends." He chose his words deliberately. "We owe them more than that."

Hook passed his hand across his face. Joseph could hear the faint rasping of dry skin over the stubble of his beard. "I don't have the luxury of choosing my own morality, Reavley. I can tell Northrup this, but he won't believe me. He can't afford to, because it makes his son a disgrace to him. And it would set a precedent that would be impossible to live with. Truth or lie, the army can't afford to grant that it is just."

"Then tell him it was an accident," Joseph demanded. "Let Major Northrup be buried with some semblance of honor. That would serve everyone."

Hook gave a sharp bark, supposed to be laughter. "I'll try!"

Joseph spent the night working with Cavan at the dressing station as casualties poured in. He snatched a few hours of sleep, then went to sit with the wounded or dying and do what he could for them. Mostly it was simply not leaving them to die alone.

At ten o'clock, Barshey Gee came and told him the colonel wanted to see him, and ten minutes later Joseph was back in Hook's dugout facing General Northrup, white-faced and standing so ramrod-stiff it seemed as if his back was arched.

"Are you saying, Captain Reavley, that my son was murdered by the common consent of a dozen or more of his own men?" His voice rasped in his throat as if he could not gulp the air into his lungs. "What in God's name has this army come to? Are we a crowd of barbarians, beyond the law? I will not surrender humanity and decency, sir, to a bunch of hooligans so demoralized by drink and terror that they turn on their own officers! Is there no morality left? How dare you stand there in the uniform of a man of God, and condone such . . . such evil!" His body trembled and he was obviously having difficulty controlling his voice.

"Sir, I did not say he was murdered," Joseph replied as calmly as he could.

"What do you call it, then?" Northrup demanded passionately. "A dozen men with guns against one unarmed officer? Pray, what does that pass for in your terminology?"

"You obviously know more about it than I do, sir," Joseph said stiffly. "What I heard was that the men pleaded with Major Northrup to listen to the evidence of more experienced soldiers, even though they were junior in rank. When he would not do so, and it was costing lives unnecessarily, they used force to make him listen, to save their own lives and those of their comrades. He was killed by accident, not intentionally. I don't know how that happened, or who was involved."

"The records of killed and injured should make that plain enough," Northrup replied. "These men all come from the same villages, played in the same football teams or brass bands, or whatever. Even a half-wit could find out who conspired together for this, if they wanted to. Whatever it began as, it ended as murder! And I shall see justice."

"Sir . . ." Hook began, but it was obvious in his face that he had already tried remonstrating with every argument he knew and had failed.

"It ended as tragedy," Joseph corrected him. "Most things do out here, sir. I believe profoundly that it would be better for everyone if we allow it to remain an honorable tragedy. Major Northrup was an officer respected by his men, who mourn their loss. Does it serve anyone to say that he was so incompetent that his men feared for their lives, and shot him in what they believed to be self-defense?"

Northrup winced as if Joseph had struck him, but he did not retreat. "I daresay that is what you would prefer, sir, but it is not the truth," he said hoarsely. "He was murdered by men who panicked and lost their discipline. I will find out who they are! If you will not assist me, I shall do it alone! And Headquarters will know that you endeavored to cover it up, to your eternal disgrace."

He gulped.

"I am forced to believe it is because the surgeon, Captain Cavan, was involved, and you are jealous of your regiment's chance of gaining a V.C.

Captain Morel, who is a renegade if ever a man was, used to be your student in Cambridge, and you are deliberately shielding him. It will not be difficult to find the others, and when I do, you will have no choice but to arrest them! Sir!" He snapped to attention, saluted Hook, then pushed past Joseph and went up the steps and out into the mud.

Hook sat down and buried his head in his hands.

Joseph said nothing. He knew Cavan and Morel at least would be arrested by morning, probably all the others within another twenty-four hours. He had done everything he knew—and he had failed.

*J*udith jolted abruptly into wakefulness. She was lying on an ambulance blanket on the floor of the tent where she had fallen asleep. She had no idea how long ago that was. Day and night had blurred into one long cacophony of guns and engines, rain-soaked darkness split by star shells and the flash of explosions.

Now it seemed to be murky daylight, and comparatively quiet, just a distant rumble. She shivered because her clothes were wet and her bones ached from the hard floor.

"Is it time?" she said automatically, blinking and trying to clear her head.

Wil Sloan was bending over her, his grip still hard on her shoulder. His face was pale and slicked with rain, his hair dripping. There were bruises of exhaustion around his eyes.

"Something terrible's happened," he said huskily.

Fear boiled up in her like a wave of nausea. Was he going to tell her that Joseph had been killed? It was the thing she dreaded most of all. She found her throat was closed and the words wouldn't escape her lips.

"They've arrested twelve men for killing Major Northrup," Wil said. "Harrison came and told me."

"Twelve!" She was both relieved and appalled. "Twelve?" She propped herself on one elbow. "That's ridiculous. How could twelve . . . all of them?"

"Kangaroo court-martial," he replied, just as she realized it herself.

"And shot him?" she whispered.

"That's what they're saying. But the thing is . . . Cavan was one of them."

Now she understood his horror. "Cavan?" It was too awful to grasp. "But they can't take our doctor away! What about the wounded? That's . . . monstrous! They . . . they can't!"

"They have," he said. "And Captain Morel."

She sat up straight, pain shooting through her muscles. "Why? How do they know it was them?"

His face was bleak. "I'm sorry, Judith. The chaplain went to Paris and found one of the men who knew, and got it out of him somehow."

"I don't believe it!" She refused to. Joseph would not do that. "You must be wrong," she insisted. "Anyway, if the man confessed to a priest, you can't use it! Joseph would never repeat a confession. He couldn't!"

"He didn't say who it was." Wil shook his head. "Just that it was twelve. Northrup worked out who was angriest with the major and took it from there."

Judith struggled to her feet. "We've got to do something about it. This is terrible."

Wil stood also. "Right now we're on duty. And we'll have to take the wounded all the way back to the field hospital because there'll be no one able to do much in the dressing station."

"What a bloody nightmare." She sighed. "We'll have to do something about it! We can't let this go on, Wil. The men'll mutiny! To lock up our best surgeon over some idiot like Northrup! Are we trying to lose this war?"

"Keep your shirt on, Judith," he said anxiously. "Don't do anything rash. We can't afford to get ourselves locked up, too. That won't help. I'll get a cup of tea. It's going to be another bad night."

It was. Judith drove in a daze, fighting to keep the ambulance on the shell-pocked road and not get mired in the mud on either side or break an axle in one of the craters. It took all her strength to hold the wheel, and twice she had to get out and crank the engine to life again after a particularly violent stop.

All the time her mind was wrestling with the thought of Cavan in military prison awaiting trial. She could picture him as clearly as if she were looking at him. She could hear his voice in her mind. If they found them guilty of having mutinied and shot Northrup, they would all face a firing squad. There was no possible alternative. The worst thing was that she knew that he could have done it. He cared for the wounded above all things; he would put them before anything else. He had the anger and the courage.

How could Joseph have let it happen? He must have known General Northrup was rabid for revenge. Why had he not simply said he couldn't find out who was responsible? Even General Northrup couldn't arrest the entire regiment.

She peered through the windshield, trying to discern what the dark shapes ahead were. The shellfire was getting heavier. The last one had landed only fifty yards away, and the debris had fallen heavily on the roof.

Maybe if she found out every stupid and dangerous thing Major Northrup had done she could widen the field of men likely to want him dead so far that they couldn't possibly arrest all of them. There couldn't be exactly twelve who had lost someone. How did they know they had the right twelve? Wasn't there some legal principle about it being better to let ten guilty men go free than punish one innocent one?

Surely the general would not want his son's name to go down in history as an officer so incompetent his men had had to kill him to save their own lives? He was refusing to believe that now, but if there was proof, he would have to. Or at least he would know that others would believe it, and that was what mattered.

They were near the front line. She slewed to a stop as a couple of soldiers ran toward her, their Red Cross armbands catching the headlights. Wil leaped out and threw the ambulance doors open. Someone was scrambling through the mud, sliding and floundering, waving his arms at stretcher bearers. Someone else was staggering across the lights, bandaged around the head and eyes, blood on his hands.

She tried to keep the engine running as she felt the weight go into the back and the balance alter. A shell exploded so close that the metal of flying shrapnel clanged on the ambulance sides. A gout of mud slapped against the window and spurted into her face.

More figures drifted across the headlights, blurred by mud and rain, and the weight jolted again.

Then Wil appeared at the door. "We're full! You'll have to back out, there's water everywhere! Don't lose the engine, you might never get it going again in this. I'll get in when you've turned." He disappeared.

It took her ten minutes, with considerable help, before she was back on the road facing in the opposite direction. She heard the door slam, and opened the throttle to push the engine as hard as she could. They lurched forward, splashing up sprays of water, hesitated a moment, then caught a purchase on the mud and gravel and moved forward.

She drove as hard as she could, knowing that because Cavan was locked up in some French farmhouse far behind the lines, they would have miles more to go before they could find help.

It was dark except for the occasional flares, and the rain became worse. They hit a deep crater in the mud, which was masked by water until it was too late. She was fortunate not to break the axle. There was no help for it but to turn off the engine and get out.

Wil came around from the back. He could see at a glance what was wrong, even if the violent lurch had not told him.

"It's too deep," she said desperately, wiping the rain out of her eyes. "You'll have to get at least some of them out. We'll have to lift it. I'll see if there's a piece of wood or something we can use as a lever, get it up, if someone else pushes." She looked around to see if there was any other light or sign of movement.

Wil pushed his hand through his sodden hair and left a smear of blood on his face. "Alf Culshaw's blinded, but he's still got both legs and arms. If we point his hands in the right place he can lift. The others are too far gone. One poor devil will be lucky if we get him there alive." His voice caught. "Jesus wept! This is so bloody senseless!" He turned and plowed back through the mud to the back of the ambulance and pulled the door open.

Judith started after him. It would take both of them to help the injured men out to lighten it enough to lift. They were heavy, awkward, and in desperate pain. Her hands slipped on the wet stretcher handles and her back ached unbearably as she tried to keep her balance and carry the heavy bodies to the side of the road.

"I'm sorry," she said to them over and over. "Got to lighten it so we can lift it out."

The first man was peacefully unconscious, blood soaking through his bandages in the rain.

"It's not too bad," the second said, trying to smile. "Don't worry, miss."

She felt the hot tears on her face as she bent to touch his hand. "Won't be long. Just got to lift a little, then we'll get you back."

Together with Wil she lifted two more out, leaving only the worst injured behind. Alf Culshaw she led slowly, warning of the puddles and ruts, until he and Wil were on either side of the stuck wheel. She placed Culshaw's hands under the edge of the frame. "Are you sure you're all right?" she asked him. "I wouldn't ask you if I didn't have to."

"I know," he said quietly. "Just don't ask me to guide you where we are going." He gave a dry, hacking laugh.

"You lift. I'll drive," she replied. "Better that way. I can't lift for toffee! Thanks." She had the wood ready—broken pieces from a dead tree and a couple of lengths of old sacking.

"Go on then," Wil directed. "One, two, three!"

The ambulance rocked and heaved level. Judith threw the wood and sacking in and it settled down again. She ran to the driver's seat and scrambled in. Wil moved Culshaw out of the way, then cranked the handle and they moved forward at last.

"Right!" Wil yelled, jumping backward. "Let's get them in again!"

She left the engine on, brake tight, and scrambled back to lift the stretchers in again to a cheer, and then to help Culshaw back into the seat.

She drove without incident the rest of the way. It seemed to take hours—but it was probably not more than forty-five minutes longer. A strange doctor, white-faced and obviously harassed, took the wounded in. The last man was already dead. Judith and Wil got back into the ambulance and started for the front again, this time with Wil in the front.

"We'll get Cavan back," he said when they were half a mile from the dressing station. "We'll find a way. He can't have been the one who shot Northrup. He must be covering for someone. It'll come out."

"Do you think so?" she asked, glancing sideways at him, although she could see nothing more than his outline in the dark.

"We've got to make it!" he said grimly. "If General Northrup could find out who the twelve most likely are, then we have to be able to find out why, as well. They'd never have done it without a hell of a good reason. We've got to find the people who'll swear to it."

"And take it to Northrup?" she asked. Her stomach knotted up with fear at the thought of it.

"You game?" Wil said, touching her arm for a moment.

She swallowed and felt her heart beating in her throat. "Of course."

On the final trip of the night she found Joseph at the field dressing station. He helped her with the last stretcher. The man was already dead from his wounds. Defeat overwhelmed her, and a sense that everything was slipping out of the last trace of control that she had.

"If we could have taken him to Cavan's dressing station he'd have been alive!" she said furiously, tears choking her. "But those men are bleeding to death because he's locked up in some damn farmhouse waiting to go on trial and be shot over that idiot Northrup!" She stared at him defiantly. "Why couldn't you leave your stupid conscience out of it and just keep your mouth shut? You didn't have to tell Colonel Hook it was a kangaroo trial! You could just have said you didn't know! Why can't you ever leave well enough alone?"

Joseph looked so tired his skin was gray in the early daylight, the stubble dark on his chin. There was no light in his eyes at all.

"I had to tell him something close to the truth, or he could too easily find out I was lying," he answered her.

"Don't tell him anything at all!" she shouted back. "Why didn't you just say you didn't know? He can't force you!"

Joseph looked down at the muddy boards they were standing on. "I thought if General Northrup knew it was at least a dozen men, a court-martial, not a private murder, he'd be so ashamed he'd let it drop rather than leave his son so disgraced. It would have been better for everyone. Otherwise he could just have found the worst enmity, the man he thought unjust, and blamed him. He isn't going to let it go."

"He isn't *now*!" she retorted. "He's charged Cavan, and we've got to take wounded men twice as far to get them treated—and they're dying, Joseph! They're dying, when they don't have to!"

"I know. . . ."

She felt guilty for attacking him when he was so obviously blaming himself anyway, but she was too angry and too frightened to stop. "We've got to save Cavan. What are we going to do?" She tried to moderate her voice a little, hearing the shrill edge to it. "Does Northrup really want it to come out that his son caused all those people's deaths? If we can prove it, find all the evidence of what a fool he was, who's dead because of him, and why there were twelve men willing to risk their own lives in order to get rid of him, wouldn't he want that silenced?"

They could both hear the sounds of movement inside, voices giving orders, stifled murmurs of pain.

"He wasn't meant to be killed, only frightened," Joseph explained.

"So who shot him?" she demanded.

"I don't know."

"Then they won't believe it. It sounds like an excuse. Were they really going to let him go again, after they'd put him on a mock trial?"

"I don't know, Judith. That's all I could get out of the man who told me."

Another ambulance pulled up outside. They saw the lights and heard the squelching in the mud, and voices shouting. Joseph moved aside and she followed him.

"Was he there? Is he in prison now?" she urged. "Why should anyone believe him? And if he told you in confession, why did you report it? He betrayed all his fellows!"

"He wasn't one of them," Joseph corrected her. "He knows because I think lots of the men do. Consider, Judith—if there were twelve men as a jury, surely others kept watch for them and covered what they were doing. There are a lot more than twelve men involved."

She saw a glimmer of hope, just a thread. "Then that's better. Everyone agreed Major Northrup was a disaster! Can't we take that to the general, and show him what it'll do to his son's reputation? Even to his own, for that matter?" Men started carrying stretchers into the dressing station. She stepped closer to Joseph. "Joe, in the general's place wouldn't you forgo revenge rather than have the name of someone you loved publicly vilified and all their mistakes proved?"

"Of course I would. Revenge is worth nothing anyway. But General Northrup doesn't feel that way."

"Then we'll have to make him!"

He looked at her blankly, anxiety puckering his brow, but he did not argue. It was only then that she realized he had intended to do it anyway; he merely needed time to gather the evidence. Perhaps her pain had made her too quick to judge.

"Hurry!" she urged. "The general could leave, and then it'll be too late. I'll help. I know Wil Sloan will, too, and others."

He drew in his breath to argue and—realizing the futility of it—let it out again without speaking.

Judith knew there was no time to wait for Joseph to speak to General Northrup. Northrup was somewhere far behind the lines. She and Wil knew who was involved and they had transport. It was not difficult to arrange to be the drivers who took several patients back to the hospital at Lille, and then divert on the way back and find Northrup's headquarters. Certainly they would be away longer than they should be, and they would have to commandeer petrol for the extra miles, but no one would have to be asked to cover for them or tell the necessary lies. A score of men were only too eager, vying for the privilege.

It required a little more bravado and finesse to find herself actually standing in the general's presence in the small French farmhouse in which he was currently headquartered. It was a comfortable place, gently domestic, once somebody's home. He was immaculately smart: boots polished, face pale and shaved to a perfect smoothness.

"You say you have further information on the death of my son, Miss . . . Miss Reavley?" he said stiffly. "Are you in a position to testify to this at the court-martial? It will not be easy for you. The whole regiment is of a sullen and mutinous nature. Discipline has been allowed to fall into laxity. Your fellow V.A.D. volunteers may make it difficult for you. Are you prepared for that?"

She had already weighed her answers. She stood to attention. "I am prepared to tell the truth, sir, because it is the truth, whoever likes me or dislikes me for it." Her gaze did not waver from his. She saw a tired and grieved man, the skin around his eyes paper thin, his shoulders held square by little more than pride.

She felt a wave of pity for him, for his arrogance and blindness, for the fragility that had stopped him seeing his son as he was, and his need to believe a lie and cling on to it even at the cost of other men's lives. But if she did not break him, then he would break Cavan, and all the others. Worst of all, he would have broken all the men's belief in justice and the bonds of loyalty here and now. And here and now those were almost the only things left that were good.

Northrup's voice was hoarse with emotion when he spoke. "You are a fine woman, Miss Reavley. You have more courage and honor than your regiment's chaplain. Is he related to you?"

"Captain Reavley is my older brother, sir." His insulting Joseph made it easier. She was angry with him herself, but that was quite different. She would have defended him to the death against anyone else. With one sentence Northrup had taken away the impediment to striking the blow.

"What is it you know, Miss Reavley?" he asked.

She replied without hesitating.

"Well, sir, in order to prove beyond question why these twelve men in particular should do such a . . . dangerous and terrible thing, the court will have to show something very special. All the hardship and loss the men have faced over the last three years has never made them . . . mutiny. And I suppose that's what it is?"

"That is what it is, Miss Reavley," he agreed. "Make no mistake."

It was time to tell him the truth, before someone interrupted them.

"Well, sir, in the case of Captain Morel, it was the order Major Northrup gave to move a field gun from one position to another across half a mile of plowed clay. The men argued that it would get stuck. They might lose the gun itself, and the wagons and the horses, possibly even some of the men, if it slipped." She watched his face and saw the muscles tighten in his neck. He knew it was a stupid order, born of inexperience and too much pride to listen to lesser ranks.

"They argued, perhaps insolently," she went on. "Major Northrup insisted. They obeyed and got stuck. They saved the horses, but two men were injured, one man's leg was broken so badly Captain Cavan had to amputate it." She hated continuing, but it was like a gangrenous limb: It must all come off or it was pointless having begun. "And Captain Morel was very upset about sending out a rescue party into no-man's-land on a day when the German snipers could simply pick them off. Some refused to go, but others did. Several men were injured. Captain Eardslie was killed. He was one of my brother's students in Cambridge, and he and Morel were great friends."

Northrup's face was ashen. She felt as if she were killing a man already wounded fatally. Still she drove it home. "I have details for all of them, sir, and men prepared to swear to every incident sufficiently to prove a motive for each one of the twelve, especially Captain Cavan. It took a great deal to break him, but I can—"

"Yes!" he interrupted her. "I see you have taken a great deal of care to have every point documented, Miss Reavley. It will not be necessary." His voice was shaking and the muscles in his neck and jaw were so tight he could not control the tic in his cheek.

Her stomach was knotted until she felt nauseous. "Don't you want to prove the guilt of all of them?" she asked quietly. "Not just the one who pulled the trigger? He may simply have panicked. Aren't they all equally to blame? The whole twelve?"

His voice was barely audible. "What is it you want, Miss Reavley? You are not a fool! Are you trying to have my son's name dishonored, to have revenge for your . . . your mutinous friends?"

She swallowed.

"No, sir. As I said in the beginning—and you praised me for it—I want the whole truth to be told, to be fair to everyone. Nobody is going to believe that good soldiers—especially exceptional ones like Captain Cavan—mutinied unless we can show what reason they had . . . or imagined they had."

He stared at her, knowing he was being manipulated. He was certain in his own mind that it was Cavan she was trying to save, and yet he could see no way out, nothing with which he could accuse her. "They are already charged," he pointed out. "Are you so bent on revenge?"

She hesitated. Was it necessary to strike the last blow? Yes it was. She dared not stop in case she was just short of victory. "Not revenge, sir, surely? Is it not justice?"

His voice dropped to a whisper.

"My son does not deserve to be buried with dishonor. Is it not enough for them that he is dead?"

"It is terrible that he is dead, sir. And Captain Eardslie, and all the others. Over half a million of them, I believe. Not counting the French, and of course the Austrians and Germans, and the Italians, and Russians. And I suppose we have to start counting the Americans, too, now."

"I will speak with the prosecutor. Perhaps the charge can be lessened."

She smiled very slightly, afraid to say anything in case she spoiled it. "Permission to return to my ambulance, sir?"

"Granted, Miss Reavley."

Mason arrived back at Passchendaele to find it worse than before. It had rained almost without ceasing, the wettest August in human memory. Men lived and died in a hell past sanity to imagine. It went on day after day, night after night, with no victory and no end in sight except the possibility that there would be no life remaining—human, animal, or plant— and finally the mud would claim everything.

He thought of his beloved Yorkshire with its wild fells, shining tarns beneath wind-ragged skies, and steep villages with cobbled streets. But the memory was too all-consuming: It robbed him of words powerful enough to capture the passion and tenderness of a love so deep. Instead he began writing of England in general.

"It doesn't seem possible." He started a rough draft. "At home the trees tower green like clouds over the gold of the harvest fields. Horses bend to the plow and the fruit ripens in the orchards. Poppies burn scarlet grazing the corn with hot color. The men are gone. Women now get ready to reap and bind, laughing with each other, growing used to their new tasks.

"Here there are no trees, only a few shattered trunks and the scarlet is blood as men are crushed and trodden back to the all-consuming clay from which we are told we were fashioned by a deity who has grown tired of us and turned away. These few terrible miles hold so much human flesh you cannot set foot without standing on some man's rotting body."

Then he tore it up and wondered how to start again. Words needed to be simple for this, clear of all sentimentality. But what was there for anyone to say? For the first time in his life, words seemed pointless, his own too small, too shallow for the burden.

"We died in hell—they called it Passchendaele." He could only quote others. "Oh, Jesus, make it stop!"

But it seemed no God was listening.

He heard the news of the arrests of Cavan, Morel, and the other ten before he reached the section where it had happened. He wanted to speak to Colonel Hook when he had the chance and to Joseph Reavley. He needed the whole story to write up, all the information he could find before the court-martial began. And of course he wanted to see Judith as well. That was at the forefront of his mind, as it had been lately, too often for his emotional comfort.

He found the ambulance parked outside a first aid station, just behind the supply trenches. It was covered with mud; he saw several scars and dents on it, and a few bullet holes. The air was soft and muggy, full of flies and the ever-present stench. The occasional fine rain did nothing to help.

He asked for Judith and was told that she and Wil Sloan were both inside the makeshift tent. There were several other men with them, all with apparently minor injuries, and they were clustered around Judith, looking at her and laughing. Most of them had mugs of tea, held up as if in a toast.

Mason's shadow across the door made one then another turn, and they froze.

He walked in. He could not help looking first at Judith. She was very slender, as if under the gray V.A.D. uniform with its long skirt she were thin enough to be fragile. She had been at the front for three years. She must be so weary of dirt and pain, and never having time for laughter, never dressing in pretty clothes, being admired, playing games and falling in love. There was something fierce and uniquely beautiful about her, a waiting passion that war had robbed her of living yet.

She was flushed and her eyes were bright. The men had been looking at her as they raised their mugs. Why? Had something happened, and he knew nothing of it?

They recognized him. Wil Sloan came forward, still smiling a little, but guarded now. "Hello, Mr. Mason. You looking for someone?" he asked.

Mason made up his mind immediately. "I was going to do a piece on your surgeon, Captain Cavan. I meant to last time I was here, but he was too busy. If he still is, I thought I'd ask other people about him. You must all have stories you could tell. It would be especially good for morale." He would have to keep up the lie to Judith, and hope she never knew he had heard about the arrests.

They stared at him, the laughter dying out of their faces. Wil turned to Judith, as if seeking her permission to answer.

"I think that's an excellent idea," she said vigorously, looking at Mason with a bright challenge. "Captain Cavan is one of the best men in the whole Army Medical Corps, and they're all good. We should tell you in detail about his holding off the German attack, which is why he's up for the V.C. But there are lots of other stories as well." Her voice was warm, vibrant with enthusiasm, her eyes shining. There was even a faint flush in her cheeks.

Mason felt an acute sensation of dismay, and then of inexplicable anger. Damn it, even after he was arrested for mutiny and murder, there was a fire in her when she spoke of Cavan that was there for no one else. Judith Reavley, the idealist, the unquestioning patriot, was going against all her convictions for this man! What was the matter with her?

Cavan was in his early thirties, and a good-looking man, fair-haired, strong, with an intelligent face. He remembered seeing him working with Judith, easily, as if understanding were there without the need for words. Should he have seen it then?

He felt shut out, cold to the core of his belly. He had been thinking of her far too often, allowing her to matter. He realized how much of the hope, the peace inside, the warmth that was worth having, had rested in the thought of her.

They were waiting for him to answer. He must control himself—hide the awful vulnerability inside him. "Thank you," he said. "That would work very well. Then a few words with him will be enough." He was not going to let them dupe him entirely. Apart from pride, he could not afford to appear a complete fool, which he would do if he wrote a piece about Cavan, apparently not knowing he was charged with mutiny and murder. When the court-martial began, that would be the biggest story of the entire British Army on the Western Front. The only thing that could overwhelm that would be for the army to break through and advance considerably. And at the moment they were paying in blood for every yard.

Judith began to organize it immediately. She directed one man to recount his memory of helping Cavan carry wounded men to shelter and set broken limbs right there in the forward trench with mortar fire all around them. Another she told to repeat his tales of good humor through long hours operating in the field hospital, patience teaching new men now to assist. And for good measure a good few long and rambling jokes were added.

Mason sat through them, making notes, watching thin, strained faces and hearing the laughter and the pain in their voices. He hated being an onlooker. There was something vaguely indecent about drawing such memories from men whose passion and nakedness of heart could be extinguished by blood and shellfire in the next week or two, while he went safely home.

And yet those who read his work were the families of those men, and countless more like them. They deserved to know.

He was very aware of their enthusiasm to keep him there, and he knew the reason. Judith might be directing the situation, but the men understood and were more than willing. The murder of Major Northrup was already known. Did they really imagine they could keep the arrest of twelve men secret? Why even attempt it? It must be only a matter of days until the court-martial. Since it was a capital charge, and twelve men accused, including two officers, the army would send a militarily appointed prosecutor from London. Even so, like every other sentence of death, it would still be referred right up to Field Marshal Haig himself before it was carried out. That rule applied to the newest private, let alone to an officer nominated for the V.C.

What a bloody horrible, senseless tragedy! Why on earth had they done such a thing? Had they really imagined for a moment that they would get away with it? Or were they driven by a power far beyond the capacity for thought?

He refused to decide at the moment exactly what story he would write, but possibilities crowded his mind. The one he knew the Peace-maker would want was to make Cavan the hero, betrayed by an incompetent and cowardly command. A bad officer had been put in charge, and a surgeon had had to get rid of him in order to stop even more pointless slaughter of his men. All the stories about Cavan that he was now hearing would help with that: the laughter and comradeship, the heroism in the face of madness.

He took it all down carefully, noting the name and rank of those who told him. Judith went outside and did some work on her ambulance, then returned an hour later. There was still the same suppressed excitement about her, and he began to realize that she was following a very definite plan of some sort. For a wild moment the thought flashed to him that it was the same as his and the Peacemaker's. She had finally seen too much slaughter and was prepared to take a small step toward ending it. She was watching him now as he finished the last notes from the men. She came over toward him. She walked with grace, the weariness under such rigid control was completely hidden. He wondered when she had last slept properly in any kind of bed, or eaten a meal that wasn't cooked in a Dixie can. She must be so tired of dirt, endless chores, and desperate jokes one hardly dared laugh at. And yet laughter and that all-consuming comradeship of those who share life and death were the only shreds of human sanity left.

"Did you get some good stories?" she asked Mason, sitting down at the other side of the small table.

"Yes, thank you. But I'd still like to hear about his stand against the German raiding party for which they've put him up for the V.C. You were there, weren't you?"

She looked at him wryly.

"You know I was. Would you like me to tell you now? I'm not back on duty for an hour." She pushed a strand of hair off her brow. "I can do it."

"What about a chance to sleep?"

"Are you telling me I look tired?"

He studied her face. He was surprised at the strength in her, and the defensive challenge in her eyes in that question. How different she was from the girl who had worn the blue satin gown at the Savoy with such infinite femininity. She must know that, too, with a different kind of regret from his.

"Actually you look beautiful." He said it deliberately, and yet it was totally sincere. "But reason says that, like everybody else, you must need to sleep."

There was a moment's confusion in her eyes, uncertainty whether to believe him or not. Then she flushed very slightly and he knew in that instant how much it mattered to her. It was a belief that if there were ever peace again she could still be the woman she was inside, before the war.

"I'll sleep next break," she answered. "You might have gone by then, and you need to get the story." Without waiting for him to reply, she told him in vivid and dramatic detail exactly what the raid had been like and how Cavan's remarkable courage had saved all their lives. He could simply take it down and rewrite it using her words, there was such a force of life in them. Never once did she hesitate or repeat herself.

As he wrote it, he began to understand at last what it was she was doing. She was re-creating in the readers' minds the situation that had brought about Major Northrup's death, and showing Cavan as a man who had had no moral choice but to act as he had. She was paralleling his courage and decision in the trenches with his decision to frighten Northrup into acting with some sense.

Did she really believe that all they had meant to do was frighten him? Or did she not care?

When she had finished, he asked the question that had waited at the back of his mind since the beginning. "Can you arrange for me to see Cavan himself, even if only for a few moments? I have to have a quote from him." He watched her, wondering what she would do.

"You can't." She looked back quizzically, trying to judge whether he was testing her, or if he really did not know.

"Can't I?" he said aloud.

"No one can," she replied, her eyes unwavering. "General Northrup found the twelve men with the best cause to kill his son, and had them all arrested, including Captain Cavan. No one confessed, and no one denied it. We don't know whether they're guilty or not. General Northrup said he would try and get the charge reduced from mutiny and murder down to insolence, disobeying an order, and accident. But it hasn't happened yet. It's bloody chaos. He was our best surgeon, and men are dying he could have saved." The misery in her voice was savage. He flinched at the sound of it.

"Why would General Northrup try to get the charge reduced?" he asked, puzzled.

She looked at him with a twist of defiance, even pride. "Because in order to prove deliberate murder he'll have to show motive, of course! Why on earth would twelve loyal soldiers without a blemish on their records get together and murder an officer?"

"Because he's a dangerously arrogant and incompetent idiot!" he responded.

"Exactly. Which I can prove. But General Northrup is not so keen to have that demonstrated. When he realized just how—"

"Yes, I see," he said quickly. "Was it you who pointed out to him how unfortunate that would be?" He knew the answer. That was the source of the fire in her eyes, and why the men were toasting her in Dixie cans of tea. No doubt it was also why she was keen that Mason should write a piece just now extolling Cavan. Was it because she cared for Cavan with more than friendship, or simply that she was brave and driven by the same passionate loyalty to her friends that bound all the fighting men together? She had charged in blindly to the rescue, without thinking of the cost or the chances of success. That is who she was, like Joseph: all pointless idealism, and dreams that were fragile and idiotic, and desperately beautiful.

The lock of hair had fallen forward again across her brow. Without thinking, he reached across and pushed it into place, only afterward realizing how intimate the gesture was.

"I'm sorry," he apologized, feeling self-conscious.

She colored as well, suddenly aware of his physical nearness.

"You're still going to write about him!" she said urgently. "Nothing that Northrup says changes that. And Cavan might have had nothing to do with it. They've just arrested the most likely twelve."

Mason reflected that, in a different age, she would have been married to some nice local doctor or landowner by now, probably with a couple of children. Her days would have been spent in a little socially admirable work, probably connected with the church, and the occasional society party, or hunts ball. Instead she was watching the carnage of a generation. It was not happiness but a kind of sublime lunacy that kept her going. It was all pointless, and it would break her in the end, and that was something he dreaded. It would be like the very last lights going out as the darkness consumed everything.

He loved her for it with a kind of hunger he dared not face. It was precious beyond his reach and like the reflection of a distant fire, a warmth he could not touch or hold. It was an illusion, what she believed in was not real, and yet the beauty of it haunted him too fiercely to let it go.

"I'll write the best I can," he promised. "But it won't change anything, Judith. I wish I could say it would. I expect it's out of Northrup's hands by now."

Her mouth tightened; she bit her lower lip. "Are you warning me to give up?" she said a little huskily.

"Never," he whispered. "Just be prepared to be beaten, at least this time." He put his hand over hers where it lay on the tabletop. Her hands were very slender, stiff now in resistance. "Cavan won't escape, unless he can prove he wasn't part of it."

"And leave the others?" she said indignantly. "He'd never do that."

Of course not. Cavan was just like her! Quixotic . . . absurd.

"Oh, Judith! Can't you . . ." He stopped. He would be asking her to deny her very nature. "No, of course you can't." He rose to his feet and leaned across the table, kissing her softly on the mouth. For a long moment of infinite warmth, as if a new fire melted every aching shard of ice inside him, he clung on to her. Then slowly he pulled away, leaving her behind, but never the memory. He turned and walked out into the incessant, clinging, suffocating rain.

Judith was right, of course; he had no opportunity to speak to Captain Cavan, or any of the other imprisoned men. He did not tip his hand to the authorities by asking for it when he knew it was an impossibility. Instead he went forward to the front line and gathered all the factual information he could. He saw how they were struggling to manage without Cavan, as Judith had told him—and for that matter, without Morel, who had been a good officer.

He asked men about Morel, and gained perhaps a slightly biased picture. But even accounting for that, he emerged as a brave and widely experienced man, which was unusual in these times of sweeping casualties. A front-line officer with three years' service was rare. He was joked about because it was the easiest way of defusing the emotion, although the men knew he was burning with anger and emotionally unreliable. However, neither his courage nor his judgment of a military situation were ever doubted. They felt his loss keenly.

Still Mason could not stand by and simply make notes of it all, like some recording demon—angels were beyond the power of his imagination. Useless or not, he went out with the stretcher parties as he had done in Gallipoli, or the Italian Front facing Austria where men also died in the tens of thousands, and on the bitter Russian Front in the east, and the sands of Egypt and Mesopotamia. The weather was different, and the terrain; death was the same.

He saw Joseph on the third day. They had both returned from no-man's-land, up to the armpits in mud from digging men out of the craters and attempting to carry them back. Off balance with the weight of the unconscious wounded, they had floundered and fallen. They had helped each other up again awkwardly, picked up their burdens again and finally reached the front-line trench. It was filled with water like a stagnant canal, with broken pieces of duckboard, and corpses of rats and men.

Still helping each other, they made it at last to a drier stretch and passed the wounded over to an ambulance crew. Then they sat shivering with exhaustion in one of the dressing station tents. Someone put blankets around them and passed the Dixie cans of hot tea laced with rum.

Joseph looked at Mason and smiled.

"Still think all this is a good idea, Chaplain?" Mason asked, waving his hand to indicate everything around them.

Joseph could see in Mason's face a darkness that would not now be won over by any word or act as it had been in the small boat back in 1915. "I think it's hell," he answered the question.

Mason looked at him curiously, an urgency behind his probing.

"I was talking to Judith," he began; his eyes flickered away, self-consciously, then back again. "She still believes there's some point to all this, some moral purpose that makes it worthwhile. Do you?"

Joseph hesitated a moment, not only as to the truth of any answer, but even to how honest he should be to Mason. "There can't be a heaven if there's no hell. But I admit, I hadn't envisioned having to spend so much time in hell."

Mason's mouth twisted a little but his eyes remained steady. "I wasn't looking for a metaphysical answer, Reavley—something a little more from the heart and the belly. Not what you want to believe, or what you think you ought to believe! What is there inside you, really?"

"When? Now? Just bewilderment and exhaustion," Joseph replied. "Tomorrow morning, or next time I see someone I love, or an act of total unselfishness, or courage more than I could manage myself? Then yes, I believe there's something wiser and better than I am, and infinitely greater. Do I know where I'm going? No. Do you?"

"I'm not sure if anywhere I wish to go exists," Mason replied.

"Then build it," Joseph replied. "If you survive, of course," he added with a smile.

"Is that what you tell your men when they're dying?" Mason would not give up.

"If it's what's needed. Usually it isn't. Just being there, talking about anything, so they're not alone."

"Saying what they need to hear." Mason turned the words over, still looking at Joseph steadily. "Because you've nothing else to say? Charging the guns, obediently, like the Light Brigade at Balaclava, because you don't know what else to do? Following orders, Chaplain? Aren't you supposed to be leading?"

Joseph saw the rage and pain in him, the knowledge of darkness closing in, not just at Passchendaele, but everywhere.

"I think the most I can do is keep going," Joseph told him.

Mason was silent for a long time. "Thank you at least for honesty," he said at last. "I don't know how you can survive on that—it isn't enough."

"As long as there's somebody you can touch in the darkness, it has to be enough," Joseph told him.

Mason did not answer. Slowly he drank the rest of his tea.

Joseph finished his also. He meant what he had said. The fact that he too needed more, just a glimmer of hope that one day there would be an answer he could understand, was none of Mason's business.

* * *

"Yes?" the Peacemaker said urgently as Mason sat in the chair opposite him in the upstairs room in Marchmont Street. "I know all about the losses. It's the epitome of all we sought so desperately to prevent. I would have given everything I've ever had, my own life if it would have helped, to prevent this. Even you don't have words to describe the horror or the futility of it. What about this trial for mutiny and murder? They have twelve men arrested, you say?"

"Yes." Mason looked up. He was haggard. His heavy black hair made his skin look even more pallid, almost bloodless, and there was a consuming grief in his eyes as if no passion would ever burn them alive again. The Peacemaker was concerned for him. Could a war correspondent suffer battle fatigue?

"The twelve men with the best motives, apparently, for wanting Major Northrup dead," Mason answered. "Or—I should say more accurately—removed from command. And since those above him either didn't know how incompetent he was, or didn't care, death seems to have been the only way. I imagine, since he was a general's son, it was beyond the power of Colonel Hook to remove him. The thing is, Captain Cavan, the surgeon up for the V.C., is one of them."

"Perfect." The Peacemaker breathed the word like a sigh. "It is so absolutely farcical we couldn't have created anything more likely to make even the sanest and most blindly loyal of men rebel against this suicidal injustice." He felt he was on the brink of something that could be used to turn the tide at last.

"There's word that General Northrup will try to get the charge lessened to one of insubordination, and that Northrup's death was more of an accident than intentional murder," Mason warned.

"Really!" The Peacemaker felt a sudden chill. "Why?"

Mason sighed. "Because to prove intent they must prove motive. Doing that will automatically expose Major Northrup's disastrous incompetence. His father does not want that. And believe me, the men are all loyal to the mutineers. If the charge is kept at murder, they'll make damned certain Major Northrup is exposed."

"And does the general know this?" The Peacemaker was fascinated. It opened up possibilities of further mutiny he had hardly dared hope for.

"Yes, of course he does," Mason replied.

"This is very good," the Peacemaker said decisively. "I shall make certain that the prosecutor appointed is a hard-liner. I have just the man in mind. He will make certain the full charge is retained, and prosecuted to the full. We need have no doubt of a capital sentence. Captain Cavan, V.C., will be put before the firing squad. It will be the spark that finally sets the tinder afire."

He smiled slightly, an unexpected regret tugging at him. "The British troops will never stand for an injustice of such obscenity. And I think the country may even be behind them, if we handle it the right way. There comes a point when people will no longer be herded to slaughter like sheep. Believe me, Mason, the Russians are very close to that point now. If the tsar does not make peace with Germany, withdraw her troops from the battle front altogether, and institute radical social reform, the Russian people will rise up in a way we have not seen since the High Terror in Paris in 1793 when the gutters ran red with blood."

"The tsar won't change—not that much!" Mason looked stunned, almost buried by the enormity of the idea.

"I doubt it," the Peacemaker agreed. "I think by next month, or the month after, we will see riot in the streets of St. Petersburg, and blood." He felt the exultation surge up inside him, catching his breath and his throat. "We are at the beginning of the end, Mason! There will be peace by Christmas! Peace! Dear God, peace!"

EIGHT

"Sir?" Joseph stood in Colonel Hook's dugout, assuming from the message that had summoned him that the news was dire.

Hook looked up from the paper he had been reading. His skin was gray and an uneven stubble shadowed his jaw.

"Ah, Reavley. I've just been informed that London is sending a prosecutor for the court-martial. I was hoping we could have someone from one of the regiments near here. At least they'd understand the . . . the pressures. But they're sending a man called Faulkner. I've heard of him." He looked up at Joseph, frowning. "He has something of a reputation, very rigid, believes in the ultimate deterrent. I don't think the bastard's ever seen action." He rubbed his hand over his head. "Sorry. I shouldn't speak of him like that. I suppose he might be able to . . ." His voice tailed off. He sounded utterly without hope.

Joseph sat down without being asked. He cleared his throat. "What are the chances of General Northrup getting the charges reduced?"

Hook was surprised. "From Faulkner? None at all. He'll make an example of Cavan and Morel. Reavley, I'm afraid of what the men will do when they hear. We've got just over three days; then it'll too late."

Joseph did not need to ask him what he meant. Once the twelve men were charged with mutiny and murder—unless they were found not guilty, which was virtually impossible—there could be no other sentence but death. The chances were high that there really could be mutiny. With the resultant loss of morale, the lines would be smashed and the forces that survived would be driven back behind the last defenses. The Germans would simply carry on straight through to Paris, and France would fall.

After that there was nothing between the German Army and the beaches of England except twenty miles of flat summer sea. Defeat would be only weeks away.

Joseph looked up at Hook and saw understanding of exactly the same thing in his eyes.

"Is it worth telling Faulkner what it would be likely to do to the men?" he asked.

"It would if he believed it," Hook replied. "Men like that usually have an excellent escape from situations they don't want to be responsible for: They simply refuse to believe it. He would say the British Army never mutinies and never surrenders. It is only the occasional soldier who does, and that sort of man has to be weeded out . . . severely. He would consider this an excellent opportunity to make an example."

"It won't make an example of anything except ignorance and brutality," Joseph said, hearing his own voice crack with emotion and something close to despair. "No matter how good men are, or how brave, there's a point beyond which they break. There's no point afterward in excusing yourself by saying you were too damned stupid to see it!"

"I know." Hook looked down at the paper again. "I'll try appealing to London, but I don't know what good it'll do."

It was dismissal. Joseph stood, excused himself from the claustrophobic safety of the mud and earth, and the few familiar objects of Hook's personal life, and went out into the faint, misty sunlight. He felt acutely guilty. At some point there must have been a time when he could have acted differently, hidden something, even lied outright so it would never have reached this stage.

He walked slowly along the track, his boots squelching in the thick mud. At this slightly higher level it was shallower, the water puddling rather than running along. Out in the craters of no-man's-land either it would be steaming a little in the August heat, or there would be low-lying mustard gas again. It wasn't always easy to tell.

If Mason had not seen Northrup's body and known he had been

shot by a British gun, there would have been no need for anyone to be aware that it wasn't just another casualty. God knew there were enough of them!

He stepped and banged into a piece of broken riveting where the earth wall had collapsed.

It was Mason again. This was playing straight into the Peacemaker's hands. Was he behind it? Or was Joseph just indulging his delusions? The last letter from Matthew had said he was chasing down the old enemy at last. There was no other way to interpret that. Now it looked as if thanks to a catalogue of stupid mistakes, the Peacemaker was going to win after all. Britain would be in mutiny and defeat, with the best part of a million men dead, countless more wounded in body and crushed in mind and spirit. It was a defeat he could not even have imagined when they first left for France three years ago, thinking they would be home for Christmas. It had been all heroism and honor then, dreams of glory. Now there was only despair.

It would have been better to have turned a blind eye to Northrup's murder, better even to have shot the man himself, than have it come to this. What was the point at which he had made the wrong judgment? Perhaps that was the secret of life, knowing when was the precise moment at which you decide to do something irrevocable, rather than being a coward, a man always thinking, poised on the edge of decision, and never making it.

Joseph went to bed in his own dugout a little after midnight and slept more deeply than he had expected. However, just before dawn he woke with a jolt, his heart pounding, the sweat pouring off his body. Everything was familiar—the books, the picture of Dante, his chair and desk—but there was rifle fire close at hand and men's voices, high-pitched, shouting.

He rolled off the bunk and stood up, his body shaking. There were more shouts, and bursts of fire rather than controlled aiming.

There was a noise immediately outside on the steps, then the sacking curtain was yanked aside and a figure blocked out the shred of light.

Joseph half expected to see the spike-crested helmet of a German officer. He made a supreme effort to calm himself and look, and realized it was a British Tommy, but bareheaded.

"Capt'n Reavley! You there, sir?"

"Yes, I am." Joseph swallowed. "What is it, Tiddly Wop?"

"They're gone, Captain. All of 'em, 'cepting Captain Cavan. Gawd knows how it happened, but they're gone!" Andrews replied.

Joseph struggled to grasp what the words meant. It could not possibly be true. "Gone?" he repeated foolishly. "You mean they've been taken somewhere else? They're going to have the court-martial at another regiment?"

"Oi don't mean been took, sir. Oi mean gone themselves! Nobody knows where they are. They escaped. Could 'ave gone anywhere."

Now Joseph was cold, as if his hands and feet hardly belonged to him. "They couldn't have got out of the farmhouse. What happened to the guard? How could they get out?"

"Guards are all tied up like turkeys for dinner, but not a hair of their head broke."

"You said Captain Cavan is still there?" Joseph was bitterly disappointed. For a moment he had believed the impossible, and now reality plunged him back even deeper. "That doesn't make sense, Tiddly Wop."

"Since when did anything in this bleeding war make sense, Chaplain? If it does to you then, whoi in't you telling anyone else?"

"The other eleven have gone? How did they get out?"

"No idea," Tiddly Wop said with a shadow of anger. "An' if Oi did, Oi wouldn't be telling. Oi just thought you'd loike to know."

"I do! I . . . I just wish Captain Cavan had gone, too."

A faint glimmer of light caught Tiddly Wop's teeth gleaming as he grinned. "Sorry. Oi shouldn't have said that, Chaplain. Course you do."

There was more shouting outside but the rifle fire had stopped. Tiddly Wop turned around and made his way out, Joseph on his heels. It was relatively quiet, the heavy guns only sporadic. Joseph stared around at the figures sprinting across the open ground, and others standing almost idly. There was a military car parked on the driest piece of ground. A man in officer's uniform stood beside it, waving his arms, apparently giving directions to the others.

"Got to look loike we want to find them," Tiddly Wop said sententiously.

"How long ago did they go?" Joseph asked.

Tiddly Wop shrugged. "How do Oi know? They could be on their way to Paris by now. Only more likely they'll go to Switzerland. Oi would."

"The Swiss border's hundreds of miles away," Joseph retorted.

"Then Oi hope they get a lift. Not that they would, of course!" he added hastily, taking a nervous glance at Joseph.

"They might have gone the other way altogether." Joseph entered the conspiracy without hesitation. "Maybe making for the sea."

"Back to Blighty?"

"No, more likely Sweden." Joseph found himself smiling. He knew it was stupid to be amused. They would be found and brought back. Cavan was probably showing more sense in staying. And it might buy more time. It could take several days to catch them all, if they ever did. Some might get killed, in the ordinary course of the war. "I wonder if we can help," he added aloud.

"Roight!" Tiddly Wop agreed. "Oi'll go an' see if Lieutenant Moore wants a hand. He don't know north from south, that one. If someone don't give him a hand he'll end up in Switzerland himself!"

Joseph offered to look for the escapees, and he spent the next hour pretending to search. Like the rest of the men, he generally made sure that all signs of which way they might have gone were thoroughly obliterated.

He shared a Dixie can of tea with Colonel Hook, sitting in the back of the supply trench on a couple of sandbags.

"Find any trace?" Hook asked, eyebrows raised.

"None at all," Joseph said immediately. He met Hook's eyes with complete candor.

"No," Hook replied. "Didn't think you would."

By midday it was a very different matter. General Northrup had returned, and word had come up the line that Lieutenant Colonel Faulkner would arrive before sunset. Northrup was furious.

"How can you be so totally incompetent?" he shouted at Hook. His face was pinched and two blotches of color stained his cheeks. "Don't you mount some kind of guard? For God's sake, your command is falling to pieces around you! Pull yourself together, man!"

They were in the small command post. It was little more than a room in a farm outbuilding, furnished with a table and half a dozen chairs. Northrup was pacing the floor, his boots scratching on the wooden boards. He swung his arms and jabbed the air.

The accusation was grossly unjust, and both tragic and absurd. Joseph intervened, although both of them outranked him.

"The men are exhausted, sir," he said to Northrup. "No one is getting more than a few hours' sleep any night. The wounded are pouring back from the battlefront and we are finding it more than we can do to get them to hospital, keep any sort of supplies coming forward of either food or ammunition. The only men we've got to spare for guarding prisoners are those who are wounded already. We don't know what happened, and blaming them is premature and deeply unfair. In any other circumstances they'd be invalided out and taken care of in a decent hospital."

"I know the conditions are hard, Captain Reavley," Northrup said with a tight little grimace. "This is not the only part of the line battered almost to breaking—although I grant you it is the worst. But it's all the more important we keep up our standards, for the sake of morale."

"If somebody is found to be culpable, it will be attended to." Hook broke his long silence, rising to his feet and picking up a pile of dispatches. "Now, sir, if you will excuse me, I must go and see to some of these things."

As soon as he had left, Northrup stared at Joseph. "This is a preposterous situation, Captain. I realize that your sympathies are with your men, and perhaps that is how you see your calling, but this cannot be ignored as if it were not a capital offense." He stared at Joseph accusingly. "You must realize that? Now, of all times, we must stand fast to those principles we believe in, when there is the greatest temptation to give in, or to cut and run. Officers must set an example. It is what we are here for."

Joseph drew in breath to argue, to tell him forcefully how absurd and cruel and utterly pointless he was, that he had lost all touch with reality.

Any day now they would lose the battle of Passchendaele, and the whole Western Front could buckle and break apart. The last thing on earth the army needed was an idiotic prosecution of one of its few heroes still alive.

Then suddenly he saw General Northrup as an old man, perhaps in years not more than fifty, but worn out in heart and mind, trying to keep up a belief in his son that he knew was false. He might deceive others, or they might concede to his view out of fear or respect—or more than that, pity—but in the end he would be left alone with the truth. He faced forward and he spoke of duty because it was the only road he had left in a world that was slipping away from him and taking with it all that he had believed in.

"Yes, sir," Joseph said gently. "I think all the men are trying to do what they think is right. When you are facing death it becomes terribly important. There isn't going to be time to try again."

Northrup stared at him, blinking rapidly several times. "What are you saying, Captain Reavley? That there is some kind of justice other than a court-martial?"

"I am saying that the men are afraid that finding Captain Cavan and the other men guilty of murder, and having them shot, will damage morale more seriously than we can survive, sir, and may even give the Germans the chance to break through and run for Paris. We have fought too long and too hard, and lost too many of our friends, for that."

"Take an easy way," Northrup retorted, his eyes never leaving Joseph's. "A wrong way, because we cannot face the enemy and stand for what we believe, for justice, and the rule of law, and each man to account for his own sins? Is that what you are saying?"

"No way is easy, sir," Joseph answered him. "And who judges what is a sin, and who is responsible for it? It is seldom only one of us at fault over anything."

Northrup shifted his weight slightly, his eyes hard and troubled. He seemed about to challenge what Joseph had said as soon as he found the words for it.

"War strips a man naked of all the ideas his brain was taught, but didn't really believe," Joseph went on. He was compelled to argue, just in case there was still a chance Northrup could plead for Cavan, and the other men if they were caught. It might be hopeless, but he could not stop trying. "These men, ultimately, were loyal to each other, and to the will to win rather than to blind obedience."

Northrup's lips were pressed tight. His eyes reflected his racing mind, and emotion filled his face, the confusion and pressure of anger and doubt inside him. Still he could not find the words.

"Legally, Major Northrup was in the right," Joseph began again. "He was the senior officer, and that gave him the power to command, whether his orders were brilliant or suicidal. But it did not make him militarily right. The men who obeyed were legally correct, and then obedience caused some of them to be killed or mutilated. Those who disobeyed are alive, but it looks as if we ourselves will kill them. And in doing so we will destroy the trust and the morale of those who look to us to lead, because they have no other choice."

Northrup was shivering very slightly; it was just a tic in his right temple, a tremor in his hands.

"With being an officer comes the duty to be right," Joseph added, knowing what he was doing to the man in front of him. "To put your men's lives before your own vanity. In peacetime you can order obedience, regardless of your own qualities, but in war you have to earn respect. Moral courage is required as well as physical—the more so of officers."

Northrup lowered his eyes. "You have no need to labor the point, Captain. I have been obliged to accept that my son's qualities fell short of the command he held, and that the army offered his men no recourse but to obey or rebel." He stood almost motionless. "And I am accountable to God for whatever part of his character made him refuse to be guided by junior men who knew better from experience. If he was weak, that was my failure—perhaps more than it was his. Perhaps I allowed him to believe that being in command is a matter of rank, not of knowing your job, or that honor is what other men say of you, not what is true even when you stand alone. If that is so, then I will answer to God, and to my son, but I will not answer to you, sir." He blinked rapidly, his face flushed and his eyes bright with tears.

Joseph ached, almost physically, to find anything to say that could comfort him. The only way to ease the pain would be to deny the truth of his part in the private tragedy of a son who had proved unequal to the final test.

"In the end it is only God's judgment that matters for any of us," Joseph said. "And it looks as if the end could be rather soon."

Northrup drew in his breath sharply as if to deny it, then let it out in a sigh and said nothing. He seemed drained of everything inside himself, as if only a shell were left which kept up the façade as an act of will. If he had been wrong and, without realizing it at the time, destroyed the son he had loved, in his own way, then at least he would not now lose the only virtue of which he was certain: courage.

"I am sure you have duties, Captain. Thank you for your time."

Joseph accepted the dismissal, saluted, and turned to leave.

Lieutenant Colonel Faulkner arrived before sunset, as he had said he would. Joseph did not see him, but he heard the comments of the men.

"Looks loike one o' them guard dogs who can't find his dinner," Alf Culshaw said sourly. "Reckon we're it!"

Barshey Gee shook his head and winced. He had a heavy bandage on his right arm, but the wound was not serious enough to send him off the front line. "Why is it they send the decent blokes up here with the guns to shoot at Jerry, poor sod, and keep the real bastards back o' the lines to shoot at us? Who thought that up, d'you suppose?"

"Some bloke as thought up hard rations an' Sunday drills and..." Snowy offered.

"An' his Ma must've knitted moi socks!" George Atherton added with his characteristic jerky laugh. "Got more lumps in 'em than Lofty's porridge."

"That's what Oi'd loike," Barshey said longingly, his eyes dreamy. "A noice hot bowl o' porridge, with sugar an' the top o' the milk on it."

George threw a dollop of mud at him.

Bert Collins arrived to tell Joseph that Colonel Hook wanted to see him. He pulled his face into an expression of disgust. "An' the new man, sir, Lieutenant Colonel Faulkner. You'll know which one he is, sir, 'cos he looked like he just ate a wasp, 'cept it's too wet for wasps. If it don't stop soddin' rainin' soon we'll all drown. What I want to know, Chaplain, is why aren't you buildin' an ark, eh?"

"No wood," Joseph said with a tight smile. "And no animals to put in it."

"An' no women," Barshey added. "Koind of more loike no point!"

Several of them laughed.

Joseph followed Bert Collins back to the command post, and went into the small room with its bare floor and sparse furniture. It smelled of damp, like everything else. He stood to attention and waited.

Hook was freshly shaved, a nick on his cheek still oozing a little blood. His uniform was comparatively clean, no more than a couple of bloodstains on the arms and mud splattered up to the thigh. He had probably worn it no more than a day.

Beside him was Faulkner. He had very short, fair hair and a thin, powerful face that seemed all brow and bone. And yet it was not a face without imagination or a degree of emotion. His uniform was immaculate, tailored to fit his square shoulders and lean body.

"Captain Reavley," Hook began, his voice formal, a warning in his eyes. "This is Lieutenant Colonel Faulkner, who is going to be prosecuting the case against the men accused of shooting Major Northrup."

"Yes, sir," Joseph acknowledged.

"As you are aware, we presently have in custody only one of those men."

Faulkner made a noise in the back of his throat. It was wordless, but his disgust was as plain as if he had spoken.

"Unless we can find those who have escaped within the next two days, we are going to have to delay the court-martial—" Hook began.

"We can try Captain Cavan," Faulkner interrupted. "And we can try the others in absentia for desertion. There can be no question as to their guilt of that."

"No, we will not try Captain Cavan separately," Hook said curtly. "And we will not try the other men for anything in their absence. Every man has the right to face his accusers and defend himself. . . ."

"They chose not to do that," Faulkner pointed out. "They gave it up; it was not denied them."

"Nevertheless, we will not try them in their absence," Hook repeated. "You are appointed prosecutor, not judge. Captain Reavley will do all that he can to trace the men's whereabouts, and—"

"For God's sake, man!" Faulkner snapped. "They've deserted! They are probably halfway to Switzerland by now."

"They may be," Hook agreed. "Or not. All we know is that they are not here, except Cavan." He looked at Joseph.

"Yes, sir," Joseph said quickly. "I will do all I can to determine exactly what happened, and if possible find the men and return them. Apart from anything else"—he studiously avoided Faulkner's eye—"it will be extremely difficult to try Captain Cavan if none of the other men are here who could testify in the matter. There will be no one to give evidence or be questioned. I believe he has not confessed to anything . . . has he?"

"No," Hook said instantly. "Quite right, Captain Reavley. Begin immediately. If there is any help you require, I'll see that you are given it."

"Report back in twenty-four hours, Captain," Faulkner said stiffly. "Although I can't imagine what you think you will find. They have deserted, apart from Cavan. And he may well also be guilty of conniving at and concealing the escape of the others. Certainly he has refused to tell us anything."

"Or he may be innocent," Joseph said sharply, a raw edge of anger to his voice. "And feel that he will get a fair hearing, and be able to prove it."

"You are excused, Captain," Faulkner told him. "The sooner you begin your inquiries, the sooner we may proceed."

Joseph saluted, then turned on his heel and left. He had no intention whatever of finding out where the men had gone, even if there had been the remotest chance of succeeding. Privately he thought Faulkner was right and they would almost certainly have made for the Swiss border. However, he was afraid that the regiment in general might suffer, especially anyone who had either positively assisted them, or negatively turned a blind eye. And profoundly he did not wish Cavan to be tried at all, but if it was inevitable, then it should be on a lesser charge, simply of having been aware that some of the men were unhappy with Major Northrup and not reporting it. The general might still succeed in getting the charge reduced.

He was also sure that Hook felt as he did, and had asked him to make the inquiries precisely because he knew he would appear to be busy, but actually do nothing at all.

Some of the men were suspicious at first, resentful that he should appear to be cooperating with Faulkner, but a couple of sharp words from people like Barshey Gee and Bill Harrison and goodwill was restored. Some even joined in a little play-acting, as if determined to help.

But of course it deceived no one. Joseph reported to Faulkner twenty-four hours later.

"I'm sorry, sir," he said, investing his voice with as much apology as he could. "None of the men appear to know anything useful. I daresay those accused were very careful to keep it all secret."

Faulkner listened to him with open disbelief, but he could prove nothing.

At noon the day after that, on Faulkner's orders, Joseph was arrested for failure to obey a direct order of a superior, and locked up in the same farmhouse from which the eleven men had escaped.

This time there were regular military police on guard, not wounded men, and in order to preserve their own liberty, they were determined that there should be no further breakouts.

They were embarrassed to lock up a chaplain and apologized awkwardly. They treated him with the greatest respect. He did not want to assault their consciences by obliging them to be other than courteous.

By two o'clock he was sitting on the floor in what had once been one of the smaller bedrooms of a farmhouse. The only window gave onto the roof, but from there it was a sheer drop to the ground, where a soldier stood on duty, his rifle at the ready. Not that Joseph had considered escaping. It would only make a desperate situation even worse.

There was nothing to do. Time crept by. Joseph stood up and paced back and forward again. Where were the men? Had they gone east, making for Switzerland? Perhaps they believed the Germans would break the line and the war was lost anyway. It was painful to accept that Morel would desert now. Joseph would have imagined him doing something more dramatic, more imaginative, truer to his roots and his nature than flight. Possibly he would have gone over the top in a grand gesture, giving his life in a way none of his fellows would ever forget.

This escape was tragic, tired and grubby, and the pain of it cut deep.

Food was brought to him at about six o'clock. It was hard rations, much the same as if he were still free. The young soldier looked embarrassed as he put it on the floor just inside, then backed away.

"I'm not going to hurt you," Joseph said wearily. "You don't need to look like that."

"No, sir, but I got to be careful. Can't afford to have anyone else go, or I'll be the one shot."

"Why? Was it your fault?"

"No!" He looked indignant.

"How did they get out?"

The soldier shook his head. "You won't be able to copy 'em, sir. Please don't try. I really don't want to shoot you. We're on the same side, sir. We all are."

Joseph looked up quickly.

"Who else is in here?"

"Just you an' Treffy Johnson, an' the doc, of course."

"Treffy? What is he here for?" Joseph was startled.

"Insubordination. Nothing much. Probably let him out tomorrow."

"And send him back up to the line?"

"Yes, of course. Poor little sod."

Joseph waited.

The soldier pulled his mouth down in a grimace. "He's only fifteen. Scared stiff, and can't hardly bring himself to shoot another man, Jerry or not."

A dozen ideas flashed through Joseph's mind: to keep Treffy Johnson in here on some other charge, to find a medical reason why he should be invalided out, even as a last resort to put him beside someone who would care for and protect him. They were all pointless. He was one of thousands. He might survive. Even if he did, he would never be the boy he was before. No one would.

"Eat it." The soldier indicated the tray of food on the floor. "It's rotten, but it's probably better than you'd get up the line. And at least it isn't raining in here." He went out and closed the door. The moment after, the lock turned and the tumblers fell home.

Joseph walked back to the window out of curiosity. How had the eleven men gotten out, then tied up the guards, and left? The more he thought of it the more obstacles there seemed to be.

He stared over the roof. A man with a good head for heights could probably manage it quite easily and reach a place where there was a down pipe. Except that the whole place was in such disrepair after three years of neglect, and the occasional bombardment extremely close by, that he could not see any down pipes left fully attached. The weight of a man, let alone eleven one after the other, would rip them off altogether. The yard below was paved. Anyone landing on it would be likely to break an ankle at the very least.

He tried to remember the other walls as he had seen them when he came in. There had been nothing to give a firm enough hold to climb down: no outhouses attached, no woodshed or apple house or milking shed. Nothing of half the height to form a safer landing. Certainly there were no trees left within half a mile. And that meant there was also no cover to hide anyone fleeing. But then they had gone at night. Still, the distant artillery lit the sky and would have made any figure on the barren landscape as obvious as a fly on a whitewashed wall.

There had been twelve men imprisoned here, and Treffy Johnson. How had they been separated? There were not thirteen rooms in the house, so at least some had been together. There were no blankets in his room, only a straw palliasse. But then one had no blankets in trenches. And it was August. Could they have used their own clothes to make a rope to descend from the window? All of them? At the same time? Were they even in communication with one another?

The light faded outside and it began to rain again. He could hear it on the window.

He sat on the palliasse in the dark. The more he considered and weighed what he knew, the more it seemed impossible that the men had all gotten out at the same time and tied up the guards. Without help, how had they escaped over the barren land and gone sufficient distance that, by the time their absence was known, they were untraceable? The escape must have been carefully planned—and it must have been effected with a vehicle large enough to take all eleven men.

Such as an ambulance! That was the thought Joseph wanted to push out of his mind altogether, but the harder he tried the more firmly it became fixed.

He lay down at last. He was cold in spite of the warmth of the air. It was probably because he was tired and miserable, and—no matter how hard he tried to quell the thought—afraid for Judith.

If the court-martial of Cavan went ahead, and they found him guilty, there would be only one sentence: the firing squad. It would be referred right up to Field Marshal Haig.

Joseph realized that in the morning he must find a way of persuading the guard to let him see Cavan. Cavan was a doctor and Joseph was a priest! There must be some argument for one of them needing the other!

When his breakfast came, the tea was at least hot. He was grateful for that.

He disliked lying to the guard, but he could think of no better alternative. He sat hunched forward, looking wretched, trying to make one shoulder lower than the other.

"Something wrong, Chaplain?" the soldier asked.

"Think I've pulled a muscle," he replied. "Thought it would be all right yesterday, but it kept me awake all night." He gave a bleak smile. "First time I've had the chance to lie down for more than a couple of hours. Could you let me see Cavan? Lock us in. Room with no window. I don't care. He might be able to put it right for me."

The guard hesitated.

"I'm not dangerous," Joseph went on. "For heaven's sake, he and I aren't going to attack anyone. And the fact that Cavan's still here should prove he's not trying to escape. I'm not charged with anything except not looking hard enough for the men who did escape."

"Yeah, all right. The doc in't no harm." The guard shrugged. "I reckon as the whole damn thing's a farce anyway! Lock up the doc an' the priest, and let the lunatics run the army! Come on. Can you stand up? I'll take you to him. Want to finish your tea first?"

"Please." Joseph remembered to drink using his left hand, and put the mug down so he could still use his left hand to eat the bread. "Thank you," he said when he was finished. He stood up awkwardly, careful again not to use his right arm at all.

Cavan was sitting on the floor when the soldier opened his door and pushed Joseph in ahead of him.

Cavan looked up in surprise, and—when he recognized Joseph— rose to his feet. He noticed Joseph holding his right arm awkwardly.

"Hurt your shoulder, Chaplain?" he said curiously, his eyes flicking to the guard and then back to Joseph.

"Yes. I was wondering if you could ease it back or something?" Joseph replied.

"No doctors on the outside?" Cavan said with a wry smile that barely reached his eyes. He looked tired and strained, deep lines scored into his face and a hollowness around his eyes. He must know that death was no longer a probability for him, but a certainty.

Joseph felt a sudden, blinding rage at the injustice of it. "I expect they're good enough," he replied, his voice trembling and sounding more strained than he had intended. "But since I'm in here and can't get out, I hoped you would help."

Cavan was nonplussed. "In here? You? For God's sake, what for?"

"I was ordered to look for the escaped men," Joseph replied. "Lieutenant Colonel Faulkner believed I was being dilatory in my duty, or even possibly intentionally obstructive."

"That's absurd!" Cavan said, shaking his head.

"Actually it's perfectly fair," Joseph told him. "If I'd fallen over them I wouldn't have told him. Not that I did! I imagine they are miles away from here. I hope so."

The guard cleared his throat. "I'll leave the chaplain 'ere with you, Captain Cavan, if I may, sir? See if you can fix 'is shoulder for 'im." He went out and closed the door. Again the heavy sound of the lock reminded them he had no intention of being held to blame for their escape.

Joseph straightened his shoulder. It was becoming painful holding it at a unnatural angle.

Cavan noticed.

"Thank you for healing it so quickly," Joseph said with a tight smile. He walked over and sat down on the floor a few feet away from where Cavan had been sitting. "He may be back soon," he went on. "I hope not, but you can't rely on him. At least, I assume you can't?"

Cavan looked confused. He sat down also, but said nothing.

"I've been thinking about how to escape," Joseph went on conversationally. "The more I consider it, the less I can see any way at all, without pretty brave and well-thought-out help from at least one person outside. More likely two."

Cavan's face was expressionless, carefully so. "Your escaping seems pretty pointless. They haven't got a charge against you that will stick. Faulkner's done this in a fit of temper, that's all."

"Yes, I know that," Joseph agreed. "I'm hoping they might even release me later today. That's why I need to speak to you now."

Cavan's face darkened.

"If you think I'm going to try and buy some kind of leniency by telling you how the others escaped, or who helped them, then you're a far bigger fool than I thought you. And a bigger knave as well. What kind of a traitor to my friends do you think I am?"

"I think you are a man too exhausted to think clearly," Joseph answered. "And actually I didn't ask you who helped them. I would very much prefer not to know. Although I have an idea, and, if I am right, then it is the last person on earth I would betray."

Cavan blinked quickly, aware that he had given himself away. He tried to hide it by lowering his eyes. "If you don't want to know that, what do you want?" he asked softly. "I wouldn't tell you where the men were if I knew! And I don't."

"I want to know what happened at Northrup's mock trial," Joseph answered. "I was told that you didn't mean to kill him. General Northrup is reasonably inclined toward having the charge reduced to insubordination and accidental death."

"Rubbish!" Cavan lifted his head, his eyes wide. "His son is dead. Apart from wanting revenge, he's a military martinet. Discipline is his catechism."

"He's a proud man," Joseph said thoughtfully. "And limited. He has little imagination, but he is not essentially dishonest. And certainly he does not lack courage. He knows his only son was incompetent and a danger to his men, which is a very hard fact for a military father to face."

"Why would he face it?" Cavan asked.

"He has no choice," Joseph explained. "If this charge goes ahead as it is, then the prosecutor will need to prove a very powerful motive for twelve men to conspire to murder an officer."

"We had one," Cavan argued, a little impatiently. "He was getting men killed and maimed unnecessarily. He was grossly incompetent, and too proud or too stupid to be guided by the men who'd been out here for months, or even years, and knew how to avoid most of the losses."

"Exactly." Joseph nodded, watching Cavan to see if he understood. "Do you imagine that is something his father wishes proved beyond reasonable doubt in a court-martial?"

A flash of comprehension lit in Cavan's eyes. "Someone has pointed that out to him? Are you sure?"

"Absolutely positive."

Cavan bit his lip.

"I see. Why do you want to know? Do you really believe it will make any difference? I like optimism, but not unreality. Shouldn't you be helping me to face the truth, perhaps make my peace with God? Isn't that what you call it?"

"It's a little early for that," Joseph said drily. "Unless that's an oblique way of telling me that you personally shot Northrup, intentionally and avoidably?"

"I've no idea who shot Northrup!" Cavan said tartly. "Except that it had to be one of the twelve of us, and it wasn't me."

Joseph asked the question to which he dreaded the answer.

"Were you loaded with blanks, or did you deliberately shoot wide?"

Cavan stared at him. "I suppose you want the truth?"

"Yes."

"Where would we get blanks?" There was the faintest smile in Cavan's eyes. "The army supplies only live ammunition."

"You wouldn't get it from supplies," Joseph pointed out. "You'd use a pair of pliers to take the heads off live bullets, then crimp the casing closed again."

"Make our own blanks. Yes, I suppose we would."

"It would be a bit rash to leave anyone to simply to shoot wide," Joseph said, not taking his eyes from Cavan's. "It would be so easy for someone to make a mistake and shoot the man accidentally. You'd be lucky if you ever found out who it was—or unlucky."

"Yes, it would be rash," Cavan agreed. "Neither I nor Morel are rash. The two of us blanked the bullets ourselves."

"So someone changed theirs for a live one." It was the unavoidable answer: deliberate murder.

"Must have."

"But you have no idea who?"

"No. Honestly, I haven't. I don't believe it was Morel, but I don't know. I'm sure I didn't, and ten of the others didn't."

Joseph believed him. He had never thought him guilty of anything but wanting to frighten Northrup into taking advice in order to cut down on the useless deaths. And now, of course, of refusing to betray whoever had rescued the others.

"Why didn't you escape, when you could?" he asked curiously, shifting position a little on the hard floor.

"I couldn't," Cavan said with the very slightest shrug. "I'd given my word."

Joseph understood. An officer's word was binding. "And the others?"

"I didn't give my word not to help anyone else escape." Cavan smiled.

Joseph had to ask. "Morel?" He was an officer, too.

"Refused," Cavan answered. "They put him in with the men. Six in one room, five in the other. That left me alone in here."

"So you helped them, and stayed behind?"

"Yes." Cavan's face was suddenly filled with emotion, as if a crippling restraint on him had momentarily broken. "Speak for them, Captain Reavley. Northrup was a dangerous man, weak and arrogant. Even when he knew he was wrong, he wouldn't listen. The men were at the end of their endurance. Someone had to act." His voice was urgent, pleading. "It was only meant to frighten him into listening. They weren't bad men, just desperate to save their friends."

"I know," Joseph said softly. "I come from the same village. I've known a lot of those men all their lives. Morel was one of my students in Cambridge." He took a deep breath. "Judith is my sister."

Cavan closed his eyes for a moment. When he opened them, they were bright and sad, but he said nothing.

A moment later the guard opened the door again. When he saw that Joseph's shoulder was apparently mended, he took him back to his own room.

In the middle of the afternoon Joseph was released and escorted to Colonel Hook in his dugout.

"Sit down!" Hook said impatiently. He looked as if he had slept little since the last time they had been here. "Don't stand at attention like a fool! Faulkner's gone, at least for the moment."

Joseph obeyed, sitting on an old ammunition box. "Is he still insisting on court-martialing Captain Cavan alone?"

"I've managed to prevent that, at least for a week or two," Hook replied. "He thinks we can find out how they escaped."

Joseph's stomach clenched. Did he already suspect someone? "Really?" he said huskily. "How?"

Hook gave a little jerk upward with his hands. It was angry, a denial. "He doesn't know the men. No one is going to tell him anything. Did you see Cavan in the farmhouse?"

"Yes. I don't know whether he knows or not, but if he does, he certainly isn't going to say."

"I don't imagine you asked him, did you?"

"No, of course not."

"Could you have escaped?" Hook regarded him curiously.

"No . . . but I didn't try."

"I'm asking you, officially, to try now."

"Officially?" Joseph wanted to be quite clear.

"Yes." Hook gave a very slight smile, so small it could even have been an illusion of the light.

"Yes, sir. Of course." Joseph stood up from the ammunition box. "I'll let you know as soon as I hear anything."

"Oh, don't wait that long, Reavley. Tell me in a couple of days. I'll tell Faulkner."

"Yes, sir." Joseph went to the step, then with one hand on the sacking he turned back. "Only one of them is guilty, you know. There were eleven blanks and one live round."

"We don't have blanks," Hook pointed out.

"They made their own. It's simple enough. The others are innocent."

"Not innocent," Hook said with a grimace. "Guilty of insubordination, not murder. But I'm glad to hear that."

"It makes a difference, sir. If they were tried and found guilty of insubordination, it might be a matter you could deal with. No need to take it higher. All inside the regiment?"

"That isn't going to help whoever sprang them out of custody, Reavley. Faulkner will still want them court-martialed. And probably shot."

Joseph felt the cold hurt tighten in his stomach again. "I realize that, sir. I imagine it will be very difficult indeed to find out who they are. Practically impossible."

"Still, we must oblige Lieutenant Colonel Faulkner. Attend to it, Reavley. Good luck."

"Thank you, sir." Joseph went out, praying that the good luck he would have would be a complete and total failure to find any proof whatsoever.

It was difficult even to find a man he could decently ask about the escape. It was not merely that no one wished to help find the men themselves; they were even less eager to add to the general misery by exposing whoever had been clever enough, and above all brave enough, to free them. Everyone was overwhelmed by the continuing battle for Passchendaele. The losses mounted, not in twos or threes but in dozens, too often scores. Sometimes the rain eased, but it always came back again until the trenches were like canals; shell craters were deep enough to drown a man and often did; and running water gouged out channels down every incline so savage they would sweep a man off his feet.

Joseph carried stretchers, when there were any, men on his back when that was all there was. As always, he did what he could for the dying and the dead. There was little enough time to think of anything else.

Still, as discreetly as he could, he began to find out where different people had been on the night of the escape. He did not begin with Judith, aware that Faulkner might follow his steps. What he could learn, so could others.

He hoped he could find that she had been miles away, with a dozen witnesses—perhaps other officers new to the area and who had no personal stake in the escape. He sensed the anger as he asked, the suspicious looks, the reluctance to answer. Men stopped talking when he approached; shaggy-dog jokes died halfway through. They did not offer him the usual tea—or Woodbines, even though they knew he did not smoke.

Most men simply said they had no idea of Judith's whereabouts. Others had observed her in at least half a dozen different places at the time of the escape, all miles from the farmhouse. She and Wil Sloan were the only ones about whom such a variety of lies were sworn to. All other V.A.D. staff were in one place only.

These men were not very sophisticated liars. If Joseph could follow that trail so easily, so could Faulkner, once he thought where to look. Then there was only one possible end: Wil and Judith would be arrested and charged. All the lies in the world would not help, because the truth was obvious. He had thought only a little while ago that it was someone extremely clever; now he thought perhaps only supremely brave, and trusting in the loyalty of the men. The guards might even have been party to it.

He walked in the late afternoon mist, his boots sodden and sloshing in the mud. He moved slowly because he had no wish to arrive. The gunfire sounded far away, over the rise and beyond the woods toward Passchendaele itself—or what was left of it. All along the Ypres Salient there were miles of mud and blasted tree stumps, craters with corpses floating in the stagnant water, some still wreathed in the heavy poison gas.

He could imagine the scene at night: Judith and Wil Sloan arriving in the ambulance, possibly even two ambulances. They would stop. One would get out, probably Judith, tired, tense, her face pale in the headlights, skirts heavy and dark with mud. She would have gone up to the guard and asked for something—perhaps fresh water or another blanket.

Wil might have waited until they were occupied helping her, and crept up. Or had they simply been honest and said what they wanted, and asked for help? Joseph might never know, and it did not matter. Without thinking about it at all, he knew if they were ever facing trial, they would say they had done it by violence and deceit. They would see that no one else was blamed.

Joseph reached Colonel Hook's dugout. He pulled back the sacking and saw the light burning inside. He knocked on the lintel.

Hook looked up and waved Joseph in. Fear was in his eyes for an instant, then he mastered it. "Yes, Captain Reavley? Have you found out anything about the escape?"

"Nothing at all, sir," Joseph said instantly. "It could have been anyone at all. The only answer is to see if we can find the escaped men. I am quite certain that only one of them is guilty of murder. The others did no more than . . . than behave insubordinately, provoked by extraordinary circumstances. Then we could have a court-martial that would be fair and reasonable . . . sir."

"We have no chance of finding the men, Reavley. They could be anywhere. Unless—" Hook stopped. "Do you believe you can?" His face puckered, gaunt with weariness. He did not daresay it, but he was begging Joseph not to tell him what he did not want and could not afford to know.

"I believe so, sir." Joseph stayed standing to attention. "If I have your permission, I would like to try. Immediately."

"They have several days' start on you," Hook pointed out.

"I know. But I think the Royal Flying Corps might give me a little help if I explain. And if you give me orders . . . sir?"

"Try," Hook said quietly. "And God help you!"

NINE

*T*he day after Wheatcroft's death, Matthew received an urgent summons from Dermot Sandwell. He had asked for Sandwell's help, but he had not expected to hear from him so soon. He went eagerly, even with a sharp flutter of excitement. He found his heart beating hard as he strode along the pavement, bumping into people unintentionally, having to apologize. He had spent three years seeking the identity of the Peacemaker, moving from one fear to another, hoping and yet also dreading the moment when he could no longer deny that it was someone he knew and liked. It had to be someone his father had once trusted, and that trust had cost his father his life.

It was a close, heavy day in late August. The air seemed to clog his throat. The sky was hazy and there were heavy clouds gathering to the west. There would be a thunderstorm by midafternoon. The armies along the Western Front would be drenched once again.

Matthew walked because it was ridiculous to try to find a taxi for the mile or so to Sandwell's office. He kept to the main thoroughfares and moved briskly.

Everything was scarce at the moment: petrol as much as food and clothes. Naval losses had severely limited all imports; nevertheless in London, if you had money, you could get almost anything, while in some areas in the country there was actual starvation.

He reached Whitehall and went in, giving his name and telling the official on duty that Mr. Sandwell was expecting him.

He was received immediately. Sandwell stood up from behind his desk and came forward, extending his hand. He looked tired. The lines were etched more deeply in his face, both across his brow and around his mouth. His fair hair had paled to silver at the temples, but his eyes were as deeply blue as ever and the grip of his long, thin hand was firm.

"Thank you for coming so promptly, Reavley." He waved to a chair and peered at Matthew intently as they both sat down. "Miserable business about Wheatcroft's suicide. Did you learn anything of value from him?"

"No, sir." Instinctively Matthew guarded the threads of impression he had of someone else behind Wheatcroft's accusation of Corracher. "I'm afraid not." It sounded too bare. "He still protested his innocence, but felt no one would believe him."

"The reason for his suicide, do you think?" Sandwell asked.

In that instant, Matthew knew what he *did* think. "Possibly. That's certainly what his note implied."

"Implied?" Sandwell picked up the word.

"Said," Matthew corrected.

"And Corracher's betrayal of him," Sandwell added quietly. "Poor man."

Matthew said nothing. It was Wheatcroft's betrayal of Corracher that lodged in his mind, and something else that eluded him, a memory of something that did not fit where it should.

Sandwell leaned forward, his blue eyes studying Matthew's face. "I'm afraid I have come to some deeply disturbing conclusions. I must swear you to secrecy before I share them with you. You will understand why as soon as I do."

"Secret from whom, sir?" Matthew asked, puzzled by such a request— in fact it seemed to be a condition. He had imagined he was being told in order to refer them to Shearing.

"From everyone, at least for the time being," Sandwell answered. "What I have discovered is more dangerous than I can begin to tell you, and I have no idea yet how far it extends. A word or a whisper in the wrong ear, and we could both be killed for it, if I am correct." He leaned forward. "Do I have your attention now?"

Matthew stiffened. "Yes, sir."

"I imagined I would." Sandwell smiled openly. "Apart from your loyalty to your country, a man such as you could never resist the sheer curiosity of it. If you could have stood up and walked away from here without knowing, I should have recommended your removal from the Intelligence Service."

"Why me?" Matthew asked. It was a bold question and to one of Sandwell's seniority perhaps impertinent, but it was not irrelevant.

Sandwell's eyes widened slightly, appreciating the perception. "You are ideally placed" was all he said. "I think you will understand when I have told you what I know and what I fear."

"Yes, sir."

Sandwell touched his fingertips lightly together in a steeple and looked at Matthew.

"You said that in the beginning you believed Corracher was not guilty of attempting to blackmail Wheatcroft, although Wheatcroft might indeed have behaved indiscreetly. I considered the possibility that you were right. If that were so, then there is only one conclusion that makes sense, and that is that there is a conspiracy behind it, formed and carried out by someone else."

He continued to regard Matthew steadily. "I weighed the likelihood of it being purely personal, driven either by ambition or revenge. I could find nothing to suggest it, and it seemed less likely than the desire to get rid of them both from their positions of political power. They are of similar beliefs in many issues, especially regarding the kind of peace we may make with Germany."

The muscles of his face tightened as if for an instant the reality of the deaths and the rage of destruction overwhelmed his mind, and the quiet room overlooking Horse Guards Parade on a great August morning was only an island, a temporary haven in the midst of ruin.

Matthew waited.

Sandwell composed himself again, but he did not apologize for his emotion. "I have noticed that two other rising politicians of similar mind have also been lost to us recently. Do you begin to understand me, Reavley?"

Matthew drew a deep breath, as if standing on the edge of an abyss and having looked down.

"Yes, sir. Someone is . . . planning ahead, maneuvering so that when the time comes they will have control over whoever is in power to agree to the terms of peace." At last he was not alone in his knowledge, but Sandwell had glimpsed only a fraction of the Peacemaker's design, just this last few months' work. Should Matthew say any more? Not yet. Be careful. Listen, only listen. And there was still the frayed end he could not place that lingered at the edge of his mind.

"Precisely," Sandwell agreed. "And doing it with very great skill. Which leads me to wonder why he is doing this *now*."

Matthew was about to point out the obvious, that now there was the greatest hope of the end to the war. But that was not true. They had hoped for it as early as the autumn of 1914. He bit back the words. Then with a catch of his breath, he realized what Sandwell really meant! If someone had these hopes and designs now, where had he been during the last three years?

Sandwell read him perfectly. "Exactly," he said in little more than a whisper. "What else? What has there been all through the years since the beginning that we have not seen?"

Matthew's mind raced. Had he found an ally at last? Then suddenly he heard his father's voice in his mind again, that last day on the telephone, warning him that the conspiracy went as high as the Royal Family. He knew now that that had been a reference to the treaty that the Peacemaker had wanted the king to sign.

"Reavley?" Sandwell's voice interrupted the sense of loss as sharp as the day of John Reavley's death. It jerked Matthew back to the present. "Yes, sir. The thought is . . . overwhelming. It is possible this is his first act . . . but . . ."

"His?" Sandwell questioned him. "Whose? Do you think it is one man?"

Matthew spoke slowly. Without having reached a decision consciously, he could not bring himself to trust Sandwell. He must weigh every word. He was acutely aware of Sandwell's extraordinary intelligence. "No, certainly not acting alone," he answered. "But it might be one man leading and others following. It seems to have a coherence about it. Forgive me, sir, if I am a little slow. The thought is enormous, and incredibly ugly."

"But not new to you," Sandwell pointed out.

Should he admit it? He saw the knowledge reflected in Sandwell's eyes. He knew at least something of Matthew's earlier convictions of conspiracy, but how much and from whom? Shearing? Someone else in the Intelligence Service?

"We're always looking for conspiracies," he said aloud, trying to make his voice sound rueful. "It's still a surprise when you find them. I did suspect that Corracher might be innocent, and if he was, then Wheatcroft is implicated, even if just another victim with less honor than Corracher, willing to ruin another man in order to escape himself. It is the other thought, of what else might have been done, or yet planned by the man behind this, that stuns me."

"As well it might." Sandwell leaned back in his chair, his eyes still on Matthew's face. "And it is that which we must address, Reavley. Saving Tom Corracher is a relatively small matter. Finding this . . . this arch-traitor is the main thing. As long as he remains hidden, with the power he has—and we have no idea how much it is—then we are desperately, per-haps even fatally vulnerable."

"And have always been," Matthew added.

Sandwell let out his breath in a slow sigh. "Tell me, Reavley, you have been in intelligence since the beginning of the war. You must have as good an idea as anyone how our enemies work. Where are we most vul-nerable? If you were this . . . this man, where would you have struck al-ready? And where would you strike next?"

Matthew saw the depth of the question and the power. If he did not answer, he would betray the fact that he did not trust Sandwell. And if he did answer, he would show that he did trust him, completely, perhaps more than an intelligence officer should trust anyone at all, especially anyone outside the service, even if he were of cabinet rank in the govern-ment. It was a position of ironic delicacy. Did Sandwell know that? He dared not assume that he didn't. He was forced to tell the truth, or some-thing extremely close to it.

"In the past," he began carefully, "I would have struck with propa-ganda aimed at morale, especially within the forces. I would have aimed it particularly at recruitment points. Next I would have struck against the navy. Without sea power we'll lose in weeks. Being an island is both our strength and our weakness."

Sandwell nodded.

"And now?" he said very softly, almost as if he feared being overheard, even though there was no one else in the room.

"I would try to neutralize the effectiveness of some of our ministers who have strong diplomatic contacts abroad, particularly in countries that might be persuaded to turn against Germany and its allies, such as Hungary. Or to hasten the withdrawal of Russia."

"Yes." Sandwell's eyes were the clearest, most brilliant blue. "That would be the natural thing."

"And of course if possible weaken the Western Front." Matthew heard his own voice loud in the utter silence. "Passchendaele is proving the most terrible battle we have ever fought. At this rate there will be a quarter of a million more dead before it's over."

Sandwell's face was white; the misery bit so deep it drove the blood from his veins. "I know . . ."

"Morale is almost at breaking point," Matthew added. "One really disastrous injustice, even a fatal mistake, and the men might even mutiny. Then the line might not hold." Instantly he wondered if he had gone too far. Sandwell looked as if he was in emotional pain so intense it had become physical. He was short of breath and his muscles were locked as if in a spasm. His face was ashen.

Matthew waited. He could hear the clock ticking on the mantel over the ornate fireplace and the first heavy spots of rain that fell against the window.

"I was right to trust you." Sandwell let out his breath in a sigh, his shoulders relaxing. "You understand perfectly. There has been an incident. An incompetent officer was shot by his own men. They know who it was, and they are up for court-martial." His voice was quite light. "Unfortunately two of these are officers; both have served the full duration of the war with distinction. In fact, one is up for the V.C. If he is found guilty and faces the firing squad for what was essentially saving his own men's lives by getting rid of a disastrous officer, then there is your incident of injustice. It could even be seen as a betrayal, if you believe sending brave men into battle led by an idiot to be a betrayal of their trust. And God knows, they deserve better than that!"

Matthew stared at him. Was it possible that at last he really did have an ally? One with power! He remembered Cullingford with a grief so sharp it brought a wave of nausea. "Be careful!" he said with sudden urgency, unable to help himself from the warning.

"Oh, I am, Reavley. Believe me, since I have become aware of this possibility, even probability, I have been extremely careful." He frowned. "But what makes you say that? Have you felt yourself in danger, personally, I mean?"

Matthew hesitated for a fraction of a moment. Again, he could not afford to be caught in a lie. But could Sandwell possibly know the truth? No, but that was not the point. Matthew had given the warning. He had to justify it.

"Yes, twice," he answered. "Once might have been an accident; the second time it was definitely an attempt to kill me."

Sandwell blinked. "You are certain? Or am I foolish to ask?"

Matthew gave a half smile. "If this man would betray his country and cause the deaths of thousands, tens of thousands, why on earth not a single one, if that one was a danger to him?"

Sandwell blinked. "Cause the deaths of . . . I was thinking rather more of someone who wants peace, even if it is the peace of defeat, rather than a continuing of this . . . slaughter. . . ." The word came out with a burst of passion which he controlled only with an intense effort of will. He bit his lip. "I'm sorry. I suppose I have no evidence for that. I just have . . ." He took a deep breath. "I have intense fear as to who this man may be, how highly placed in order to have done what he has. I had not considered his motives. I admit, Reavley, I find the whole thing shattering."

"You have some idea who it is?" Matthew asked, unable to stop his voice from trembling.

Sandwell looked away. "I would rather not say anything yet. It . . . it is so appalling. But I will give you all the information I have, as well, of course, as placing copies in my safe where they will be available to the prime minister if anything happens to me. But it is your safety I am concerned about, Reavley, because it is your skills that will unmask the man, if anyone can do it."

"But why not reveal your suspicions now?" Matthew insisted.

Sandwell met Matthew's eyes unflinchingly. "I would prefer you reach your own conclusions. You may see the same facts as I do, and place some different interpretation on them. But I am correct regarding the catastrophe about to happen on the Western Front when this court-martial takes place. Begin by looking at the record of the military prosecutor they have appointed to the case."

"Yes, sir," Matthew said very slowly, his mind grasping at sudden reality, a course to pursue. "I'll begin immediately." He rose to his feet.

"Reavley!" Sandwell stood up also. "Be careful! No one must know what you are doing, even in your own office. In fact"—he sighed—"especially in your own office."

Now there was a chill in the room, in spite of the August closeness of the air. "I understand, sir."

"Do you?" Sandwell questioned. "I hope for your sake, for your life's sake, that you do."

Matthew did precisely as Sandwell had warned him, and told no one that he was going back to see Mrs. Wheatcroft again. As before, he found himself obliged to use the weight of Sandwell's name in order to be received.

He stood uncomfortably in the withdrawing room. The bay windows overlooked the immaculately groomed late summer garden.

Mrs. Wheatcroft entered with only the briefest acknowledgment of him. She stood pale and graceful in a long muslin dress.

"I don't know how I can further assist you, Captain Reavley," she said coldly. "If it were not that apparently you have some connection with Mr. Sandwell, I should not have seen you at all."

"So much you made clear, Mrs. Wheatcroft," he replied. "However, I assume that if there is a conspiracy to ruin your husband—and Mr. Corracher—in the interests of German victory, then you will be as keen as Mr. Sandwell and I are to uncover it."

She bit her lip, momentarily confused. "Do you think it is such a thing? I had assumed it was simply Mr. Corracher's greed, both for money and personal advancement."

"Mr. Sandwell does," Matthew answered. "If you doubt that, call him and ask. I understand you are acquainted with him?"

"Socially," she said, the chill returning. "I would like to believe that I could trust an officer of our Intelligence Services, but if you wait here, I shall place a call to Mr. Sandwell. Then I shall consider what he advises."

"An excellent idea." He sat down in the armchair before she left the room. She saw his ease and her face tensed with disapproval at the liberty.

It was half an hour before she returned, looking considerably chastened. Now the hinted aggression was gone, replaced by fear, and for the first time she met his eyes candidly.

He had risen as she came in, but she waved him to sit down again, and sank into the chair opposite him, barely bothering to straighten her skirts.

"I apologize," she said briefly. "Mr. Sandwell has advised me to tell you the absolute truth, so that is what I shall do." She took a deep breath. "My husband had a weakness. I did not know it when I married him, but I learned it within the first few years. If you repeat this, I shall say you are a liar." For an instant the defiance was back in her eyes.

"It is not in my interest to repeat it, Mrs. Wheatcroft," he told her. "Nor to make judgments of him. I am happy to accept the story that he was no more than naïve and unfortunate. What I do not accept is that Tom Corracher tried to extort money from him in exchange for silence on the matter. Nor do I believe that it was his own idea to put up that defense." He was watching her closely, and saw the flicker in her eyes.

"His letter—" she began, then stopped abruptly.

Then he remembered the element that did not fit. It was a matter of timing. He was cold as the confusion fell apart, leaving the beginning of a picture even uglier.

"I read it," he agreed. "He had obviously written something—the pen and ink were there, freshly spilled and blotted. But the letter I found was written days ago, before he knew about Marlowe being transferred."

She looked confused. "Who's Marlowe? What has that to do with Alan's death?"

"Nothing. Marlowe was the man he thought would take over from him, but by the day before he died, when I saw him, he knew it was Jamieson."

She stared at him, frightened and unable to hide it now.

"You destroyed his real letter, didn't you?" he said grimly. "Because he admitted that Corracher was innocent, and he had accused him to save himself . . . and of course you. But he couldn't live with the lie, and couldn't face you if he told the truth."

She drew her breath in sharply to protest, but the guilt was hot in her face and she saw no escape. There was something else in her eyes as well, an acid, corrosive hate.

He was glad to see it. It made it easier to crush her.

Something must have relaxed in him and looked to her like retreat.

"You can't prove that," she pointed out. "I burned his second letter, and he did write the first, just not then. He wrote several. It wasn't hard to put one together. He always used the same ink and the same paper. There's nothing you can do."

"Whose idea was it, Mrs. Wheatcroft?"

"Mine!" she said quietly.

"If you had said it was his, I would not have believed you," he told her. "You had to force him into it, if not for your sake personally, then for your sons."

"If you like!" She had regained her composure. "But when Alan realized what his disgrace would do to them, he was willing."

"I doubt it," he said drily. "But it's irrelevant now. It was the guilt of lying that killed him."

"It was the guilt of being so unbelievably stupid!" she snapped.

"How did you know to blame Tom Corracher rather than anyone else?" He remembered Sandwell's words about political ideology, and the Peacemaker's plan behind the ruin of all four men.

For an instant she hesitated, then grasped after an answer. "That was Alan's idea. I just said to think of someone."

"Someone with the same political beliefs about the terms of any possible peace treaty with the Germans," he elaborated.

Again there was confusion in her eyes, then a sudden new understanding. "They worked together. It made sense."

She was guessing. Actually they had not worked together, simply held the same opinions. Someone else had suggested the idea of blaming Corracher to her. Perhaps she knew who it was and why. More probably she was simply a willing tool, caring only to save herself and her sons. Anyone would do as a sacrifice, and the larger cause was irrelevant.

"Was anyone else aware of this, Mrs. Wheatcroft?" he asked casually, as if it were no more than a passing thought.

Again the half-second's hesitation, then she denied it. "No, of course not."

He looked at her chiseled face. It was beautiful in a hard, brittle way, but without yielding, without forgiveness. Perhaps she was a knowing tool after all. In protecting her own, she was not open to the vulnerability of mercy or conscience.

"Thank you, Mrs. Wheatcroft." He rose to his feet. "You have been most civil. I shan't need to trouble you again."

A faint smile touched her lips. "It would be courteous to say I regret that, Captain Reavley, but I do not. Good day."

He also took Sandwell's other piece of advice and made inquiries about the man who had been sent to prosecute the twelve soldiers accused of murdering Major Northrup. The answer that came back was exactly what Sandwell had warned. Faulkner was known to be a stickler for the law in every detail. He believed justice, and therefore society, was best served by following procedure to the letter. The innocent were protected by the unfailing punishment of the guilty, and there was no room for personal interpretation of the law.

Matthew arranged to meet an old friend, Errol Lashwood, for luncheon at the Ivy Restaurant in Covent Garden. They received excellent food, and the atmosphere was easy and charming. The restaurant was highly popular with all manner of people, especially the theatrical community. Matthew had on occasion seen Bernard Shaw there, and Ellen Terry and Gladys Cooper last year when they had been playing in J. M. Barrie's *The Admirable Crichton* at Wyndham's Theatre.

This time Lashwood smiled and pointed out the amazing profile of Ivor Novello, who was sitting only a couple of tables away.

"Faulkner." Matthew returned him to the subject.

"Not a bad man," Lashwood said wryly. "Just highly unimaginative, and very little sense of joy in the absurd. I think, personally, that he is rather afraid of change, and therefore feels threatened by anything he does not understand." He shrugged. "Or perhaps I am thinking beyond the mark. The man infuriates me. He could be so much better than he is. I believe he once fell in love with a highly unsuitable woman, and the whole experience soured him for life. His father was the same." He smiled. "But his mother is as different as could be. Delightful woman, charming and eccentric and full of life. Still wears rather old-fashioned clothes, almost prewar, very feminine. Has a famous collection of gorgeous parasols and hats with flowers on them. Loves the horse races . . . and a good champagne."

"What on earth does she make of her son?" Matthew said in amazement. "I presume he is scandalized by her?"

"On the contrary," Lashwood assured him with a smile. "She is his only redeeming feature. He adores her."

"But she has never managed to imbue him with her own joy in life?"

"Never." He speared a succulent morsel of meat from his plate and put it into his mouth. "He considers it his duty, and his privilege, to look after her, and indulge her, which she accepts with the utmost grace."

Matthew's heart sank. It was far too little information to be of any use. "How the hell did we get lumbered with having him prosecute the men accused of killing Northrup? And how do we get him changed for someone with a little more compassion and imagination, possibly amenable to considering the larger picture?"

Lashwood pulled his mouth into a grim line. "Difficult, old fellow. He's a friend of your boss. Sorry, but for all I know, it could have been he who picked him out."

Matthew was suddenly cold. "Picked him out? You mean for this prosecution?" Was this at last what Sandwell had been wanting him to find out? It was the fear that had rested like poison at the back of his mind almost from the beginning—the Peacemaker was Shearing himself. He had hated the Peacemaker for killing John and Alys Reavley, and all those since then: good people, men who had trusted him.

But how many more had died fearful deaths on battlefields all over the world? How many were shot, frozen, gassed, drowned in mud, or carried to the bottom of the sea in the millions of tons of shipping lost? How many starved to death, even here at home? How many more were maimed in mind and body or crippled by grief? How much of the whole world was ruined in blood and fire and grief?

The Peacemaker had wanted to prevent it and, when that was too late, to stop it, at any cost! He was an idealist who had lost his balance. He had worked to save lives, but had taken to himself the power to decide what cost was to be paid.

He could hate such a man, but he could also understand him.

"Reavley!" Lashwood's voice cut across his thoughts.

Matthew jerked himself back to the present. "Yes. You are quite sure? No possibility of a mistake?"

Lashwood frowned. "I've known Faulkner for years, and his mother." He leaned forward across the table. "You look a bit green, old boy."

Matthew struggled to compose his face and respond noncommittally. "So you think there's no chance of getting him changed?"

"Not really. Bad show. Wish I could think of something helpful. But from what I hear, he actually requested the case."

"No point in going over it. Spoil what's left of a good meal," Matthew said, trying to smile. He left the thoughts raging in his mind until he could escape and find privacy to think.

That opportunity came as he walked back across the park. It took him a mile and a half longer than necessary, but he could not yet bear to face Shearing. Lashwood would not have lied, nor could he have been mistaken. Shearing knew the man, knew his rigidity, and had allowed this, possibly even contrived it. Was that something Sandwell had also known Matthew would find, and be driven to the inevitable, hideous conclusion?

He found himself taking the other path across the grass, not in the direction of his own office, but back toward Sandwell's.

He had to wait most of the afternoon to see him, but at four Sandwell returned from a Cabinet meeting in Downing Street, and admitted Matthew immediately.

"I see by your face that you have followed the trail to its bitter conclusion," he said quietly. He walked over to the table at the far side of his office and picked up the crystal decanter from the tantalus, pouring two glasses of brandy and offering one to Matthew. "I'm sorry. It's the worst of all answers."

"Why would he do such a thing?" Matthew asked, taking the brandy. "Who is he? What is he? There's nothing in his office—no pictures, no mementos, nothing from the past at all! He never mentions family, or even friends, where he went to school or university, or any other place that matters to him."

Sandwell's face was bleak. "He wouldn't," he answered, motioning Matthew to sit down and sitting opposite him. "He sounds like an Englishman because he's taught himself to, and he's nothing if not thorough. Actually he's an Austrian Jew. Settled here thirty years ago. No idea what happened to his family. None of them are here in Britain, or ever were." He sipped his brandy. "Unless they came in under forged papers, but I'm as certain as I can be that they didn't. His name was originally Caleb Schering." He spelled it out, in the German way.

Matthew drank a mouthful of his brandy. It was a waste of a fine spirit, but he needed its fire more than its savor. "How in God's name did we come to have him in the Secret Intelligence Service at all, let alone as head of it?"

"Because he started when we had no cause to fear Germany, let alone the Austro-Hungarian Empire," Sandwell said simply. "And there's no proof of a single error or slip of any kind against him. English sense of fair play, I suppose!" He shrugged slightly. "Added to which, I daresay he knows where a few bodies are buried. No one will want to be the first to suggest anything. He's an agreeable man. People like him. One doesn't want to seem paranoid, seeing ghosts where there are none."

"God Almighty!" Matthew swore. "How . . . how bloody amateur!"

Sandwell smiled, his expression suddenly warm and extraordinarily charming. "The English disease," he said ruefully. "And at times our genius."

Matthew closed his eyes. "Not this time."

"What are you going to do?" Sandwell asked after a moment or two.

"Collect evidence," Matthew replied. "There's nothing else I can do."

"Where will you take it?" Sandwell's face darkened. "Be careful, Reavley. There have been murders already. I don't know how many, but he is playing for empires, even millions of lives. Yours would be nothing to pay for victory."

Matthew grimaced. "I'll remember."

*　*　*

Matthew spent a wretched night. Unable to sleep, he sought every kind of escape from the only conclusion now possible.

He lay staring at the ceiling. He was safe and comfortable in his own bed. The silence surrounded him, cocooning him from the world. He began to think about his brother.

Joseph, if he was sleeping at all, would be in a hole dug in the sodden earth of Flanders. There would be no silence there. The guns never entirely stopped, least of all now with the battle for Passchendaele raging on. Now and then phosgene or mustard gas would be pervasive. Death and decay would be everywhere—the smell of it, the taste of it. Those Joseph shared tea and bad jokes with tonight might be torn apart by shrapnel tomorrow, and he would bury what was left of them.

And here was Matthew in silence and clean sheets, tossing and turning because tomorrow he would begin proving that Calder Shearing was the Peacemaker, the idealist turned betrayer who had killed John and Alys Reavley.

He finally gave up trying to sleep and made himself a cup of tea. Then he sat in his armchair noting all he knew already, and what he needed to learn from a reputable source who would not take the inquiry back to Shearing.

The second was the more difficult. He remembered Sandwell's warning that Shearing would not hesitate to kill if he was threatened. Matthew already knew that. He had never forgotten Cullingford, and his loss still hurt. Looking back now he was certain that the attack in the alley when he had so nearly been knifed himself was not an attempted robbery but a murder foiled more by luck than skill.

Why? He had not suspected Shearing then. In fact it was barely twenty-four hours since they had eaten a hasty supper together of ham sandwiches and coffee, set up over maps of safe houses and escape routes for saboteurs. He could see it exactly in his mind's eye: the lamplight on the table, Shearing's dark head bent over the diagrams, his sudden smile when he had seen the solution, and then the eagerness in his voice. It had been one of the rare betrayals of emotion in him. Matthew had felt an intense companionship at that moment. They had even joked afterward; Shearing had told some long-winded story about a dog and a newspaper. They had laughed, mostly from relief.

There was really only one person he could speak to, and that was Admiral "Blinker" Hall, the head of naval intelligence. He had gone to him before when he had had knowledge that was sensitive and painful. He was used to harboring secrets that would make or break nations, and that could never be revealed.

It was still a little after one the following afternoon when Matthew was shown into Admiral Hall's office. Hall was sitting behind the desk, papers spread in front of him. He was a stocky man with an eaglelike face and thick white hair. His narrowed blue eyes blinked rapidly every now and then, as if he could not help himself.

"Well, Reavley, no preamble. No time. What is it that you must tell me that cannot wait?"

"Not tell you, sir," Matthew corrected him. "*Ask* you."

"You had better know a good reason for this. Sit down, man. I'm not spending my time straining my neck looking up at you! Spit it out."

Matthew sat obediently.

"Information has come to me, sir, from a source high in the government that casts doubt on some of Colonel Shearing's actions and decisions." He felt like a traitor saying it aloud.

"For example?" Hall asked, blinking several times.

"His explicit approval of Lieutenant Colonel Faulkner as prosecutor in the court-martial against Captain Cavan, and the other men, if they are caught," Matthew answered. "Faulkner is an absolute hard-liner, and if Cavan is found guilty and shot, it will be a disaster to morale, possibly beyond our ability to cope with. It could even become a full-scale mutiny." He had no need to elaborate for Hall what would follow that disaster.

"Have you asked him?" Hall raised his eyebrows.

"No, sir. I realize I know nothing about Colonel Shearing except that he is an Austrian-Jewish immigrant. He arrived some thirty years ago, and none of his family is in this country, as far as we know."

"No, they aren't," Hall agreed, leaning back a little and making a steeple of his fingers on the desk. He regarded Matthew over the top of them. "All his family are dead. Both his parents were killed by the Austrian police. The woman he loved—Ingrid, I believe her name was—was raped and killed in a particularly brutal incident on the Serbian border. He and his brother, Baruch Schering, escaped to England, but Baruch went back, working for British Intelligence, to see what information he could gain about political alliances in the Balkans at the time. He was especially concerned about Austrian treaties with Russia which might affect us in the future."

His eyes were steady, the blink forgotten. "He was caught and tortured, but he died without giving away any of our other men, although he knew the names of at least a dozen of them. It is because of Baruch and our debt to him that we trusted Caleb . . . Calder Shearing. He has never let us down. I am prepared to stake Captain Cavan's life, and the outcome of the court-martial in Passchendaele, on his honor in this, if not his judgment. If, indeed, he really did propose Faulkner."

Matthew sat still, his face burning, his brain trying to accommodate all he had heard, and decide what he believed. He had come in accepting at last that Shearing was the Peacemaker. Deeply as that hurt, he no longer fought the idea. Now all was confusion again.

Hall must have seen it in his face. "I understand your concern, Reavley. On the face of it, to send Faulkner seems the worst possible choice. He may have reasons we are unaware of. Find out, and bring me the answer."

"I have no authority with which to question him, sir," Matthew began.

"I said find out, Reavley, not ask him," Hall snapped. "Learn what you can about any friendship between them. Is it possible Shearing is so burdened with other issues he has been misled, careless, or used by someone else? And do it quickly. We have no time to spare. Report to me in forty-eight hours. Or less, if you find a satisfactory answer."

Matthew stood up. "Yes, sir." His head was swimming. He heard every tick of the clock on the desk as if it were consuming the seconds until Cavan should be shot, and the whole Western Front collapse.

Judith also had very little sleep, and even in those brief hours snatched here and there she was troubled by memories and fears. She was accustomed to physical exhaustion and the discomfort of being bruised by the constant jolting of the ambulance over rough ground, her muscles aching from floundering in mud and trying to lift stretchers awkwardly. She was also, like everyone else, accustomed to being wet most of the time, having her feet hurt as her rough shoes scraped where the leather had become twisted and hard from being soaked and caked with mud. She felt permanently filthy. Like everything along the entire Western Front, she almost certainly smelled stale and dirty. She felt about as feminine as a road navvy or railway stoker . . . or a soldier.

Over the last year, that had not mattered. Seeing the wounded, thinking about the war in general and this Salient in particular was all that anyone had time for; helping friends, and friends were whoever was near you. But Mason had looked at her with that tender, aching intensity, the softness in his eyes so naked it tore through her like a fire, destroying complacency and balance.

Before the war she had been beautiful. She knew it from the reflection in men's eyes. Now they looked on her as one of the chaps, something of a mascot even: a good driver, a good sport, brave, reliable, someone to trust. And yet still not really one of them.

As she lay curled up in the back of the ambulance, she could dimly see the outline of Wil Sloan a few feet away. He was breathing evenly, almost certainly asleep. She had never admired anyone more. Wil was brave with a casual air as if it were ordinary, and he made off-beat silly jokes, told long stories about the American West that no one else understood. But he laughed at the English tales that must have been equally obscure to him. He shared his food and blankets, when there were any, and he never complained. She would have trusted him with anything except the vulnerability of her emotional need and confusion at the moment.

He had helped her free the accused men from the farmhouse, and that could have cost him his life. It still might, for that matter. Colonel Hook had asked Joseph to find out how the escape had been effected, and he had been so obviously dilatory that Faulkner had insisted he be imprisoned for his collusion.

She turned over in bed carefully as her muscles tweaked with pain. Poor Joseph. He had been so wretched over realizing that Northrup had been shot by his own men, even though this time there was no way he could have avoided it. Mason knew, and that was the end of his chance to conceal it.

The last time she had seen Mason there had been a bitterness in his words, an anger that was not at the Germans just beyond the ridge, or at circumstances that had brought them all here. It was as if he had expected incompetence and futility, and hoped for nothing better. His faith in the world was gone.

She huddled a little tighter, remembering their conversation.

"Do you know *Through the Looking Glass?*" he had asked wryly.

"Yes, of course I do," she had answered. She had loved it, possibly even more than *Alice in Wonderland.* There was an extra absurdity to the logic, and the poetry stayed in her mind, especially the White Knight. " '... fingers in a pocket full of glue. Or madly pushing my left-hand foot into my right-hand shoe.' " Aloud she had said "Why?"

" 'Walrus and the Carpenter,' " he had replied. "Walking along the beach, 'wept like anything to see such quantities of sand.' "

She picked it up. " 'If seven maids with seven mops swept it for half a year. Do you suppose, the walrus said, that they could get it clear?' "

" 'I doubt it, said the carpenter, and shed a bitter tear,' " he finished. "How many women, in how many factories, their backs aching, feet sore, labor all day and all night, to make the shells that are shattering this land and sending mud into new piles, for someone else to blast all over a slightly different place tomorrow, and tear apart a few more human bodies in the process? That's real absurdity. A world that makes no sense."

She had longed for something to say that would explain to him the will to fight, the love of all the remembered sweetness of life: small things like a walk in the woods at bluebell time; lark song early in the morning; sunlight on shaven fields in autumn when the air is gold; and big things like laughter with friends, and faith in tomorrow. But she did not want him to damage her faith with his disbelief, and paint gray over her dreams. They were too precious to risk. Without them she might not survive.

Now there was a darkness in Mason that saw no point in their efforts, almost as if he derided them in his own way. She remembered his words as they had stood together in the dark, talking in between the crashes of mortar fire and the heavy shells exploding less than a mile away. Even in the clouded night they could see the great gouts of earth and mud flying into the air. Judith perceived his anger—not only what he said, it was the edge of despair in his voice.

It was at that moment that she had realized how small a part of his life she was. Yes, he could laugh and need and give like anyone else. But how much courage had he to hope when it was almost impossibly difficult? To lay the soul bare to the darkness, with the knowledge that it might not end? All the intelligence, the imagination, and pity, the moments of tenderness, were not enough without hope as well.

She sank into a kind of sleep at last, and by five o'clock she was awake again in the gray light. A splash of cold water on her face brought her to attention. Wil gave her a large mug of hot tea. She picked a bedbug out of it, then drank. It was so strong she could barely taste the strange mixture of things that had been in the Dixie can before it.

She was doing a little maintenance on the ambulance when she heard footsteps across the cobbled farmyard. At first she assumed it was Wil again, returned from his errand, but when he spoke she swung around in amazement to see Joseph. He looked tired, as always, the shadows around his eyes making them look even darker.

"Sorry," he apologized. "Didn't mean to startle you."

She saw an intensity in him that sent a wave of fear through her. In spite of all his care not to, had he found undeniable evidence that it was she who had organized the escape of the prisoners? Would he lie to protect her—tell a deliberate, outright lie? Maybe he couldn't. Maybe he had some kind of priestly oath, or a covenant with God. Perhaps he would not break that oath for her, or anyone.

"Hello, Joseph." Her voice croaked a little.

"I know I'm interrupting, but I need to speak to you," he said. "It's important."

She put down the rag with which she had been cleaning the carburetor.

"About the escape," he went on.

She tried to look as if she had no idea why he was asking her, and knew that she failed.

He smiled bleakly, his face tight, his eyes gentle. "Be careful what you tell me," he continued. "So far I have ideas of who was involved, but I don't know for certain, and without proof I wouldn't say anything."

"Oh." She let out her breath in a sigh. "I see. What is it you do not want to ask me?" She was puzzled. "I wouldn't tell you who it was, even presuming I knew."

"Of course you wouldn't," he agreed hastily. "I imagine you have an intense admiration for them. It was clever, simple, and took great courage, and of course a loyalty as deep as that of any of the soldiers on the line." He was still looking at her intently, eyes so shadowed with weariness she could not read them. "They are willing to die for one another. And that is what it would come to. If that person, or two people probably, were to be caught, it would be a firing—" His voice cracked, too. "A firing squad matter. I wouldn't ask you to tell me . . . if you know. That kind of betrayal is unthinkable."

Her mouth was dry, her heart pounding. He was playing a game, but what? And what for? "Joseph—"

"But I want you to use your imagination," he cut across her. "I've just spent a little time in the farmhouse where they were kept. And I spoke with Cavan. I know more about what actually happened now. I think only one of them is guilty of murder, the rest of . . . let's say 'conduct unbecoming.' "

She cleared her throat. "Does it make any difference?"

"I think so. I'm going to go after them and try to persuade them to return and face court-martial."

"They won't!" She was appalled at his naïveté. "For heaven's sake, Joseph, they'd be shot! Guilty or innocent, the army's after blood! You know that."

"Not if they come back willingly," he argued. "If they stay away then they're deserters and fugitives. Worse than deserters, actually: mutineers and murderers."

"Then they'll just stay in Switzerland! Or—" She stopped abruptly, realizing she had told him which direction they were going. But they had at least three days' advantage on him. "Or wherever they go," she added lamely.

"Yes. Or South America, or wherever we have no treaties of extradition for murder," he said grimly. "They can never come back to England. Never have careers, never stop looking over their shoulders, never be honest with anyone. That's a heavy burden to carry all your life."

She almost said that there might not be an England to come back to, but that was a terrible possibility she refused to harbor. Then the enormity of their situation began to sink in: the endless state of not belonging; the loneliness for anything deeper than passing acquaintance; the knowledge that you were forever a stranger.

"Think of their families," Joseph said quietly. "They're not cowards, not ruthless or without honor. I think they would rather try to prove their reasons for acting as they did, their innocence of murder, than run for the rest of their lives."

"Maybe. But it would take almost impossible courage."

"If anyone on earth has it, it's the men here," he said simply. "All I want to do is give them the chance, Judith," he said. "Where were they making for? Were they going to travel alone, in separate groups, or all together?"

She did not bother to pretend anymore. "Switzerland," she answered. "Pretty well all together, although if anyone got hurt or wanted to drop out, the rest would go on. They went on foot, so as to look as much like ordinary soldiers as possible. There was no way of making them look like civilians. Also, only Morel really speaks French, and anyway they're all of military age and obviously perfectly fit enough to fight, so there wouldn't be any explanation for their being out of uniform anywhere but a neutral country."

He gave her a sudden hard embrace and held her for several moments. "Thank you," he said gently. "Thank you very much."

"Be careful, Joseph," she said, clinging onto him. They were always in danger, but this mission was particularly unsettling. This time he was going away from Passchendaele and into country neither of them knew. He would be among strangers, and no one would bring word of him. "Be careful!" she said again, more urgently.

"I will," he promised. Then he broke free and gave her a quick salute. "You, too," he said huskily. He turned and walked across the cobbled yard without looking back.

TEN

*J*oseph realized that his only chance of finding the escapees before they crossed into Switzerland would be with the help of one of the reconnaissance planes from the Royal Flying Corps. They were fast enough to cover the distance in hours, and skilled enough to spot a group of men moving eastward instead of with the rest of the troops.

For this, of course, he had a letter of authority from Colonel Hook. Other than that, he took only a shaving kit, toothbrush, the minimum of clean underwear, an extra pair of socks, a pocket copy of the New Testament, and the regulation soldier's first aid equipment and hard rations.

When the staff car dropped him off at the Royal Flying Corps airfield, the sun was breaking through the mist and it looked like a good day for air reconnaissance. He felt a sudden lift of optimism as he thanked the driver and started walking toward the huts that served as headquarters.

Joseph spoke to the first officer he met, a good-looking young man with dark hair brushed back off his brow, deep-set eyes, and a shy smile. At the moment he had a pipe clamped between his teeth.

"Lost, Padre?" he said, looking at Joseph's dog collar and squinting a little in the sun. "Or are you an answer to someone's prayer?"

"I doubt it!" Joseph answered drily. "At the moment, I'm looking to receive help rather than give it."

The man extended his hand. "Captain Jones-Williams."

"Captain Reavley." Joseph shook the offered hand.

"What can we do for you, Captain Reavley? Looking for a trip up to find God?" Jones-Williams gestured into the milky blue of the sky.

"Actually I'd settle for eleven escaped prisoners," Joseph replied with a rueful shrug. "Sounds a little disrespectful, but I've got a few things to do before I meet God. Not really ready for that yet."

Jones-Williams laughed outright. "A priest who'd rather find eleven escaped prisoners than find God is worth getting to know. Will any eleven do, or do you have a particular set in mind?"

"Sorry, I have a very particular set in mind," Joseph replied. "They were held in a farmhouse just this side of Passchendaele, and—"

Jones-Williams's face was suddenly desperately grave. "From that poor bloody regiment that's being slaughtered? Can't you let 'em go? Turn a blind eye? Wouldn't your faith allow you that much mercy?"

"They've been accused of mutiny and the murder of an officer, Captain."

"Sorry, old fellow," Jones-Williams said with a brief smile. "We're pretty shorthanded ourselves. Lost quite a few lately. Got to keep what we have for taking a look at Jerry and what he's up to. Can see troop movements quite well from up there. I'd give it up, if I were you."

Joseph knew exactly why the captain was refusing, and he understood the pity and the revulsion behind it. He liked the man the more for it. "That's not the whole picture," he said, meeting his companion's eyes. "They would be fugitives for the rest of their lives. Never go home again. And I think all but one of them are innocent. I want to give them the chance to come back and clear their names."

"Of murder and mutiny?" Jones-Williams's eyebrows rose in disbelief. "They'll shoot them. They'll have no choice."

"I think the officer's father, who is a general, might push pretty hard to get the charge withdrawn."

"Really?" Jones-Williams still looked skeptical.

"A capital charge has to be pretty thoroughly proved," Joseph pointed out, "and the defendants given every opportunity to put their case."

The drone of an airplane broke the silence above, sounding like an angry insect. Automatically Joseph glanced upward as it made its way lower and sank toward the airfield, sputtering now and then.

Jones-Williams chewed his pipe stem a moment. "I'd have thought in this instance those two were rather the same. Their defense that the man was an ass, and a dangerous one at that, gives the prosecution their motive on a plate. Doesn't excuse shooting him, though, even to save their own lives. On that score they could get rid of half the officers we've got!"

"Thing is," Joseph went on thoughtfully, "General Northrup won't enjoy having the court-martial drag out and prove each point of his son's incompetence, and exactly how many men were maimed or killed because of it. Even the surgeon, Captain Cavan, soon to be V.C., felt no alternative but to put him on trial."

The plane landed at last, and Joseph felt his shoulders ease with relief that it was safe.

Jones-Williams took the pipe out of his mouth. "So what do you want from us? A lift as far as possible along the line to look for them?"

"That's exactly what I'd like. I realize it's only a chance I'll find them, but it's worth a try. You'd better see my authority." He fished in his pocket for the paper.

"What?"

Joseph smiled. "Well, I could be a deserter looking for a damn good start eastward myself!"

"No point. Your dog collar could be real or not, but at your age you could reasonably beg out anyway."

Joseph winced. "Depends how desperate we are. You won't have them in the R.F.C., but we have fourteen-year-olds in the army. Lied about their age, of course, but we know. Sooner or later they say something that gives them away." He stopped abruptly.

"That was a bit tactless of me," Jones-Williams said by way of apology. "Come on and I'll find you someone to take you up for a look, and drop you off as near to the Swiss border as you think you want." He turned and sauntered over toward the line of hangars beyond the smaller buildings of offices and control tower.

Joseph followed him, catching up quickly. He glanced once at the three planes drawn up on the strip, including the one just landed.

"Take you in something much bigger than those," Jones-Williams said cheerfully. "Two-seater. One of the observation planes. Keep low much of the time. Hedgehopping, we call it. D'you know how these fellows of yours went? Got a car or anything?"

"On foot, at least to begin with," Joseph replied.

"Won't have got far, then. Hey, Vine!" he called to a slender young man in R.F.C. uniform, goggles and scarf around his neck, flying jacket slung over his shoulder and helmet swinging from his hand.

"Yes, sir?" Vine paused a few yards away from them, more or less to attention.

"Chaplain here is from the army," Jones-Williams explained. "He's looking for a hand to find a few fellows gone AWOL. He thinks if they come back they'll have a chance of doing better than if they keep on running. Wouldn't like to take him along the lines a bit, would you?"

"Of course," Vine agreed obligingly, turning to look at Joseph curiously. "How far, Chaplain?"

"Until you find them. Or Switzerland," Jones-Williams said cheerfully. "Good. All set then." He turned to Joseph. "Come and have a cup of tea. Officers' mess is over there. We'll find you some decent goggles and a jacket. Chilly up there. Vine will come for you when he's all ready."

"Thank you." Joseph found himself off balance with the speed of the decision, but he could not afford to question it. He thanked Vine again, and followed Jones-Williams over to the low, rather rambling buildings at the side. He felt grateful now for time to prepare himself for the flight.

But all the imagination of his life was futile compared with the reality. First there was climbing up onto the wing and into the small seat and fastening the harness to hold him in. The engine was started with a tremendous roar, then a moment later the tiny, frail craft went racing over the grass, bumping on every tussock, before lifting off jerkily. The plane bucked slightly, catching the light wind and clearing the neighboring stand of trees by what felt like no more than a few feet.

It was an appalling sensation, being out of touch with the earth—and apparently completely out of control. Joseph felt he was a prisoner.

He was sitting behind the pilot. A lightweight machine gun—a Lewis gun, to be precise—was mounted beside him. He had been told cheerfully that it was just in case they should meet any opposition.

They seemed to veer around quite badly as they gained height. Joseph had the very alarming feeling that he could be pitched out any moment and find himself falling through the air. Was he high enough up that it would kill him outright? Or might he be left broken but alive? Why on earth could he not have left well enough alone and stayed on the ground?

Then there was the question of keeping his stomach in place.

They were a few hundred feet up now and steadying. He could see nothing but trees slightly below him. The airfield and control tower were somewhere over to the left.

He steeled himself to look down, afraid of an overpowering sense of vertigo, but below him and stretching into the distance he saw a landscape that took his breath away. There was a strip of desolation a few miles wide, ruined, it would seem, beyond recall. It was cratered with shell holes that steamed in the August warmth—or perhaps it was poison gas that curled yellow-white in the hollows.

Blasted tree trunks poked up here and there. The wreckage of vehicles and guns was easy to see by outline rather than any difference in color. Everything was gray-brown, leached of life. Shape also distinguished the corpses of men and horses, too many to count. From up here the sheer enormity of it was overwhelming. So many dead, enough men to populate cities, and all destroyed.

Faint sunlight gleamed on the watery surfaces of trenches in recognizably straight lines, zigzagged to block the lines of fire. Two long stretches were waterlogged, like some gray mire, dotted with corpses.

He could see men moving around, foreshortened, dun-colored like the clay. Up here it was ridiculous how anonymous they seemed, and yet he probably knew all of them. He understood what they were doing only because he knew; he had done it all himself: shoring up walls, carrying supplies, cleaning weapons. A few cars chugged slowly on pockmarked roads, sending little puffs of exhaust out behind them. Judith might be in one of them, seeming to crawl along compared with the crazy speed of the plane. Ambulances were easy to spot. Columns of men moved on foot, reinforcements going forward, wounded going back. It was also easy to see the field guns, the huts and tents, the dressing stations, and the first aid posts. Some of the humps in the ground he knew were dugouts.

The plane gained more altitude, and Joseph could see the German lines as well. He knew their trenches were deeper, their dugouts better organized—and better furnished, so he had heard. But the land was the same: shattered and poisoned. The men, such as he could see, were engaged in the same activities. They, too, when motionless, catching an hour or two of sleep, blended into the earth and became almost invisible.

The terrain was becoming less distinct as they climbed higher. Beyond, the green was visible again, in both directions: Trees had leaves; there were patches of grass. On toward the horizon to the south and west there were the dark scars of roads and railways, but they lay across cornfields and meadows, and soft, blurred patches of woodland. Here and there Joseph saw the silver curl of a river.

It was like looking at the track of a wound across the land, or the scorched path of shrapnel through flesh, leaving the rest oddly whole.

For three long, terrible years they had faced each other over those few thousand yards of ground, and killed—and killed—repeatedly. It was madness! In the silence up here with nothing but wind and sun and the shattering roar of the engine, it was so obvious he wanted to lean over and shout invectives at them. But of course no one could hear him. He might as well scream at an anthill.

They were moving east and south. He saw railway tracks and marshaling yards. He thought he recognized some of the features of the land, the curve of hill and river. He saw what he thought was Lille, but he was not sure how far they had come.

Half an hour passed in silence. He searched the sky nervously, but there were no other aircraft visible. The French lines below them looked the same as the British or Canadian: just gray mud, wreckage, what one could make out of men moving about the same midday duties.

When was Vine going to go low enough for him to have any idea if there were men moving eastward? So far they had followed the battle line southeast as it curved away from the advancing German army.

Had they not gone far enough yet? He had lost any sense of where they were. The ground was so far below he could barely make out the roads, let alone who was moving on them. Perhaps this was an idiotic cause anyway, and Jones-Williams had let him come only because he had no imaginable chance of succeeding.

He leaned forward and shouted at Vine, and as he turned for a moment, Joseph pointed downward.

Vine held out his hand, thumb up, and obediently swooped the plane low, hedgehopping, as Jones-Williams had called it. Details became sharper—roads, the colors of men, horses, and artillery—but Joseph saw nothing to indicate the presence of his eleven men. He thought they would have moved much farther eastward by now. They could have covered twenty or thirty miles a day with a little help—a lift here or there. They were all fairly fit and used to marching.

Suddenly and with absolutely no warning, the aircraft pitched and yawed like a tub in high seas. One minute the sky was above them, the next they rolled so the earth swung around, over their heads, then right and left wildly. Finally it fell away as they reared up and climbed steeply, racing toward the faint shreds of cloud, which were still far above.

Joseph thought he was going to fall out. Only the harness jerking violently on his body held him in. Bruised and shocked, he was sick over the side. They were still climbing. He clung onto the cockpit, knuckles white. Even yesterday, it had never occurred to him that he would die this way.

They swiveled around and dived, then climbed again. That was when Joseph saw them, black outlines against the sky like dragonflies, swooping and diving. They seemed angry, turning on each other, always going back again into the heart of the swarm. It was a great aerial dogfight, high above them, up almost to the thin layer of cloud.

Vine was keeping their plane lower, probably hoping that against the darker background of the fields and interlacing support trenches they would be almost invisible. The pilots in the dogfight would be concentrating on each other, looking for who was in their sights and who was on their tails.

The seconds seemed to stretch forever. They climbed a little. Joseph did not know why, but he assumed it would be to give them space to dive and evade if they were seen.

Joseph touched the Lewis gun experimentally. He was a noncombatant, a man who served the fighting soldiers, but did not possess a weapon himself. But if they were attacked now, not only Joseph's life but Vine's as well would depend upon Joseph shooting and doing it effectively. He did not even think of trying to find an escape from it.

The dogfight was still above them and only a short distance behind.

Vine put the aircraft into a climb again, trying to gain height in case they needed the speed of a dive to make a run for it.

From the whirling dance of the dogfight one plane exploded, red fire and black smoke staining the sky. The pieces of it plummeted downward. Another blossomed a long trail of smoke, smearing across the blue. Then it cartwheeled over and over, hideously slowly.

They were climbing again, then without warning another plane roared above them. It was probably fifty feet away, but seemed barely to miss them. It was so close Joseph could see the pilot's face for an instant—his head bent forward, his muscles tense. Then it was gone, swinging away and up again. On its tail was a red-winged triplane, guns blazing.

Vine suddenly swung wide also, and for a moment—there and then gone again—Joseph had the red-winged plane in his sights. Too quickly it was away and there was nothing there but blue sky.

He was dizzy as they soared up, and he realized there had been another plane above and behind them. Bullets ripped through the very edge of the wing as they slithered sideways, around, and then up even higher.

Now there were planes all around them. The maelstrom had descended. More bullets streamed overhead and struck the tail of a plane above them.

Joseph was galvanized into movement at last and gripped the gun. Next time he saw anything in his sights, if it was German he would fire. If he had long enough to be sure.

The need came before he expected. Vine swung the plane around, over in a roll too close to a somersault, pitching Joseph almost over the side. He straightened up, bruised, heart pounding, and raised the barrel of the gun. It turned easily. He found he could follow the course of a plane for seconds. Long enough to hit it.

Except that Vine never kept them still. They surged and slithered across the sky. One minute Joseph was staring at fields, the next at gray trenches, then the sky. Other planes crossed his vision and by the time he was certain they were German, they were gone.

Then bullets tore the wing again, and the red triplane was there.

Joseph squeezed the trigger and bullets exploded out of the muzzle. They just caught the very edge of the red tail. An instant later it was gone.

Joseph sat hugging the gun, his heart pounding. It was the first time he had ever fired a gun at a human being, intending to kill. It was an extraordinary feeling, decisive, shameful, exhilarating. He had passed a certain barrier. How much did it matter that he had not hit the man? The wind rushed past him as the plane banked.

They were in the middle of a swarm, like angry hornets, engines roaring, bullets stuttering. Another plane whirled and cartwheeled, spiraling down with a black plume of smoke trailing behind it. He saw it strike the ground and explode in flames. He realized only then that he had not noticed whether it was British or German, only that the pilot would die.

There was another rattle of bullets. Several struck so close to him that he flung himself backward with a jolt, mouth dry, gasping to regain his breath. Then he grabbed the gun savagely. When the next German plane came into his sights, he let off a stream of fire in return and was elated to see the tracer bullets strike the back part of the fuselage. It tipped the balance wildly, the plane yawing like a sailboat in a bad sea.

Vine raced after the damaged plane, turning wide to give Joseph another shot. He hesitated, almost lost aim, then at the last second shot at the engine. It was a senseless distinction from shooting at the man. If the plane went down the pilot would be killed anyway. The difference was a sophistry.

On it went, almost like a three-dimensional dance. Up here it was noise, engines, bullets, wind ice-cold on the skin. They wheeled and climbed, juddered on the top of the ascent, careened sideways, swooped, guns chattering. Then they increased speed until the wind was screaming in their ears and the ground seemed to race up toward them. They struggled to break out of the dive and bank around again, caught the enemy in the gunsights and shot.

He lost all count of time. He shot in short, rapid bursts at other planes with no idea if he hit them or not. He was hardly even aware of it at first when the bullets struck them. It was even a moment or two before he realized with mind-numbing clarity that the smoke was their own. This long dive was not going to end in the swift turn and banking up into a climb again.

The ground came closer and closer. He could see trees clearly and a farmyard. Then he realized Vine was making for the fields beyond. He was going to try to land.

The seconds were endless. Joseph had no doubt that he was going to die in seconds now. He had expected to die in Ypres, certainly, but this was France now, a summer cornfield ready for harvest. Almost like Cambridgeshire. Almost as good as home.

Now he had no more time to do better, try harder. Soon he would know the truth, whatever it was. He ached with a blinding pain for what he left behind.

They leveled out, lower than the trees. There was nothing but fields ahead. Something tore at the wheels, pitching him forward so violently for a moment he could think of nothing but the weight of the blow. He felt bruised in every part of his body. They were still moving, tearing through the corn, ripping a path in it toward the little copse of trees.

Then everything was still, eerily silent after the noise.

He heard Vine's voice shouting: "Get out! Run! Reavley, get out!" There was fear in it—high, sharp-pitched fear.

He was jerked out of his stupor. Awkwardly, oblivious of the pain, he scrambled to release himself and get out of the cockpit. He clambered over the edge and dropped into the corn. The black smoke was still pouring out of the engine.

He staggered to his feet. He must get as far away as possible. Then after a couple of steps he turned. Vine was still in his seat.

"Come on!" Joseph yelled at him. "Get out!"

"Can't!" Vine called back. "Got a bust leg, old boy. Get going while you can. This thing could go up any moment. Good luck."

Whatever it cost, Joseph knew he must try to get Vine out. He could not run for his own safety and leave the pilot to be burned to death. Vine was only here because of him. He stumbled back the few steps, climbed up onto the wing and over to the cockpit.

"Get out!" Vine said sharply. "Don't you understand? I can't stand anyway. My whole right leg is shot up. Go on!"

"I'm used to carrying wounded men," Joseph told him. "It's mostly what I do. Get that harness off and grab hold of me. This is not that much different from a mud crater, and God knows how many men I've pulled out of those."

Vine hesitated.

"Come on, damn it!" Joseph shouted suddenly. "Don't be a bloody hero. You'll get us both killed! Hold on to me!"

Vine unfastened his harness and gripped Joseph. His face was white under the smears from the smoke, and there was a sheen of sweat on it.

Joseph looked down to see the blood-soaked leg, wanting to cause as little extra pain as possible. He was hideously aware that any moment the engine could catch fire and the fuel tanks explode, killing them both. He took hold of Vine and tried to heave him up. It was far more difficult than he had supposed. He knew he was hurting Vine, but the only alternative was to run and let him die. He could feel his own muscles tearing with the strain, and the sweat of fear running down his body.

Vine rose a little. The seconds were ticking by. Smoke billowed out, sharp, hot, and acrid.

Joseph pulled again, putting all his strength and weight behind it. Please God he could do it! He must!

With a bitten-off scream of pain, Vine came out of the cockpit. Joseph collapsed backward onto the wing and slid down it to land on his back in the corn, Vine on top of him.

Then he felt hands pulling him and heard voices. For a moment he did not understand. Then with blessed relief he realized people had come from the farmhouse and he was being lifted up. He and Vine were half-dragged, half-carried across the ripe ears of corn, their stalks catching and poking at them.

They were seventy yards away when the plane exploded. The blast knocked all of them off their feet, scorching them with its heat.

Joseph sat up slowly, at first his vision obscured by the tops of the corn. Then he saw the flames and the black column of smoke going up.

"Thanks," Vine said hoarsely from beside him. "Thanks, old fellow. Wouldn't have liked to be in that. Bit of a mess, eh?" His face revealed a pain so intense he could barely keep consciousness.

A couple of yards away an elderly man rose to his feet, muttering expletives in French. He was gray-haired, his shoulders sagging, and the stubble of a beard darkened his chin. He shook his head and looked re-gretfully at the scorched and trampled field, then he turned to Vine and apologized in broken English.

Vine was lying on his back. He looked crumpled, smaller. His eyes were closed, and it seemed as if the agony of his leg had finally overtaken him.

A broad-shouldered, handsome woman—possibly the old man's daughter—staggered to her feet, yanking her skirt out of her way impa-tiently. She was clicking with her tongue, her face anxious.

Joseph spoke to her in French. "We need to stop the bleeding, and see if we can splint where the bone is broken," he said urgently. "I expect there'll be an army hospital not far away, but he'll die if we don't do that much immediately."

"Yes, yes," she agreed. "It looks bad. Poor man. And you, are you all right?"

"Fine. Only a few bruises," Joseph replied. "He made a good job of landing. Sorry about your field."

She waved her hand, as if dismissing the subject. Then she looked up in the sky where they could just make out the tangle of planes wheeling around each other. "Circus of the Red Baron!" she said disgustedly. "I suppose you are lucky to get out alive."

Joseph remembered the red triplane. He had actually taken a shot at it himself! Even hit a piece off the tail. Manfred von Richthofen—but he would have time to think about that later. Now they must look after Vine.

It was an arduous job, but one at least that Joseph was accustomed to. With the help of the French farmer and his daughter—as she proved to be—they splinted Vine's leg and then stopped the worst of the bleeding, at least for the moment. Then they put him in the one decent wagon left and hitched up the ancient horse.

It took them two hours of driving along mud-rutted lanes to get Vine to the French military field hospital behind the lines, but he was still alive—and conscious again—by then. The surgeon looked at the leg and said he thought he could save it.

"Thanks," Vine said when he was alone with Joseph, after the farmer and his wife had gone. He was lying in a hospital cot, a sheet up to his neck. "Good luck in finding your fellows. Tell them from me they'd better come home and face the music. They owe you that."

"They owe *you* that," Joseph corrected him. "I'll be sure to tell them so. Good luck."

Vine's face tightened in momentary pain, then relaxed again into a smile. "I expected you to say 'God be with you, my son,' or something of that sort."

"God be with you," Joseph replied wryly. "I trust God. It's the luck I'm a bit dubious about!"

He went to the commanding officer of the section, no more than half a mile from the hospital.

"We'll find someone to give you a lift back to your regiment, Captain," he said in excellent English. He was a slender man with a dark, intelligent face. He had an air of weary resignation, but he was unfailingly courteous.

"Thank you, sir," Joseph replied, also in English. "But I was making my way to Switzerland, or at least in that direction." And he explained his errand, showing him Colonel Hook's letter as proof. Without it he could hardly expect anyone to think him other than a deserter himself. He said that the men were wanted for the murder of Major Northrup, a grossly incompetent officer, but it was his belief that only one of them was actually guilty. He skirted around the issue of mutiny, aware that it might be a sensitive subject for a French officer, especially if introduced by an Englishman. He had no idea what this particular man's sympathies were. He was aware of sounding rather stilted. Then he saw the smile on the Frenchman's face and appreciated that he had understood Joseph rather better than he had intended. But to apologize would make it worse. Instead he simply smiled back.

"So you are going east after the eleven men?" the Frenchman asked.

"Yes, sir."

"Let me give you a good dinner and a night's rest first," he offered. "Then if you wish to proceed, may I suggest that you change your attire? You appear to speak French at least adequately." He pulled a slight face. "Not enough to pass for French, unless you claim to come from some other region—Marseille, perhaps?" His tone suggested that to him Marseille was barbaric, barely French at all. "Have you any other language? German, perhaps?"

"Yes. And rather better," Joseph admitted. "But I don't think passing for German would be very clever."

The Frenchman gave a particularly Gallic shrug.

"Of course not. I was thinking German-speaking Swiss," he said. "That would account for your accent. A Protestant priest, Swiss, and therefore neutral."

The idea was very appealing, except that if he were captured out of uniform he could be shot as a spy rather than held as a prisoner of war. He pointed that out.

"Indeed," the Frenchman conceded. "I was considering your chances of success in traveling unnoticed, and finding your eleven men. We can get you some suitable clothes. Stay as far back as the supply trenches, or even farther, and you are unlikely to be taken by Germans. Do what you think best."

When Joseph set out in the French staff car the following morning he was well fed, by trench catering standards, and well rested.

It was not raining and the late summer air was soft and bright. He was so accustomed to the smells of overcrowding, open latrines, and too many dead to bury that he barely noticed them. He thought instead of the sun on his face and—at least to the south—a land that held some echo of its prewar glory. Farms were ruined, villages bombed and burned as everywhere else, but on the horizon there were trees and the hills rolled away green in the distance. He could even see cattle grazing here and there when he veered farther away from the trenches and the incessant sound of guns.

Just as in his own lines on the Ypres Salient, there were men returning to battle after brief leave, often because of injury. There were columns of wounded making their painful way back to field dressing stations, and there were supply trucks, munitions, and ambulances on the crowded roads.

The car took him another thirty miles. After that he had to walk. He stopped only to ask directions or seek information of anyone who might have seen a group of men together who were going along the lines rather than back or forward to fight. He was appalled how easily it came to him to invent lies to explain his errand. The only part that did not vary was his physical descriptions of the most noticeable of the men, particularly Morel, the one he was sure could speak French fluently and would be the natural leader.

He slept where he could. Men were unfailingly willing to share the meager rations they had. Any thanks he offered were inadequate, but gratitude was all he had.

When he finally found someone who seemed to have seen them the day before, he was dubious. The description he received in return could have been almost any soldier.

That evening the sighting was much more positive. Crouching in one of the rear support trenches, Joseph listened to a group of French soldiers describe someone lost and badly frightened. Apparently the man had admitted considering mutiny, which they sympathized with wholeheartedly. The man had divulged that he had an idiot for an officer, that he had rebelled against his orders. As a result he was now a fugitive, cut off from his friends and all his connections with home. Worst of all, even if they won the war, he could probably never go back. He had stuck with it for three years, gone through hell, and one stupid useless officer had ruined it all.

Since Joseph was pretending to be Swiss, they did not think he had any serious interest in the issue, so they were prepared to talk about it to him, and he did not disabuse them. He set out again with quickened hope and moved more rapidly than before, believing the escaped men were not far ahead of him.

Directly to the east was the German border. He was past the field of Verdun, where 350,000 Frenchmen had been killed or wounded the previous year, and still the battle raged on. Joseph had no idea how many Austrians and Germans had been killed there, but he knew it must be at least as many. The Russian Front he had only heard about, and the Italian, and the Turkish fronts, and the arenas of war in Africa, Egypt, Palestine, and Mesopotamia. He refused to think about them. All he could do was this one tiny contribution: give Morel and the other fugitives a chance to come back. Even that might be beyond him, but trying had become almost as important for his own sanity as for their survival. It would mean that in this endless destruction there was something within his control.

In the end, he found them in the ruins of a bombed village, so little of which was left that even its name was obliterated. He had followed a rumor: a joke about someone's French being notoriously bad. Some young men, worn out and with several days' beard, had asked for directions to a farm where he and his friends could sleep. Only he had mispronounced it as *une femme*—a woman. He had met with much bawdy laughter, and remarks about all ten of them.

The joke was told with pity for their desperation but then everyone was desperate. It was not that they were unwilling to share what they had, but they too had nothing. They were gaunt-faced, exhausted young men with eyes that stared beyond the mark, seeing a hell they would never forget. The images lay inside the eyelids, waking or sleeping, and coiled into the brain, pounding in the blood. The sound of guns never stopped; even in the rare silences it was still there in the head.

The escapees saw Joseph at the same moment he saw them. He knew Morel instantly, even in silhouette against the sunlight on a stretch of wall still standing. He was thin, and his uniform was filthy—perhaps on purpose to disguise its markings. But the way he stood was characteristic. Even now the grace had not left him, the natural elegance he had always had. Trotter and Snowy Nunn were sitting on piles of rubble. Snowy was drinking from a tin can. The others were out of sight, perhaps asleep somewhere.

Morel saw Joseph and froze, his hand on his revolver.

Joseph stood motionless. He did not have a weapon, but even if he had he would not have used it. He took a step forward experimentally.

Morel raised the revolver.

"That would change everything," Joseph said quietly.

Morel stiffened, recognizing him now, even though Joseph was wearing borrowed French civilian clothes, and Morel was facing the sun.

"Would it?" he asked. "Who would know?"

Joseph stood still. "You would," he answered. "You might forget shooting me, although I doubt it. In hot blood now, it might be all right, but peace will come eventually, of one sort or another. . . ."

"I can't count the number of men I've killed," Morel told him wearily. "Most of them were perfectly decent Germans doing no more than I'm doing, fighting for their country. What choice do they have, any more than I?"

"None," Joseph said honestly. "I expect it hurts them just as it does most of us. But you know me. I'm part of your peacetime as well as your war. But even if you can live with it, can Snowy? Can he ever go back to St. Giles, to his family and his land, if you kill me?"

Morel gave a sharp burst of laughter. "What the hell is so special about you? You're ridiculous!" There was deep, wounding pain in his face. "A million Englishmen are dead. God alone knows how many French and German. Why should it make any difference if you're dead, too?"

"Not *because* it's me," Joseph corrected him. "As you say, that's nothing. It's the circumstance. To shoot an armed soldier is one thing, albeit he's a mirror image of yourself. To shoot your priest is different. Ask Snowy."

Snowy rose to his feet slowly, the sun catching his pale hair. He looked older, his young face etched with tragedy.

"Stand still," Morel ordered him.

"Or what?" Snowy asked, lifting his shoulders and letting them drop. "You'll shoot me, too?"

"Because I damn well ordered you to!" Morel snapped.

"What's the matter, Captain?" Snowy said quite casually, although his voice shook a little. "Don't you approve of men thinking for themselves when it's a moral issue? What's that, then—mutiny?" He took a step forward, then another.

Morel raised the gun a little higher. "Don't be stupid!" he warned. "Whatever he's come for, he hasn't deserted. He's here to get us to go back, and you know as well as I that if we do, we'll be court-martialed and shot. There's no way on earth they'll let us get away with killing Northrup."

"Did you kill him?" Joseph asked, doubt in his voice.

"No, I didn't!" Morel said with sudden anger. "But it's academic. I arranged the mock trial and I was in charge. It's my responsibility. That's how the army works. It's how life works. You want to lead, then you take the glory—*and* the blame."

"True," Joseph conceded. "To do less is without honor. Did Snowy shoot Northrup? Did Trotter?"

Trotter was still sitting in the rubble, staring from one to the other of them. There was a bandage on his arm, but it had bled through.

"No," Morel replied.

"Are you sure?"

"Yes, I'm bloody well sure!"

"How can you be?" Joseph persisted.

"Don't be idiotic!" Morel's patience was shadow thin. "You know Snowy. He fires high at the bloody Germans. He couldn't kill anyone except by accident."

"And Trotter?" Joseph's voice wobbled a little with fear of failure, now that success might be so close. It was hot here in the sun, and quiet. They were miles from the guns; they could hear them only in the distance.

"Are you sure about him?"

"Yes, I am! It was Geddes who killed Northrup."

"Why?" He had to say something, and he wanted to know, to be certain.

"I've no idea, and I don't care," Morel replied, still holding the gun steady. "And the court-martial won't care, either. Don't soil your dog collar by lying, Captain. I'd rather take my chances in Switzerland than come back and be shot by my own. Can't go home anyway, so it's all pointless."

Snowy took another step toward Joseph.

"Stand still!" Morel snapped at him, jerking the gun toward him. "Think, Snowy! It might be all very heroic and honest to go back, but if they shoot us, what do you think that's going to do to morale, eh? Do you want a real mutiny? All along the line?" His voice caught and there were tears on his face. "The Germans would make mincemeat of us— those of us that are left of the Cambridgeshires. Is that what you want?"

Snowy froze.

"They'll shoot Cavan anyway," Joseph pointed out.

It was so quiet now that they could hear birds singing in the summer sky.

Snowy Nunn walked slowly over to Joseph. Not once did he turn to look at Morel. "I want to go home," he said simply.

Joseph waited.

Morel put the revolver away. "They'll shoot all of us," he said again, but there was an exhaustion in his voice so intense that pity gripped Joseph like a vise.

"General Northrup wants to reduce the charge," Joseph told him, his own voice gravelly, slipping out of control. He explained what the general had said.

Morel shrugged. "It won't make any difference. What a bloody fiasco. We must be the stupidest people on earth. You won't get Geddes back so easily, supposing you ever find him."

"Where are the rest of you?" Joseph asked.

"I'll tell them what you said," Morel smiled bleakly. "They can make up their own minds. You go for Geddes; he's the one you want."

"Did he go on to Switzerland?"

"That was his intention." Morel hesitated. "Look, Reavley, you're a decent man, but you haven't a ghost of a chance of bringing Geddes back. You aren't even armed, for God's sake! He'll shoot you if he has to, to get you off his trail. I'll come with you. That way you've a chance."

"No—" Joseph began.

"Snowy and Trotter can put your arguments to the others," Morel cut across him bluntly, all the old respect and acknowledgment of seniority gone. "They'll get back. You'll give your word, won't you?" He turned to Snowy, Nunn, then to Trotter.

"Yes, sir," Snowy said immediately. Trotter agreed also, rising stiffly to his feet at last. Only then did Joseph notice that his left leg was hurt as well.

"I'd give you my gun," Morel went on, looking at Joseph. "But I don't suppose you would know which end to fire."

"Actually I nicked the tail of the plane of the Red Baron," Joseph said with some dignity.

Morel stared at him.

"From another plane, with a Lewis gun," Joseph added. "How do you suppose I got here so quickly?"

Morel began to laugh. It was a wild, hysterical sound, very nearly out of control.

Joseph came to a decision immediately, although possibly not a sensible one. He stuck out his arm, pointing.

"Right. Snowy, you and Trotter go and find the others, or as many of them as you can. Get them back to the regiment. Make sure you give yourself up and aren't taken!" He looked at Snowy closely, his eyes hard. "Do you understand? It could all rest on that!"

" 'Course Oi understand, sir," Snowy said gravely. "It shouldn't be too bad. Nobody'll be looking for us going the other way. Good luck, Chaplain. But you watch for Geddes, sir. He's a hard one, an' he's got nothing to lose now."

Joseph and Morel turned south and made the best time they could. Joseph managed to persuade Morel to change clothes with a middle-aged man invalided out of the army and now mending shoes in a small shop. They continued with Morel looking less like a British officer on the run. Joseph also convinced him to speak German, and say that he too was Swiss, heading back home. No one was interested enough to challenge them seriously. They all had their own troubles.

Joseph and Morel were tired and hungry. They were within thirty miles of the Swiss border when the trail they had been following petered out. The village they arrived at had not suffered as much as many, and they were treated with courtesy, although less than the profound kindness that Joseph had received earlier when he was still in uniform. The people were war-weary, robbed by circumstance of almost everything they had. Still, they faced the possibility of invasion and occupation, and the loss of the only thing they still possessed: the physical freedom to be themselves—Frenchmen who owned their own land, blasted and burned as it was. Joseph did not blame them if they were less than wholehearted friends to men going back to a land that chose to fight on neither side.

"Can't find any trace of him," Morel said despondently.

Joseph's feet hurt and his back ached. The late August sun was hot, and he was thirsty enough to have been grateful for even rainwater in a clean ditch. "No," he said honestly. "I think we've lost him."

Morel sat down on the grass, waiting silently for Joseph to make a decision. The sunlight on Morel's face showed not only the ravages of emotion but the physical exhaustion that had almost depleted him. He was so thin his bones looked sharp beneath his skin.

Joseph, too tired to remain standing, sat down in the dust. He felt empty. He had not allowed himself to plan against the eventuality of losing Geddes. Consequently, he had no reserve strategy now to fall back on. If he had been alone he would have prayed, but it would be awkward in front of Morel, who had no faith left in God.

Was Joseph any better? What did faith mean? That everything would turn out right in the end? What was the end? Could any overriding plan one day make sense of it all?

"I don't think he's gone to Switzerland after all," Morel said, interrupting Joseph's thoughts. "If he were just a deserter, it would be one thing; but he's wanted for murdering an officer, and that's quite different. Any Englishman there, and maybe even many of the Swiss, would turn him in anyway."

"Well, the French certainly would," Joseph agreed. "No question."

"Yes, but the Germans wouldn't," Morel pointed out.

For a moment Joseph barely breathed. "Through the lines?" he said softly, understanding at last.

"Why not?" Morel looked back at him, his dark eyes steady. "The ultimate escape."

Joseph climbed to his feet slowly and dug his hands into his pockets. He stared beyond the lines in the distance, at the German trenches beyond. "Perhaps," he murmured. "You speak German. So do I."

Morel rose to his feet also, his eyes wide. "Really?"

Joseph knew what he was asking. "I want him back, to get the rest of you off. Especially Cavan. Are you game to try?"

"Of course," Morel responded. He gave an abrupt little laugh. "What use would you be by yourself?"

ELEVEN

As darkness came, Joseph grew more and more apprehensive. Crossing the lines was likely to get them killed. Maybe Geddes was already dead and they would never know why he put live ammunition in his gun and deliberately betrayed his fellows by executing Northrup instead of merely frightening him.

The only plan they could form was to lie low until the first attack, then join with the French soldiers going over the top, keeping as far from the lights as possible. Become separated from the group as if by the fighting, and in the general turmoil press farther and farther forward. At least no one would be likely to suspect anyone coming up from behind and going on over.

The more Joseph thought of it, the more suicidal it seemed. But was it worse cowardice still to back out now and simply go home with Morel and hope he was believed.

"We should go now." Morel's voice came out of the darkness. "We might need all night to work our way into the French force and join them. We don't know when they'll go over. I don't suppose they know, poor sods."

That was the decision made. To argue now would look like fear. At the very least it would leave Morel to go alone, and that was unthinkable.

"Right," he said as if Morel were in charge. Perhaps he should be. Joseph had been into no-man's-land more often than he could count, but as a chaplain, in order to pick up whatever bodies he could find and help the wounded. After the worst night's fighting he had been as far as twenty yards from the German trenches, but he had never faced an enemy soldier in anger, never fired a gun at a man.

"Are you all right, Chaplain?" Morel asked, the use of his occupational title betraying the uncertainty he felt of Joseph's mettle.

"Yes, I'm right behind you," Joseph said. "If we go over just behind the first attack, we can look like stretcher bearers. Attract less attention, and go as far forward as possible."

"Won't fool anyone for long," Morel replied over his shoulder. "But maybe by the time they realize it we'll be through. Just hope they don't take us for deserters."

"Deserters usually go the other way," Joseph pointed out. "That's what makes Geddes clever."

"He's a clever bastard, all right," Morel agreed dourly, his voice low in the darkness in spite of the guns in the distance. He did not add anything more, and they went the rest of the way in silence, dropping down the slight slope toward the field dressing station a thousand yards away.

They curved around it, keeping as far away from the light as possible. Joseph, with his priest's collar, did not need to account for his presence. For Morel it was harder. He had no rifle, only the revolver.

All around them were French soldiers, their outlines in the near dark little different from the men of the Cambridgeshires: helmets smooth, the occasional peaked cap, rifles stark. Their voices were muted, a little harsh with tension. Many smoked and the smell of Gauloises was different from Woodbine, but the long, slightly sour jokes were similar: self-mocking, the laughter quick.

There was coffee in their own version of a Dixie can. It was offered generously and both Joseph and Morel took it. It was bitter as gall.

A little over an hour later the order was given to advance, and without guns they rose with the other men and charged forward. Like the Ypres Salient with which Joseph was familiar, no-man's-land was desolate, but drier than the thick Flanders clay. There was the same greasy film of chemical residue from shelling. The earth was strewn with the wreckage of guns and half-sunken vehicles. The same stench of decaying corpses filled the nose and mouth. Drowned men, bloated and inhuman, rose to the surface of water-filled craters when they were disturbed.

They moved forward as fast as possible, struggling in the mud, crouching low to avoid the return fire of the enemy. Star shells lit the sky, rose high and bright, then faded away again. The noise of guns was everywhere, and now and then the dull *whoomph* as a shell sent earth and mud flying up only to fall, crushing and burying everything it landed on.

There was a surge forward again. There were men running all around Joseph, bent forward, flailing in the mud. Every now and then one would stumble and fall. Sometimes they got up again, sometimes not. Instinct and long habit made him want to go back and see if he could help. Once he stopped and Morel lunged at him, half dragging him forward, all but wrenching his arm out of its socket.

They were far closer to the Germans now. When the flares went up they were clearly visible running and firing. Joseph realized with sudden, stomach-jarring horror that in a few moments he would be fighting for his life. He would have to kill or be killed, and he had no idea how to do it. He was not a soldier, he was only playing at it—wearing the uniform, eating the food, sharing the grief and the hardship, but never doing the fighting, never seeing the purpose for which a soldier lived and died.

Ahead of him a figure stumbled and fell forward into the mud. Automatically Joseph stopped and knelt beside him, almost tripping Morel in the process.

"Are you hurt?" Joseph shouted in French at the man on the ground. He tried to turn the man to see, and realized his chest was torn away.

"Come on!" Morel lunged at him to pull him up.

Joseph tore the rifle out of the dead man's hands. *"Merci, mon brave!"* he said briefly. He took the ammunition belt as well, putting it on with clumsy fingers as he stood up again. *"Pardon,"* he added.

"Get on with it!" Morel yelled at him. "We've got more pressing things to do than get shot or bayoneted here. We've got to get that son of a bitch back and clear the rest of us!"

Joseph moved forward, following on Morel's heels. He had grown up in the country. He had no pleasure in shooting, but he knew how. He could understand overwhelmingly the ordinary young soldier's desire to aim wide rather than at a living man.

The next moment they were almost at the German trenches. The noise was indescribable: gunfire, the scream of shells and the roar of explosions, shrapnel flying—all alternating between darkness and glare.

Suddenly there was a man in front of Joseph. He saw the light on the blade of bayonet and in trying to avoid it he slipped in the mud and staggered forward. It was all that saved him from having his stomach ripped open. Immediately there was someone else in front of him. He saw the high point in the center of the helmet, and lifted his rifle to fire. The man fell, but he did not know if it was he who had shot him, or someone else. There seemed to be gunfire everywhere.

He plowed forward, sliding into the trench and running along it toward the supply line leading backward. He shouted in German at Morel to follow him.

The trench was deeper than he had expected, and drier. It startled him and he felt both ashamed and resentful. It was several minutes before he realized that he needed to change identity. Now he must be German. Being covered in mud was an advantage. He threw the gun away and looked around for a wounded man, any wounded man, to make it look as if he were helping.

Where the devil was Morel? There was no time to go back and look for him. What if in those last few seconds he had been shot? What if he was lying wounded, maybe bleeding to death just beyond the parapet, while Joseph was pretending to be a German soldier and running for the supply trench?

He turned back just in time to see Morel fall over the parapet and raise his gun to fire at him.

He froze. It was the final absurdity. They had made it, and were going to shoot each other! He started to laugh, crazily, idiotically.

Morel lowered the gun and came toward him. "Chaplain, are you all right?" he asked sharply.

"In German!" Joseph snapped back at him, using that language for the command. "Are you badly hurt?" he went on.

"I'm not . . ." Morel began, then as a German corporal came around the corner of the trench he doubled over and all but collapsed in Joseph's arms.

Joseph took his weight with difficulty. "It's all right, I've got you," he said in German. "I'll take you back to the dressing station. Here!" He half-lifted Morel over his shoulder and, ignoring the corporal, set out along the supply trench.

"Can you manage?" the corporal called after him.

"Yes, thank you," Joseph answered. "I'll carry him to the surgeon, then I'll be back."

Morel muttered something into his ear, but he did not catch enough of it to make sense.

Joseph kept his head down, easing Morel's weight higher—both because it was easier to walk, and because it allowed him to hide most of his face without arousing suspicion. He hurried, as if Morel were bleeding to death and he had to get him out of the range of fire and then attend to him.

He passed other people: stretcher bearers, medical aides, even another priest. There was enough noise from gunfire to make conversation difficult and everyone had their own duties. Even so, there were more offers of help, which he refused.

It was eerily like a mirror image of the British trenches he was so used to where he knew every yard, every bend and turn, every rise to stumble over or pothole to turn your ankle in. He knew every ledge and shallow dugout where a man could curl up and snatch an hour of sleep.

These trenches were deeper, drier. He passed a dugout with electric lights. It was harder going out into the darkness again. Morel was growing very heavy.

Suddenly there were two figures black in the gloom ahead of him, talking softly in German. Cigarette ends burned brightly for an instant, then disappeared.

Suddenly panic seized him and he slithered to a stop. Morel dropped over his shoulders to land in the mud, cursing roundly, but having remembered to do it in German.

"Bless you," Joseph replied. "Are you hurt?"

"Bruised to hell." Morel stood up slowly, wincing. "You might have warned me."

"Geddes," Joseph whispered, pulling Morel away from the men. "Which way?"

Morel looked around carefully. "There." He pointed forward. "He's getting away from the lines as fast as possible."

"Does he speak any German? He must, or he wouldn't dare come through."

"Picked up some, but he won't want to put it to the test this close to the firing line." Morel started along the trench again and Joseph caught up with him, moving swiftly now.

They kept out of sight as much as possible, but always as if priests ministering to the wounded. Reluctantly, Morel had gotten rid of his gun also. It was too dangerous to keep if he wanted to maintain his disguise.

By dawn they were two or three miles behind the lines. The light came early in a clear sky, which held only a few shreds of gray cloud, lit from beneath with pale brilliance. It showed a land shattered by war. Trees were splintered, their naked trunks leafless, some scarred black by fire. Farmhouses were roofless, walls fallen away. Fields were scoured up, crops ruined.

Joseph glanced at Morel but did not speak. It was time he thought more clearly. Now they were through the German lines they needed to plan, and first to deduce what Geddes would have done.

"Change clothes," Joseph said slowly, thinking aloud. "Eat. More important, drink. Water would do, anything clean. Need strength." He imagined Geddes giddy with freedom, but so tired he could barely stand, and knowing he was a fugitive who did not even speak the language and understood very little of it. "Might have to fight later," he went on. "Need a safe place to rest first. Exhausted now, and need to plan."

Morel was staring at him, frowning. "We have to find Geddes," he said awkwardly, his face twisted with sudden and startling pity, so deep it gave him pain.

Joseph saw it and it took him by surprise. Morel had misunderstood, thinking he was speaking of himself. The pity was for him, and perhaps for what he had once been, in another age, in Cambridge. He realized something would be broken between them if he said the wrong thing now. The emotion must be acknowledged, then put away as if it had never happened. He looked over toward the fields and the road, away from Morel's eyes. "You know him better than I do," he went on, as if considering deeply. "What do you think would be his first priority?"

Morel answered after only a moment's hesitation, and he kept his voice very nearly expressionless, as if he had known what Joseph meant from the beginning. "As far from the lines as possible," he said, relief making his voice a little high. "He's not a coward, but he wouldn't look for trouble. He's strong. He grew up in the country. If any man knows how to survive on the land, he does."

Joseph turned to look at him for a moment, then at the fields again.

"I know." Morel lowered his voice, almost as if in the presence of the dead. "It looks pretty bad, doesn't it? I should think if there's anything to eat in that, the locals will have had it. Turnips, wild berries, even roots, nettles. God! What a . . ." His voice caught. "I don't know. I haven't got a word for it. *Tragedy* doesn't seem big enough." He pushed his hands into his pockets. "If one man with the potential to be great is brought to his knees by a single weakness, we call it tragedy. We haven't got a word for an entire continent committing suicide."

"It's mutilation, not death yet," Joseph said softly, willing himself to believe it.

"Isn't it?" There was little hope in Morel's face.

Joseph started forward. "Let's see if anyone's encountered Geddes."

They walked in silence for more than a mile. They passed only one person: an ancient man leading a plow horse, a dog at his heels.

Then Joseph picked up the conversation. "What are we going to say? I should be able to make them believe I'm a priest. And that I'm nearly forty. They'll believe I'm that old."

Morel gave him a wry look. He was in his mid-twenties, but he looked gaunt and there were deep lines in his face. "Or more," he said drily. "But so are plenty of fighting men. I'd better think of something, and before we reach that farm." He gestured toward a group of buildings perhaps half a mile away. One side was black from fire.

"The simplest is best," Joseph answered, having already given the matter some consideration. "You are a priest also."

"What happened to my collar?" Morel asked the obvious. "German priests wear them, too."

"Swiss," Joseph corrected him. "Your accent isn't good enough for a native. You were helping someone and got blood all over it. You could wash yourself, but your collar and tunic were ruined. Don't forget the tunic, nobody gets blood only on their collar. They'll know you're lying. Another tunic is no problem from a dead man, but he wouldn't have a priest's collar. You know enough from your prewar studies of biblical languages to pass as long as you don't try to conduct a service."

Morel smiled. "You lie better than I expected."

"Thank you!" Joseph said sarcastically. "Geddes won't get away with that. So what would you do in his place?"

The farm was only a hundred yards away now. It was dilapidated, mended with old boards and clearly whatever had come to hand. There obviously had been no glass to replace the shattered windows, and perhaps no putty either. It must take either courage or desperation for the inhabitants to have remained here.

"He doesn't have more than a few words of German," Morel said dubiously. "But he's a fly bastard. He'll have thought of something."

"If you don't understand, best to pretend you can't hear," Joseph observed. "Maybe he'll pretend to be shell-shocked and deaf."

Morel looked at him with a flash of respect, but he said nothing. They were at the entrance to the farmyard. An elderly woman was putting out kitchen scraps for a few scrawny chickens. She was raw-boned and thin, her face seamed with grief. She looked up at them with alarm.

Joseph smiled at her. "Bless you, mother," he said quietly in German. "Can you spare us a little clean water to drink?"

She saw his collar, and the fear melted out of her eyes. Joseph was ashamed at the ease of the deception. "Of course," she answered him, only glancing at Morel. "And food? Are you hungry?" That was a gracious formality. Of course they were hungry. Everyone was hungry.

Joseph hesitated. Which was worse—to take her food or to insult her by implying that she had too little to give away?

"Come," she directed, and led them into the farmhouse kitchen. It was stone-floored, with heavy wooden rafters across the ceiling from which in better times there would have been a flitch of bacon and strings of onions, as well as the few dried herbs there were now. Being late August there was no need to heat the room, and she had allowed all but the embers to go out in the big black range. She had probably been going to eat whatever she had cold. Now she opened up the door of the range and prepared to put a small piece of wood inside.

"It is hot walking," Joseph said quickly. "Pastor Morel and I would both be grateful for cold water, if that is possible? My name is Josef..." —he picked the first name that came into his head—"...Bauer."

She introduced herself shyly and then turned her attention to cutting dark rye bread into slices and finding a small portion of cheese and half an onion. She served it carefully on polished plates, and with glasses of cold water, presumably from the well. They were far enough back from the battle line for the water to be unpolluted.

Joseph began the conversation by explaining their presence. He said they were looking for a young man, a parishioner in peacetime, who was badly shell-shocked and who had run away, terrified. They were afraid if they did not find him he might be shot as a deserter, but since the incident he had been deaf and would not understand. Had she seen such a young man pass this way?

She said she had not seen him herself, but her neighbor three miles to the south had mentioned just such a man to her only yesterday. They thanked her profusely and took their leave. She had given them directions to the nearest village, and then to the small town beyond. She felt certain that anyone in the young man's position would head in that direction, hoping to hide and find shelter and possibly food before making his way home.

They thanked her and left.

They passed munitions and supply columns going toward the front, men on foot going back from leave and brief recovery after minor injuries, and raw recruits going to join the front. Most of these last were painfully young and their faces soft with the last remnants of childhood. Now they were struggling to mask fear and honor their commitment, and their families' faith in them. Many would already have lost fathers and older brothers.

"Jesus wept!" Morel said under his breath. "That blind boy on the right looked just like Snowy Nunn! What the hell are we doing here, Chaplain? What are we doing anywhere except at home?"

Joseph did not bother answering. Platitudes were no use anyway, and there was nothing else to offer but words that had all been said before.

They found shelter for the night in someone's byre. Even though it was dry, clean, and perfectly comfortable, the owner apologized, quite unnecessarily. The next morning they were offered a kind of gruel for breakfast. They ate it gratefully and without asking what was in it. Everyone they saw was hungry, frightened, trying hard to hang on to some dignity and a shred of hope.

Morel knew nothing of the Peacemaker, and for a few moments Joseph was overcome with the longing to talk to Matthew, to try to explain why looking at this land, these people, he could understand the dreams and the pain that had driven a man to want peace at any price. The world in which right and wrong had seemed so obvious was gone like a bubble grasped at by a hand, disappeared in an instant.

But he could not say as much to Morel. Morel needed him to be certain of at least something—therefore he must seem so.

Finally it was Morel who broke the silence. "Will you go back to St. John's?" he asked, staring straight ahead, avoiding Joseph's eyes.

Joseph was appalled. Is that what Morel thought of him, that he would go back to the same old escape, exactly as if nothing had happened? Build himself another cocoon!

"I don't imagine there'll be much to go back to," he said a little sharply. "I can't see many people wanting to learn biblical languages in the aftermath of this, can you?"

"They have their uses," Morel said with a frown. "Perhaps if we'd studied the past a little more diligently we'd have seen further into the future."

"That's a leisure pursuit," Joseph said. "I don't think we'll have much leisure in the years after the war. It isn't going to be the same."

"*Nothing's* going to be the same," Morel agreed with intense earnestness. "Women are doing half the jobs men used to. A woman's life isn't defined by who she marries anymore. It won't go back to that, not now. Think of your sister."

Joseph knew he meant Judith, but even Hannah was changed. All over Europe there were women who had learned to manage alone, to find courage and learn skills that had not been imagined before the war.

"You can't turn time backward," he said aloud.

"Good God, no!" Morel was suddenly savage. "Not in anything! I've fought beside men who used to wait on me at table or clean my boots. We can't and mustn't go back to that."

"We won't." Perhaps because Joseph had been home on leave so little, and then only to St. Giles, where social barriers were as old as the land and who owned and worked it, most of the change had made little impression on him. He had always known men like Barshey Gee, Snowy Nunn, and the others. He had played with men like them in the village school, knowing they would go on to work with their hands, and he would go up to university.

"There'll be a new government," Morel said thoughtfully. "If they don't care for the sick and disabled, then we'll force them to. There'll be legislation so it's every man's right to work, or if there's no work, then to be cared for, to have medicine, food, a roof over his head regardless, and over his children's. And the right to be taught because he has the brains to learn."

He was walking with his shoulders hunched, muscles tight. "Not out of charity, but because it's every man's right. We're quick enough to call him up to fight in the blood and filth of the trenches and to die for his country. And he came in the millions, without a question or a complaint. We owe, Chaplain! And by God, if I live through this, I'm going to do what I can. Not just for them, but for ourselves. What are we worth if we don't?"

It was a challenge. Joseph knew he meant it. It was for the men he led that he had been willing to mutiny against Northrup, and that was blazingly clear now. It was not one isolated anger or a personal rebellion. It was his nature, and he would be as true to it in civilian life as he was now. Joseph could imagine him in the future, a firebrand politician fighting for social justice, with a decency man to man that owed nothing to charity. The loyalty in the face of horror would not fade just because the guns were silent.

Nor would the suffering. Only a fool could imagine that. The dead would never return, nor would most of the crippled or blinded ever be whole again.

Was Morel waiting for him to say what he would do? The silence within his own head demanded it. There was only one decent answer: to go back into an active ministry, if there was one that would have him. What faith would there be after this? Millions would be desperate for help, comfort, and hope in the future, a belief that there was meaning to the ruin of so much. But would they look to God for it? Or would the Church seem as much an anachronism swallowed in the past as the golden afternoons of cricket and tea on the lawn in that last gilded summer of 1914?

And could he do it alone, without a wife to encourage him, explain the village gossip, the relationships he did not even see, to pick up his mistakes and oversights, simply to believe in him?

Joseph had no answer for himself, never mind for Morel. "In any event I'll not go back to St. John's."

"Didn't think you would." Morel smiled.

It was the second night, after a gaudy sunset painted across the southwestern sky, that they arrived at the bombed-out part of a small town where they hoped to find Geddes. They were moving carefully, aware that he was a fugitive and although he would not expect them, he would be wary. He spoke little German and knew he was in enemy territory, and a hunted man.

For their own safety they had long ago discarded their French rifles, and even Morel's British Army revolver. As priests they had no justification for carrying them, much less for using them. Geddes, on the other hand, would certainly have armed himself with a German pistol to go with his masquerade as a German soldier.

There was little light in the sky and it was several moments before Morel was even certain that the man they had spotted was Geddes. He waited, watching as the man looked one way then the other, preparing to settle himself for a brief rest. His face was haggard, stubble growth on his cheeks. He could easily have been what he pretended: shell-shocked, exhausted, terrified because he could not hear.

Deliberately Morel tapped his boot on the stone lintel of what was left of the house. The man spun around, facing the last of the light from the fading west. He saw only Morel's outline in the archless doorway. There was a second when he was uncertain what to do. His movement had betrayed that he could hear. That ruse was lost to him. He could not recognize Morel, who was deliberately standing with his back to the light, and one hand near his hip where a gun would have been—had he still had one.

Joseph was at the far side, closer to Geddes. When he saw Morel nod, he moved to stand close enough to Geddes that he could push a small piece of wood into his side, like the barrel of a gun. "Don't move, Geddes," he said quietly. "I'd rather deal with you alive, but if need be, dead will serve."

Geddes froze. He might not have known Joseph's voice, but the fact that he had spoken to him in English was sufficient.

Morel strode forward and took the piece of wood. "Thank you," he said easily. "Now I think we should all start off home while it's still dark. It's a long hike. But as long as we make the lines before dawn, we have as good a chance as we'll get."

"I'm not going anywhere," Geddes said flatly. "Shoot me if you want to."

Morel was not in the least perturbed. "Actually I do rather want to," he said quite lightly. "If you hadn't shot and killed Northrup, we wouldn't all have this present spot of bother. What the hell did you do that for? We could have made our point without hurting him."

"Maybe you could," Geddes said sullenly. "What about the poor bloody soldiers he was going to order into the next stupid piece of action? Wouldn't be you, would it, Major! Your skin's safe."

"Not now, it isn't," Morel answered. "But a little testimony from you would help."

Geddes sat down deliberately. "Too bad." His sneer was visible in the half-light. "Because I'm staying here. Shoot me, if that's what you want. It won't get you anything—no testimony, no defense. Please yourself."

"I wasn't thinking of shooting you to death," Morel told him. "Something rather more painful, but not fatal—at least not yet."

Geddes was motionless. When he spoke, his voice wobbled a little. "You wouldn't . . ."

"The Chaplain might not," Morel admitted. "But I would. The way I see it, Geddes, it's your life or mine. And not only mine, but Cavan's and all the others'. Put like that, and you bloody bet I would!"

"If you get me back, what makes you think I'll tell the truth?" Geddes stayed where he was, but there was no ease in his body now. His back was stiff and the muscles were corded in his neck. "I could say it was you! More than that, I could tell them how we got out of that farmhouse." His smile widened a little. "I could tell them all about that nice V.A.D. driver who rescued us and her Yank friend. Do you want to see them shot, too? And make no mistake, they would be. Can't have V.A.D.s deciding who faces court-martial and who doesn't!" He turned slowly to peer at Joseph in the near dark. "Isn't that right, Chaplain? You'd better go while you can. You're in enemy territory!"

Did he know Judith was Joseph's sister? Probably. The enormity of the situation washed over Joseph like a cold tide. What had he been thinking to imagine they could get Geddes home and that he would simply confess rather than take as many people down with him as he could? He was desperate—a murderer, a mutineer, and now a deserter as well. He had nothing to lose. If he were to survive at all, it would have to be this side of the lines.

"Maybe you can't see it in this light," Joseph said quietly, hating doing it. "But we are dressed as Swiss priests. We both speak German. You don't, and you are in German uniform. Who do you think the Germans will believe if we're caught?"

Morel did not move. Geddes sat still on the floor.

Outside, a car engine rumbled in the distance. They were not far from the road.

Geddes cleared his throat. "You wouldn't do that, Chaplain. Isn't that against your oath or something?"

"You're planning to let Cavan be shot for your crime if we don't get back, and to betray the V.A.D. who helped you if we do. What do you think, Geddes?" he asked.

"You tell the Germans who I am, I'll tell them who you are," Geddes replied, sitting a little more upright

The red in the wash was fading to pink and the shadows were impenetrable.

Joseph changed direction. "Why did you kill Northrup, anyway? You've made it very clear you don't give a damn about the lives of your fellows, so it can't be that, which is almost the only thing that would be understandable. What is it? Money? Hate? Stupidity?"

"Because he deserved it!" Geddes snarled. "He was an arrogant, incompetent fool as an officer, and he wouldn't listen to anyone. Always had to do it his way, even if it cost other men's lives." He was facing Joseph now, ignoring Morel. "But I know more about him than you do. Scare the hell out of him, he still wouldn't have learned." He jerked his arm toward Morel. "They all thought you could talk sense into him. I know better. He was born that way. His father thought the sun shone out of his ass, indulged him rotten, let him do any damn thing he wanted. Lorded it over the rest of the village, ran up debts, then when he hadn't the guts to admit it to his father, lied in his teeth."

Joseph did not interrupt. Geddes's voice had the bitter ring of truth—at least the truth as he saw it and felt it burning like acid inside him.

"He ruined my father that way," Geddes went on. "My father trusted him, the more fool he. I could've told him Northrup was a liar and a coward, but he wouldn't hear ill of the old general's son. Cost him his house. Our house!"

"So Northrup dies a hero, shot by mutineers, and Cavan goes to the firing squad for it," Joseph said with equal bitterness. "Who was it you said was the fool?"

Geddes was silent.

"You'll not make it here," Joseph went on. "You'll starve, if they don't shoot you as a spy first. Nobody likes spies. They might question you a bit first, to see what you can tell them about our positions. Or is that what you're going to bargain with, betraying your regiment?"

Geddes swore viciously.

"Then they'll shoot you," Joseph went on. "They don't regard traitors any more highly than we do. You can come back to Passchendaele and at least tell your story."

"If you come back you'll get revenge," Morel added. "If you stay here, you'll get nothing at all. Although actually I'm not going to let you stay here anyway." Without warning he walked forward and raised his arm. He gave Geddes a hard clip on the side of the head with the butt of the gun, and Geddes crumpled over without a sound. "Do you really want to take him back?" Morel asked quietly. "On the chance that he could still betray the V.A.D. who let us out? It was your sister, you know? Maybe you didn't realize that?"

"Yes, I know," Joseph replied. It would be ridiculous to deny it now. "Anyone looking into it could prove it pretty easily. But we're not going to shoot Geddes. We're going to get him back to the lines, and then through them."

"How?" Morel asked. "He's out cold now. Who knows what he'll say when he comes around again, but whatever it is, it'll be in English, because that's all he knows."

"Then we'll have to see that he doesn't say anything," Joseph replied. "We'll take him as a wounded man. We're priests. That's reasonable. We'll be heroes. Who knows—they might even help us. We'll tie his head and face up, with a gag underneath the bandages, so he can't speak. Cut him a little so there's blood. Just hope to hell that whoever helps us isn't a surgeon!"

"We can't carry him that far," Morel pointed out reasonably. "We've come four or five miles at least!"

"If we go back on the road we'll find some debris. With luck, something with wheels. We can cannibalize it and make a carriage for him."

"I realize how little I knew you at Cambridge," Morel said drily. "I was a child!"

"We all were," Joseph replied. "Let's tie him up first. We don't know how soon he'll come around."

They used Geddes's own shirt to bind him for lack of anything better. They slit it with the knife he had and tore it into strips. It would be enough to hold him until they found better. Then they took turns carrying him as far as the road. He was a young man, heavy-boned and well muscled although any surplus flesh had long since gone, and he was dead weight. In fact, twice Joseph was anxious enough about him to stop and make sure he was still breathing. He was not certain how hard Morel had hit him.

They had to carry him another laborious half mile along the road before they came to a car that had been blown to bits. But no matter how they tried to imagine it, there seemed no way to take any of it apart. Reluctantly they abandoned it and again began the arduous task of carrying him.

They were still three or four miles from the nearest trenches when they were passed by a couple of soldiers who had apparently become separated from a relief column. It was a summer night, cloudless with a three-quarter moon, and light enough for Joseph to see how gaunt they were. He judged them to be veterans who had been wounded, and sent back too soon out of desperation. He had seen the same in the British ranks. In so many ways this was a mirror image of home. It tore at him with a familiarity, an acute understanding he would rather not have had.

The two men stopped. Neither looked strong enough to help carry Geddes, for which Joseph was grateful. Geddes was going home to face trial. He would never fight again, but still it would be one deceit too far.

"Looking for the nearest field station?" the taller one asked.

"Yes," Joseph replied. "Not sure how bad he is."

Geddes must have been conscious. He started to wriggle and become extremely awkward to hold. Had they been alone Joseph would have threatened to drop him, and done it. Geddes was trying to shout.

"He's in a lot of pain," Morel offered. "We're looking for something to wheel him on, if we can find anything."

"There's bound to be something with wheels," the shorter man said hopefully. "Even something broken might do. We could fix it to take the weight. He's nothing like as heavy as field artillery."

"Nothing like as useful, either," Morel said under his breath.

They walked together, alternating Geddes's body from one to another. The Germans insisted on taking their turn, and there was no way to refuse them without offense.

They had gone another half mile when they came to a pony cart at the side of the road. One wheel was blown to bits and what was left of the pony's carcass was still between the shafts. They put Geddes down, Joseph adjusting the gag to make sure it was not working loose, and also retightening the binding around his body so it was less obviously a restraint and rather more like a bandage.

The other three undid the harness and lifted the broken trap off, then hauled it up onto the road. It sat sideways because of the missing wheel.

"Got to find another wheel for it," Morel said thoughtfully. "Even one a different size would be better than nothing. Pity we have no tools. It won't be so easy. Have to make do with lashing things together. Still, not far to go."

The Germans had introduced themselves as Kretschmer and Wolff. Wolff and Morel now wandered off to see what they could find. Joseph and Kretschmer set about getting the three good wheels clean from the rubbish and making sure they could turn as freely as possible.

Wolff reappeared with a small wheel from a barrow of some sort, and Morel had a length of rope and a short piece of chain. Using everything, and considerable ingenuity, they lashed together a fourth leg for the cart, with the wheel on the end. It still did not make the height exactly, but it was a great help. Pleased with themselves, they laid Geddes on it as comfortably as possible, and set off on the road, taking turns, two at a time, carrying the shafts. The wheels squeaked appallingly.

"Here," Kretschmer said cheerfully, digging into his pocket and bringing out a small bottle. "Have some schnapps." He offered it to Joseph.

Joseph thanked him and took a mouthful. It felt as if a fire had exploded in his stomach. He was sure he could belch flame. Coughing hard, he thanked Kretschmer and passed it on to Morel, who took it rather more easily, then offered it to Wolff.

A mile later, after a couple more changes of shift as to who was pulling, they passed the schnapps around again. Joseph realized with a smile that they were marching in time to the squeaking of the wheels. The last shreds of cloud had gone and the moonlight shone pale on the cratered road, making black skeletons of the few shattered vehicles and broken trees. In the distance they could make out the standing walls of a burned house.

Wolff began to sing a drinking song. His voice was light and pleasant. Joseph remembered a little of the tune from his visits before the war, and he joined in.

An ambulance passed them going back, and a munitions supply convoy passed going forward to the lines.

They found a second song, and a third. There were still at least two miles farther to go. Joseph started to worry about how they were going to explain leaving these two men who in some absurd way had become friends. The last drop of schnapps was gone and none of them had any food. The squeaking of the wheels was incessant, and they were all unquestionably a little drunk.

Wolff began to sing again, this time in English, and they all joined in.

"There's a long, long trail a-winding, into the land of my dreams,

"Where the nightingales are singing and a white moon beams . . ."

They went through all the verses, then began again. The three-quarter moon lit the road, but the only sound apart from their voices was the squeaking of the wheels, and the guns roaring a couple of miles ahead. The odors of bodily waste and putrefying flesh were already strong, and in the distance there was the flash of red and yellow mortar fire.

Joseph had no idea how they would get through the lines, other than the same way as they had come. Additionally, they would have to untie Geddes so he could run. But first they would have to find a way of parting from Kretschmer and Wolff, who with luck, would have a specific place to report.

But for this moment, his feet hurt, and his hands were blistered from holding the cart. His back and his legs ached and he was so hungry he could have eaten a raw turnip with pleasure, if he could have found one. But he was light-headed with schnapps, singing in the moonlight, and there was a kind of happiness in it that was desperately, passionately real.

TWELVE

*M*ason returned to London with a heavy sense of oppression. His mind should have been crowded with thoughts of the slaughter at Passchendaele and the impending farce of the court-martial of Cavan, the only one of the twelve men who was actually in custody.

But all the way across the Channel, and then standing crowded in the troop train from Dover to London, jostled and jolted, kept upright largely by the press of other men's bodies around him, he felt a deep and abiding misery that was almost paralyzing. There seemed no light in his inner landscape at all. Had he really imagined the court-martial would solve anything?

Rationally, perhaps the idiocy of it all, the casualty toll climbing toward a quarter million men for the gaining of one shattered town, would have been enough to make sane men call a halt to it, at whatever cost, on whatever terms. But was there any sanity left? No one looked at the whole monumental disaster. They all looked at their own little patch of it.

Perhaps it was too big for anyone to comprehend the ruin that stretched right from the Atlantic waves that swallowed men and ships off the battered shores of Britain right to the blood-soaked sands of Mesopotamia, to the snowbound graves of Russia. Europe was a charnel house. No one could count the millions of dead, let alone those maimed forever.

And yet Judith Reavley was prepared to risk her life to help eleven mutineers escape and flee to Switzerland, and Joseph was equally willing to risk his life to bring them back! In the scheme of things both actions were equally pointless, and just as likely to end in death.

Perhaps that was what hurt? Joseph had hardly any chance of succeeding, which—if he were a logical man—he would have known; but he wasn't logical! He was an idealist, a dreamer, seeing the world he wanted more clearly than the real one.

Mason wished he did not like him so much. He had wit and imagination, courage to the point of stupidity—no, actually beyond it. And compassion, again beyond sense. You could not argue about honor with him because he did not listen. He followed his own star, even though it was an illusion; beautiful, better than the truth, but a mirage. And when he reached the place where he thought it was, he was going to discover that there was nothing there. That was what Mason hated: the disillusion he knew had to come. No one would be able to help them. What does a man do when he climbs the vast heights, struggles his way upward to heaven, and when bleeding and exhausted he gets there and finds it empty?

He was furious with Joseph for being so vulnerable, and leaving people like Mason to be wounded by his pain.

The train jolted and threw him against the man beside him, knocking him off balance. He apologized. They stopped somewhere in a siding, crowded together, hot and exhausted, legs aching.

The minutes dragged by. He was impatient, although it made little difference when he reached London. He was going to see the Peacemaker, and he would be admitted whatever time he got there. He was going to report on the court-martial and the mood of the men. The Peacemaker would not be pleased. The court-martial was not only going to be absurd, it was going to appear so. Might someone step in and prevent it even now? Was there anyone who could? If so, it would be obvious they had, and that would be absurd also.

The train started to move, lurching with a clang of couplings, then stopped again. Someone swore under his breath. There was another lurch and bang, and another. Then slowly they picked up speed.

Mason was lying to himself: It was not really the thought of Joseph that weighed him down, it was Judith. He could remember the touch of her lips, and her eyes as she looked at him when he drew away at last. He wanted to hold that forever, and he knew he was losing it already. Even if no one ever betrayed the fact that it was she and the American volunteer driver who had rescued the mutineers, she had been willing to do it. That was the division between them that was uncrossable. She was impulsive, quixotic, rushing in like a fool to do something noble without thinking of the inevitable result.

He should force himself not to care. He would only be hurt. She was not going to change. Possibly she was not even going to live through the war! That had always been a risk. Ambulance drivers did get killed, of course they did! Anyone on the battlefront ran that risk.

Why did that thought all but make him sick with despair? She was not part of his life. They had no commitment to each other. They had met only a few times, shared intense emotions of terror and hope and pity, laughed too much, to the edge of weeping, and kissed just once.

He was lying to himself again. She was part of his dreams, of the quiet places inside him that fed his strength, the things for which he struggled and climbed to his feet when he fell, the thing that gave the journey a purpose, a distinction, a place to belong.

The train was moving swiftly now, swaying with a kind of rhythm, everyone so close they held each other up, and all lost in their own thoughts.

How had he allowed himself to do something so stupid? Why could he not have chosen any of a dozen pretty, intelligent, and reasonable girls he had known? Because to persuade himself that he cared for any of them was one lie he could not get away with. There are parts of a man that will accept only the truth.

The train slowed going over the bridge, and finally pulled into Waterloo. They spilled out onto the platform—stiff, dirty, their bodies aching and so tired no one spoke. Mason pushed his way to the entrance to find a taxi, but there was a queue so long it would take hours, and many of the men standing there had injuries far worse than the few cuts and bruises he had. He went instead to the underground train, and an hour later was walking along Marchmont Street in the warm evening air. He passed a newspaper seller and ignored him. Their chief correspondent on the Western Front was a man he knew well. He could imagine what he would make of the court-martial story, and he would be bound to get it. He would make Morel look like a traitor, and Joseph Reavley like a fool.

He reached the Peacemaker's home and was let in by the same manservant as always, and received in the upstairs sitting room. A moment later he was joined by the Peacemaker. He was wearing a smoking jacket, as if possibly he had been reading a little while, having a last cup of tea, or whisky and soda, before going to bed.

"You look tired," he said sympathetically. "Rough crossing?" He gestured to Mason to sit down. He had already asked the manservant for sandwiches and fresh tea.

Mason sank into the familiar chair. "No. Calm as a millpond," he replied. "But no room to sit on the train. Stood all the way from Dover. Hardly room to lift your elbows." He was not looking forward to reporting on the state of the court-martial. He did so briefly, almost tersely, to get it over with.

"What a mess," the Peacemaker said with little expression, surprising Mason by his control. "I assume someone helped the mutineers escape? Any idea who?"

"None at all," Mason lied without compunction. "Could have been any of a thousand people. Nobody wants this court-martial to go ahead."

"Any chance of capturing the escaped men?"

"One in a thousand, maybe," Mason said, leaning back in his chair. "But I can't see that it would improve matters. Just increase the chances of someone saying who helped them." He spoke honestly, then felt the pain grip his heart and knot in his belly as he thought of Judith in the dock beside Cavan. It was a sense of loneliness as if the lights had gone out in the world, or in his part of it. But it was also jealousy. Judith admired Cavan, and surely he must admire her, too. They would stand side by side, ready to be crucified for loyalty to the men they served. Everyone else was shut out, especially someone like Mason who thought the whole thing was a pointless sacrifice.

He looked across at the Peacemaker, expecting his reaction to be one of fury, perhaps most of all for the waste of good men of just the kind of nobility, courage, and loyalty he himself so valued. But the Peacemaker was smiling bleakly, his eyes bright. He saw what Mason was describing, understood the words if not the heart of it, and was ready to move on to the thoughts that obviously took precedence with him. It was as if he were not really even surprised.

"Thank you," he said aloud, crossing his legs comfortably. "It is exactly as you say: a final piece of idiocy. I wish we could prevent it, but I know of no way. I believe they are sending Faulkner to prosecute, and he will carry it to the last degree. A narrow man full of fears. He worships the letter of the law, because he has neither the courage nor the imagination to see the spirit behind it."

Mason remained silent, not trusting himself to speak. His mind raced, skittering around, crashing into ideas in his search to think of anything at all he could say or do that could save Judith, or even save Cavan! Would he save Cavan, for her, knowing that it would exclude him forever?

That was a stupid and crassly sentimental thought. There was no *forever*. The darkness had begun in August 1914, and now, three years later, it was almost complete.

"I have more news from Russia," the Peacemaker was saying. He was leaning forward again in his chair, fixing Mason with the intensity of his eyes. "They are on the brink of a real revolution! Not the halfhearted affair of Kerensky and his Mensheviks, but one that will change everything, sweep away all trace of the old regime. They will get rid of the tsar and all his family forever." He made a short, jerky movement with his long hand. "Lenin is back, and he and Trotsky will lead it. It will be violent at first; there is no alternative." His face pinched for a moment. "There will be many deaths, because the old guard is strong—they have been there for centuries and the corruption runs deep. No one gives up power unless they are forced to." The light came back into his face. "But think of the future, Mason! Think of all that the Bolsheviks can do with their passion and ideals. A new order, started from the beginning! Unity, equality, an end to war."

"It will drown Russia in blood." Mason was appalled. He should have guarded his speech. He knew his protest was pointless, or—worse than that—dangerous, but the words were out in spite of himself.

"No, it won't!" the Peacemaker argued, too excited to be angry. "It will be violent to begin with, of course it will. The tsar had warning after warning but he took no notice. What else can they do, Mason? As long as the Romanovs are alive there will always be the old nobility, the property owners, the oppressors who will try to return. They are of the old aristocracy of privilege and violence who know no social justice. They use the ordinary man as cannon fodder in a war the people of Russia have no interest in. It must stop! It is not the tsar or his supporters who are dying out there in the bitter snows of the Eastern Front—it is the ordinary man! It is the family of the ordinary man that is starving at home."

He leaned farther forward. "Well, no more. The people will rise. They will refuse to fight. Mason, we are at the beginning of the end. By Christmas there will be peace in Europe. We can begin to rebuild, not just materially but socially as well." His face was alight, his eyes burning.

It was a dream again. Mason had a sudden terror that he was being swept along in a fantasy in which everyone else believed, and only he could see the bitter truth. Individual ambitions would always play their part; men would build on towering visions and subsequently forget the details that would undo them.

The Peacemaker had lost sight of the individual in his sweeping plan, as if one man's ideas could command the loyalty of millions, and their obedience.

For the first time Mason began to wonder if the Peacemaker was mad. No man had the power to do what he dreamed, and no man should.

Perhaps he had seen too many dead and become tired, his own passion exhausted. Judith would hate everything the Peacemaker had said. She would tell him it had nothing to do with reality, the way people actually were.

The Peacemaker would say her sight was too small, too ordinary.

She would say that his was too far from the human heart to see into it: too overweening, exercising not leadership but dominion.

"Mason!" the Peacemaker said sharply. "It is the beginning of the end! Can't you see that? Peace! There need never be this abomination of war again!"

"Yes, sir," Mason said a little flatly. "Well, not here anyway."

The Peacemaker was not to have his spirits damped. "You're tired. Go home and sleep. Write your article. Then go back to Passchendaele. Attend the court-martial and write the truth about it. The men deserve that. Cavan deserves it."

Joseph and Morel, with Geddes in tow, made the crossing back through the German lines, over no-man's-land and then through the French lines. They had great difficulty but achieved it in the same manner as they had crossed the other way: running, crawling, scrambling the moment it was dark enough between the star shells. Perhaps they had been a little less frightened, thanks to the schnapps, and for the same reason also a little clumsier.

They had found parting from Kretschmer and Wolff had occurred naturally because the German soldiers had had to report to their units. In the darkness and the tension before an attack, other people's minds had been more preoccupied with what was to come than identifying individuals. Like the British and French armies, their regiments had also been decimated. The losses were staggering, and men were assigned anywhere just to fill in the numbers and make up a platoon or a brigade. There were more strangers than friends left. No one questioned Joseph or Morel closely, and the clerical disguise did the rest.

Getting through the French lines was more difficult. They were taken prisoner at the point of a rifle—in fact several rifles.

"We've got a German prisoner," Morel said immediately, in French, indicating Geddes, whose mouth and lower face were still bound. He was still in his stolen German uniform, so there was nothing to make the statement appear untrue.

The French lieutenant in command looked dubious, but he accepted the story, at least on the surface. Joseph was so covered in mud that his dog collar was all but invisible.

When they had been taken farther back to a dry dugout suitable for interrogation, they told the truth, more or less.

The French lieutenant shook his head. "I suppose you want to take him back to Ypres now?"

Joseph smiled. "Yes, please. If you can help it would be enormously appreciated."

The lieutenant shrugged. "Well, you can barely walk! And I don't suppose your prisoner is very keen. We'd better have somebody drive you." He rolled his eyes. *"Entente cordiale,"* he observed, making an elegant gesture of despair with his hands, but he was smiling. He might never admit it, but he obviously found it secretly rather entertaining. It was something different, and a story to tell.

He must know, just as Joseph did, and any other soldier anywhere would, that war is frequent terror, occasional hideous violence, sometimes terrible pain, a lot of exhaustion and discomfort and hunger, but it is mostly boredom. It is the comradeship, the laughter, the stories and bad jokes that make it bearable, the sharing of the glorious and the absurd, the dreams and memories, and the letters from home through which one clings to sanity.

Thus it was with the help of the French lieutenant, after a meager but well-cooked meal, and armed with a new stock of tall stories, they were driven the long way back to Passchendaele. They arrived the following day, with Geddes still bound but no longer gagged since there was no necessity for it.

They thanked the French driver profusely and offered him a tin of Maconachie's and a bar of decent chocolate, which he accepted reluctantly but with grace.

Before reporting to Colonel Hook, Joseph had a brief moment alone with Morel. There was a military police sergeant in the doorway; there would be no second chance to escape. He wanted to ask Morel what he intended to say about his original escape. Faulkner would ask, and if Morel refused to answer he would add to the original charge that of concealing the identity of his helpers who had committed a criminal act in aiding him.

It was a crime Joseph was guilty of as well.

Far more urgent, however, was the matter of what Geddes would say. It would have been pointless trying to persuade him not to betray Judith and Wil. He was already facing the firing squad. There was nothing they could offer him or threaten him with. It would depend upon what the other men said. There was a faint glimmer of hope that if they all stuck to the same story, it would be believed over Geddes's testimony. It would be suggested that he named Judith as accomplice out of revenge, because it was Joseph who had brought him back.

But he could say none of that now. He and Morel had traveled together, shared laughter and pain. Each man's survival had depended upon the other; but now Joseph was going to resume his duties, and Morel was facing court-martial and perhaps dishonor and death. Nothing was equal between them anymore.

"Thank you" was all Joseph could think of to say that was not condescending, false, and completely pointless. He offered his hand.

Morel took it, held it hard for a moment, then turned and walked over to the sergeant. Without looking back, he went out of the door.

Admiral Hall had given Matthew forty-eight hours before reporting back on Faulkner, and Matthew knew that they could afford no more. He toyed with the idea of simply asking Shearing why he had chosen him, but in spite of what Hall had told him of Shearing and his family, he still could not silence that last whisper of doubt. Sandwell's words stayed with him. Whatever he learned, it must be from his own investigation, his own sources. And it must be discreet.

But all the searching he was able to do swiftly and discreetly only confirmed that Faulkner was an extreme disciplinarian, rigid in his interpretation of the law, a man who seemed unfailingly to have pushed for the letter of the law above mercy. He had served all his career in England and had, so far as was known, never seen the battlefield or had the slightest knowledge of life in the trenches, let alone death in no-man's-land.

He seemed the worst possible choice to prosecute Cavan, Morel, and the others. If Faulkner was single and he had any weakness, or even any redeeming factors, whatever it was, Dermot Sandwell had not known of it. He believed Faulkner was invulnerable, and Shearing had agreed to him for precisely that reason.

Matthew had no time left, and now no alternative but to face Shearing.

As they sat facing each other in Shearing's office, Matthew began without apology or preamble. "Sir, I recently had a matter which I took directly to Admiral Hall. He gave me instruction to investigate it and report to him within forty-eight hours. That time is up today, and I have no satisfactory answer. I need to know if you have any knowledge on the subject."

Shearing put down his pen carefully and sat back, staring at Matthew. "I assume this is about your vast conspiracy again," he said slowly, his face tight and wary.

Matthew evaded the answer. "It is about Lieutenant Colonel Faulkner, sir," he said. "He is going to prosecute Cavan. And any of the other men, if they are found."

Shearing's eyes were cold. "I told you, Reavley, that matter is in hand. You are not to interfere with it. That is a direct order. If you disobey me, I shall have you transferred to the front—immediately. Do you understand me?"

Matthew felt the chill as if a window had been opened onto an ice storm. "Yes, sir. But I have been studying his past record . . ."

Shearing sat upright sharply. "Who gave you permission to do that? You could have jeopardized the whole court-martial! You—"

"Admiral Hall, sir," Matthew cut across him.

Shearing's eyes were like black stones. "Do you think me incompetent, Reavley? Or that I am involved in this conspiracy of yours?"

Matthew stared at him and felt guilty for the spark of pain he saw in Shearing's face. It took him by surprise and he found himself speechless.

Shearing breathed a faint sigh. "There is no good solution, Reavley. Faulkner is simply the best we have—"

"I don't see how," Matthew interrupted him bitterly. "He's—"

"I know what he is!" Shearing snapped. "If you think about it a little harder, use your brain rather than your emotions, you might see it yourself."

"He'll insist on the charge of mutiny and murder," Matthew said wretchedly. "General Northrup might have moderated it, to save his son's reputation, but from what everyone says of Faulkner, there isn't a cat in hell's chance he'll go for anything less than the full thing, and a firing squad—no matter what a rank injustice it is, who gets executed, or even what it does to the regiment, or even the whole damn Western Front! He's an obsessive, single-vision martinet." His anger and helplessness made him louder than he had intended.

"That is precisely what he is, and it is the single weakness that may, with great skill and luck, be turned against him." Shearing's voice was elaborately patient as he held up his hand, fingers stiff. "There are three possible verdicts: guilty of mutiny and murder, guilty of mutiny and manslaughter, or guilty of gross insubordination and accidental death— for all except the man who deliberately front-loaded the live round. He alone is guilty of murder."

"Faulkner will insist on mutiny and murder," Matthew interrupted him. "Even mutiny and manslaughter will get the firing squad. They might be able to delay it a while on appeal, but what use is that? The end is just as inevitable, and everyone knows it."

"Which is why there is no use finding a prosecution who will go for the middle charge," Shearing said grimly.

Matthew still saw no hope. "There's no way Faulkner will accept gross insubordination!"

Shearing's lips were drawn into a tight line. "Of course there isn't! He will insist on murder, and if we can get the right man to defend Cavan and the other men, he will force Faulkner to prove it, to the very last act and word, even thought, beyond any doubt at all, reasonable or unreasonable. He will hang on like a bulldog, until the arena is swimming in blood, but he won't let go."

Matthew was stunned.

Shearing's voice was very low. "It will destroy Howard Northrup's reputation, but for his father it will be like seeing him killed again. It will show the court exactly why Cavan and Morel and the others felt they had no choice whatever, no morally acceptable choice, but to take an action which they believed would save the lives of at least some of the men they led, and who trusted them, for whom the army had made them responsible."

At last Matthew understood. He breathed out very slowly. "It's a hell of a risk, sir."

"Can you think of something better?"

"No," Matthew admitted. "Have you got a military lawyer with the nerve to do that? And the knowledge of the front line?"

Shearing smiled with a bitter irony. "No. It's customary for an officer from the regiment to defend on lesser charges. I think the very best they can do is pick one of them this time. . . ."

Matthew was appalled. "Against Faulkner? His opponent will be crucified!"

There was a bright, hard light in Shearing's eyes. "It doesn't need a brilliant student of the law, Reavley. It needs a man of passion, courage, and undeviating loyalty, a man who knows the accused and what they have endured, and why. A man who will be prepared to sacrifice himself before he will stand by and allow an injustice to be done. A man whom the court will respect as one of their own."

Matthew could feel his heart pounding in the oppressive room with its still, hot air. "And you have such a man?"

"Naturally! He knows the case better than anyone else, and he believes in their moral innocence. Also, he does not know when he is beaten, so he will not give up."

"Joseph . . ."

"Precisely," Shearing agreed. "I have an excellent man there to brief him. Let's hope he does not get himself killed in the meantime!"

In Passchendaele the fighting wore on. A sense of foreboding filled the air they breathed, the clothes they wore, the food they ate, and darkened the vision, like the rain, everywhere. It was all hopeless, as if the final insanity had seized the world. Rescue was pointless. Whoever did not die today would die tomorrow, or the day after.

Colonel Hook sent for Joseph. It was late. As August moved into September, the nights were drawing in. Summer was fading.

"The court-martial is going ahead," Hook said gravely. "The preliminaries are tomorrow, the real stuff the day after."

Joseph had expected it. It was unrealistic to hope for anything different. All the arguments and pleas had been made and rejected. The desperate state of the battle had been argued, as had the morale of the army, the possible effect of such a trial and the verdict on the entire Western Front, and therefore on the war as a whole.

"Rubbish!" Faulkner had dismissed it. "We are winning the battle of Passchendaele," he had insisted. "The discipline of the entire army depends upon never, in any circumstances, being seen to allow mutiny and murder. If disgruntled men who think they know better than their officers can take the law into their own hands and commit murder and get away with it, then no officer will be safe from now on. It is impossible that you can be so stupid as not to see that. If we do not serve justice both when we wish to, and when we do not, then we serve nothing. The essence of justice is that personal feelings do not enter into it. Either it is impartial, or it is meaningless."

Alone with Hook, he was at a loss to know why he had called him to tell him no more than they already knew.

The briefest of smiles touched Hook's face. "I know you are already aware of that, Reavley. What you don't know is that it has been requested from London that you represent the accused men."

"Of course I shall be there," Joseph said quickly. "But it would be far better if their defense did not call me. Much of what I know I cannot testify to. Let Morel tell them about finding Geddes and bringing him back, and anything he said about Northrup and his father. He knows it all as well as I do."

Hook pushed his hand through his hair. "I have no intention of letting you testify, Reavley. I know perfectly well that you know who helped them escape. I have a damn good idea myself. I am not calling you as a witness. You are to defend them."

"What?" Joseph was horrified.

"You are to defend them," Hook repeated.

"Me? I have no experience—and no natural ability," Joseph protested. "I don't know the first thing about military law. They need an expert. In fact they need the best there is."

"No," Hook said wearily. "They need a man who believes in them, and doesn't know when to give up. They need a man who knows what it is to fight, and what our losses have been." The briefest flicker of amusement touched his eyes. "I would also prefer it if you were not called to testify. I'm sure you'd lie in your teeth rather than implicate . . . whoever it was who helped them escape." His gaze did not waver. "Even if it was a civilian, such as the V.A.D., for example, and not subject to military law, only ordinary imprisonment. They were not worried about betrayal of anyone. Morel in particular thought you would lie, possibly hating doing it, but lie nevertheless."

"I must remember to thank him," Joseph said drily. "That doesn't alter the fact that I have no experience. Faulkner would make mincemeat of me."

"I don't think so," Hook told him. "But regardless of that, it is you they have chosen, and I agree with them. And London is satisfied."

"That's hardly enough!" Joseph exclaimed, desperation rising inside him, and a hard, stomach-twisting fear. He would fail! He would let them all down!

Hook did not flinch. "They're facing the firing squad, Reavley. They've a right to ask for whomever they wish. I'm assigning you, so you'd better go and prepare. You've got tonight and probably most of tomorrow. You've seen courts-martial before. You know the drill. There'll be people there to keep you straight on the law. If you're still on speaking terms with God, you'd better ask Him for a little help. You'll need it."

"Yes, sir." Joseph saluted a little clumsily, and walked out into the darkness wondering if he was actually still on speaking terms with God. He had once believed that he knew the truth of doctrine, and morality, and that he could argue it with conviction.

But that was a long time ago. Now he was confused, torn by emotion, and above all afraid. He stood in the mud and looked up at the enormity of the September sky, for once glittering with stars.

"Please help me" was all that came to his lips. "Father, please help me."

THIRTEEN

*J*oseph's mind was racing, and yet the words poured over his head uselessly. He was sitting in his own dugout with an army legal officer trying to help him understand the legal niceties of what he could do, or not do, in order to defend the twelve men. Outside in the distance the gunfire was sporadic, mostly sniper fire, but it was growing dark and the rain was starting again. In an hour or two some poor devils would be going over the top.

The air was heavy and close; it seemed to cling to the skin. The oil lamp on the table burned steadily with a small, yellow flame, casting highlights and shadows on the familiar objects, the few books, the picture of Dante, a tin of biscuits, the pen and paper.

They had been through the procedure three times. Joseph was feeling as if the whole trial and verdict were as inevitable as the tides of the sea, and anything he did would make as little difference as he would to them.

"Remember the difference between civilian and military law," Major Ward said urgently, leaning forward, elbows on his knees. "Civilian law has the right of the individual at the front, the first concern. Military law is at least as much about the good of the unit. You'll have soldiers in active service on the panel. The president will be a major general from a division just like this one, who's fought along the Ypres Salient since 1914, just as you have. Give him half a chance and he'll be on your side. Never forget that, Reavley, and you could save them."

Joseph rubbed his hand across his brow, pushing his hair back so hard it hurt. "Why on earth did they choose me? You know the law. You'd do a far better job. I'm a priest, an ordinary soldier!"

"Haven't you been listening?" Ward demanded, frustration and weariness sharpening his voice. "That is exactly why you might succeed! You don't need to know the law, man! You need to know the army, the trenches, the reality of death and loyalty and what it means to be part of a regiment."

Joseph wanted to believe him but he had no faith in his ability to overcome the unarguable facts of the law. The men were placing a trust in him that was born of faith and desperation, and possibly some hope he had given them falsely, and beyond his ability to live up to. He would have betrayed them as deeply as the whole war had. In his own way, he was as incompetent as Northrup, another man put into a job for which he had not the skills.

"Nobody wins them all," Ward said to him drily. "But you damn well fight them all!"

An ugly suspicion flashed into Joseph's mind that they had put him onto this case because they did not want one of their own to be seen to defend mutineers, and of course to fail.

"Yes, sir," he answered.

Joseph got little sleep. By the following day, when the court-martial proceedings were under way with the usual declarations, and the accused men's right to challenge all the officers was in progress, time had assumed the character of an infinitely slow nightmare.

There was a farcical element to sitting in this airless room in what was now September heat, and hearing all the prescribed questions put to each man as if somehow it were going to make any difference. As Ward had said, the president was major general Hardesty from a nearby section of the line, and the other officers were Colonel Apsted from the regiment immediately to the west, and Major Simmons from a regiment to the east. It would have been pointless to object to any of them, but the protocol had to be followed.

Throughout, Lieutenant Colonel Faulkner sat behind his table, backbone like a poker. His face was tense, only a tiny muscle twitching in his cheek betrayed the looseness of his hands in front of him as a calculated pose.

The twelve accused stood together. It was an unusual circumstance for there to be so many, but the prosecution had chosen deliberately not to divide them. To present one accusing another might allow an intimidated or overcompassionate president to say he could not choose between them. He could excuse all on the argument that it would be better for the army to let guilty men go free than to be seen to punish the innocent. But *innocent* was a word Joseph already knew Faulkner did not allow easily. He believed that the authorities hardly ever accused innocent men, and in this particular case the evidence was overwhelming.

Joseph felt the sweat trickle down his sides and soak into his tunic, and yet he was cold. He looked around the room. He must not avoid their eyes. Morel and Cavan were easy to distinguish at a glance because they were officers. The rest of the men were noncommissioned. Most of them had been in the army since late 1914 or early 1915. That alone made them worthy of some respect, especially from a man like Faulkner, who had never seen a shot fired in anger. He had never gone over the top at night, into the mud and darkness, knowing that the men facing you had guns as well, and the murderous shrapnel could tear a man's body in half and leave his head and chest a yard away from his legs, and his guts streaming across the ground.

Joseph forced his mind back to the present. These men had asked him for help, not pity. Anger only clouded his thinking.

The charges were being read out: mutiny and murder. He had known it would be, but it was still a crushing of ridiculous hope to hear them.

He looked around to see General Northrup. Had he really tried to get the charge reduced? Or had his grief and anger at the death of his son overridden everything else, and he had dismissed the ruin of his reputation?

Despite Joseph's sympathy for General Northrup, it was the sight of Morel that bit most deeply into his emotions. He could remember the youthful Morel arriving at Cambridge his first year. The man he was now—honed hard by mental and physical suffering, the isolation of leadership, the rigor of living with his own decisions—was not even foreshadowed in him then. That had been only five years ago, but when the world was still young.

Morel should have been graduating this year, and wondering what to do with his life! Instead he was standing in a farmhouse near Ypres expecting to face a firing squad of his own countrymen, because he had rebelled against what he believed passionately to be wrong. Was there any way on earth Joseph could make that argument in his defense?

Morel stood straight now, at attention as the charges were repeated.

The farmhouse room was full of men, and a few women from among the nurses and V.A.D. corps. The three officers were seated behind the wooden table. Joseph and Faulkner were at separate tables immediately in front.

Joseph still had only the barest idea what he was going to say. He was reluctant to think of departing from the truth on moral grounds, and in practical terms that course was far too dangerous. To be caught in even an evasion would destroy the only advantage he had, which was the hope of understanding. If they had any defense at all, then it was that their act had been driven by a moral necessity.

The preliminary formalities were over. Faulkner rose to his feet, but did not move from behind his table. He had a curious quality of stiffness that was apparent from the very beginning. He made no gestures with his hands nor did he even seem to alter the weight of his body from one foot to the other.

He called his first witness: the medical orderly who had initially examined Howard Northrup's body. The man was manifestly unhappy, but the facts were not contestable. Northrup had died as the result of a rifle bullet to the head. It had struck him through the brow. He had to have been facing forward at the time.

"Let me understand you clearly, Corporal Tredway," Faulkner said heavily. "Whoever fired the shot was standing in front of Major Northrup, looking straight at him?"

"Yes, sir." Tredway gulped. He had no room for evasion, although he would clearly like to have had.

"Head up?" Faulkner persisted. "Head down? Turning, ducking?"

"No, sir," Tredway said wretchedly.

"And you know this how?"

"Path of the bullet, sir. Straight through and out at the back, sir."

"And the distance the man with the gun stood from Major Faulkner when he fired the shot?"

General Hardesty looked inquiringly at Joseph, but Joseph made no objection.

"The distance?" Faulkner repeated.

"Hard to say, sir," Tredway answered.

"Touching him? Fifty feet? Half a mile?" Faulkner raised his eyebrows.

"Most like fifty feet, sir."

"How do you know this, Corporal?"

" 'Cos o' the wound, sir. An' how far the bullet went through."

"And can you tell the kind of gun it was fired from? At least whether it was a handgun or a rifle? A British gun or a German one? Or French, perhaps?"

"We've got no French 'ere, sir," Tredway said tartly. "They're up farther to the east." There was clear contempt in his voice for Faulkner's ignorance. He was a man who shuffled papers, not one who fought.

"I was thinking of the gun itself, Corporal," Faulkner corrected him. "Not the nationality of the man who fired it."

There was a rustling in the room. Someone coughed.

Tredway flushed. "A rifle, sir."

"British?"

"Couldn't say, sir." His jaw set hard.

"A rifle, possibly British, fired at apparently fifty feet," Faulkner summarized. "Thank you, Corporal." He gestured to invite Joseph to ask his questions.

Joseph stood up. Now that the moment had come he felt a sort of calm hopelessness. "Corporal Tredway, your knowledge is impressive, although I imagine after three years' active service you have seen a great many wounds of all sorts? Rifle, revolver, pistol, shrapnel, shell splinters, even injuries caused by explosions, overturning gun carriages, panicking horses . . ."

Faulkner stared at him with mounting irritation.

Hardesty winced but did not interrupt. His expression suggested pity more than anger.

"Yes, Chaplain . . . I mean . . . Captain Reavley," Tredway said, frowning.

"Any way to tell if they are caused by accident or by malice, Corporal?" Joseph asked.

"No, sir," Tredway said, meeting Joseph's eyes squarely. There was a flicker in them, as if he might have thought of smiling. " 'Cept for horses panicking, like. That's almost always accident. They don't often do it maliciously. They're better than people, that way."

There was a slight ripple of laughter in the room.

Faulkner's face tightened.

"And gun carriages," Tredway added. "That's more likely accident, down to stupidity . . . sir. They don't have no malice neither."

Joseph preempted Faulkner. "But gunshots would be most likely intended, I assume. Is there any way you can tell, from the injury itself?"

"No, sir. None at all, sir."

"Thank you."

Faulkner declined to pursue the issue. General Hardesty also did not take up his right to question the witness. He looked around slowly, gauging the emotion of the court, and perhaps judged correctly that almost to a man they were in sympathy with the accused. They would have to be forced or tricked into giving any evidence against them if it could be withheld, misinterpreted, or simply denied.

But Joseph knew it was a shallow victory. In the end it was the officers who would decide, not the men who crowded the benches or stood at the back waiting, their hands clenched, faces tense. There was no jury, no public opinion. Those who attended were either witnesses called or men who were off the front line due to injury.

The next witness took the stand. He recounted who he had seen—and where—on the day of Northrup's death. He was neatly tricked by Faulkner into stating that most of the men charged, and Cavan in particular, had not been at their usual posts in the early evening. In fact, Cavan had not been in any of the places he usually was at that hour. The man's testimony, intended to help, went to indicate that Cavan behaved out of character, and that no one knew where he was.

Joseph knew he would not improve the situation by questioning the man; more likely it would make it more obvious that he was lying in an attempt to save Cavan.

Hardesty looked as if he was aware that emotion was having a far larger effect than the facts, but he did not intervene.

Faulkner called more men and elicited similar responses, building a picture of curious and unexplained behavior that night. Each piece was minute, but placed carefully together, as Faulkner did, they were like the fractions of a mosaic, and the picture was chillingly clear. Twelve men were unable to find a single witness as to where they were. The conclusion was only implicit, but it sank with deeper and deeper weight on everyone in the hot and overcrowded room.

There was a brief recess. Joseph saw Judith come in. Actually what he saw was the crowded men move to make space for her, and then the light on the fair streaks of her hair, bleached from when the summer had been bright, before the battle at Passchendaele, and the rain. Their eyes met. She was frightened, but had he not known her so well he would not have seen it in her pale face.

The court resumed.

Faulkner began calling his other witnesses. This was the most difficult part for him, far worse than any defense Joseph might mount. He must prove some kind of motive for such a terrible and self-destructive act as mutiny, and by officers, in particular, who had until that time shown exemplary service. There cannot have been a man in the room, or beyond it in the regiment, who was not burningly aware that Cavan had been put up for the Victoria Cross. Compared with him Howard Northrup was both a moral coward and a military fool.

At the same time Faulkner must not allow anyone to suggest that Northrup had deserved his fate, or even that he was seriously incompetent. It must seem that every other man faced with the same situations might have given the same orders, with the same results. There must be motive, but no justification. It was a delicate balance, but he stood on the balls of his feet, weight slightly forward, voice confident.

Joseph looked over to where General Northrup sat, his face so pale the shadows under his eyes looked like old bruises. His lips were tight, his nose pinched as if he had long carried an inner pain which had finally come to a crisis.

Joseph turned away. To stare at a man in such distress was intrusive, the more so because Joseph would only add to it when circumstance allowed him. There was little room for compassion here, perhaps none at all. It was deeply against his instinct to strike at a man whose grief he had seen so openly, who had possibly even trusted him. But gentleness toward one now might yield the death of the others, and his loyalties could not be divided. Everyone else in the court might be evenhanded, but his duty could be only to the men whose champion he was.

Faulkner was careful in his questioning, almost to a fault. He called men as witnesses who had been on the edge of incidents, and were not caught up emotionally. By presenting such a bland view he showed that he was not ignoring the incidents. He conceded that they had occurred, robbing Joseph of the need to and if Joseph were to then call men who gave very different accounts, they would be seen as biased.

Their closeness would in itself color their views and they could easily be suspected of leaning too far in the opposite direction, of seeing fault in Northrup simply to justify the actions of their friends who now faced judgment. Joseph saw the trap, and yet he still feared overbalancing into it.

His hands clammy and his chest tight, he rose to cross-examine the third witness, a young soldier who had been at the front only a matter of three months. He came from the Derbyshire Peak District and had no ties with Cambridgeshire.

"Private Black," Joseph began. "You have given us a clear account of this unfortunate accident with the gun carriage, which you say some of the men felt was Major Northrup's fault. You saw nothing to suggest that it was?"

"No, sir," Black replied. He looked uncomfortable and confused. He was very young, perhaps sixteen.

"But you say they were extremely angry?"

"Yes, sir. At least, they were cussing a lot, and swore he was . . . well . . . not up to much as a soldier."

"Did anyone suggest that he should take advice in the matter from some of the more experienced men?"

"I dunno, sir."

"Are you quite sure about that, Private Black?"

Black glanced at Faulkner, then back at Joseph. It seemed to occur to him for the first time that he was out of his depth, and that whatever

Faulkner promised him, it was the men of his own regiment whom he would have to live with, and very possibly die with. He stood fidgeting slightly, clenching and unclenching his hands.

Joseph could not afford to be sorry for him. Everyone in the room—and especially the officers who would have to make the judgment—must surely have seen that look.

"Do you know why you in particular were asked to give evidence today?" Joseph pressed his advantage.

"No, sir."

"You did not have a particularly good view of the accident?"

"No, sir." Black was now visibly unhappy.

"Nor much knowledge of field guns, horses, mud, bad weather?"

Black was sweating. "No, sir. I only just got here, sir."

"Did you volunteer to testify?"

"No, sir!" That was from the heart.

"I see. Perhaps you simply represent a certain point of view, a very impartial one?" Joseph suggested.

"I think impartiality is what we are seeking, is it not?" Faulkner interrupted coldly. "It is the indulgence of emotion and personal opinion over obedience, discipline, and loyalty which has brought us to this place."

"Impartiality perhaps," Joseph said, knowing his voice was rough-edged with the power of his own feelings. "But not apathy, indifference, or, above all, total ignorance." He stopped himself from continuing only with an intense effort. In spite of himself, of seeing it open in front of him and knowing its exact nature, he was still overbalancing into the trap.

Faulkner smiled. "I have nothing further to ask Private Black," he said.

Hardesty turned to Black.

"Did you hear talk of mutiny, Private?"

"No, sir!"

"Simply distress at an accident?"

"Yes, sir!"

He was excused, and Faulkner proceeded with perhaps a little less assuredness. He called more witnesses of military misjudgment, lack of knowledge or foresight, but always making it seem like no more than the misfortunes of combat that happened all the time, and to other men as well as Northrup. He built up a careful picture of resentful men who were desperate to escape the battle line, to blame someone else for their pain and fear, and their helplessness to alter the terrible fate ahead of them.

The case closed for the day.

Joseph left the farmhouse and walked alone back toward his dugout. It was more than four miles, but he wanted the time alone to think. If there was to be justice then eleven of the twelve men would be found guilty of no more than insubordination, and that even with understanding; but Howard Northrup would not be exposed to the whole army as an arrogant and incompetent man, a failure. He had been placed by circumstances into a position he was not suited to fill. Possibly an ambitious father who saw what he wished to was additionally responsible. But was there any justice served by forcing him, publicly, to see every bitter moment of his own mistakes, and what they had cost?

Joseph would like to have saved them all.

He trudged through the mud in the dying sun, refusing to accept that it was impossible. Was he capable of virtually crucifying General Northrup?

If he did not, then his evasion, his cowardice, would condemn Cavan and Morel and the others. And it could also betray the rest of the regiment who trusted him to fight for them all. And they did see the fate of them all in whatever happened to the twelve, he had seen that in their eyes, the tension in their movements, the questions they did not ask. They believed they knew him.

Perhaps that was the decision made. He could strip the defenses for Howard Northrup, and those from his father, as far as he had to. He would be careful to say nothing but the truth. That was bitter!

No, it wasn't! The fact that in one man's opinion something was true, or part of a truth, did not rob him of judgment whether to speak it or not. The responsibility was still his. It was the ultimate hypocrisy to shelter behind morality instead of standing before it.

He reached the lines, ate a brief meal of stew and hard bread already beginning to mold, then walked through the mud to his dugout. He read for a little while, and finally fell asleep after three in the morning, with the words crying out in his mind "Father, help me!" but no idea of what that help could be.

The next day began with Faulkner once again calling witnesses from among the men who had been at the front only a short time and had no personal loyalty to Morel or to Cavan, and no friendship with the other men of the Cambridgeshire regiments.

Within the first half hour, his questions turned in the direction Joseph had dreaded from the beginning. "Why," Faulkner asked, "if the accused men were not guilty as charged, did they escape custody and flee the battlefield, and try to reach neutral Switzerland? And what is more interesting—how did that escape occur?"

Joseph was cold to the pit of his stomach. Had he underestimated Faulkner in thinking he did not know that Judith and Wil Sloan had helped them? Was he looking for someone to betray that? Was he trying to apply pressure on Joseph that would force him to lie to protect them both, and thus expose himself as a passionately interested party doing everything he could to conceal a crime out of personal motives?

Was that why they had chosen Joseph to defend the men? Because he had the ultimate weakness and they had known it all along? How blindly, arrogantly stupid he had been! Yet again he had walked, open-eyed, into total betrayal! And not only Cavan, Morel, and the other men, but Judith and Wil Sloan would pay for it with their lives.

Now he was angry, deeply and passionately angry. He was sweating. The room seemed to roar in his ears as if he were underwater. Surely the Germans had not advanced far enough to make the room ring and tremble like this?

Faulkner was questioning one of the guards who had kept the prisoners in the farmhouse rooms. The man stared back stolidly, answering exactly as required.

"Yes, sir, Captain Morel refused to give his word, sir, so we had no choice but to lock him up."

"But separately, not with the other ranks?" Faulkner clarified.

"That's right, sir."

"And he escaped?"

"Looks that way, sir."

Faulkner's eyebrows shot up. "You have some doubt, Corporal Teague?"

"Only know he was there in the evening, an' gone the next morning, sir," Teague replied blankly. "Don't seem likely he was abducted."

There was a snigger of laughter around the room.

Faulkner flushed. "You find this amusing, Corporal?" he said icily. "We are investigating a man's death!"

"Holy God!" Teague exploded, his face suddenly white. He swung his arm out in a generally northeast direction. "We got a thousand men out there dying every single bloody day!" he shouted. "One idiot officer gets a clean bullet in his brain, or what passes for one in his case, and you become righteously indignant, as if it never happened before? I got no bloody idea what happened to him, and I don't sodding care!"

His voice was growing more strident. "Good men got crippled or killed because he was too stiff-necked to let anyone tell him what he didn't know. And God 'elp 'em if they tried! If someone bust them out, I don't know who it was. They give me a clip on the back of the head, an' I don't blame them one bit, but I never saw their faces." He flung his arm out to point at the accused men, but still stared defiantly at Faulkner. "Haven't you got something better to do than stand here arguing the toss over those poor sods? We're going to lose the war 'cos you lot shot us from behind!"

Faulkner's face was burning with rage, but General Hardesty stepped in before he could speak.

"Corporal Teague, one of the reasons we fight this war is because we believe in the rule of law, not of barbarism. We appreciate that you have been tested to the extreme by seeing the deaths of your comrades, some of them perhaps unnecessary deaths, but you will apologize to the court for your disrespect, and then answer Captain Reavley's questions, should he have any for you."

Teague controlled himself with an effort. "Sorry, sir." His voice was strangled. He turned attentively to Joseph, his expression changing to one of utmost respect.

Joseph stood up, an overwhelming sense of belonging surging through him, and a passionate will to succeed.

The tension in the room was teetering, willing Joseph to defeat

Faulkner, but the law was even more tightly around the accused men now than before Teague had spoken. But Joseph's mind was racing with fear for Judith. Did everyone know it was she who had rescued the prisoners, just as surely as they all knew Northrup was a fool?

They would not execute Judith, but they'd send her to prison. Even after all she had done here, the years of hardship and danger, pushing herself to exhaustion, living in hunger and filth. Would prison finally destroy her? Would bitterness at the injustice of it break her spirit?

"Corporal Teague," he began. What could he ask this man who so fiercely wanted to help?

"Yes, sir." Teague stood smartly to attention.

"You guarded these men during their imprisonment?"

"Yes, sir." There was disappointment in Teague's face. He had been hoping for something brilliant.

An idea flashed in Joseph's mind, partial, a hope only. "Did you hear them talking to one another at all?"

Teague hesitated. "Yes, sir." His eyes were wide, tentative. He wanted to be led.

It must be done with exquisite care. Joseph breathed in and out slowly, steadying himself. "Were they always aware of you overhearing them?"

"Er . . . no, sir."

Good. He dared not smile, not give the slightest encouragement. "Did you ever hear them say that they had intended to kill Major Northrup?"

"No, sir." The disappointment was back again in Teague's face, deeper.

Faulkner gave an exaggerated sigh of exasperation.

The silence prickled in the room.

Joseph plunged on. "Did you ever hear them say that they had wished he would listen to advice from men who were familiar with the battlefield? With horses, for example? Or the peculiar nature of the clay mud here?" Faulkner objected, but Joseph ignored him. "Or when it was more dangerous," he said clearly, "or *less*, to go over into no-man's-land to try to recover wounded or dead? Or even the lie of poison gas. Or sniper fire, visibility, any of the things the rest of us have learned by experience over the years."

Teague was following him now. "Yes, sir," he said cautiously. "Yes, I did hear them say as it would've been better if he would've listened, but no one could make him. 'E were dead stubborn. . . ." He blushed. "Sorry, sir. But 'e were a very proud, unbending sort of man. The ignorant ones often are."

There were several gasps in the room, followed by a moment's silence.

"Why did they want him to take advice, Corporal?" Joseph needed him to nail it home.

Teague blinked. " 'Cos we were getting hurt bad, or killed," he said with incomprehension at Joseph's stupidity. "No man sees his mates getting killed for nothing an' stands by with his fingers up his arse . . . sir."

"You mean the army is built on loyalty to the men beside you, whose lives depend upon you and yours upon them, even more than upon obedience to discipline?" Joseph made it doubly clear.

"Yes, sir, I do mean that," Teague agreed. "Being obedient isn't enough. When you're out there with Jerry firing everything he's got at you, you got to be right as well."

"Yes," Joseph agreed. "Yes, I know. I've carried the bodies home."

"Yes, sir. I know you have. And a lot o' the ones still alive."

Joseph thanked Teague and resumed his seat at the defense table.

Faulkner knew well enough to remain silent. His face was pale, the freckles standing out.

Hardesty asked Teague again if he was certain that he did not know who had let the prisoners go. Teague repeated that he had no idea.

Faulkner called upon the testimony of other men, particularly those who had searched for the escapees afterward, asking about how the escape could have been effected, and drew from them the answers he wanted. It required a vehicle large enough to transport all eleven men, and of course a driver. No vehicle had been reported lost or abandoned. The conclusion was obvious: An ambulance had carried away the prisoners.

The room seemed to be hotter, smaller, the walls crowding inward.

Joseph accepted the possibility that he would have to lie under oath to defend Judith. Could he? Could he swear on the Bible that he knew so well, not only in the poetic glory of the King James version but in the Hebrew and Greek and Aramaic as well?

Yes, he could. Words were strong and beautiful, but it was the reality they spoke of that mattered. What were all the scriptures in the world worth if he placed his own emotional comfort first and let Judith suffer, even be broken, for doing what she believed was essentially the right thing? And the fact that all the men of the regiment whom he knew, whose lives and dreams he shared, thought so too eased the decision. Yes, he would look Faulkner in the face, and lie to him. If he had to.

Judith was wondering the same thing, and yet it did not frighten her as much as it should have. She had known the risk when she took it, and would have done it again. It was Cavan and Morel she was afraid for, and the other ten, not herself. She had known Teague would lie about knowing who was behind the escape.

She looked at General Northrup's face and saw the pain in it. He must be realizing now that every rank and file man in the room, every man who actually went out into the mud and death of battle, would risk his own freedom, perhaps his life, to lie for the men accused of Major Howard Northrup's death. Could there be a loneliness, a failure more bitter?

There was a stir in the crowd to her left and automatically she turned to look. It was Richard Mason. As if he felt her gaze, he turned toward her. He must be here to report on the court-martial. He looked tired, more than physically exhausted, as if there were a weariness inside him. The ridiculous thought flashed into her mind that he had been wounded and what she saw was the debilitation of pain. But she knew that was not so. She had seen him too recently for such a wound to have been sustained and then healed enough for him to be here now.

As soon as there was a break in the proceedings she looked for him, to find him also looking for her. When they met outside the farmhouse only a few yards from other war correspondents, drivers, and witnesses, she could think of nothing to say. She knew from the fine lines in Mason's face dragging downward, and the tiredness of his eyes, that he had lost something. Immediately her mind went back to what Joseph had said about a darkness in Mason that would prevent him from making her happy, and the coldness of that thought touched her now. Since she had seen him last, a fire had gone out of him, as if some hope or trust had been betrayed.

She was suddenly angry. All hope might be betrayed, all trust soiled, used and thrown away. It did not alter the value of all the things that were loved, or the need to go on fighting for them. What was the alternative? To deny that they were infinitely precious, whatever the cost proved to be? There was no second best, no fallback position worth having.

"Hello, Judith," he said quietly. "Joseph is putting up a better battle than I thought he would."

"What did you think he was going to do?" she said with unexpected bitterness. "Fold up like a deck of cards? You should know him better than that."

"Not fight a battle he can't win," he replied, but he said it softly, as if it caused him pain.

She searched his face and saw not triumph or any vindication of his earlier views but a sense of loss that startled her. It seemed so immediate, as if the erosion were happening as she watched.

"Sometimes you don't win battles," she answered quietly, but with unwavering certainty. "But your side wins the war. People get lost, soldiers get killed. Do you only fight if you know you'll win? That sounds like a coward to me."

He winced. "I choose my battles," he answered. "There are not many of us fighting my war. Every loss counts."

"What is your war?" It was a challenge and she meant it as such. She looked at his dark face with its powerful lines—the shadowed eyes, the emotions within—and she remembered the joy and compassion they had shared. And she remembered how he had kissed her, as if she could smell the warmth of his skin now, and taste him. She had given him more of herself than she had realized.

"What is your war?" she repeated. "What is it you're fighting for? Or have you given up?"

"Sanity," he replied, the hurt in his eyes deep. "And yes, I probably have given up. I ought to. Joseph can't get these men off, and if he isn't careful they'll take you down with them as well."

She felt a sharp grip of fear, like a cramp in the stomach. Would Mason betray her, thinking the truth worth more than individual loss? Exactly what did he believe in? Had she ever known, really? She found herself staring at him, searching, trying to dig deeper than she had any right to, tear off the protecting mask and understand the dreams and the pain underneath.

"Judith!" he said desperately.

What did he want? Trust? She could not give that to him. There was a dark, unknown void inside him that could swallow the things she loved: Joseph, Wil Sloan, Cavan, the men she had known as friends all these years, the men who trusted her. If she let them down there would be nothing left of herself, either.

She turned away from Mason, tears stinging her eyes. There was not anything to say, nothing words could capture or enfold. Either he understood already, or it was too late.

He watched her go with a sense of a door having been closed against him, shutting him out. The blow was not unexpected. He had known she helped the prisoners escape, and he was exasperated with her but not surprised. It was the sort of insane, thoughtless, idealistic thing she would do. She still had the same heroic ideals that the young men had had who went to war three years ago, believing it was glorious. Most of them were dead now, or crippled, shell-shocked, disillusioned. Rupert Brooke, the epitome of them all, the golden poet, had died of blood poisoning before the battle of Gallipoli. The poetry now was of realism, of destruction, of anger and loss. Only dreamers like Judith refused to grow up, clinging to a paper-thin mirage.

And Joseph, of course, trying to defend the morally just and legally indefensible! He would go down with it, like the captain of a sinking ship.

So why did Mason, standing in the sun watching Judith's gaunt, square shoulders and the light on her hair, feel as if he had been shut out of Paradise? The pain of it caught him by surprise, taking his breath away, taking his hopes, and he was naked without them.

Early in the afternoon Faulkner closed his case for the prosecution. It was legally perfect, and he knew it. There was no doubt that the twelve men accused had mutinied, regardless of their motives, and that as a result of their act Major Howard Northrup had been shot by one of them, and it could not have been accidental. Which one had fired the bullet that killed him was immaterial to the charge. He turned to Joseph, inviting him to attempt a defense.

Joseph stood up, forcing himself to keep calm, to try to look as if he knew what he was doing. This was his last chance.

Hardesty asked him the usual questions. Did the accused wish to testify in their own behalf? Did they wish to call any witnesses?

"Two of the accused will testify on behalf of them all, sir," Joseph replied. "And we have two witnesses." Please God this was the right decision.

He had racked his brain, considered every possibility both likely and unlikely. He had prayed about it, but no sense of ease came to still the gnawing doubts in his mind or comfort any of the fear. If that was a sign the decision was wrong, that left him with no answer at all. Every other alternative was worse.

Hardesty nodded grimly. "Very well. Proceed, Captain Reavley."

"Thank you, sir." He called Cavan first.

Cavan swore to his name and rank and exactly where he served and for how long. Joseph had considered listing some of Cavan's achievements, but decided it would give the impression that he was desperate. He was, and probably Faulkner knew it, but bluff was all he had to play.

Carefully, and in sparse, verifiable detail, he drew from Cavan a list of men he had treated and what their injuries had been. Every time he asked if Cavan knew whether the men had survived or not, and if so, if he had lost limbs or eyes.

The court listened in silence. Every man Cavan named was known to them, a friend, possibly even a cousin or brother. If Faulkner could be unaware of the feeling around him then he was truly anesthetized to life. He was at least wise enough not to challenge Cavan.

"Thank you," Joseph said gravely. He turned to General Hardesty. "Sir, it is a matter of record which I will be happy to have Colonel Hook verify that each of these men was injured while obeying the direct orders of Major Northrup. I shall call other witnesses to confirm that the orders were given against the advice of more experienced but junior men."

"That will be necessary, if you wish to make this evidence of any value in these proceedings, Captain Reavley," Hardesty replied. "So far all you have achieved is to illustrate for us the tragedy of war, of which we are all wretchedly aware."

"All except Colonel Faulkner, sir," Joseph replied. "I believe he has not seen action."

"It is irrelevant!" Faulkner snapped, his face pale except for two spots of pink in his cheeks. "This court-martial is to address the crimes of mutiny and murder, not to praise or blame the war record of the officers concerned, or to comment on the tragedy of young men's deaths."

"It is to exercise the circumstances, Colonel Faulkner," Hardesty responded coldly. "You will have your opportunity to contest any of Captain Cavan's testimony, if you wish." He turned to Joseph. "Continue, Captain Reavley. You have a long way to go before you have made this relevant to the charge." There was warning in his face and sadness. Was it for the dead and injured, or because he believed Joseph could not succeed?

Joseph reached the moment of decision. He turned to Cavan again. "When you realized that Major Northrup was not going to take the advice of the men familiar with the conditions and the dangers, Captain Cavan, what did you do?"

"I knew there were many other men who felt as I did," Cavan answered quietly. "Particularly Captain Morel. We decided to use force to make Major Northrup listen. We decided to frighten him badly enough he would feel he had no choice. Morel devised a plan that we hoped would make him see that it was both wisdom and his duty to act on advice, and I agreed immediately."

"What was that plan, Captain?"

"To take him by force to a place where we could hold a mock drumhead court-martial and charge him with the mutilation and deaths of the men who suffered because of his arrogance," Cavan replied. "If we proved to him that it was his fault, we believed he would be willing to change. He was a stupid man, arrogant and out of his depth, but he was also frightened, and I believed he wanted to succeed; he simply didn't know how. He wasn't actually cut out to be a soldier, but then most of the men here wouldn't be if they had a choice." His voice was quiet and clear, the anger in it almost hidden. "We thought it was a way out for all of us."

"And why wasn't it, Captain Cavan?" Joseph asked.

There was complete silence in the room. No one even shifted position.

Cavan's face was white, but he stood stiffly to attention, his eyes fixed on Joseph's. "He was terrified. We found him guilty of gross negligence, and followed it through with a mock execution. We thought it was necessary at the time, in case once he was free again he reneged. We all loaded with blanks—"

"Blanks?" Joseph interrupted sharply. "The army doesn't issue blanks. Where did you get them?"

"We didn't," Cavan said. "We made them. It's easy enough."

"Is it safe?" Joseph pressed. "How did you know they wouldn't still fire bullets? It looks as if one did."

"No sir, it's not possible. The bullet that fired was a live round." Cavan again explained carefully exactly how a blank was made.

"Then one of the men replaced his blank after you had seen him load it?" Joseph deduced.

"Yes, sir."

"Did you know that at the time?"

"Of course not!" Cavan clenched his fists, and his voice shook. "Do you think we wanted this?"

"No, I don't think so," Joseph replied. "But we need to demonstrate it to the court. Who shot the live round?"

"I have no idea, sir, except I don't believe it was I."

"Why not?"

"The kick from a live round is different. I'd have felt it. From a blank there is no recoil."

"You are a surgeon," Joseph pointed out. "How do you know what firing a live round feels like?"

Cavan blushed faintly. "I've fought as well, sir. I have fired a rifle many times."

There was a murmur around the room. Many knew of his V.C.

"Thank you, Captain Cavan."

Faulkner rose to his feet.

Joseph swallowed, his mouth dry. He sat down.

"Yes, thank you, Captain Cavan," Faulkner said. "I'm not sure how much of your story I believe, but I can think of only one thing further to ask you. Regarding these various men and their injuries, I imagine you will only repeat what you have already told us." He smiled bleakly. "However, I am interested in the fact that when your eleven coconspirators in this . . . disciplinary action of yours chose to escape and run for a neutral country, leaving the battle front altogether, you did not. Why was that, Captain?"

"I had given my word not to, sir," Cavan answered.

"And you are a man of the utmost honor?" Faulkner gave the question only the barest lift of interrogation. "So much so that you will remain to face a firing squad rather than break your given word?"

"Yes, sir. I would have imagined that as an officer yourself you would have understood that," Cavan replied, the faintest edge of contempt in his expression.

Cavan had not seen the trap, but Joseph did. He felt the sweat break out on his skin and his stomach clench.

Faulkner smiled. "I do, Captain, I do. Who organized the escape of the other eleven men held prisoners with you?"

The heat in the room prickled. Someone shifted their weight and a board creaked.

"As you observed, sir," Cavan replied. "I am an officer and I gave my word. I was not imprisoned with the men. I did not see them go, nor did I see who assisted them."

"That was not exactly what I asked, Captain Cavan," Faulkner pointed out. "I asked you if you knew who it was, not if you saw them. But as a matter of fact, Captain Morel went, and he is of the same rank as yourself, an officer! Were you not billeted together?"

"No, sir. Captain Morel was with the men."

"Indeed? Why was that?"

"You must ask him, sir."

"I will. You have not answered me as to who effected this . . . rescue. I accept that you did not see them. I asked you if you know who it was!"

Joseph rose to his feet, his legs stiff. "Sir!" he said to Hardesty, far too loudly. "If Captain Cavan did not see who it was, then he cannot know. Anything else would be no more than an educated guess, or what somebody else had said, and not evidence." He had phrased it badly, forgotten his legal terminology.

"Quite," Hardesty agreed. He looked at Faulkner. "You may consider the action reprehensible, Colonel, but hearsay evidence will not stand up. Captain Cavan has told you that he was imprisoned separately and did not see anyone. That is the answer to your question. Proceed."

"I have nothing else," Faulkner said curtly. "For this witness."

Now it was Morel's turn. He stood as stiff as Cavan had, but he was far leaner, almost haggard, all taut muscle and bone, his face thin, dark eyes hollow.

Joseph found his throat too tight to swallow. He had to clear it to speak. "Do you wish to amend anything in what Captain Cavan has said, Captain Morel?"

"No, sir." Morel's voice was hoarse. He straightened his back even more.

Joseph knew he must address the escape first. The knowledge and the fear of betrayal was in the room like an unexploded bomb.

"When you were arrested and imprisoned in the farmhouse you refused to give your word that you would not escape. Did you expect to be rescued?" he asked.

"No, sir."

"Do you know who rescued you?"

Morel hesitated. He was so tense he was swaying a little with the concentration of keeping control. He knew he must be believed. Joseph had told him everything rested on that.

"Yes, sir."

Joseph could hear his own breath in the silence of the room. The walls seemed to swell and then recede, as if they were the chest of some sleeping monster. "Who was it?"

"I refuse to say, sir. They risked their lives for us. We do not betray our own men."

"Just so." Joseph felt his heart pounding. "Did you fire the shot that killed Major Northrup?"

"No, sir."

"Do you know who did?"

"Yes, sir."

"And will you refuse to tell us that also?"

"No, sir. He did not act for the good of the regiment or to save the lives of his men. It was a private vengeance for a civilian matter and had no place here."

"Who was it?"

"Lance Corporal John Geddes, sir."

There was a rustle of movement, indistinguishable voices.

Hardesty looked startled.

Faulkner was taken aback, angry.

"And how do you know this, Captain Morel?" Joseph asked loudly.

"I heard him tell the whole story when we were returning from our escape," Morel replied. "It would be easily verifiable. I expect General Northrup, who is here in court, would testify to most of it, since it happened in the village where he and his family live, and so also does Geddes's family. I daresay General Northrup would find it painful, but I believe he would not lie."

A score of men in the room turned to look at Northrup who sat ramrod straight and ashen-faced.

"The motive might be easy enough to check," Joseph agreed, his voice husky. He loathed doing this, but he was aware that he must raise all the objections before Faulkner did—bite first and draw the poison. "That does not prove Geddes's guilt. Why would he tell you this? And if he was indeed guilty, why would he return to stand trial rather than simply continue in his escape? Was he not already far beyond British jurisdiction when he made that decision?"

"Yes, sir." There was not a flicker in Morel's face. Now everyone had turned toward him. "He was in German territory, sir," Morel continued. "Hurt, alone, starving, and unable to speak the language. If the Germans had caught him, I think it possible he would have been treated as a spy. He might not have been shot cleanly, and we can do at least that for him."

"How do you know this, Captain Morel?"

"I was there, sir."

"Do we have anyone's word for this, apart from yours?"

"Yes, sir." Again there was not a flicker in Morel's face. "There are a number of French officers who could testify to various points of our journey. And you yourself could testify to all of it."

There was a rustle around the room, a murmur of voices, one or two gasps. Then Hardesty leaned forward. "Is this true, Captain Reavley?" he demanded.

"Yes, sir."

"And are you willing to testify? If you do so, you will, of course, be subject to cross-examination by the prosecution."

Joseph cleared his throat. He had no choice. He had struggled to avoid it from the beginning, but there was no way around it that did not make him look like a liar. "Yes, sir," he said hoarsely.

"Very well. After Lieutenant Colonel Faulkner has questioned Captain Morel, we shall have you testify."

Faulkner obtained nothing further from Morel that was of any use and Hardesty adjourned the court for the long, miserable night. Joseph spent most of it awake, trying to think of a safer way to introduce the evidence he needed. It all depended on the understanding of morale, of the loyalties that bound the men together, their trust in Morel and his knowledge of it, the obligations he felt. His own testimony of that was useless. Faulkner would judge it self-serving and dismiss it. Only men like Morel could know what he believed and why.

A jury of his peers. The phrase flashed into his mind in burning clarity. It was still only a chance. Faulkner might still trip someone and catch them out over Judith, and of course Wil Sloan. Although since Wil was American, the consequences might be less severe for him.

Finally, almost as the sky was paling in the east, he fell asleep.

FOURTEEN

*T*he next morning Joseph called his first witness. Snowy Nunn stood scrubbed and stiff, answering with surprise to his given name, almost as if he did not recognize it. He had been called "Snowy" since before he could talk.

"Private Nunn," Joseph began, addressing him formally.

"Yes, sir." Snowy was so rigid Joseph could see where the fabric of his uniform was strained by the unnatural posture.

"How long have you been in the army?"

"Since the autumn o' 'fourteen, sir. Oi soigned up immediate."

"Why?"

Snowy looked startled. "Roight thing to do, sir. Same loike everyone, you know that, sir. You did the same thing. And your sister, to droive ambulances."

"Yes, I do know," Joseph agreed. "But perhaps General Hardesty and the other officers on the panel did not. And of course Colonel Faulkner. Does that mean you have known most of the accused men for all that time?"

"Yes, sir, most of them. Known the rest since summer of 'fifteen, just after the gas attacks started. Came to replace . . ." He swallowed. "Some o' those we lost."

"How long have you known Captain Morel, for example?"

Faulkner rose to his feet, addressing General Hardesty rather than

Joseph. "Sir, the prosecution is happy to concede that Private Nunn, and indeed the majority of the men in the Cambridgeshires, all know each other and have a loyalty greater to the men of their own villages than to their king and country, or to the laws thereof. It is wasting the court's time for witness after witness to attest to it."

Hardesty looked deeply unhappy. Beside him Apsted grimaced.

"Sir," Joseph responded. "I object profoundly to Colonel Faulkner stating that any man in the Cambridgeshire regiment has a greater loyalty to his fellow soldiers than to His Majesty, or to England. On the battle-field a soldier's loyalty is to the men who fight beside him, and to those for whom he is responsible. We fight for king and country, give our lives if necessary, endure injury, hardship, and sometimes appalling pain, but we do it here. These are the men whose backs we defend, whose lives we save, or who save ours, whose rations we share, with whom we laugh, and weep, and face the evening, and whose wounds we will try to stanch if we can, or who will carry us back from no-man's-land—dead or alive. Loyalty is not an idea here, sir, it is the price of life."

There was a murmur of approval from the body of the court. One man raised his hand and shouted out his agreement.

"For God's sake!" Faulkner snapped. "This is not the place for a sermon. We are dealing with facts, and the law—not emotionalism. We are only too well aware that the chaplain is partisan; I may say, highly partisan. He comes from the same village and has known these men all their lives. I do not question his honesty, but I do most profoundly question his ability to separate the law from his personal loyalties."

"Thank you for not questioning my honesty," Joseph said with considerable sarcasm. "The fact that you raise it at all suggests that you might."

"If you give me cause to, I shall, sir," Faulkner retorted. "I believe Captain Morel was a student of yours in your Bible teaching days in Cambridge? And one of the better-known women ambulance drivers is your sister? Your personal loyalties are deep enough to make questions not unnatural, Captain Reavley."

The attack on Judith had come at last, and not to answer it would be to signal his vulnerability. Joseph dared not ignore it. The challenge had been very cleverly made, discreet, oblique enough not to seem deliberate, and yet of course it was. He had walked into the trap. Had there ever been a way of avoiding it?

"My sister is one of the ambulance drivers," he agreed. "And yes, Captain Morel was one of my students, of Biblical languages, actually, not of the Bible itself. And certainly I have known most of the men in the regiment all their lives, or if not them, then men exactly like them, from villages like my own. That makes me better able to understand them than you are."

"I understand the law, sir, which it seems increasingly apparent you do not!"

Hardesty drew in his breath, as if to speak. There was a sharp snap as Apsted broke a pencil, accidentally twisting and turning it too hard.

It was time for Joseph to play his only card. He looked unblinkingly at Faulkner. "One of the few things I know about the law, and have admired the most, is that a man is entitled to be tried by a jury of his peers. Not men who are higher or lower than he is, or who are of a different nature or class, or who have never walked a step along his path and know nothing of his faith, the trials he has faced, or the burden he has carried. We cannot be judged fairly by the arrogant or the ignorant. I hope to demonstrate that I am not too partisan to see the truth, but partisan enough to understand it, and the men who have lived for it, or died for it."

He steadied himself. It must be done. "And that includes the grief of General Northrup, his desire for justice, and perhaps for revenge, his guilt that he pushed his son into a rank and a position for which he was not equipped, and which ultimately destroyed him. And for Major Northrup who was sent to a miserable death by men who did not understand him, and circumstances that are beyond the control of any of us."

Faulkner was furious. "Sir, you exceed your own position! You are a captain. You are a priest in uniform, because the army must offer what spiritual comfort it can to men who face death. You have no right and no remit to judge your superior officers, or the military ability or record of any man at all. To insult General Northrup from the safety of your appointment to this court is a despicable act. I hope the court will see fit to admonish you."

Hardesty was pale, his face tight with anger. "Colonel Faulkner, I will exercise my own discipline, without suggestion from you, sir."

He waited, but Faulkner did not apologize. He inclined his head and then straightened his shoulders as if he would have taken a step backward, but the room was so crowded men stood pressed against each other; there was nowhere for him to go.

Hardesty turned to Joseph. "For goodness' sake, Captain Reavley, ask your questions and get on with it! Does Private Nunn have anything to contribute or not?"

"Yes, sir," Joseph replied. He looked at Snowy, doing his best to hide the helplessness he felt. He was not sure now if calling him was wise—in fact if the entire strategy, which had seemed in the night to be possible, was not a disastrous idea. "Private Nunn, do you know all the men who are here accused of mutiny and murder?"

Snowy's face was almost as pale as his hair. He stared at Joseph, desperately seeking guidance. Joseph dared not give him any, and was too transparently honest—it would show instantly.

"Do you?" Joseph repeated. "Just answer truthfully."

Snowy relaxed a fraction. "Yes, sir."

"Including Captain Morel?"

"Yes, sir."

"You are a private. He is a captain. How do you know him, other than to take orders?"

Snowy hesitated, unsure how much Joseph wished him to say.

"Your brother Tucky was recently killed," Joseph prompted him.

Snowy swayed, struggling to get his breath.

Joseph waited. He felt brutal, but he knew even worse could be ahead.

"Yes, sir. He was shot going over the top," Snowy answered. He took another shuddering breath. "Oi suppose that was when Oi got to know Captain Morel a bit more. He was . . . he was very good to me. Knew how Oi felt. Tucky an' me . . ." He stopped again, unable to go on.

Joseph had to rescue him. "Were very close. I know. I think we all know a great deal about loss, comforting one another . . . the responsibility."

Faulkner rose to his feet.

"Yes, sir!" Snowy said loudly, before Faulkner could speak. "Captain

Morel took it very hard when any of his men got killed . . . or injured, either. He's a good man, sir. Oi hope—" He stopped abruptly, aware that he had nearly said too much. He blushed scarlet.

Hardesty had the briefest of smiles, little more than a softening of the eyes.

"I hope so, too," Joseph said softly. "It is my responsibility to look after my men, and I will do everything I can to fulfill that duty. In your judgment and experience serving under him, did Captain Morel feel that same sense of duty to his men, Private Nunn?"

"For heaven's sake!" Faulkner said furiously. "That's an idiotic, self-serving question. The man's a private! He's hardly going to say *no*. He's talking about his officer! And one who showed him some compassion when his brother was killed. Sir!" He appealed to Hardesty.

Joseph cut across them both. "It's also an excellent opportunity to earn credit with his new commanders, and at the same time get a certain revenge, if he felt Captain Morel had been less than the leader he wanted. Private Nunn risks far more speaking for him than he would against him, sir."

"You have an excellent point, Captain Reavley," Hardesty conceded. He looked at Snowy. "Private Nunn, will you please tell me, in your own words, not Captain Reavley's, what was your experience of Captain Morel as an officer."

"Yes, sir." Snowy stood very straight. "He was a hard soldier and he didn't like any lip, but he could see a joke like anybody else. He expected you to be obedient, jump to it instant, loike, no slacking, no hesitating once you'd gone over the top. Always look after your own, help the wounded, bring everyone back if you could. Always looked out for his men. Be loyal to him, an' he'll be loyal to you, even to his life. Sir."

"Thank you, Private Nunn." Hardesty looked at Joseph.

For a moment Joseph hesitated. Was it better to reinforce what Snowy had said, or leave it as if Hardesty had done enough? Leave it. The deference to Hardesty was wiser.

"Thank you," Joseph said aloud. "That was my point precisely, sir." Awkwardly, still not quite sure, he sat down.

Faulkner stood up. He looked at Snowy with weary disgust.

"Do you believe mutiny is wrong, Private Nunn? Or let me put it this way, is your loyalty to your country, or to the Cambridgeshire regiment?"

"Oi reckon as they're the same, sir," Snowy answered.

"Well, Cambridgeshire may be your whole world, Private Nunn, but I assure you there is a great deal more of England than that!"

"Oi expect there is," Snowy agreed steadily. "But all Oi know is Cambridgeshire and here, and maybe it's all Oi'm like to know. Cambridgeshire'll do me."

There was a rumble of approval from the men in the room.

"So your loyalty is to a Cambridgeshire captain before the king!" Faulkner challenged, his face pink.

"Oi don't know the king, sir," Snowy told him unblinkingly. "An' Captain Morel's from up Lancashire somewhere."

Faulkner stood motionless, unable to decide whether it was worth pursuing what seemed to be a fruitless course.

Joseph waited also, terrified Faulkner would go on and try to provoke Snowy into a mistake, or worse, into losing his temper. He had tied himself irrevocably to Morel, and through him to all the accused men. It would be disastrous. He stared across at Snowy, trying to will him to stay calm.

"Private Nunn," Faulkner said again. "I ask you, do you condone mutiny? A simple *yes* or *no* will do."

"Oi never thought of it, sir," Snowy answered. "Oi trust Captain Morel. Oi know him. Oi'd go over the top if he told me to, any day. Oi have done. He wouldn't order it if it weren't necessary. He knows what he's doing, and he respects his men, sir. Loike they do him."

"That wasn't what . . ." Faulkner began.

"You have the best answer you are going to get, Colonel Faulkner," Hardesty told him. "If you have any further questions for Private Nunn, ask them."

"No, sir. It seems pointless to ask. Except one thing." He turned again to Snowy. "Private Nunn, do you have any idea why Corporal Geddes, alone among the accused men, should have wished to kill Major Northrup? You seem to know all your comrades so well, surely you know that?"

"No, sir, Oi don't know," Snowy answered. "But Oi don't think Corporal Geddes is stupid. If he had a good reason in his own mind for thinking of something like that, he isn't daft enough to tell me about it. He'd know Oi wouldn't go along with it, sir." It almost amounted to insolence, but not quite.

Faulkner gave up. "That's all, Private Nunn." He looked at General Hardesty. "Sir, since this defense claims that only Corporal Geddes was guilty of murder, perhaps Captain Reavley will provide a credible witness as to what possible motive he could have had. I have questioned him myself, and he denied it. I do not find Captain Morel credible, since his interest in the issue is that his own life depends upon it. Captain Reavley would testify, since he was apparently present when Geddes allegedly admitted to the crime. Then in the interests of both law and justice, I may cross-examine him on his testimony."

The trap was sprung, tidily and completely. Joseph could not refuse him or he would appear to be denying what Morel had said, and the whole defense would collapse. And once Joseph was cross-examined, Faulkner would find a way of raising the escape again. Could Joseph lie? And if he did, would that jeopardize everything in the defense so far?

He had no choice. He was sworn, and briefly told them all that Geddes had said on the long journey back. No one interrupted him.

"A most interesting tale," Faulkner said finally. "Did you believe him, Captain Reavley? Or is it Chaplain, in this case?"

"If you mean, am I breaking the sanctity of confession, no, I am not. If you remember, Colonel, Captain Morel was also present."

"Oh, yes, of course, your onetime student, Captain Morel. You have a great loyalty, Captain Reavley. How does your loyalty to your calling, to the truth and honor you have spoken about so eloquently, compare with your loyalty to the ambulance driver who helped the mutineers to escape, and of course the murderer Geddes, as well?"

All movement in the room ceased. Everyone looked at Joseph.

He stared back at Faulkner, terrified that he might accidentally look at Judith.

The slightest misstep now, even a word, and Faulkner would have him.

"I do not know who helped them escape, Colonel," he said.

"Come now," Faulkner said tartly. "Is being disingenuous to this degree not morally the same as a lie? You may have taken great care not to have anyone repeat news to you, but are you telling this court that you really do not know who it was? Be very careful precisely where your loyalties lie, Chaplain!"

"You are quite right," Joseph admitted. He could feel the sweat trickle down his face. Deliberately he relaxed his hands. Was Judith afraid he would betray her, even accidentally? "I have taken very great care indeed not to know who it was. And I have been successful," he said levelly. "I can guess, but as you yourself have pointed out, most information comes to me in the way of confession, and I cannot repeat it. Not that anyone *has* confessed to that."

"And you do not consider it your duty as an officer to report such a crime?" Faulkner said in amazement.

"No, sir. I consider it my duty as an officer to go after the men who escaped, and bring them back to face trial. Which I did. It redressed the situation, without betrayal of any trust."

"Bringing them back for trial, and possible execution, was not a betrayal of their trust? You amaze me." Faulkner's voice was heavy with sarcasm.

"I persuaded them to come back freely," Joseph corrected him, feeling the heat burn up his face. "For trial. I believe them to be innocent of mutiny or murder, and I hope this court will find them so."

"Except Geddes! He didn't come willingly!"

"He admitted to murder. That is different."

"Not one of your village men, Chaplain?"

"No." Joseph knew what was coming next. But at least they had left the subject of the escape, for a moment.

"Could that be why he is guilty?"

"If you are suggesting all Gloucestershire men are murderers, that is ridiculous," Joseph retorted.

"I am suggesting, sir, that your loyalty to your own men supersedes all honor or balance or judgment on your part. Fighting together in these appalling circumstances, and your fearful losses, have warped your judgment and upset the balance of your thinking. We have no one's word for it but yours and Captain Morel's that any of these events in Major Northrup's home village ever took place."

"Are those your last questions to me?" Joseph found his voice was trembling and there were pins and needles tingling in his fingers. The last chance, the one he had been hoping to avoid since the beginning, was now facing him.

"They are," Faulkner replied with a gleam of satisfaction.

Joseph turned to Hardesty. "Sir, I need to call one last witness who can substantiate the greater part of what I have said."

"Who is it, Captain Reavley?"

"General Northrup, sir."

Hardesty stared at him, eyes wide, questioning.

Joseph stared back. The fact that he had made the decision did not lessen his revulsion at it.

"Very well," Hardesty agreed. "General Northrup, sir. Will you take the stand." It was an order, not a request. There was no choice for either of them.

Slowly, as if his whole body ached, Northrup rose to his feet and walked forward, back straight, shoulders angular and rigid. He was sworn in and turned to face Joseph. There was nothing gentle in his face, no silent plea for mercy. He looked like a man facing his execution. It seemed Faulkner had convinced him that Joseph was utterly partisan, a man without justice, only blind loyalty to his own, regardless of innocence or guilt.

Joseph wavered. He longed to be able to prove him wrong. He had mercy, honor, a sense of justice being for all, as it was for none. But his calling here was to fight for his own men, and that did not allow him space to cover Major Howard Northrup's weaknesses with mercy. He wanted General Northrup to know that, to understand. He realized in the same moment that to do the right thing was necessary, to need to be seen to do it was a luxury, even a self-indulgence, and completely irrelevant.

"General Northrup," he began, his voice firmer than he had expected. "Would you confirm for the court that you live at Wood End Manor in Gloucestershire, and that your son Major Howard Northrup grew up there, and lived there until the outbreak of war in 1914?"

"That is correct," Northrup replied coldly.

"Did Corporal Geddes's family live in the same village at that time?"

"Yes."

"Did Corporal John Geddes's father become involved in a business venture with Major Northrup?"

General Northrup stiffened, his face pink. "I did not concern myself in my son's financial affairs," he replied quietly.

Joseph loathed doing it, but his voice was perfectly steady. "Every man in this court would understand your desire to protect your son's name, sir, but you are under oath, and other men's lives depend upon your honesty—good men, soldiers like yourself. Are you swearing on your word as an officer that you at no time involved yourself, financially or otherwise, in your son's business affairs?"

Northrup's face burned scarlet. "I . . . I lent him money when it was . . . necessary. Once or twice. Not . . . not as a habit, sir."

"Would it be truthful to say that you indulged many of his desires, and that when he overspent, you paid his debts?" Joseph pressed. "Or did you never do that?"

"I did it. . . . It was a matter of honor," Northrup said savagely. His eyes blazed in sockets so shadowed as to seem hollows in the bones of his head. He had aged bitterly in the weeks since his son's body had been found.

"Did the Geddes family lose their home?"

Northrup's hand jerked up. He drew his breath in as if to deny it, then remained silent.

"Is the Geddes family still in the home in which Corporal Geddes grew up?" Joseph insisted. "If necessary we can find out, but it will delay proceedings, surely pointlessly. The answer will be the same. Is it something you wish to hide?"

Faulkner rose to his feet, and Hardesty waved him sharply down again.

"No, sir," Northrup said very quietly. "I believe they were evicted."

Joseph chose his question very carefully. "Did your son's business succeed or fail?"

"It failed."

Joseph was aware of Faulkner tense in his seat, ready to spring to his feet any moment. He would need only a shred of a chance.

"Might it be possible that Corporal Geddes could believe that was Major Northrup's fault, whether it was or not?"

"It . . ." Northrup swallowed, a flash of gratitude in his eyes, there and then gone again instantly. "He might have believed it, yes."

"Thank you, General Northrup. That is all I have to ask you, sir."

Faulkner shot to his feet, stared at Northrup's ashen face, then very slowly sat down again. "I have nothing to add to this . . . this fiasco," he said angrily.

Hardesty looked at Northrup. "Thank you, sir," he said quietly. "The court has nothing further to say, either."

In a room electric with hostility, Faulkner made a closing speech demanding justice against one man who had committed murder, and eleven others whose act of mutiny had condoned it and made them accessories both before and after the fact. He requested that the court sentence them all to death, for the sake of law, justice, and the values the army and the country stood for. He demanded that they not allow sentimentality or fear of the enemy to dissuade them from doing their duty.

He sat down again, still with the court in utter silence.

Joseph stood up.

"The circumstances of this war are unlike anything we have ever known before," he began. "A man who has not floundered in the mud of no-man's-land, faced every fire, and seen his friends and his brothers torn apart by shellfire, riddled with bullets, or gassed to death, cannot even imagine what courage it takes to face it not just day after day, but year after year. Many of us will never leave here. We know that, and we accept it. Almost all of us came here because we wished to, we came to fight for the land and the people we love, our own people."

He took a deep breath. He realized with surprise how passionately he believed what he was saying. "But in order to walk into hell, we need the loyalty of our brothers, whether of blood and kin, or of common cause. We have to trust them without question, trust that they will share with us their last piece of bread, the warmth of their bodies in the ice of winter, and that they will never sacrifice our lives uselessly, on the altars of their own pride, or expect us to pay the price of their ignorance. If you will follow a man into the darkness and the mouth of the guns, then you have to know beyond question that he will do the same for you, that he will give all he has to be the leader you believe him to be."

He was speaking to Hardesty and the two men beside him, in whose hands judgment rested, but he faced the body of the court.

"Captain Morel and Captain Cavan, and nine of the other ten men here, took the action of trying to curb Major Northrup in order to fulfill the duty of trust they know their men placed in them.

"They were guilty of gross insubordination. It was the price they were willing to pay to save the lives of their fellows. They will accept judgment for that at the hands of their peers, of men who know what it is to be a soldier at Passchendaele, and they will serve whatever punishment those men decide is just, because they have walked the same path."

He sat down again, the sweat prickling on his skin, his heart pounding.

"Thank you, Captain," Hardesty said quietly. He looked at the men on either side of him. "Gentlemen, we shall return to the farmhouse kitchen in case there are any points of law you wish to consider." He rose to his feet and Apsted and Simmons went out after him.

Not a man or woman left the court. No one even spoke. Minutes ticked by.

Hardesty, Apsted, and Simmons returned.

Joseph found his heart beating so violently he gagged on his own breath.

As the junior officer, Simmons gave his verdict first.

"I find Corporal John Geddes guilty of murder," he said quietly. Then he listed the names of all the others, which seemed interminable. No one moved a muscle. "I find them guilty of gross insubordination, sir."

Hardesty thanked him and turned to Apsted.

The tension was almost unendurable. It was like the minutes before men go over the top into the enemy guns.

"I find Corporal John Geddes guilty of murder." Apsted swallowed hard. "And all the other accused, guilty of mutiny."

Joseph felt the sweat run down his body and his hands clench till his nails drew blood. The room swayed around him.

Hardesty spoke last. "I also find Corporal John Geddes guilty of murder." He listed all the other men. "I find them guilty of gross insubordination. By a majority decision, that is the verdict of this court. Sentence of death on Corporal Geddes will be referred up through the usual channels. The others accused will be dealt with at regimental level."

Then at last the cheering erupted. Men shot to their feet, shouting, holding hands high, gasping, laughing, with tears in their eyes and on their cheeks. Morel and Cavan were saluted, the others grasped by the hand, hugged rapturously by friends.

Mason waved his notebook in the air, his eyes bright, although he knew that in London the Peacemaker would be white with rage, uncomprehending that somehow, yet again, the Reavleys had beaten him. Judith wept openly with relief and overwhelming joy.

Joseph was hoisted up and carried out on the shoulders of Snowy Nunn, Barshey Gee, and he knew not who else. He had found a decision within himself and been prepared to pay the price of it, bitter as it was. He had not flinched. He had repaid the trust. Now he was dizzy with hope and a searing promise of faith, a belief in the possibility of the impossible, even out of utter darkness.

And to the north, toward Passchendaele, the big guns continued their relentless pounding of the lines.

PHOTO: © JONATHAN HULME

ANNE PERRY is the *New York Times* bestselling author of the World War I novels *No Graves As Yet* and *Shoulder the Sky*, as well as five holiday novels: *A Christmas Journey*, *A Christmas Visitor*, *A Christmas Guest*, *A Christmas Secret*, and *A Christmas Beginning*. She is also the creator of two acclaimed series set in Victorian England. Her William Monk novels include *Death of a Stranger*, *Funeral in Blue*, and *Slaves of Obsession*. The popular novels featuring Thomas and Charlotte Pitt include *Long Spoon Lane*, *Seven Dials*, and *Southampton Row*. Anne Perry lives in Scotland.

Visit her website at www.anneperry.net.

Praise for

ANNE PERRY

and her Victorian Mysteries

"Intelligently written and historically fascinating."
—*The Wall Street Journal*

"[Perry is] the most adroit sleight-of-hand
practitioner since Agatha Christie."
—*Chicago Sun-Times*

"You can count on a Perry tale to be superior."
—*The San Diego Union-Tribune*

"Few mystery writers this side of
Arthur Conan Doyle can evoke Victorian London
with such relish for detail and mood."
—*San Francisco Chronicle*

"[A] master of crime who rarely fails to deliver a
strong story and colorful cast of characters."
—Baltimore *Sun*

By Anne Perry
(*published by The Random House Publishing Group*)

FEATURING WILLIAM MONK

The Face of a Stranger
A Dangerous Mourning
Defend and Betray
A Sudden, Fearful Death
The Sins of the Wolf
Cain His Brother
Weighed in the Balance
The Silent Cry

A Breach of Promise
The Twisted Root
Slaves of Obsession
Funeral in Blue
Death of a Stranger
The Shifting Tide
Dark Assassin

FEATURING THOMAS AND CHARLOTTE PITT

The Cater Street Hangman
Callander Square
Paragon Walk
Resurrection Row
Bluegate Fields
Rutland Place
Death in the Devil's Acre
Cardington Crescent
Silence in Hanover Close
Bethlehem Road
Highgate Rise
Belgrave Square
Buckingham Palace Road

Farriers' Lane
The Hyde Park Headsman
Traitors Gate
Pentecost Alley
Ashworth Hall
Brunswick Gardens
Bedford Square
Half Moon Street
The Whitechapel Conspiracy
Southampton Row
Seven Dials
Long Spoon Lane

THE WORLD WAR I NOVELS

No Graves As Yet
Angels in the Gloom
We Shall Not Sleep

Shoulder the Sky
At Some Disputed Barricade

THE CHRISTMAS NOVELS

A Christmas Journey
A Christmas Guest
A Christmas Visitor

A Christmas Secret
A Christmas Beginning